HALF NATION
UNDER GOD

HALF NATION
UNDER GOD

A NOVEL

Under religious rule
who will fight to keep women free?

CORA CORBETT

This is a work of fiction. All the characters and events portrayed in this novel are either fictitious or are used fictitiously

Published by Eru Books
7014 E. Golf Links Rd. #176
Tucson, Arizona 85730

www.EruBooks.com

Illustration by Peggy Jackson

ISBN 0-9720936-0-5

Library of Congress Control Number:
2002092163

Printed in the United States of America

First Edition October 2002

FOR
KAYLA, HAILEY, OLIVIA, AND IVY

May you grow up in a world where women are free to be the authors of their own destiny

ACKNOWLEDGEMENTS

Nothing is ever done alone. Without support and encouragement from family and friends novels would never be written. I'd like to thank Jennie, Bruce, Sandey, Brian, Bertha, and Jared for the years they listened to my dreams and encouraged me to pursue them.

Special thanks go to five women in my life that have worked to define this novel, who spoke openly about its merit and it mistakes, who propped me up and pushed me forward from one rewrite to the next. They are as much a part of this work as I am. So thank you:

Faith, Kim, Libby, Peggy And Denise

I would also like to thank my critique group at Borders. Our time together was a constant reminder of where I wanted to go and the only path to get there.

But a short time elapsed after the death of the great reformer of the Jewish religion, before his principles were departed from by those who professed to be his special servants , and perverted into an engine for enslaving mankind, and aggrandizing their oppressors in Church and State
Thomas Jefferson to Samuel Kercheval, 1810

PROLOGUE

Huddled in the shadows between two buildings, the young girl shivered. The night air was hot, but it did nothing to lessen the cold fear that ran through her body. She closed her eyes and forced herself to take long deep breaths. *No one can see you. They don't know you're gone.* Her heart settled and she slowly opened her eyes.

Cracked dry earth lay between her and the chain link fence that surrounded the prison. When she first ducked out of the congregation, she didn't know where she would go, or how she would get out. All she knew was, the opportunity she had patiently awaited appeared and she might not get another before it was too late.

As she stared out at the mountains in front of her, a plan, born in desperation, began to develop. She knew where she was; she had driven by the prison thousands of times in her young life. The Salt River was only a few miles away. It was Friday, and it was summer. If she could make her way to the beach and hide out until morning, she could blend in with the thousands of partygoers who showed up each weekend to go tubing. There she would be just another face, a deserted wife looking for a ride home. Someone, some guy, would be more than willing to take her to Phoenix.

The spotlight lit up the courtyard, stopping inches from her feet. She held her breath until it passed. For fifteen minutes she watched the light, trying to distinguish its pattern and timing.

The beam followed a counterclockwise circle around the perimeter of the prison. Each time it passed, she counted, *one, one thousand, two one thousands*. Each pass took approximately, three hundred seconds.

The chain link fence stood sentry against the desert only a few hundred feet away. Barren ground, daily raked rock and sand, barred her way. Even though she had been on the track team in high school, and didn't doubt her ability to make it across the courtyard, she knew the direct approach was not the safest.

Searching from her hideaway, she assessed the buildings between herself and the fence. There were three sand colored adobe structures, each with only one story above ground. None offered much shelter, but her chances of staying in the shadows as she tried to out run the searchlight were better than a straight path. Her eyes scanned the fence. Even in the moonlit night she could see the knotted barbs threateningly coiled at its peak. A new shiver, colder than the first, ran down her spine. If she made it through, she would be scarred for life – not that she wasn't already. The new scars would be external, the kind all could see, unlike like the emotional ones she knew would haunt her for the rest of her life.

She rubbed the distended belly that protected her child, hoping to warn it of the impending pain. Hoping it would forgive her for the anguish she was about to cause. *We'll make it. I won't let them have you.*

As the light slowly approached, she ripped the hem of her hot pink maternity dress and wrapped it around her hands. She would let the light circle one last time and run at its next pass. She pushed the air out of her lungs and took one long deep breath in anticipation of the race. She stretched her wrapped hands, knowing it would be the last time they would be pain free. The light slowly approached. She readied herself. Set position, down in the blocks. The light drew near. *Ready*, an inner Starter called out. *Set.* She squatted in position, her belly causing her to rise higher than she normally would. She watched her breathing as she had been trained. There would be no start gun and she must be sure, surer than she had ever been before, not to anticipate the start, not to fly out of the blocks before the light completely passed.

The light drew closer, only three feet away. She took a long deep breath and waited.

"Hey, you. Girlie," a man's voice urgently whispered.

She faltered, almost falling into the beam as it passed. She was caught. Without being consciously prompted, her body began to shiver once again, and she fell back into her corner. A small man in jeans and a white tee shirt approached her.

His head jerked left then right as he walked towards her. His small eyes beat frantically as if in a nervous twitch. "You thinking of escaping?" he asked as he held out his hand to help her up.

Her head shook, "No, no" she stuttered as she tried to stand up on her own. Her legs wouldn't support her, and she took his hand. It was clammy and callused.

The little man smiled, exposing what had been perfect teeth. "I can get you out. My truck's over there." He said pointing towards the cafeteria.

She thought she misheard him. "What?" she whispered.

His smile grew wider. It was one sided. His left check rose higher than the right, but his mouth remained closed. He released her hand, letting the back of his brush up against her abdomen and breast. She felt a chill run through her as he touched the bare skin on her neck and face. "I'll get you out. But you have to promise to be good to me."

She opened her mouth to speak, not sure of what to say. He placed his finger over her lips. "I'm not saying forever, just for a while. A month or so. Then you can go wherever you want. I'll even help you and your baby get out of the state."

She had only been with one man before, a man she loved. Sex was not something she doled out freely, but what this man wanted was nothing in comparison to what she had to have. A month of fornication was well worth escaping four and a half more years in prison and the adoption of her child. She nodded her head and forced a smile. His finger slowly moved away from her mouth, down the neckline of her dress, and around her belly. He placed both hands on her stomach and gently rubbed. "Baby, climbing you is gonna be like scaling Mt. Everest." He reached his hand down between her legs and smiled. "We're gonna have a good time."

She forced a smile and nodded.

"Let's get going." He took her hand and gently pulled on it.

She looked past the little man, unsure she wasn't dreaming. Had God heard her prayers, had this man been sent to protect her? She gave thanks with a skyward glance, and saw the searchlight. It was only feet away. "The light," she frantically whispered, pulling him into the shadows with her.

He plowed his face between her breasts and came up smiling. "I think I'm gonna like you."

Her heart pounded against his. His hands explored between her thighs, but she didn't care. She held her breath and closed her eyes as the beam passed.

"Okay, now," he said as he righted himself and stepped away. "My truck's over there. There's a space between the front seat and the cab. They've never checked it before. There's a tarp back there you can hide under."

She nodded her head again and let him lead her across the paved course between the prison chapel and the cafeteria. They stopped when they thought they heard voices and pressed their bodies up against the stucco wall of the cafeteria. A door closed and the voices disappeared. The man placed his hands on her shoulder and pressed her back towards the wall. "I'll get the truck. You stay here. When I pull up, get in the passenger side and get your ass behind the seat."

"I'll be fast," she whispered. As he stepped away from the wall, she grabbed his arm and pulled him back to face her. "Thanks."

His eyes scrolled her body, and he smiled. "There'll be time enough for thanks when we get home. Now stay put." He squeezed her hand then let go.

The little man turned the corner and disappeared. Cleaned up, maybe he wasn't so bad – she didn't really care. His escape route would be a lot less painful than her original idea of going over the fence and becoming tangled in razor wire. She'd give him what he wanted, but not for a whole month, a few days, maybe even a week, but then she'd make a second escape.

The tired coughing of the truck's engine as it attempted to start echoed through the yard. "Please," she heard herself say as it squealed once more and died. Again, it choked and coughed. She held her breath and prayed. After the fourth try, it caught. The soft murmur of its engine was more soothing than any man's passionate words. She released her breath and waited, but the truck didn't slip into gear.

"Hey, Mac, you get the piece of shit started?" a deep voice called from somewhere beyond the truck.

"Fuck you," her benefactor yelled back. "This ol' doll's been better to me than your wife."

"I hope so," the other voice laughed. "What are you doing here so late?"

"Kitchen overflowed. I don't know why you let them girls work in the kitchen. They backed up the whole system with potato skins. Took me over an hour to get it cleaned up."

"I hear ya. Every week it's something else. I swear they do it on purpose. Last week in the sewing shop, four machines were jammed. One so bad it had to be sent off-sight. With what the state tries to do for these women, you'd think they'd be appreciative."

"Well, if they're not," Mac said in a more serious tone than he had used so far. "I am. It's state accounts that carry me. Don't know what I'd do without them."

"I hear ya," the man with the deep voice said. "Wish I could stay and chat, but I've got to go round up the strays. Seems some of these bitches don't think they need to hear God's Word and aren't in tonight's meeting."

The young woman's heart sank. No one ever took roll in the meetings. The way they herded them from one building to another, it was next to impossible to break away. Her eyes perused the visible buildings and shadows. How many others like her were hiding in the night waiting for an escape route to miraculously appear?

A large sun faded red truck, with the name McCorvey Plumbing stenciled in dirty white lettering along its side, pulled up beside her. It was bigger than she anticipated, and she took an involuntary step back.

Mac reached over the front seat and opened the passenger side door for her. She yanked it open wide enough to slip her body through and pulled herself up onto the footstep.

"Hurry up," he urged as he pulled the back of the seat forward, revealing a small hiding place. He lifted a dirty tarp and motioned for her to crawl under it. She wasn't sure she could fit in the tight space, but was damned if she wouldn't. She jammed herself and her unborn child into the cubbyhole, feet first. He threw the tarp over her and pushed the seat back, pinching her belly between hard warm metal and soft torn vinyl.

"Okay, now keep quiet. The guards hear everything. We get past them and we're home free."

She didn't answer him. She laid her head back on the dirty floor, closed her eyes and pretended not to be overwhelmed by the musty air beneath the tarp. *It will all be over soon*, she promised her child. As if in answer, it turned inside her.

"Here we go," Mac whispered then rolled down his window. The truck came to a stop.

"How'd it go?" a female guard's voice asked.

"Great, once I scraped all the potato skins out of the drain. Someone needs to give these women a good kick in the ass."

"We do our best," the guard said. The young woman couldn't see the flashlight as it searched the contents of the cab and truck bed, but she could feel it in the pit of her stomach. She tried not to breathe as she fought the urge to jump from her shelter and give herself away.

"You're good, Mac," she heard the guard say. "All clear."

The squeal of the gates as they started to open put her heart in over-drive. She couldn't believe it could be this easy. Tears began to form and run down the sides of her face.

The tires beneath her moved. Small rocks were crushed beneath the truck's weight. "Looks like we made it," Mac whispered from the front seat.

"Thank you God," she whispered back as she pulled the tarp from her face. For the first time in six months, she felt safe. She envisioned herself holding her child, singing soft lullabies as it looked up at her with total trust and adoration. The image contorted, twisting into a hideous scream. She pulled herself up as best she could and looked out the back window.

Sirens wailed, and lights flashed, screaming the announcement of a won prize. "No, God, please. Please, no," she whispered.

"Fuck," Mac screamed then slammed on the brakes. Her body was thrown hard against the back of the seat. She pulled herself up again. He had stopped.

"What are you doing?" she shouted. "Get us out of here."

"Sorry, babe." His door opened, then the seat fell forward. His hand was around her arm and he was pulling her from the back. "Get out," he screamed.

"But Mac. We had a deal," she cried.

"Deals over. I need their friendship a hell of a lot more than yours."

"No, please," she cried as he held firmly onto her with one hand and shot the other straight up into the air in a sign of surrender.

"I got her. I didn't know she was there," Mac screamed into the oncoming barrage of lights and guards.

He had betrayed her, sold out to the other side, sacrificed her freedom for friendship. She wouldn't go back, she couldn't. The grip he had on her arm was tenuous at best. She wrestled free, and knocked him to the ground.

"Fucking bitch. You better start running," Mac yelled as he pulled himself up. He turned to the gate they had come through. With both arms over his head he ran towards the prison, screaming over and over again, "I didn't know she was there."

"Bastard," she yelled as she looked back at the prison, turned and ran. Lights danced across the desert. A cacophony of bells and whistles drowned out the sobs that escaped her lips.

She headed toward the mountains. Forcing away the tears, she focused on the silhouettes ahead of her. Dozens of giant saguaro cacti, arms up-stretched in surrender, stood frozen in the night. Clumps of cholla, yellowed and ready to spurt their jumping spines, taunted her as she dashed around them. Dry sharp grass and sagebrush sliced at her legs. In the distance, faint against the night, but still real, was a small hut, and, though in her heart she knew there was no safety there, she headed towards it.

Behind her, engines roared. She didn't turn. She didn't stop. Holding her abdomen tightly, she ran the greatest race of her life.

Tears fell from her eyes and snot from her nose as her stomach began to ache. Blood ran down her legs. She longed for the security of her father's arms. "Daddy," she mumbled through the spit that filled her mouth.

The sound of approaching Jeeps forced her to run faster. Ahead of her was a thick crop of Pagoda trees. She ran towards them hoping she could outmaneuver her pursuers. She lost sight of the hut. Her muscles, flaccid from months of inactive confinement, wanted to give up. The baby stabbed her, reminding her why she ran. She forced herself to run faster.

"Stop," a woman's voice screamed at her over the sound of the Jeeps.

"Maim her," another screamed back.

One of the Jeeps sped up beside her. A guard grabbed for her arm, but missed. She darted to the right, missing a cholla by an inch, though some of its barbs managed to find her ankle.

"Shoot her. Get her in the knees," a voice behind her demanded.

"What about the baby?" someone shouted back.

"It's the baby I'm trying to save. She'll kill it if we don't stop her. Aim low. Billings, tell them to get the doc out here."

Two shots rang out. She darted to the right, but was too late. Her right shoulder exploded, then her right knee. Her body was swung forward by the impact. Instinct caused her to reach down with her good arm and protect her child before dropping onto a cholla plant. The spines tore through her neck, scalp, and back. She thrashed in pain, giving the inch and a half long spears more flesh to skewer. Her checks once pale and vibrant were a pincushion doused in blood. Her tongue caught on the inside of her braces as she screamed and fell to the ground.

Her body calmed as the pain peaked and the shock left her numb. Her eyes fluttered with images. Her mind was deluged with voices. She felt a spray of dirt from the Jeep's tire as it pulled up next to her. Someone's feet landed by her blown out shoulder.

"Oh, shit," the person screamed. "Where the fuck is Doc? Don't anyone touch her."

Another Jeep came to a screeching stop nearby. Two women in white rushed up beside her. "Oh my God," one of them said. "Get a blanket, we've got to get her inside."

Someone grabbed her good leg and arm and pulled her out from under the cholla. The spines dug deeper, but she couldn't feel them. Saliva oozed from the corner of her mouth as she mumbled words of confession to her unborn child, and cried for her daddy to help her.

"How's the baby?" a heavy raspy voice ordered.

"In stress. We've got to hurry or we'll lose it."

"How far along is she?"

As her eyes fell in and out of focus, she saw a small, hand held scanner pass over her face and back behind her ear. A small beep, like those at the grocery store, went off and the arm and scanner were drawn away. A second passed and then more computerized clicking held her attention. "Twenty-nine weeks," someone above her said.

That's right. Twenty-nine weeks. I'm twenty-nine weeks.

"Get my kit, and call back for an incubator. I'm going to take it here," the heavy voice ordered.

"Here? What are you nuts? You'll kill her. She'll bleed to death out here," the voice above retorted.

"Not if I can help it. Now wrap something around her so you can hold her down."

Warmth and peace crept slowly into the young woman's consciousness while a dark fog settled around her. She barely felt the knife as it cut open her abdomen or the pressure on her shoulders that kept her from jerking. A baby screamed a thousand miles away and she opened her eyes. The face of a remorseful stranger fringed in short black hair hovered above her. She heard a whispered plea for forgiveness, and tasted the salt of some unknown tear before stepping into nothingness and finding peace.

1

Sharon lay in bed, her eyes closed, her hand slowly caressing her firm moist belly. He was no longer on top of her, but she wasn't ready to release him. The smell of his neck, and the soft nap of his hair as it brushed her face were lingering memories that enticingly hovered about her. She was addicted to his passion, and wanted more.

"When do you leave?" he called from the bathroom.

The words didn't register. She was in a different place, a private zone, too busy relishing the past to pay attention to the present.

"I have a meeting this morning," he continued. "But I can take an early lunch if you want to get together before you take off."

His voice slipped into her consciousness, and she slowly opened her eyes. He was standing in front of the sink, naked. She stared at his tight black buttocks and smiled. Slowly she crept from her tangled sheets and moved up behind him. Pressing her body against his, she leaned her cheek on his back. "Stay home," she said as she reached around him and caressed his chest, rolling his nipples between her fingers.

He put his razor down and turned to face her. "I have to go," he whispered in her ear as he gently bit it. "We're meeting with the final auditor this morning."

"I know," she said lazily. "But I'm going to be gone for at least three weeks. Can't you have someone else handle it?"

"No," he said gently pushing her away. He reached down with his mouth encasing hers. His hand slid between her thighs, his fingers probed the warmth and moistness he had recently left behind. She tugged at him gently, urging him back to bed. He lowered her to the floor and took her, more violently than the time before, and she came once again beneath him, lusting to unite their energies and soar, if not forever, then for the rest of the morning.

As they finished he pulled her up with him, their bodies still melded in sweat, and stepped with her into the shower. Warm water poured down on them as he pulled her tight in against him one last time. He picked her up by her ass, and kissed her hard. "I love you," he said as he put her down.

She kissed him, then fell away letting the water take her. Slowly the pelting spray calmed her, and her ravenous lust turned into excitement for the weeks that lay ahead.

"Are you sure about this trip?" He asked as he turned off the water.

"Yes," she said smiling as she absorbed the outline of his body while he dried it.

"I don't know, babe. I'm worried about you. Has it occurred to you this could get out of hand and you could end up in trouble?"

"I'll be fine." She stepped out of the shower, dried herself off and wrapped a towel around her shoulder length flaxen hair. "Actually, I'm pretty excited," she admitted as she walked back out to the bedroom and lay on the bed.

"I could tell."

"Uhm," she said, propping herself up so she could watch him dress. His body was finely toned. Not excessively, no bulges, but a six-pack that took three days a week at the gym to maintain. She loved his body. It was what had attracted her in the first place. The sex came shortly after and was so powerful, so addictive, she couldn't help breaking her three month love them and leave them rule. He had gotten to her. He had become part of her, and though she had never told him she loved him, in her heart she feared she did.

Now, as she watched him, she realized just how miserable she was going to be without him. Besides her granddad, who had died a few years back, Thomas was the only person Sharon had opened her heart to. It was a small opening, but it was a start. She had been raised by a cold, un-nurturing mother and her half-crazed Aunt Theresa, a woman convinced the government was conspiring with aliens behind everyone's back and kept detailed records of what every citizen ate, read, bought, and thought. Aunt Theresa was certifiable; her mother too caught up with herself. There had never been enough time for Sharon. The hugs, kisses and constant approval all children want came from only one source, her granddad. Now that he was dead, she was trying to let Thomas fill his vacant spot.

"When are you leaving?" Thomas asked as he zipped his fly and walked over to the dresser, scooping up keys and his Id card.

"Around noon, but I won't be able to meet with you for lunch. I have a meeting with Derek at eleven."

"So this is it then?" He said as he turned and tightened his tie.

"Yup, I suppose it is."

He looked her in the eye, and shook his head. "You're not the least bit nervous?"

He had already asked her this at least ten times since she told him about the assignment, and each time she had lied. Sure she was nervous. She would be touching tender nerves wired into the heart of Arizona's legal system. But she had to go. In the four years she had worked at the Sentinel, this was her first assignment with substance. Previously, it was always local politics, community news, or award ceremonies. Finally, she had been given something with the potential to catapult her career. There was no way she was going to let her nerves stand between her and the next Pulitzer. So, once again she told him what he needed to hear rather than the truth: "No, I have no reason to be. Everything's already lined up. All I have to do is show up, take their statements, and come home."

"Sounds too easy," Thomas said. "If I lived there, I wouldn't be keen on talking to the press. The state is so militarized; it's probably illegal to discuss the penal system with anyone, never mind a reporter from one of the Free states."

Sharon initially shared those fears, but Derek, her editor, had come through for her. "I made some good connections," she said with a smile. "Derek hooked me up with an old school chum from his ASU days. She's given me a great list of contacts."

"Yeah, but are they willing to talk?"

"It's amazing," Sharon said, still surprised herself that so many women were willing to be interviewed, especially the ones who had been incarcerated. "It's like they need to tell their stories. They all seem scared, and yet at the same time excited about speaking to me. As long as I give them aliases."

"Of course," Thomas said smiling at her. "I'm not too sure you shouldn't use one yourself."

"No way," she said laughing. She stood up and walked over to him. A smile played on her lips as she pulled him towards her by his tie.

"You know, this could be Pulitzer material."

He smiled and kissed her. "God forbid. You'd never marry me then."

"You never know," she said teasingly, "fame changes a person."

He laughed. "Oh, then maybe you would marry me."

"No, promises," she whispered, then kissed him.

Thomas pulled away. His smile faded. "I wish you would reconsider."

Sharon's shoulders sagged. "This isn't the time..."

"No, I was talking about Arizona. There have been cases where people actually killed themselves in lieu of going to jail."

Sharon laughed. "I can assure you, I won't be going to jail. They can't arrest me for asking questions. First Amendment, remember? Freedom of the press."

"Yeah, well from what I hear, they have their own Constitution, and it's not filled with too many freedoms."

"Thomas, listen to yourself. It's not like I'm going to some third world country where they can lock me up without anyone knowing. This is the United States. Even if they don't like it, they still have to abide by the Constitution. I have rights, and whether I'm in a Free state or a Religious one, I'm protected."

"I don't know," Thomas said pulling her back into him. He ran his fingers through her hair. "I'm worried that's all. I have a horrible feeling about all this, like I'm going to lose you. I couldn't bear that."

Sharon let him hold her for a minute. Emotions always made her uneasy, it was one of those personality traits so imbedded in her that no matter how much she wanted to change, she couldn't. But, for his sake, she would endure it. Thomas had come from a loving home, a home full of kisses and 'I love you's.' His needs were different from hers.

"It's not like I'm going to get an abortion, sell drugs, or steal babies," she said into his chest then looked up at him. She gave him a cursory hug and stepped back. "I hate to say it, but I think you've bought into the propaganda the *Times* keeps dishing out. I'm sure the truth is probably somewhere in the middle.

"Of course, if it's not," she smiled, "and I break what's really happening. It will be bigger than the destruction of the major party lines." She vividly remembered the headlines that year. Spader and Kelly, journalists for the Washington Post, with the aid of a woman cloaked in purple, had produced numerous video tapes where three members of the White House staff were seen handing money over to known terrorists. No one had been too surprised. Rumors had been going around for years. Spader and Kelly were touted as heroes. There had even been a movie.

"Well," Thomas said, as he put on his jacket. "When you meet American Violet, tell her I said if anything happens to you, I'll be up there to kick some righteous ass."

"I'm sure I can do enough kicking for both of us. So stop worrying. Plus, the paper's behind me. If I do get in any trouble, Derek's prepared to bail me out." *God, why did you say that?*

"Prepared? You never said you anticipated any trouble."

"Calm down. We don't. It's just precautionary," she lied.

"Are you sure you'll be okay?" he said taking her hands in his. "If anything happened to you…"

He was starting to irritate her. No matter how much he thought he loved her, he had no right to make her beg for his approval. She pulled her hands away and backed up half a step. "Nothing's going to happen to me. This is my big chance, Thomas. Don't try and make me feel guilty for taking it."

"I'm sorry. You're right. I guess I'm being a little over protective. It's just that sometimes your mouth gets you in trouble. Remember the day at the Mayor's luncheon when he decided to support the removal of women from the city fire departments? You accused him of, let me see how did you put it, 'viewing women from the end of his dick instead of through their contributions.' You almost got banned from covering his re-election."

Sharon smiled. Mayor Renault was a pompous, sexist, ass and she a reporter with a low threshold for arrogant men. Thomas was right. Her mouth had gotten her into messes before, but she was prepared for the type of men she would be dealing with in Arizona and was sure she'd be able to control her flippant remarks. "I've grown a lot since then," she said. "And that's not the point. The point is I'm going and I don't want to be constantly worried that you're upset with me for taking this assignment. This is my career, Thomas. Don't louse it up for me."

"Okay. All Right. I promise. I won't say another word."

"Good. So go to work. Meet with your auditors. I wouldn't want to be the cause of your contract being canceled."

Thomas laughed. "Is that a joke? Four terms of Moralists, and three-quarters of the world still not knelling in front of the US god just about insures the defense industry's pocketbook up until the twenty-second century. This is just to make sure we stayed within our budget on the prototype. We're actually expecting an order of at least twenty more jets to come out of today's meeting. That's why I have to be there. Fred said he wants me to spearhead any technical questions they have."

"All right. If death and destruction are more important than me," she said, stepping back into him. "Go, but I'm warning you, by the end of the week, you'll be missing me so much you'll wish you stayed."

He took her into his arms and kissed her hard. "I'm already missing you," he whispered.

Sharon smiled and pulled him towards the bed. "It's not too late to change your mind," she said falling backwards and pulling him down on top of her.

"You don't give up, do you?" he asked, pulling himself off her. "I can't." He bent and kissed her one last time. "But if you're here when I get home, I'll be glad to accommodate you."

"Fat chance," she said, looking up at him, trying to memorize every curve in his face. "I'm going to go nuts until it's time to leave. If you really loved me, you'd stay and keep me company."

"Oh, no you don't," he said looking at his watch and then backing away from her. "I'm going, and you need to get dressed. Call me. Tonight."

"I will."

"I love you," he said, then turned and left the room.

She listened as his footsteps descended the carpeted stairs. His keys rattled, the front door opened, then closed. She heard the motor of the garage door and his car as it pulled out. She rolled over and hugged his pillow. Drowning in his smell, she tried to relive the passion between her thighs.

2

The clock moved slowly, and the condo fell silent. Sharon resorted to daydreaming, to pass the time. She saw herself interviewing the president, asking how he felt about the fall of the Moralist party, now that the world knew of the human rights violations going on in the religious states. "Why, Sharon," he said, smiling for the TV cameras, but secretly giving her the finger. "The Moralists had nothing to do with what was going on in Arizona. You of all people should know that. Our government, as well as our party, was founded on the rights of the people. Never would the American government, or I, stand for such atrocities to occur."

"But, Mr. President," she would say, smiling back at him with contempt. "Weren't you Governor of Arizona while the prison systems were being designed?"

"I had nothing to do with that," the dream President curtly answered. "As you know, the penal system was completely privatized by the time I took office."

"And the anti-abortion laws, sir. Didn't you support the incarceration and sterilization of women attempting to obtain an abortion?"

"That was a Legislative action. Plus, it was what the people wanted. You have to understand, Ms. Clark, as Governor and as President, I do as my constituents demand."

"My ass," Sharon said out loud. She pulled herself from her bed.

Her clothes were laid out for her, her suitcases packed and in the car. It was nine-thirty when she started to dress, ten when she left for the paper. The half hour drive only took fifteen minutes. The day was moving too slow.

Sharon waited patiently at her desk for eleven o'clock to roll around. At ten-fifty she got a call from Derek's secretary, Tonja. He was going to be late. "Damn him," she said when she hung up the phone. She wanted to leave; she could feel this story, it was simmering already. What she didn't need was to sit around and waste time waiting on Derek.

Ten more minutes dragged on. That was it, she couldn't do it any longer. Grabbing her purse, Sharon headed up the stairs to Derek's office. He wasn't there yet, so instead of taking a seat she paced, back and forth in front of his door, as if her walking would hasten his arrival.

Tonja looked up from her computer, "Anxious?"

"A little," Sharon replied, not wanting Tonja to know just how anxious she really was. She liked Tonja, they all did, but she reported every word, every movement back to Derek. Sharon stopped in front of Tonja's desk, picked up the picture of her two kids, and absently studied it. "Is this recent?"

"You could say that. I had them done a little over a month ago."

One of the boys had high cheekbones and full lips like his mother. The other's face was softer, rounder. They looked about ten and twelve. "Nice looking boys. This one looks like you," Sharon said pointing to the taller of the two. "The little one must look like his dad."

"Who remembers," Tonja said taking the picture back and looking at it herself. "He took off two weeks after Tyrone was born, the bastard. Just left us. Thought I'd lose them to the state."

Sharon looked at Tonja and how gently she rubbed the picture of her sons. "The state? How come?" she asked.

"I wasn't living here," Tonja said putting the picture back in its cluttered spot on her desk. "I was still back in Texas. Neighbors turned me in when they found Marcus eating out of the garbage. Didn't take but a day before Children's Services was on my doorstep."

"Shit," Sharon said and meant it. Children's Services had become the present version of the dreaded SS division of the Nazi government. They had gotten so bad in the past decade or so that there was even an illness attributed to them – Parent Fear: stress related ailments such as ulcers, high blood pressure, and mental fatigue due to the constant supervision of one's children. "How'd you get out?"

"Derek. He pulled lots of strings for me. He and my dad go way back. My sister came up with the money for our airfare, and proved she had a home the boys could come to, but it was Derek who saved my ass. He signed all sorts of affidavits stating there was a job back here in California for me and that my salary would be enough to support my two sons and me.

"I was damn lucky too. Now, with all the friction between the Free states and the Religious ones, there's no way they would have let me move my boys here. You know the stories, once the state moves in, there's no getting your babies back."

"No kidding. It makes me glad I'm childless," Sharon said, a tinge of guilt crossing her face, one she hoped Tonja didn't see. "How long ago was this?"

"Four and a half years. I started here about six months before you did."

Six months? That was hard to believe. From day one, Tonja had seemed like a solid fixture – Derek's armament. Sharon had been warned up front, no one got to Derek without first going through Tonja, and at times, getting through Tonja had been impossible. That made sense now, even if she had only arrived six months before Sharon. Derek had been Tonja's champion, and now Tonja was his. Sharon's respect towards the sometimes-abrupt secretary rose four levels. She was about to ask how Texas's Foster Care program works, when her name was called from across the room.

"Sharon!" It was Derek. He half waved at her with one hand as he sipped from his brown ceramic *Dad* mug, the one his daughter had finger engraved when she was in the seventh grade, twenty years ago. He was an unkempt man, his shirt always loosely tucked in his pants and stained with remnants of breakfast or lunch, but he was a good editor. He had taken the paper from being a small local weekly, twenty years earlier, to a daily with a circulation of over seven hundred and fifty thousand.

Sharon waved back, trying not to let her irritation at having been made to wait show. She liked him and respected him, but she hated it when people wasted her time. Thomas once told her she was too self-centered and lacked tolerance for others. She didn't see those traits as failings. Thomas measured success by the number of friends he had and the size of his paycheck. He didn't share her passion for being the best, regardless who or what got in the way. Derek understood these things, that was one of the reasons she stayed with him, but now it was him who was in her way and though she would try not to let him know, she was mad. *Patience,* she could hear Thomas chiding her. *Tell him where to get off,* her mother countered. Of the two, Sharon knew too well which offered the best advice, and decided to take it. One more sharp edge, ingrained by Mother, and sanded smooth by Thomas' good sense.

"Sorry, I'm late," he said as he approached her. "I knew you'd be waiting." He ushered her into his office. Newspapers were stacked in piles along the walls, his desk covered with scattered papers and dust from a sugarcoated donut. "Punctuality is one of the things I've always liked about you, Sharon. I was in an impromptu board meeting. They're thinking of down sizing the paper."

Sharon's agitation subsided – she was one of the most junior reporters on the staff. "Down sizing?"

"Yeah. All that shit about us not being able to compete with the *Times.* I'm sick of hearing it," he said as he put his coffee mug on top of a stack of papers and sat down. "I've got a damn good staff, and our circulation is growing. They said they're worried about all the God damn money that's being pulled out of Southern California."

Sharon sat down on the wooden chair in front of Derek's desk. Her excitement over the assignment deflated as she considered the consequences of losing her job. She picked up his embossed brass nameplate, Derek Robinson, Editor-in-Chief, and played it back and forth in her hands. "That could be bad news for someone with as little time in as me," she said looking up at him for support.

"You? Shit. You make peanuts. It's the old timers they'll let go first. Walter and probably Mary Ellen. They're both in their mid-fifties and about to become fully vested. You know Sharon," he said leaning over his desk and pushing his mug to the side. "We may be living in one of the Free states, but we're sure as hell being paid by a group of God damn Moralists. I've known for a long time Art was waiting to come up with a reason to get rid of those two, he doesn't want to pay their pensions."

"No pension," she thought out loud. Since they abolished Social Security and Medicare, all anyone had was their pension. The paper had a twenty-year program. If you stayed that long, you'd get matching funds in your IRA and forty percent salary. If not, all extra money was withdrawn. "Is that legal?" she asked, not really concerned with Walter or Mary Ellen, but contemplating her future investment with the paper.

"Yup. He just has to say he needs to down size. Who he chooses to ax is up to him." He looked up at her and raised an eyebrow. "I don't expect this to leave my office."

"No. Of course not," she said, absently replacing the nameplate.

Wait until I tell Thomas. Nineteen plus years of service, then whack, you're out on your ass.

"I knew I could count on you. You know, Sharon, I've always had high expectations of you. If you bring back the story I think you can, you could give this paper the boost it needs. Maybe even save Mary Ellen's and Walter's jobs."

"Sure add pressure," she said half jokingly. She couldn't afford to worry about her co-worker's future. She had taken this assignment to boost her career, not to save someone else's. *Stay focused.* "I'll do my best. I have fifteen women lined up for interviews. Five had self-induced abortions before anyone knew they were pregnant, two were smuggled out of the state, and then back in, five were incarcerated and had babies taken from them, two were jailed for visiting a suspected abortionist even though they weren't pregnant, and one was turned over to the police by her grandmother, a head figure in the early part of the new millennium's right-to-life movement," she said in one long breath. She took another breath, stopped and smiled.

"Pretty impressive," Derek said. "What else?"

Sharon's face lit up. "Three abortionists, and," she said pausing for effect, "a priest who supposedly used the confessional as a means of singling out women at risk for abortion. He's something else. He would convince the women to join a support group the Church sponsored, so they could make sure they were making the right decision. What he didn't tell them was that anyone who joined the support group was automatically monitored and flagged as at risk by the state."

"And he got away with it?" Derek asked.

"In the Church's eyes, he did no wrong. He didn't break confessional."

"What a racket."

"Tell me about it. Anyway, tomorrow morning I'm meeting with a Baptist Minister who teaches a class called The Sanctity of Life to women incarcerated at Arpaio Women's Penitentiary. Friday I'm scheduled to tour the prison with him, and then on Saturday, I'm meeting with Senator Listner. He's leaving Sunday for Washington, but he agreed to meet with me for an hour at his office."

"Good job. What about the traders? Have you been able to contact any of them?"

"No. But I'm sure I can get connected through the two women who used them."

"Great. I had Tonja get you an advance. It should already be credited to your account. End your trip by getting them to take you on a run. Get a feel for what's happening. I also want you to try to move around the prison without an escort. I think there's a lot more going on there then just protecting fetuses. Remember those five women who were on the Cheryl Myers show?"

How could she forget? They were the impetus for the assignment. "I saw the tape. They said it was pretty tough."

"Tough, sure, but there was something else. Two of them said they couldn't account for some of the time they were there. I want you to see if the women you talk to have similar stories. I also want you to find out what happens to all those babies once they're born."

"I thought they were adopted out?" Sharon said. She hadn't thought much about them, the babies. They seemed more inconsequential to the story, but he was right. Their dispensation, if it wasn't wholesome adoption, could be pivotal to the assignment.

"Not all of them. See if any of them are ending up in the state foster homes. If so, I want to know how those conditions are, what type of education those kids are getting, and if once placed in the homes they're still available for adoption."

"This could take longer than I thought," she said excited, seeing for the first time the scope of the assignment. It wasn't just about women, it was about how a system worked, or didn't work. It could prove conclusively that the Moralist party, considered life more important than living.

"I don't care how long it takes. You just make sure you get the goods on these fanatics, so we can blow their religious asses out of the water. Elections are coming up in five months, Sharon. If someone doesn't expose what's really going on, four more states could go totally Moral. If that happens, they'll have the thirty-five states they need to start ratifying the Constitution.

Sharon was aware of what could happen in the next election. She knew her story would have an impact on the abortion issue, but hadn't seen it keeping voters away from a Moralists ticket. A chill ran through her. This was the assignment she had been waiting for – the career maker. Not only was she excited and anxious about getting started, she was ready for it. The apprenticeship was over. Once she stepped out of Derek's office, she would be a real journalist – a writer with the power to cause upheaval and change.

"I'll do my best," she said.

"I want better than your best. And here," he said pulling a folder from his top middle drawer and shoving it across the desk at her.

Sharon opened the folder. In it was an eight by ten glossy of a young blonde, blue-eyed woman in braces. With her square jaws and full face, she could have been Sharon's younger sister.

"Who is it?" she asked.

"Bethany Collins, seventeen. She's the daughter of an old college friend. She disappeared over a year ago when she thought she was pregnant. Her father believes she was picked up for attempted abortion. He hasn't heard from her since. I want you to see if she's in Arpaio."

"Hasn't he inquired?" she asked, staring at the girl's crooked smile.

"Yeah, but he can't get any straight answers. They say they may have picked up someone matching her description, but not her name, and that if it was her she was released after miscarrying."

"He doesn't believe them?"

"No, and he has no connections to get any answers."

"Except you," she smiled.

"Except me. And you, my dear, *are* my connection. I want you to find out one way or another if she's in there."

Sharon envisioned herself going up to every blonde blue-eyed inmate and asking if she was Bethany Collins. In reality she didn't think she'd be given the opportunity to talk to any of the inmates. Reverend Samuels had only promised entrance, never impromptu interviews.

"That won't be so easy," she said a little put off by Derek imposing a personal favor. "I doubt I'll see every woman there during my tour." She put the picture back in the folder.

"Just, keep your eyes open. I didn't promise him anything, but I owe him Sharon. All he wants to know is if she's there and if she's safe. Once he has confirmation, he can pursue it himself."

"I'll try. Anything else?" She put the folder in her bag, and looked up at him.

Derek shrugged his shoulders, "No. Just good luck, and bring me back a story to put a halt to those damn Moralists."

"I will." Sharon stood up and looked at the disheveled man who was about to give her the career boost she had plodded through four years of tedium to get. "I want you to know Derek, I really appreciate you giving me this assignment."

"You're the best person for it," he said, shuffling through the papers on his desk.

Personally she agreed with him, but was surprised he felt that way. In the four years she worked for him he had never excessively praised any of her stories. For a while she had worried she would drown in local politics and job fairs. She hesitated for a moment, then said, "I didn't know you thought so highly of my work."

"Sure I do." He looked up at her for a second as if pondering whether or not to continue, and then he said it. He brought up the dirty little secret she had shared with him in private over too many tequila sunrises. "Well, there's your style, which you know I love. But I had to take into consideration your personal insight. I'll be honest and tell you Marion wanted this assignment, and she has five years seniority over you. I would have given it to her too, except I believe you can tell it better. How old were you then, twenty?"

Sharon didn't answer him, but yes that's exactly how old she was. It had been about eight years now, and still the mere thought of it made her knees week. She looked down at the floor.

"I'm sorry, Sharon. I know it still must hurt. But it gives you an insight the rest of us just don't have. You can see this from the eyes of someone it could have happened to."

Sharon tried to brush the memory away, but the knot forming in her stomach was barely climaxing. She looked up at the boss she thought was her friend. "I thought a good journalist was supposed to stay detached, you know remain objective," she said in a weak, sarcastic voice. She put her bag down on the chair and backed up against the door.

"They are, you're right, but it always helps to have an inside view of a subject. Those women will trust you if they know you've been there, if they think you understand their reasons for taking such risks. It's your *in*, Sharon. Use it."

She didn't like being used, and yet a piece of her had known all along. She just didn't want to acknowledge it. He wasn't sending her in because he thought she was the best, he was sending her in because she was the only reporter on staff who had had an abortion. *Fuck it,* she said to herself, *this is your big break. If it takes using the most painful memory of your life to pull it off, so be it.* She gave her boss the upbeat smile she knew he was waiting for. "I'll use it," she said, stepping away from the door, and picking up her bag.

"Great!" Derek got up, walked around his desk, and put his arm around her shoulder. It wasn't a lecherous hold, or even an *I'm counting on you* hold, but rather a *take care of yourself* fatherly hold that Sharon had only experienced from her granddad. It was nice knowing he cared. It lessened the sense of betrayal. He opened the door and led her to Tonja's desk. "Tonja has everything you'll need. You need anything else, you call me. I want to know what's going on." He removed his arm from her shoulder and turned to his secretary. "She's all yours, Tonja." He gave Sharon a quick smile, an almost nervous smile, then turned back to his office.

"I made your reservations central to where I thought you'd be working." Tonja. said, gaining Sharon's attention. "Here's directions." Tonja offered a sheet of paper with Sharon's itinerary. "They're going to bill us for the room. I told them you might be staying past the anticipated three weeks, so don't worry about it. Just call me and I'll arrange it."

"Thanks," Sharon said, giving the paper a cursory look before folding it and putting it in her purse.

"Be careful." Sharon looked up. Derek hadn't gone into his office. He was standing in the door, looking at her. "They take this stuff seriously over there."

"I know," Sharon said, sure she was above any real danger, yet slightly disturbed at his apparent apprehension. "What kind of trouble can I get into by interviewing people? Like I told Thomas, they're still part of the United States. People have rights. The Constitution hasn't been ratified, yet."

"Don't you trust them." Tonja shook a pencil at her. "Their idea of what those rights are, are way different from what you're used to."

"I'll be fine," Sharon assured them, hoping the conviction in her voice would calm their nerves as well as her own. As for trusting anyone, no need to worry about that. Trust wasn't in her vocabulary.

"I'm sure you will. Keep in touch." Derek gave her one last smile then turned his attention towards Tonja. "Get Ted Johnson on the line for me will you."

"Sure thing." Tonja put on her head set. "Ted Johnson." She held up her hand for Sharon to wait, so she did. Derek closed his door.

"Derek Robinson calling for Ted Johnson," Tonja said into the mouthpiece. She picked up a large padded envelope on her desk and handed it to Sharon. "Here," she whispered.

"What is it," Sharon whispered back as she took it.

"Mr. Johnson, please hold for Derek Robinson." Tonja pushed a button on the headset and looked up at Sharon with a big smile. "High tech spy stuff."

"No way." Sharon opened the envelope and dumped the contents onto Tonja's desk. There were five leather headbands, a silver cross on a chain, a watch, a pen light, a worn black leather bible with her name embossed in gold, and an ID with her picture on it. She picked up one of the headbands and examined it. "What is it?"

"A camera and face distorter."

"Face distorter?"

"Pretty cool, huh? It's to use when you don't want your face recognizable through the street monitors. I'm not sure how it works, but it somehow deflects light so the points are slightly off from your real face."

Sharon tried it on. "So whenever I'm wearing it, it's on?"

"No. Only when it's at a about a fifteen degree angle. Here." Tonja reached up and pulled the front of the headband to Sharon's brow line. "There isn't a detectable light, but supposedly it works. Only thing is, be sure not to use it all the time. We're pretty sure you'll be put on the watch list the minute you enter the state. They need to think they're tracking you, so save it for when you move around with the traders."

Sharon took off the headband and looked at it more closely, then gently rubbed her hands up and down its spine.

"I can't feel anything."

"That's why they call it high tech."

"And the camera? How does that work?"

"You have to have the headband back in place, then…" Tonja picked up the necklace and put it on. "The cross acts as a remote for the camera. You nonchalantly play with the cross in your hand, like this." She fondled the cross and ran it back and forth along the bottom of the chain. "When it crosses the chain about an inch from where it normally hangs the headband snaps a picture. It works by movement and body heat, at least that's what the instructions said. You have to make sure your fingers are touching more than one side."

"Where's the lens?" Sharon asked, once again examining the headband.

"They said it's centered on the top edge and that it's focused for about six feet out. So, don't get too close, and make sure your hair stays flat."

"How do I reload it?"

"You don't. Each one of the headbands holds a hundred and ninety four pictures. You use it up, you start with a new one. Use your regular camera most the time. Save these for the incriminating shots. Also, since we were given five, try and alternate which ones your using. If one gets lost we won't lose a whole segment of the story."

"Where'd you get this stuff?" Sharon asked handing the headband back to Tonja.

"Who knows. It was brought by courier yesterday morning. Derek and I spent all afternoon going through it and reading the instructions. He wasn't so surprised with getting the stuff, just how sophisticated it was."

Sharon smiled. It was sophisticated, way beyond the Sentinel's budget. Whoever was sponsoring her trip took the assignment much more seriously than she or even Derek had, and had planned for the worst. That was good.

Sharon put down the headband and picked up the bible as Tonja took off the cross. "I suppose this is some type of listening device?"

"Only if you're wanting to hear the Word of God. Sorry. It's just a Bible. My grandmother's as a matter of fact. We had your name put on it, just in case anyone goes through your things. Looks better if you're a God fearing woman."

"Of course. And the watch?" Sharon said, putting down the Bible and picking it up.

Tonja reached over and started to unbuckle Sharon's watch. "It's a recorder. Wear it all the time. If you pull out the stem, it will record everything that's being said."

"I love it," Sharon laughed as she turned it over in her hand. "Can I keep it when I'm done?"

"Yeah, right." Tonja took the watch from Sharon and turned it over. "See this?" she said pointing to a small round cell firmly seated in the watch's back.

Sharon picked up a few of the handful of matching cells off the desk. "What are they, batteries?"

"No. Digitized recorders. Each lasts twenty hours. You fill one up, and pop it out like this. See?" Tonja demonstrated by pulling the small cell from its holding place and putting in a new one.

"This is going to be fun." Sharon took the watch from Tonja and put it on.

Tonja held up the penlight. "This is very important. You'll need to activate it when you get out to your jeep. It tags on to your car's GPS system and records your exact positioning." Tonja handed Sharon two batteries. "You activate it by loading the batteries, but you need to be in your jeep. Once it's activated, if you push this button it will log your exact coordinates, and then return those coordinates instead of your real ones. Like the face distorter, only use it when you really need to. Make sure you return to where you activated it, before pressing the button again to deactivate it. General vicinity is okay, it will make the correction for you the next time you move the vehicle."

Sharon shook her head. "They didn't miss a thing."

"Good thing, too. I'm thinking this assignment is a lot more dangerous than any of us thought. Derek's scared too. I think that's why he wanted me to give it to you when he wasn't around."

Sharon looked back at his closed door and wondered if he was sitting at his desk regretting sending her, worrying about her, or just talking to Ted Johnson and dismissing her. A slight knot formed in her stomach. *Damn him for worrying.* She turned back toward Tonja.

"So what's the ID for? It looks exactly like mine."

"Yeah, except for the number."

Sharon looked down at the number on the ID. It was way off.

"I don't get it."

"Derek's afraid that if you use your ID and get stopped for any reason, they'll pull up your medical records. He wants them to think you're writing an article leaning towards criminalizing abortion here in California. Didn't he tell you that?"

"He did. But what do my medical records have to do with anything?"

Tonja looked around the office then leaned over her desk. In a hushed voice she said, "The minute you step into that state, they're gonna know everything about you and almost everything you do. Just coming from Southern California's going to be a big enough strike against you. If they knew about your abortion they probably wouldn't let you in."

Sharon's head jerked up so fast a bone cracked. "How'd you know about that?"

Tonja grimaced. "Sorry. Derek told me. You gotta understand, Sharon, Derek, he tells me everything. I didn't mean to offend you."

Offend, no. Shock was a better word for it. How could Derek have shared such a personal piece of information? Armament or not, there had been no need to tell Tonja. Not only was he using Sharon, but now come to find out he had betrayed her confidence. *Never trust a man*, she could hear her mother warning her.

"I'm sorry," Tonja said.

"No. I'm not offended," Sharon finally said. "It's just that I've worked hard to keep that part of my life private."

Tonja held up her hand. "I've never told anyone. I promise. But I can't speak for Derek," she said lowering her hand. "You know him. He'll use anything if he thinks it will get him what he wants."

"Yeah, I know he will," Sharon said with a smile. It was one of the qualities she admired most in him, but she didn't like the idea of him using her. She'd have to re-examine that specific attribute when she had more time. For now, there was nothing she could do about it, so it wasn't worth worrying about. Tonja already knew and maybe that was for the best. When Sharon got back, she'd consider pursuing a friendship with the girl. It would be a relief to have someone to share secrets. Someone who had some of her own, like why her son was eating out of a garbage can.

"See if you can keep him from telling anyone else," Sharon said, as she picked up each of the items, put them back in the large envelope, and then placed the envelope into her bag with the folder containing

Bethany Collin's picture.

"I'll do my best, but no promises. I'm not with him outside the office."

"Good enough." Sharon looked at the stairwell. "Well, if that's it Tonja, I think I'm going to head out."

"Not so fast." Tonja pushed a form in front of her. "Sign here. I don't want to be responsible for any of that spy shit. They're on loan. On what I get paid, one missing link of that chain could break me for a month."

Sharon smiled, knowing by their earlier conversation that Tonja was probably better paid than half the staff. She signed it and handed the pen she had picked up off the desk back to Tonja. "You're all clear."

"You too. And I don't want you coming back here all full of religion. We get enough of that down at the AME."

"Not to worry. I brought my anti-religious ear plugs."

"Good for you," Tonja laughed. "Now get out there and save some souls, sister friend before the Moralist crusade sticks it to the rest of us."

"I feel a revival coming on," Sharon said in her best Evangelical voice then waved good-bye to Tonja and headed for the parking garage.

Her heart raced as she approached her Jeep. Silently, she cursed Derek for putting doubt in her mind about her ability and safety, then she cursed herself for falling for it. Everything would be fine. She'd get her story, then she'd get out. They couldn't do anything to her for pursing the truth, even if they wanted it hushed. Until the Moralists changed the Constitution, she was protected by it. That was *her* armament and by God, she'd sure as hell use it if she had to.

The back of the Jeep was stuffed with clothes and equipment. She had everything she needed. "This is it," she said as she placed her thumb in the door lock. "No turning back now."

Once in the jeep, she pulled the penlight from the envelope and put the batteries in. Nothing happened. It was an innocuous penlight. She thought to push the button to activate it, but thought again. She'd have to trust it when she needed it. Blind faith, wasn't that what everyone had these days? Well she'd put hers in technology, and hope it'd get her ass out alive.

She put one of the headbands and the necklace on and then shoved the rest of Tonja's toys in her purse before typing in her destination and putting the jeep on autopilot. It would take about seven hours to get to her hotel in Phoenix. Plenty of time to strategize, and to decide just how much of her life she wanted to share with strangers.

Derek was right. It was a powerful card she held. Used correctly, it could get her into places no other reporter on staff would be able to go. For the first time in her life she saw a bright side to the rape that had haunted her for so many years.

3

It was a long trip through the desert. Out of boredom, she had taken the car out of autopilot and drove herself. Memories of the rape flooded through her. "Damn you Derek," she said out loud. These were the ghosts of painful pasts she didn't want to revisit. But it seemed she had no choice. The wall that protected her tumbled easily and every detail of the rape came back. She could smell the oil from the street where he had attacked her, feel the tip of the knife under her ribcage as he pounded inside her. She hadn't screamed. She did as she had been taught. *Lie there and take it. Come out alive.* Worse than the rape, she relieved the fear, the fear of dying. The fear of having someone rip away her control, of enforcing his will without giving her a chance to fight back. Then there was the humiliation. Walking down the empty street, naked and bruised looking for help. She had never felt so vulnerable in her life. He had stolen so much from her. Back then she didn't think she would ever recover, but she did. She was stronger than him. He had only been able to subdue her for one night. When she was safe, she promised herself not to allow him to destroy the rest of her life, but then the worst she could imagine happened.

She was pregnant. Pregnant with a rapist's child. And though she knew it wasn't the child's fault, she couldn't help viewing the fetus as a festering wound, an impure parasitic infection. There was no way she could have carried it to term. No way she could have ever loved it.

She did what she believed was best, and though the rape hadn't scarred her, the abortion had. It was her darkest secret. She could still feel the doctor's cold dry hands, hear the suction of the vacuum that had disposed of her attacker's spawn, feel the loss of a child that had never sinned.

Sharon had regrets, but in her heart she knew she had done what was best for both her and the child. She would give no more thought to what it could have been, because as far as she was concerned, it never was. She was at peace with her decision and with her God. No one could take that away from her or force it on her.

It was past four when Sharon pulled up to the California border checkpoint. It had been a long time since she had crossed this particular border. The last time, on a boating trip with her granddad when she was seven, there were only California Agricultural checkpoints. *Any fruit or vegetation, sir?* Things had changed. Now there were two check points, one at both the California and Arizona border. They were strategically placed on either side of the connecting bridge that crossed the Colorado River, a yellow line painted across the center of the bridge, marked the division, not only of states, but of thought and law.

Sharon pulled up to the California checkpoint. A female guard waved her on, but pointed to two large bold signs. One warned the motorist to adhere to Arizona's laws, citing California's inability to act on the individual's behalf. The other showed a picture of a pregnant woman with a red slash through her. Below the picture was a sign. *Pregnant woman cannot be guaranteed safe passage out of Arizona. If crossing the country go through Nevada.* It reminded Sharon of the signs she had seen while hiking in bear country. *Active bear path, menstruating women take alternate trail.* It also reminded her of why she had come.

As she crossed, her gut tightened, her palms began to perspire, her foot rose off the gas pedal. "No getting cold feet," she warned herself in an attempt to push the feelings of trepidation aside. It didn't help much.

The Arizona border was imposing. It was made up of four inspection booths, computerized and manned by uniformed guards with guns. There were four Arizona State patrol cars in the parking lot. Two officers stood sentry on either side of the freeway, their weapons exposed and at ready, as if they were guarding a treasured gem.

Sharon approached the Arizona inspection booth. A man and woman dressed in tank tops and cutoffs were being escorted into a building in the center of the freeway. A guard was getting into a faded orange Volkswagen bug. "I wonder what rule they broke?" she said out loud as she pulled into the inspection bay.

"ID," an older man with thick black hair implants demanded.

"Sure," she said fumbling in her bag for her wallet. She could see the woman through the row of booths. Her long dark braid swung frantically about as she looked over her shoulder, her eyes darting, in what Sharon took as an attempt to get someone, anyone to help her. Sharon couldn't concentrate on the feeble search her hand was making in her bag. She wanted to know why the couple was being detained? What had they done? Then a strange sensation hit her, fear. She could feel it creeping up from the base of her stomach and welling in her chest. She didn't think she'd be this scared, this soon, but she was. She silently wished Thomas was with her as her hand found the wallet, then as if touching a rattlesnake, she dropped it. *Fake ID, you idiot,* she chided herself. *Don't make your first mistakes before getting into the damn state.* She couldn't afford to be careless. Closing her eyes for half a second, she regrouped, pulled her purse onto her lap, and opened the envelope with the fake ID. She smiled when she turned back to the guard and handed him the card. "Sorry, I should've had it ready," she said.

"No problem," the guard said as he eyed the ID then took a good look at Sharon.

"What's going on over there," she asked, nodding her head towards the couple as they disappeared through the door of the center building.

"Couldn't say, ma'am," the guard said without looking out his window. He ran Sharon's ID through an electronic reader. She held her breath, wishing she had checked the card out in LA, leery of the counterfeit data. "Look into the camera please." He swiveled the face scanner to point directly at her face. Within seconds the calculations were complete, the digitized reading of her face was blocked out in bright blue by the word CONFIRMED. "Purpose of visiting Arizona?" he asked.

She let out the held breath. "I'm a reporter."

"So, I see." The guard looked down at her and brushed his hand back along his sprouting hair. "And what exactly will you be reporting on, Ms. Clark?"

Derek had prepared her for this. There was no getting in without a good reason. Reporters were frowned upon, especially ones from Free states. Derek had arranged it with the authorities though, they knew she was coming. He had told them she was going to write an anti-abortion piece.

"I'm writing a piece on the abortion issue," she said with the most sincere smile she could conjure under the circumstances. "Elections are coming up and we want to see how things are working in Arizona."

"Pro or Con?" he asked.

"Con," she said, still keeping the plastic smile on her face.

The guard turned back to his computer and typed. Sharon craned her neck to see what he was writing, but couldn't. It seemed like a lot.

"Where will you be staying?"

"Phoenix."

He gave her a look she believed was meant to convey his annoyance with her. "Where in Phoenix?"

She stared at him for a second, unsure of what he meant. She looked up at him and squinted. "Do you mean, which hotel?"

"Yes, Ma'am."

Holy Shit. Fear was starting to turn to anger. They wanted to strip her of her rights, her privacy, right there at the border. No pretenses, no happy welcoming committee, just register your movement, and obey all laws. "I don't see why you need…"

"Destination, please, or I can't let you enter."

She was about to tell him it was none of his G D business, but decided against it. It was better to stay calm, go with the flow. What did she care if they knew where she was going to stay. She reached into her bag and pulled out the directions Tonja had given her. "I'm staying at the Desert Suites on McDowell," she said then threw the itinerary back in her bag.

He took a few seconds to type, then without looking at her asked, "Length of visit?"

"Jesus." She shook her head and looked back at the building where the couple had been escorted. Maybe they had stayed a day longer than planned.

"Length of visit?" the guard asked again this time louder and more direct.

"Three or four weeks," she said slowly and with too much emphasis. She sounded like a fifth grader talking back to her math teacher.

He typed then handed back her ID. "Enjoy your visit. Remember you can't take any fruit or plants out of the state."

She took, or rather grabbed, her ID back. "Don't worry," she said as she threw it back in her bag and put the Jeep in gear.

"So much for self-control." She slowly pulled out of the orange-coned lane. She looked at the guard through her rear view mirror. Her picture flashed on his screen. He was still typing.

The rest of the trip was uneventful, the scenery boring. Sharon filled the long drive by recording a list of questions she would ask at each interview. Later in the evening she planned to transpose those questions to paper as she prepared for her first day's schedule.

Finding the hotel was easy. It was only a couple of miles north of the airport. She checked in without incident, though she did have to show her ID again. She hoped they hadn't noticed the sweat on her brow as she fumbled in the bag for the right one.

Her room was on the third floor of the hotel. It had a queen sized bed, a dresser, and a writing table. The art on the walls was the type you could buy for fifty-nine dollars at the starving artist sales held monthly at various hotels throughout Los Angeles. Good, but nothing original. There were three desert landscapes throughout the room, their rust and sand hues picking up the colors of the Aztec pattern on the bedspread and matching side chair.

She pulled her files from one of the suitcases and spread her notes all over the bed. Tomorrow she had three interviews scheduled. Two with woman who had been incarcerated and one with the Baptist minister, Reverend Samuels. She transposed the notes she had made on her drive and changed the batteries and disk in her recorder before climbing into the soft bed and calling Thomas.

She didn't tell him about the couple being detained at the Arizona border, but did mention the guard. Thomas reminded her to stay safe. A warning she had heard all day, and was just now starting to take seriously. But she was too tired to think about what might happen. Instead she let his voice calm her, his handsome face seduce her. With each word he spoke, another muscle relaxed. Thomas was a gift. It would be a long assignment without him.

4

Martha looked up from the space on the floor where she had fixed her gaze. There were three other people in the room, two girls and one boy. Each wore the required state uniform, sand colored cotton pants with a matching short-sleeved work shirt, tightly buttoned to the collar. They sat silently. One of the girls stared at the wall, the other at her feet. The boy watched his hands as they nervously fiddled with the ID tag on his brown duffel bag. In the hour they had been sitting there, no one attempted to converse. No secret looks were exchanged, no reassuring smiles given. They had been taught well.

Martha knew the boy. He was Indian, Pima she thought by his large size. She had seen him in the nightly meetings – the only time boys and girls were allowed to associate. He had been singled out many times and ordered to refrain from his fidgeting. She looked at his constantly moving hands and remembered the time when she had sat next to him.

The reverend was talking about the purity of the soul, and how all have fallen short of the glory of God. His message dulled in her ears as her attention was drawn to a quiet scratching sound to her left. She turned her head slightly towards the large Indian boy beside her, and watched him out of the corner of her eye. His eyes were on the pulpit. His fingernails scratched incessantly at the knees of his starched cotton pants. His right leg jiggled as if he had to pee. A guardian walked up to the row in which they were seated. Martha faced forward. She had been caught not paying attention. The guardian stood there for a few minutes. Martha could feel his presence like a weighty pull, tempting her to acknowledge him, to admit her guilt. She tried to hear what the reverend was saying, but his words wouldn't filter. In a quick single movement, the guardian's arm reached over and above her. Her gut tightened. Her eyes shut tight. Her shoulders pulled in towards her spine. The firm wood of a paddle stick swished by her face, landing firmly on the boy's hands. She involuntarily jumped from the loud slap, the words "oh, h," escaped her lips as air gushed from her constricted lungs. Her body shook, but she kept her eyes glued to the reverend.

Without saying a word, the guardian removed his hand and paddle as quickly as he had presented them. He stopped for an instant. His fist hovered close to Martha's face. She didn't flinch. It was a test and if she failed, she knew she'd be next to feel the heat of the paddle. Seconds passed like hours, then the guard withdrew to his stance in the aisle. The sermon continued as if nothing had happened, but Martha didn't hear it. From the corner of her eye she watched the curl of the boy's hands as his fingernails dug into his lap, and a single tear slowly slid down his face.

That had happened her first week. She had always felt a sense of camaraderie with the boy. He had seen her fear as clearly as she had seen his shame. But there were no feelings of friendship today as they sat waiting to hear their names. There was too much apprehension, too much hope and fear of the unknown.

Martha shifted her gaze to the two other wards.

She knew one of them, LaShana Syas. They had been in the same dorm. The other was LaTasha, LaShana's identical twin. They were indistinguishable, except for the four inch raised scar that ran down LaShana's cheek. Martha touched her cheek, remembering the day the girl had been marred.

They were getting ready for bed. LaShana was in the bathroom supposedly brushing her teeth when two guardians burst into the dorm. They tore open the bathroom door and dragged LaShana out of the room. Her screams could be heard all the way down the hall. The mirrors, told. LaShana knew that, they all knew that, but she had done it anyway. She had spent more than her allocated two minutes in front of the mirror. Self-admiration and primping were serious infractions; and this wasn't LaShana's first violation. That next morning a special meeting was called. All wards were pulled from training, chores, and sick beds, forced to attend LaShana's punishment, dolled out by Reverend Ames, in the name of God.

"We have before us. A sister who tests God's virtue," the reverend said while LaShana, cloaked in a white cloth robe, was escorted up to the pulpit. "She mocks the very God who has created her. She has deemed her own image more beautiful than the glory of God. How can this be?" He shook his head and lowered it. "How can this be?"

"'For if a man think himself to be something, when he is nothing, he deceiveth himself,'" the reverend yelled as he pounded his hand on the pulpit. Slowly, he lifted his head and stared out at the congregation. Raising his arm, he pointed at LaShana. In a soft voice he quoted scripture. "'Favour is deceitful, and beauty is vain.'" At that, guardians stepped up on either side of LaShana and held her by the arms. Reverend Ames walked over to her and drew a short blade from under his robe. "'But a woman that feareth the Lord,'" he yelled. "'She shall be praised.'" He put his hand on LaShana's forehead and pushed her head back, placing the tip of the knife an inch below her eye.

LaShana screamed.

"Don't move," Reverend Ames warned her. "I could poke out your eye."

LaShana closed her mouth, but Martha could still hear her whimpering and see the trembling of her chin.

In a hushed, but loud voice, Reverend Ames said, "'Let the woman learn in silence with all subjection,'" then he sliced LaShana's face from cheek to jaw.

LaShana's knees buckled. Blood fell down her neck and chest. The congregation sat silent. The reverend, stepping behind her, placed his hands on LaShana's head and spoke above her cries. "Dear Father," he prayed. "Forgive this creature, who thou art inclined to call daughter. Cast the demon Satan from her soul, and release her from the bondage of vanity. Make her pure again in your heart and forgive her her transgressions. She is but a poor soul tempted by the Devil's enchantments. Guide us, as her brothers and sisters in Christ to show her the way of your Word and to instruct her on the righteous path. Amen."

"Amen," the wards mechanically repeated.

Martha stared across the waiting room at the broken beauty of the young woman's face. She had never really spoken to LaShana, but she knew something of her history. The Syas twins had been in the home for almost eight years. The only time they were allowed to be in the same room at the same time was during the nightly meeting, and then they were not allowed to speak, touch, or look at one another.

Sara, the girl who occupied the bed next to Martha's had once told her that when the twins first arrived one would always sneak into the other's bed. Finally someone told on them and they were severely punished and separated. As a rule, Living Trust frowned on tight relationships. They believed no one should come between the ward, God, and the state. If a guardian felt you spent too much time talking to or being with one particular person, you would be put through the rite of disassociation. Forced to sign an agreement that you would never speak to that person again and in front of all your peers vow never to be seen within twenty feet of each other. "It's one of their ways," Sara had said, "to keep us from plotting against them."

Martha thought of Sara, and her wide-eyed smile, and realized she was going to miss her. Though most of their conversations had happened in snippets, Martha admired Sara's spirit. She was the only one Martha trusted.

Sara had been in the home for ten years, by her account, but had not fallen prey to the bombardment of demoralizing verbal abuse that was thrown at them every day. Sara told Martha that even though she touted the state dogma, she didn't believe a word of it, nor did she believe she was worthless. Martha envied Sara's strength and determination to maintain a sense of self – two things Martha had lost by the end of her first week at Living Trust.

As she stared around the room, noticing the sterility she was about to escape, she remembered that awful first day when she was brought in, handcuffed like a criminal, and stripped searched by a female guardian.

"Go to hell," she had told the guardian when ordered to strip.

"Right behind you," the guardian said. She grabbed Martha's hand and twisted it up behind her back. "Strip or I'll have it done for you."

"Fuck you," Martha whispered.

Martha's feet were kicked out from under her. The guardian let go of her arm and she fell. Her head hit the concrete and bounced. Stunned, Martha lay on the floor starring at the ceiling, not quite sure what was happening to her.

"Gus," the guardian called. "Gus, get in here. We have another one."

Four white men, all only a few years older than Martha, moved into the room. Strong hands grabbed her hands and feet. Martha began to refocus when she heard the first cuts made into her favorite jeans.

"Bitch," she yelled. "You fucking bitch."

The scissors came up above her face. "You're mine, ward. Whatever happens in here is up to me. You want to keep that pretty face, then shut up."

Martha let her body go limp. She looked at each of the men. They turned their heads. There would be no help, no sympathy from them. The female guardian was brutal. She nicked Martha five times, drawing blood. But Martha didn't respond, she didn't cry out. She wouldn't give the woman the satisfaction.

Strips of cloth were yanked out from under her, exposing naked skin. It was the first time a man had seen her without clothes since she reached puberty.

"Roll her over," the guardian ordered.

Hands were everywhere. Martha didn't fight, nor did she help as she was mauled and turned.

"Gus, lift up her back end for me, will you?"

One of the men sat on her shoulders. He put his arms around her naked belly and lifted her ass into the air. The guardians holding her legs, spread them. Cold petroleum jelly attached to someone's fingers explored the inside of her vagina, then rectum.

"Clean," the guardian said.

She was dropped to the cold floor.

The guardian and her henchmen left without saying another word.

When the door closed behind them, Martha began to sob. Strips of her clothing, the only thing she had been able to count as hers for the past five days, lay in a heap beside her. She pulled them towards her and cradled them around her head.

After a few minutes, the door opened, and she was ordered to get up. Two of the men who had held her down watched and waited while she pulled herself from the floor. As soon as she was standing, one pulled her hands behind her and cuffed them. The other took a pair of scissors and cut her waist long hair to an inch above her shoulder.

Raggedly shorn, naked, and smeared with petroleum jelly, she was paraded down a long hall, in front of guardians and other wards on her way to the showers. Everyone looked away. At the time she had thought it was out of empathy, but later she learned that looking would have meant punishment for the wards, and that the guardians, protégés of the state foster care system themselves, looked away out of years of reinforced moral obligation.

"A woman's body," she heard the reverend repeating in her mind while she sat in the waiting room, "while beautiful in the eyes of the Lord, inspires lust and is therefore a sin to behold."

As she sat in the cold barren room with the three other wards, she thought about the girl she had been out on the streets of Phoenix, and wondered how she had been lost so quickly.

"Clean it up," she remembered the guardian ordering her on the last day she had rebelled – her second day at Living Trust.

She looked at the diarrhea that covered the floor and bed. She felt sick and turned away. "I can't," she said. "I'll throw up."

"I said clean it," the guardian shouted throwing a mop at her.

She didn't reach out to catch it, she just let it fall. "Go to hell," she murmured.

He grabbed her by the back of her neck and pulled her over to the mattress. She struggled, but he was too strong. Without a word, he shoved her face in a puddle of liquid shit and held it there. Martha held her breath for as long as she could. He hadn't let up, and she had to breath. She opened her mouth and gulped for air, sucking shit beyond her lips as she did so. The guardian let go. She slipped and fell in more of the diarrhea.

Her stomach revolted. "Oh, no," she cried. She turned from the mess, her hand seeking out clean flooring. She pulled herself free of the mire and threw up.

The guardian said nothing. He just stood there watching.

"Bastard," she said as she tried to pull herself off the floor.

The guardian placed his foot between Martha's shoulder blades and shoved her down into her own spew.

"You're going to clean this all up," he said calmly. "There is a bucket in the bathroom. Rinse the sheets out by hand and put them in the bucket when you finish. Do you understand me, ward?"

Martha nodded her head, strips of diarrhea and vomit drenched hair fell over her face.

As she sat looking back at it now, she knew it had been the day they had stolen her soul, and she had become like all the rest, fearful and without will.

Hopefully the same thing hadn't happened to her brother, Anthony. He was much stronger than she was, he would have held up better. *But would that be a good thing?* Martha asked herself looking at the vacant dull eyes of the boy sitting across from her. *It doesn't matter* she decided, *because by the end of the month I'll have you out of there.*

The last she had seen of him was at their mother's trial.

"Mr. Foreman, have you reached a verdict," the judge had asked that warm winter day.

"We have your honor."

"On two counts of illegal possession of a controlled substance. How do you find the defendant, Suzanne Garcia?"

"Guilty, your Honor."

Martha screamed. She knew the consequences. It was the third time her mother had been charged with possession, and just like in baseball, three strikes were all you got.

Martha remembered pleading with her mother. Her grandmother was no longer alive, and their father dead many years before. "If you get caught again," she had screamed that day, "what happens to Anthony and me? Do you ever think of what you're doing to us?"

"Don't be so selfish," her mother yelled back. "I'm the closest thing this community has to a doctor. What do you want me to do, sit around and watch them die?"

"Better them die than we end up in a state home," Martha cried before running through the door. She felt guilty for those words, but in her heart it had been exactly the way she felt. The community had used her mother. Without medical care, they were reliant on the few free clinics set up by churches in the area. Clinics with lines going out the door, few supplies, and fewer doctors. Her mother filled the gaps. She had become known as the healer, learning her craft of herbal remedies when she was a teenager from an ancient Navajo Shaman hiding deep in the Grand Canyon.

Martha loved her mother, she was proud of who she was and what she did, but she had been scared. The FDA controlled medicinal herbs. It was illegal to purchase them without a doctor's prescription, and no doctor prescribed them. Martha's mother had her sources though. She grew batches of innocent looking weeds and flowers in alleys between the apartments. She was fearless. But no one is immune to the law or to the church. It had taken them six years to catch her again, but they did.

Martha was with her when the cruiser pulled up beside them. "Suzanne Garcia?" one Posse member had asked as the other stepped out of the car brandishing his gun.

"Yes," her mother hesitantly responded.

"Put your bag down ma'am and turn around, hands on your head."

"What's this all about?" her mother asked while complying with their demands.

Martha stood perfectly still, frozen to the pavement, as the Posse member with the gun came around from the passenger side of the car, picked up her mother's bag and emptied it on the urine stained sidewalk. Make-up, candy, papers, and tampons, rolled and blew down the street.

"Nothing," the would be detective said, throwing the bag down and under the cruiser.

The other got out of the car and stepped up behind her mom. His hands poked and prodded her mother's body as he frisked her. "Found something here," he said as he stuck his hand inside her shirt, exposing her breast to the street and pulling out a bag of dried lobelia. Throwing it to the other Posse member, he continued his search. He reached up under Suzanne's dress and pulled down her panties, exposing a blood free sanitary napkin. "What do we have here?" he asked, pulling the pad free of her underwear.

Martha looked over at her mother. Suzanne gave her a quick short shake as if to tell her not to respond to what he had found.

The civilian vigilante examined it for a minute, then turned it around and sliced open its back, exposing a cache of fresh comfrey. "We've got you this time, witch. Check that one out," he ordered his partner, nodding at Martha as he cuffed her mother and threw her into the cruiser, her panties still at her knees.

Martha clenched her teeth as the Posse member ran his hands up and down her body. She prepared to be probed. She held back her tears and took a deep breath as he reached the hem of her tee shirt and felt around the waist of her jeans. But he didn't go beneath her clothes. He didn't penetrate her private parts. She had been let off easy. It was her mother who had received the thorough treatment. Which was only fair, since it was *she* who was the chronic offender.

"You the daughter?" the man with the gun asked.

Martha nodded.

"You have a brother, don't you? Where is he?"

"I don't know," she mumbled. *Family is power, protect them at all cost,* she heard her father telling her when she was little. *We're each other's power.*

"Bull shit. You tell me where he is, or we'll get it out of your mother here." With that he moved over to the cruiser and raised his gun to Suzanne's head.

"Don't tell them," her mother whispered.

"Shut up," he yelled at her.

"Look," the other Posse member said as he stepped in front of Martha. He took her face in his hand and pulled it up, stretching her neck so far that she had to stand on her tiptoes. "Mommy's going to go to jail for a very long time, and since you and your brother are minors, it's up to us good, law abiding, folk to protect you. Now you tell me where your brother is or I'll let him blow your mother's fucking brains out right here and now."

"At home," she cried. "He's at home."

For five days they sat in separate cells as their mother was arraigned and tried. Only on the final day, the day of the verdict, were they allowed to be in court.

Anthony had not left the room easily. He kicked and screamed as the bailiff cuffed him and dragged him away.

Martha didn't know what had happened to him, and no one seemed willing to tell her. She had stopped asking after the first week.

She thought of him and his quick temper, now, and smiled. Today was the day, May fifteenth, the day to set things right. She was eighteen, of legal age to be on her own, and to petition for custody of her brother. He had been her power to get through the past four months; she would now return that power by freeing him.

A door opened and a white man holding a clipboard stepped into the room. *Call me, call my name first,* Martha internally pleaded.

"Martha Garcia?" The clerk asked looking directly at her. Martha tried to contain the smile, but couldn't.

"Present," she said standing up, back straight, shoulders square.

"Get your things and follow me."

Martha picked up the duffel bag that had been handed to her as she entered the room. It was not very heavy, and she had no idea what was in it. All she knew was it held her name, personal identification number, the one she had been given at birth and made to memorize before she was three, and her birth date. She hoped it contained a new pair of jeans and at least one piece of colorful clothing.

The man held the door for her as she walked through it into a long empty corridor. "Third door on your right," he said, then disappeared into an office immediately inside the door to the waiting room. Martha slowly walked down the hall, fearful what the exiting process would be. The door was open. She stopped two feet before it, took a deep breath and stepped forward, turning to face the lone occupant.

A heavy set woman, with orange dyed hair, a deep green scarf, burgundy jacket and navy blue dress sat behind the desk eating french fries and a burger. Like Pavlov's dog, saliva filled Martha's parched mouth. It had been a long time since she enjoyed anything but the dry stale food served in the cafeteria. "Have a seat," the woman mumbled through the food in her mouth. She quickly wiped her hands on a napkin and opened a thin file on her desk. "Martha Garcia?"

"Yes, ma'am." The chair was gray, metal and armless. It was cold against the warm colors of the large woman's wardrobe.

"I'm Mrs. Jordan, your social worker. Before we get started, let me wish you happy birthday."

Martha smiled at her. She didn't expect to hear those words today. She had imagined the head guardian, one last time, screaming her worthlessness in her ear and then shoving her out the door. She never envisioned a Mrs. Jordan, overweight and colorful, could exist inside the Child Services system. "Thank you," she said.

Mrs. Jordan flipped through the few pages in the open file. "I'm afraid you don't give me much to work with. Seems you've only been here for four months."

"Yes, ma'am." *Four months of hell.*

Mrs. Jordan leaned over her desk, planted her elbows firmly on its wood, folded her hands and leaned her chin on her knuckles. "Tell me, what skills do you have?"

"Skills?"

"Yes, part of the release requirement is that I find you a job."

A trap. It's a trap. They aren't going to release me. She adjusted her seat, too afraid to ask, but too afraid not to know. She stammered. "Wha, what do you mean? If you don't find me a job, they won't let me go?"

"Oh, don't worry." The woman waved her pudgy hand. "I'll find you a job, even if its slinging burgers at Wendy's."

Mrs. Jordan's eyes were large and dark brown, the light flickered off them, making them twinkle. She reminded Martha of the fairy god-mother in the Cinderella story she had read when she was a child.

"I'm here, Martha," she said more seriously, "to make sure you get the best start possible as you re-enter society. The more you help me, the better I can help you." She looked down at the file and shook her head. "It's a shame you weren't here long enough to get into one of the training programs."

Martha knew of the so-called training programs. Girls were offered clerical, assembly line, housekeeping, and child-care. The boys were automatically entered into the Armed Services. A few of the lifetime wards, the most disciplined and pious, were hand picked by the head guardian to join the guardian apprenticeship program. The training, she had heard, was stricter than living in the state's custody or the mandatory four year enlistment. She thanked God in her daily prayers for making her ineligible.

"No. They said I wasn't going to be here long enough to benefit from them, so I spent most of my time mopping floors."

"Hhm. Mopping floors isn't really a skill. Did you have a job before you came here?"

Martha thought back to the streets she came from. She could smell the fresh tortillas frying in the back room of the grocer.

"I delivered groceries for a market near my house," she said.

"No. That won't do. Our aim is to get you out of those kinds of neighborhoods and into a more civilized existence."

More civilized? What could be more civilized than her own small community where everyone knew each other and looked out for one another? People like Mrs. Jordan just didn't understand community. "They live in boxed houses, ten feet away from their neighbors with high walls. God forbid they ever see each other for more than a minute or two," Suzanne Garcia had said many times when talking about the moral decay of Arizonians.

"My neighborhood is great. I plan on going back there. It's my home."

"Martha, my dear. There's no home there for you. Our records show your father is dead and your mother is in prison for life. You have no family."

"My brother." Martha sat straighter in her chair, her eyes widened.

"Oh yes, your brother. My records show he is also a ward of the state. No, you must not think of the past. You're a part of the state family now, we'll take care of you." Mrs. Jordan pulled a print out of names and phone numbers from under her desk blotter.

Martha never expected wards were seen as anything but a burden. Maybe she was wrong. Maybe Mrs. Jordan would help her make a future for herself, so her children wouldn't wind up like she had – property of the state.

"I've always wanted to go to college," Martha said, her spirits lifting for a brief second. "I was a B student in high school. I have enough money saved for my first year's tuition. If I could get a grant from the state, I could go to school and work part-time to help support us."

"Money?" Mrs. Jordan said. "You don't have any money. Any holdings in your name became property of the state the minute you were made a ward."

Martha's mouth dropped. "What? They can't do that. That's my money. They can't just take my money. I planned on becoming a doctor."

"Oh, honey." Mrs. Jordan leaned over her desk and reached out for Martha's hand. "If only you had been here longer, we could have helped you to understand and accept your position in life. Even if you still had your money, where is one year of college going to get you?"

"But with grants…"

"What grants? They'd never give a girl with your background a grant? I'm sorry, Martha, but it's a known fact your kind just don't have the motivation to stick out eight years of college. You're best suited for service jobs, or assembly manufacturing."

Martha didn't know about the rest of *her kind*, but she knew herself. She had worked hard to get good grades while attending one of the last schools in Arizona that required no additional funds beyond the state and federal voucher. In a school with overcrowded classroom, twenty-year-old textbooks, and no air-conditioning, she had worked hard for her education. Mr. Ramirez, her tenth grade science teacher, told her she had potential, and she believed him. Her dream was to become a doctor, to follow in her mother's footsteps. Only she, Martha, would get the respect and pharmaceuticals her mother lacked.

"But, I've wanted to be in the medical field for a long time," Martha pleaded. "My teachers even said I'd make a great doctor."

Mrs. Jordan shook her head. "I'm afraid, Martha, the closest you'll get to that dream is by being an orderly or a receptionist. There's just no money out there to put you through college. Trust me, you'll be much happier in a less taxing position. And soon, you'll meet a man, get married, and have children. All in God's good plan, dear.

"In the meantime, the state needs you to work in other types of positions. By law you have to work and make payments to the state for four years. After that you're free to do whatever you want with your life. So let's see." Mrs. Jordan ran her finger down the short list on the printout. "Here's a good one. This is perfect for you. It's a maid position up on Camelback Mountain, in one of those lovely homes. I've actually met Mrs. Sanders. I think you two will get along famously."

Martha knew about the four year commitment and that she had no way of fighting it, but she did not intend to be forced to do menial labor. She stood up quickly, the metal chair toppling backwards crashing against the open door. "A maid," she yelled. "I can't be a maid. Just because my skin's a different color than yours doesn't mean I'm stupid. I need a career not enslavement."

Mrs. Jordan leaned over the desk and pointed her finger at Martha. "Sit down. How dare you yell at me. I'm trying to help you, young lady. If you're not willing to work with me, then maybe you need to stay here for a little longer. Is that what you want? Jesus, Mary and Joseph, don't you kids learn anything while you're here?"

Martha stood, saying nothing. Her body shook with anger and fear. She was angry with herself for jeopardizing her freedom and afraid it may be too late to be contrite. "I'm sorry," she said. "I just need a better job. I have to be able to support my brother. I can't do that if I'm someone's maid. Isn't there anything else on that list I could do?"

Mrs. Jordan straightened her scarf and rearranged the papers on her desk. "I'm sorry, too. I shouldn't have blown up at you like that. It wasn't very professional of me. Now, what's this about your brother?"

"My brother, Anthony," Martha said, sitting back down. "I'm eighteen. Legally I can become his guardian. I want to petition the courts for custody."

"Custody?" Mrs. Jordan folded her hands on the desk and bowed her head. She sat quietly for a few seconds in what looked like prayer.

Martha held her breath.

Mrs. Jordan slowly unfolded her hands and looked up. "I'm sorry, Martha," she said in a quiet solemn voice. "I'm sorry if anyone has led you to believe you could get your brother out of the state system. It just isn't done. Once a child is registered with the state, they're wards until their eighteenth birthday. No one is granted custody."

"What?"

Mrs. Jordan reached her hand across the desk. "There's nothing you can do. You have to forget about him."

Martha went to speak, but Mrs. Jordan held up her hand. "I know it won't be easy. But what are you going to do, Martha, take on the state of Arizona all by yourself? Others have tried and they've failed. This job with Mrs. Sanders, its a good job. She's a wonderful woman and she treats her help with respect and dignity. We have two other girls already working there. You get complete medical, and she pays eight dollars an hour. That's a dollar seventy-five over minimum wage. Why that's more than many of your grown men make. Take it and be grateful."

Martha's shoulders fell, as did her head. Finally they had beaten her. Without hope of rescuing Anthony, her power was gone.

She moved through the rest of the interview docile and degraded, the perfect product of the Arizona State Foster Care System.

5

Sharon pulled up to a two-story track home in Mesa. It was one of the larger models, with its sand colored walls, and oversized windows. Its small front yard was neatly landscaped with colored rocks and cacti – identical to all the other homes she had seen as she drove through the development. She parked by the curb and looked down the deserted street. Not a child, or a child's toy was visible. All the little yards were immaculate, no weeds, no spilled rocks marring the smooth gray concrete, no life.

"Too sterile for my tastes," Sharon said as she turned off the Jeep and grabbed her purse.

A cement walkway, lined by small path lights, led from the driveway to the front door. Sharon got out of the Jeep. The dry Arizona heat embraced her. It was mid-morning, in mid-May and already ninety-five degrees with a promise of hitting one hundred and three. It was going to take a few days for her to become acclimated to the heat.

The door to the house opened before she had a chance to step onto the walkway. "Sharon Clark?" a small woman, dressed in a crisp teal tank top and pressed white shorts asked.

Sharon smiled. "Dorothy Merrill?"

"Yes. Please, come in." The woman pulled a cigarette from behind her back and inhaled deeply.

Sharon hoped the slight grimace she made when she saw the cigarette had not been noticed. She hated the smell of cigarettes. "I thought cigarettes were banned?" she asked the woman as she stepped past her into the living room, hoping Dorothy would take the hint and put it out.

"Only in public. We can still smoke in the privacy of our own homes. I picked the habit up from my grandmother when I was twelve. I've never been able to break it."

"Oh," Sharon said as she moved farther into the house. The smell of stale tobacco and dusty ash permeated the house. Sharon's nose itched, but she fought the impulse to scratch it. Cigarettes had been taken away from prisoners in the first sweep of inmate policy revisions – back in the beginning. Back when a Sheriff ruled and the populace was being brainwashed, bit-by-bit, to believe it was okay for criminals to live in tents in one hundred and twenty degree weather, denied coffee and TV, fed tasteless slush, and used as laborers to support the county's Posse. It was hard to believe a state that modeled its prisons after their infamous county jail system would allow inmates, especially pregnant ones, to smoke.

"You weren't allowed to smoke in prison, were you?" she asked.

"No, no." Dorothy said, blowing smoke out her nose and mouth. "I went nuts in there. I picked it up again my first day home. Have a seat." She pointed to a peach colored leather overstuffed sofa, then put her cigarette out in a crystal ashtray sitting on a glass covered coffee table. Dorothy looked at Sharon and smiled weakly. "I almost canceled you know. I'm not sure I should be doing this at all. My husband is really against it, and so are my parents."

All the women Sharon had contacted originally conveyed the same sentiments. They were all afraid to talk, yet, most felt compelled to do so. She couldn't afford to have anyone back out at the time of the interview, so she had prepared herself to reiterate reassurances. "Well, as I said over the phone, you will have complete anonymity. No one will ever know you spoke to me."

"I know. It's just that they can make it so hard when they want to," Dorothy said, walking over to a small cabinet and pulling out a pack of cigarettes.

"Who's *they*," Sharon asked pulling the hand held disk recorder out of her bag and holding it up to Dorothy. "Do you mind?"

"You're sure no one will ever know?"

Sharon looked at the lines forming around the woman's nervous mouth, and forced a smile. "I promise. After I take notes off the disc tonight, I'll erase it."

"They'll know you were here though."

Sharon smiled, yes they would know she had been here, that she had talked to Dorothy Merrill, but unless the house was bugged, they would never know what was said.

"When we're done here, I'm going to change the tape and ask you questions that I want you to answer as if everything was great. If they question our interview, I'll show them that tape. Okay?"

Dorothy sat down in a peach and cream striped recliner, took another long drag off her cigarette and nodded at the recorder. Sharon quickly turned it on, not wanting to give the woman a second longer to back out.

"By *they*, I mean the Posse. I'm constantly watched. Once they catch you, they never believe you're truly reformed. Everything I do is up for discussion. I once lingered too long in the baby aisle at the grocery store. The next day my social worker called to see how I was doing and scheduled me for an extra check-up. They have spies everywhere." Dorothy took another rapid drag off her cigarette, and looked over her shoulder.

Dorothy could quickly turn out to be a waste of time. Her neuroses would taint the story and it would prove worthless. If she wanted to get anything out of this woman, she would need to calm her down and make her think rationally. She needed Dorothy to realize how important it was to tell the story unembellished by her fears.

"I'm very interested in what you have to say, Dorothy," Sharon said. "Southern California is about to have a major election, and could easily wind up with all the same laws and restrictions you have here. I need you to give me solid facts, so our voters can make an informed decision. There aren't too many of you from Arpaio willing to talk, so I need to get as much factual information as I can from each of you."

"No one wants to talk because they make you believe what they're doing to you is for your own benefit." Dorothy said.

Sharon thought she knew this time who *they* were. The penal system was made up of more than just guards and wardens. After welfare was abolished, Arizona had taken all the social workers and turned them into social police for the state. Their job, or what Sharon understood of their job, was to instill and maintain social morality among released offenders and law-abiding citizens. She had hoped to make their role an integral part of her story, and needed solid examples to demonstrate how controlling the state had become in its resident's lives.

"How can they do that?" she asked. "Do they invade your privacy? Do they bombard you with subliminal messages?"

"Heaven's no. They just watch you. They watch you and they confront you. The problem is, you never know who's one of them and who isn't. It gets so you don't trust anyone, or you're so afraid to do anything you just sit home and behave. I've gotten to the point that I don't dare say or do anything in public anymore. My husband says I'm paranoid, but I'm not."

Sharon offered a reassuring smile, though she wasn't willing to choose sides just yet.

"Sometimes I think I was better off in prison," Dorothy continued. "At least there I knew exactly what I could and couldn't do. I was in for five years, you know." Dorothy looked past Sharon towards the bay windows that faced the street. I was only seventeen. I didn't mean to break the law. It wasn't even my idea. It was my boyfriend's father's plan. He set the whole thing up. You know it's against the law to have a child if you're not married?"

Sharon nodded her head. In the late twentieth century many states had begun enforcing premarital sex laws written in the seventeen hundreds to prevent teen pregnancies. Many of the younger states, like Arizona, had drawn up newer, harsher ones. So far California hadn't adopted any of the morality laws. And it was a good thing, Sharon laughed to herself. She would have been sentenced to life years ago.

"Mr. Garris said his son had too much going for him to be saddled with a wife and baby. I remember," Dorothy said dreamily as her hand slowly lowered, the cigarette coming too close to the arm of the recliner. "I cried all the way to Phoenix. I really loved Sam. I really wanted to have our baby. But his father insisted. I was three months pregnant at the time. Sam was scared of getting caught, so he dropped me off three blocks from where I was suppose to go and made me walk the rest of the way."

Sharon looked at the woman and tried to envision her as a young seventeen year old. She couldn't be much older than twenty-three, but she looked forty. Her skin was loose and seemed to sag from her face and hands. Her hair was straw colored and wiry. It looked as if it had been set earlier, but then slept on. Her fingernails were bitten to the quick, yet showed signs of having recently been polished a coral-orange. At one time she may have been considered pretty, but not anymore.

"And, you know," Dorothy continued. "They were waiting for me." She looked up at Sharon. "I've always believed it was a set up. I've always believed Sam's father had me arrested. I don't think there even was a doctor. I think Mr. Garris was one of *them* and in trying to keep his son from being arrested for premarital sex, he sacrificed my baby and me."

Dorothy paused, as if waiting for a response. Sharon sat motionless, expressionless; it was the same old story every convict cries. *It wasn't my fault. I was framed.* She had hoped for more.

"Anyhow." Dorothy took another drag off her cigarette. "I was taken into custody, tried that very day, and sent immediately to Arpaio Women's Penitentiary."

"What?" Arizona's court system was known for its quick expediting of cases, but the same day seemed unbelievable. No one could have prepared a case in a day. "Didn't you have an attorney?"

"Of course I did. A public defender, anyway. He told the judge my story. He even tried to get me the lighter sentence for premarital sex."

"And the judge didn't buy it?"

"No. He called Mr. Garris and made him come in to testify. Sam was conveniently out of town."

"And he denied everything, right?" Sharon asked, already knowing the outcome of the story.

"Everything. He called me a liar. He said he didn't believe it was his son's baby, but some other boy Sam had seen me flirting with over the past six months. That was all the judge needed to hear. He sentenced me on the spot and sent me to Arpaio. I didn't even get the chance to see my parents."

Sharon shook her head in disbelief. "They just took his word over yours? No questions asked? How could they have done that?"

Dorothy lowered her cigarette and looked at Sharon, she almost seemed to laugh at her. "He's a man, of course they're going to take his word over mine. That's not what bothered me. It was the timing. I think if my own father had been able to come into court and stand up for me, then things would have gone differently."

"Unbelievable. How did they ever convince you it was better for women to return to the home and let men rule?"

"Oh, it's definitely better this way," Dorothy said. "There's less crime. Our children are healthier, happier. I don't know what I would do if I had to work. I'm just not smart enough to hold down a job. That's what men are for. Women are too emotional to make it in business. We're nurturers, we lack the aggression needed to succeed."

Sharon's first reaction was to deck Dorothy Merrill, but then she decided pitying her was more appropriate. It wasn't Dorothy's fault how she saw herself. She was just a product of her environment. Nature versus Nurture, where brainwashing won out over instinct and intuition. It was an old religious tradition. There was nothing Sharon could do about it, so she decided to bring the conversation back to Dorothy's time in prison.

"Tell me, Dorothy. What was it like at Arpaio? How did they treat you?"

"Fine. Actually, it wasn't as bad as I had anticipated. I got three good meals a day, plenty of exercise, and there were enough day time activities to keep me occupied."

Sharon looked at Dorothy. What theme park she had visited? This was not how the others had described Arpaio. Supposedly, there was excellent treatment of the pregnant women, but after the babies were delivered, the mothers were treated similarly to any other female convict.

"That's odd," Sharon said. *Unless you got your hands on some great hallucinogenics.* "Other women have complained of harsh, almost brutal treatment. You're saying that wasn't the case?"

"Not where I was. Maybe other units were treated differently, but everyone in my group was treated well. I don't remember anyone being beaten or mistreated in any way. The only real hardship we had was not being allowed visitors and having our babies taken away from us."

"You didn't see any mistreatment?" Sharon asked.

"No, but I never saw anyone outside my unit."

It didn't make sense. Either Dorothy was lying or she had preferential treatment. But why? What would have made her unit so special? Sharon looked at Dorothy. She wouldn't know, not consciously anyway.

"You said earlier, that they make you believe what they're doing to you is for your own benefit. What did you mean by that?" Sharon asked.

"Oh, you know. The constant monitoring. Every three months for five years I have to go in for a mental health check-up and attend a women's issues seminar. Then once a month I have to report in with my social worker. " Dorothy paused. She looked into Sharon's eyes as if wondering how much to tell, took two drags off her cigarette, flicked the ashes in the crystal ashtray and continued. "Last month she told me they have decided to stop my quarterly injections of Depo-Provera. It seems the state has deemed, since I'm married now, that I should start having babies and build a family. My 'Godly duty,' as she called it."

"Babies?" This woman was a surprise a minute. Either she was living in a fantasy or had been somewhere other than Arpaio. "How can you have another child? According to all the articles I've read, sterilization is mandatory for woman convicted of attempted abortions.

You're telling me you weren't sterilized?"

"Sterilized. Heavens no. This is a Christian state. According to the Bible, it's our responsibility as women in Christ to multiply. Whatever gave you the idea they would sterilize us?"

"I could have sworn I read the law verbatim. It said that every woman convicted of attempting an abortion would be sterilized."

"Oh, well that doesn't apply to everyone. Just to those women the State sees as unrehabilitatable. During your stay you undergo intensive therapy and counseling. If the reverend thinks you're truly remorseful for your decision, and would eventually make a good mother, they don't sterilize you. Personally, I don't know anyone who was sterilized, but then my unit was special. Every one of us was forced or mislead by parents and lovers into attempting our abortions. None of us really wanted one. We weren't bad, just easily manipulated."

Sharon looked at Dorothy for a full minute, trying to hold back the chuckle that wanted to escape her lips. What an understatement. Dorothy was a sponge. She was the type of woman that if you told her nothing bad had happened to her even if she had the scars to prove you wrong, she'd believe you. What an ideal inmate she must have been. No wonder her unit had been treated special. Now the only question was, what did the state want with these gullible women?

"I don't understand, Dorothy," Sharon said, hoping to draw more information from her easily led informant. "If everything went so well for you, why did you feel you needed to talk to me and why are you so afraid of getting caught?"

Dorothy pulled another cigarette from her pack and lit it off the end of the butt she had just finished. She got up and paced back and forth in front of the sofa, looking at Sharon for a moment, taking a puff of her cigarette, and looking back at Sharon.

"Everyone thinks I'm nuts," she said. "But I'm positive. I just know it's true."

Sharon was inclined to agree with everyone else, Dorothy was nuts, but at least she really did believe she had something important to say. Now, if she could only get her to say it.

"What Dorothy?" Sharon stood up and placed herself in front of the woman, who was now visibly shaking, and put her hand on both of Dorothy's shoulders. "What's true? What really happened in there?"

"I had babies," she whispered.

"What?" Sharon pulled away. She had heard Dorothy use the word babies one other time, but thought it meant individual women's babies, not multiple births on Dorothy's part. She smiled at her, wanting to keep her coherent and focused. "You mean you had your baby, right, Sam's?"

"Well, yes. I had Sam's baby. I never got to see it, but I remember going into labor. I mean more babies. Two, I think. But I'm not sure. So much is in a haze. It was like I was always pregnant. I'd ask how long I'd been there and they would say only a few months. But it was years."

Sharon moved over to the recliner and sat down. It wasn't so unbelievable. Visitors and cameras hadn't been allowed in any of the religious state's prisons since the early part of the century. What would prevent them from using these women as incubators? It would be the perfect breeding ground.

"Why do you think they would do this?" she asked Dorothy, not really believing the woman would have an explanation.

"I don't know. I just don't know. But, it happened. I'm sure of it. You think I'm crazy, I know. Everyone says I am. But I swear. It couldn't have been a dream. You just don't forget those kinds of things. Each pregnancy was different than the others. But when you're locked up inside all the time, you don't know if it's day or night. You don't know how many months or years have passed. All you know is what they tell you. But I remember giving birth three times when I was there, I swear it."

She could swear all she wanted, but her word would get them nowhere. "Do you have any proof?"

"No." Dorothy's eyes watered. She put her cigarette out and turned her back to Sharon. "My husband thinks I'm nuts. My parents won't even discuss it with me." She turned around. "I thought if I talked to you, you could find out for me. You know, see if other women had the same thing happen."

Sharon studied the woman's face for a moment. One of her greatest skills as a reporter was reading people, and from what she could tell, Dorothy Merrill believed every word she said. Sharon leaned back in the chair. A part of her wanted to pass off Dorothy's rantings as part of her psychosis, the other half, the reporter half, secretly wished it was true.

"That's a pretty big accusation, Dorothy," Sharon finally said. "You know what it would mean if you're right?"

"That we were used as breeders. I think about it all the time. I always wonder whose babies I had and where they are." Dorothy walked over to the bay windows, hugging herself tightly. "I feel as though I were raped. Not just physically, but mentally. They did something to my brain. They fucked up my mind, and then clouded it over with happy thoughts. Help me," she said, turning around and facing

Sharon. "I need to know. Am I crazy, or did it really happen? I can't have another baby until I know just how many others I've already had."

"I don't blame you," Sharon said as she got up, turned off the recorder. She pulled a clean disk from her bag, and inserted into the recorder. "Okay, now for the lies."

Sharon and Dorothy rehearsed then recorded. Dorothy told her story of Mr. Garris setting her up, of not being sterilized, and of having been treated well while at Arpaio. Almost everything she had said before, except the fact she thought she had been an unwilling participant in starting a baby boom. After about fifteen minutes, Sharon turned off the recorder, she didn't want to hear any more, nor could she sit through one more cigarette. It was time to go.

Sharon held her hand out to Dorothy. "I don't know what happened to you, Dorothy, but if I find any evidence that women are being used as surrogate mothers, you'll be the first I'll tell."

Dorothy walked over to the door and opened it. "Thank you. Actually I feel better for the first time in a long time. You're the only person who hasn't laughed at me."

It seemed awkward, but Sharon gave her a quick hug. "I'll do what I can." As she pulled away, Sharon repressed a shudder and feigned a smile. Dorothy Merrill's story if told by a woman who was not paranoiac, meant that women weren't just being incarcerated they were being impregnated. If that were true, Sharon's piece on abortion just took a dangerous left turn.

6

Sharon's second meeting was with a black woman named Phoebe Washington. Phoebe didn't want to meet at her home, so Sharon arranged to meet her at the Indian Bend Park in Scottsdale. It was a long narrow park formed around a man-made lake that stretched for a few miles through apartment complexes, residential neighborhoods, and a golf course. Sharon waited for Phoebe in a small parking lot in the area of the park where the lake turned into a stream.

When she first talked to Phoebe to arrange the meeting, Sharon asked her how she would recognize her, Phoebe had laughed. "Don't worry, you'll see me." Sharon hadn't believed she would be that intuitive and made sure she gave Phoebe an accurate description of herself: twenty-eight, five foot seven, a hundred and twenty pounds, shoulder length blonde hair, and blue eyes. Phoebe laughed even harder. "You know the old saying," she said. "Seen one blonde, blue eyed whitey and you've seen them all."

Sharon had laughed with her, but she still didn't trust her ability to pick Phoebe out in a crowd until she had driven around Scottsdale in search of the park. She was half an hour early and used the time to walk around nodding her head and smiling at those she passed. Phoebe had been right. She would be easy to find. Everyone was white. They were all different, unique in their own way, from the older couple sharing bottled water, to the teen-age boys playing basketball, and the group of mothers playing with their children. Distinct individuals linked by their common denominator, the color of their skin.

Sharon thought of Thomas. How he would feel by her side amidst so many Anglos? "Like a fly in milk," he would say as he had the first time he had gone to one of her mother's extended family picnics when they first started dating. Even in California, everyone in her supposedly liberal family had stopped speaking and turned to stare as they approached, arm in arm. Her mother was furious at first. "What of the children?" she had cried. But Thomas with his big smile, and effervescent charm, had won her, and everyone else in the family, over quickly. Now her mother was begging for grandchildren, something Thomas would love to accommodate, but Sharon refused to discuss.

Sharon walked under a large iron wood tree to get out of the sun. It was hot, but not unbearable. If she were in Southern California, she would be sweating profusely, but here a good fifteen degrees hotter than she was accustomed, she felt dry. A slight breeze circulated the air, making it pleasant. The park was clean and fresh, unlike the graffiti smeared one around the corner from her condo.

A yellow-breasted finch landed in a branch above her head. Sharon looked up to watch as it fluttered from limb to limb. She considered the melodious chirping, finding in it a tune of complacency that seemed to match that of the other occupants of the park. She was just getting into its song when she was distracted by the sound of a car pulling into the lot. A small, white BMW parked next to her Jeep. The front window was heavily tinted, so she couldn't make out the face of its occupant. She waited and watched. The driver's side door opened and two long black legs, shod in thin white-strapped thongs appeared beneath it.

Everyone in the park turned to watch Phoebe Washington make her entrance. Sharon stared with them, stunned by the woman's beauty. Phoebe was at least six feet tall, thin, with small high breasts, dark even skin, and a chiseled face enhanced by a starched helmet of short black hair. She wore a tight white tank top and a bright orange skirt that barely covered her backside. Phoebe had been right, she was not someone who would become lost in a crowd, and it had nothing to do with the color of her skin.

"Phoebe?" Sharon asked as she stepped up to the woman and held out her hand. "I'm Sharon Clark of the Sentinel. You certainly know how to make an entrance."

"Who? Me?" Phoebe said touching her hand to her heart then burst out laughing.

Sharon laughed with her then pointed to a picnic table under a pagoda. "You want to sit over there?"

"Hell, no," Pheobe said stepping over a barrier. Sharon thought she caught a glimpse of the woman's white underwear. "I need to walk."

"Sure," Sharon said then started toward the path. Pheobe was right beside her, though Sharon's head only reached the top of Phoebe's shoulder. It seemed awkward staring up at the woman as they walked, so Sharon let her eyes roam across the landscape, towards the birds, the children, and the long stretch of green grass. Phoebe started to talk about her morning, what time she had gotten up, what she ate for breakfast, nothing important. It was a good way to start the interview. Sharon needed time to get a feel for this woman, to know how to approach her.

She was just about to start asking more personal questions about Phoebe's time at Arpaio, when a small girl, about four years old, in a blue floral sun dress and purple harness ran towards them, her tether dragging behind her. A woman ran after her, trying to grab the girl's strap and secure her, but the child evaded her. She ran through a flock of sleeping ducks and laughed. When she finally approached them, she stopped inches from where Pheobe stood and stared up at her.

"What's wrong with your skin?" she asked.

Phoebe cocked her head to the side, and looked down at a the little girl. Sharon held her breath. "Nothing honey," she said as she patted the girl's head. "I just have a really good tan."

The girl looked up, and then reaching with her small index finger, she poked Phoebe's leg. "Does it hurt?"

Phoebe's head rolled back and she laughed. It was a loud guttural laugh. Sharon couldn't tell if it was from annoyance or sheer joy.

"Deidra," the woman screamed as she ran up to the child and grabbed her arm. "You mustn't bother the lady. "I'm sorry," she told Phoebe as she picked up her daughter's leash and pulled her away.

Phoebe's laughter stopped in mid-breath. "You ought to be more careful," she told the woman. "I saw two mothers being arrested yesterday for letting their kids run free."

The woman scanned the park quickly and tugged on the child. "I, I don't know how it happened. One minute I was holding her, the next she was gone."

"They're a lot of responsibility," Phoebe said.

The mother nodded her head and pulled the child along with her, careful not to let her get too close to the water's edge.

Phoebe exchanged waves with the little girl, and then shook her head. "That woman's going to have a break down before the kid's seven. That's one disease I don't have to worry about."

"Parent Fear," Sharon said in a hushed tone. "I haven't figured out why anyone gets pregnant on purpose anymore. Imagine going to jail because your kid tore his leg open going down some slide."

"See over there." Phoebe pointed across the lake at a fenced off cement rock and a pile of sand.

"Yeah, what was it?"

"Used to be a fountain for the kids to play in, next to it were swings and a Jungle Jim. Some guy sued the city because his daughter slipped on the cement and hit her head. Instead of charging the mother with negligence, the city decided to take away all possible hazards. They even posted signs over by the rocks warning parents they'll be cited if their children are found playing on them."

"It's amazing mothers let their children outdoors at all," Sharon said looking at the fenced off rocks.

"Amen to that," Phoebe said.

They walked in silence for a few moments, each, Sharon supposed, contemplating the responsibility behind parenthood. It was such a risk, yet women still had children, and as impossible as it seemed, many of them survived childhood without getting their parents arrested.

It was time to get back to the interview. Sharon pulled the Pheobe notebook from her bag and studied it for a moment. "So, over the phone you said that after the baby was born, you were only fed twice a day, and forced to work in a sewing shop for ten hour shifts."

"At least ten hours. There's a real market for prison garb out here. They call it Redemption Clothing. The women prisoners make it and the State sells it to the public. All the proceeds are used to support the prisons. It's not much better than slave labor. "

"And the public allows it?"

"Sure. No one has much respect for criminals here, regardless of the crime. People believe that once you're incarcerated you're nothing more than tainted meat. They'd like to throw you away for good, but just can't bear to do it. Instead of letting you just sit and rot though, they make sure you're productive for the State. Everything here is done for the good of God and the State and to hell with you if you disobey."

Dorothy Merrill might disagree with that assumption. "I just left a woman who was released only a year or so ago, who said nothing about being forced to work. She made her stay sound more like a retreat than a form of punishment."

"Oh yeah? What color was she?"

Sharon looked up at the woman, a piece of her not wanting to offer the answer, but she did. "White."

"I knew it. You know, there wasn't one white woman in our unit." Phoebe laughed. "They got us. Wouldn't you know it. The white women were getting all our food and we were doing all their work."

"I don't know," Sharon said, uncomfortable with her attempt to minimize the obvious racist implications. "I didn't think to ask her if all the women in her unit where white. I assumed the penitentiaries were mixed just like other prison systems."

"And me," Phoebe said pointing to herself. "I was just as ignorant. I convinced myself that white women were too Christian to try and abort their babies. Shows you," she said gently patting Sharon's back. "Hey, look at that."

Phoebe pointed to a group of ducks lying in the shade of a large pagoda tree. "That one over there's rolling its egg." Both women slowly approached the duck. Phoebe broke out laughing and slapped her knee. "I'll be damned. It's a golf ball. Wouldn't you know it, only a duck from Arizona wouldn't be able to tell the difference between a golf ball and a baby."

People in the park had stopped their activities again and were looking over at the laughing black woman. "Phoebe," Sharon said trying to quiet her down so they wouldn't be so visible.

"Oh, hush. Everyone's been watching us since I got here. I swear some come just to see if I'll show up. I live nearby and make a habit of parading myself up and down the path in an attempt to exercise. It makes them all feel kind of exhilarated, I think. The mothers pull their children closer to them, the boys stop playing basketball, even the regular joggers give me a wide berth."

"Is all of Scottsdale like this?" Sharon asked.

"Scottsdale? What blinders have you been wearing? It's all of Arizona. Only about one half of one percent of the population is black, and most of those live in Tucson." Phoebe looked around and smiled approvingly. "But I tell you what, our measly half percent sure can send a shiver down these white folks' spines. They don't say anything, but you can feel it."

Sharon hadn't noticed the sharp contrast of race outside Scottsdale, but she had only been in the state for a little over a day. She promised herself to be more observant and to check into the state's demographics, but, as she reminded herself, this wasn't a piece on racism. This was about abortion. *Or maybe, it was about both.*

They walked up to a covered table and sat down. Two air stream skaters, properly padded and helmeted, passed them. A group of teenage boys appeared and began throwing a flying disc a few yards off. After a minute of introspection on both their parts, Sharon decided to get back to the abortion issue.

"Phoebe, that other woman I talked to said she'd been impregnated two other times during her five year sentence. Do you have any memories of your pregnancy lasting past the original nine months, or is there any time during your five years you can't account for?"

Phoebe shook her head and looked over at the children's canceled playground. "I don't know what was happening in those other buildings, but I can tell you none of us had second pregnancies. I was sterilized the day my baby was taken, and I remember vividly each and every day I spent at Arpaio. Look," she said turning around, lifting up her shirt and showing Sharon her back. It was criss-crossed with scars. "I wasn't one of the rehabilitative. I fought for what I believed every chance I could. I never thought I'd get out of there alive."

Sharon examined the scars. Corporal punishment had made it back into the prison system as well as the school system after the privatization had occurred. She had had her share of welted buttocks as a child, but had never seen scars like the ones on Phoebe's back. Sharon pulled out her camera. This was the type of mistreatment she had hoped to find. "Do you mind?" she asked. Phoebe shook her head no. Sharon snapped three pictures.

"I don't get it," Sharon said as she pulled down Phoebe's shirt. "If they've done all this to you, why do you stay? You're free to go, aren't you?"

Phoebe stood up and walked over to the small stream near their cars. Sharon followed. The stream was shallow, its banks deep, and it stank of algae. Sharon's gaze followed the green ooze and the small fish that swam below it as she waited for Phoebe's answer. A dull brown bird, resembling a starling, pulled a four-inch fish from the stream. They watched in silence as it moved the fish back and forth in its mouth, breaking its spine one section at a time, before dropping it and pulling out a piece of its flesh.

"I was born here," Phoebe finally said not looking at Sharon. "This is my home. My dad came here, from California, as a matter of fact. He was a young man full of dreams. There were still plenty of scholarships for minority children back then. So, even though he was poor and black, he was able to get into ASU on a scholarship. From there he went on to law school." She turned and faced Sharon. "He always says Arizona gave him his life, and he has no intentions of ever leaving it."

Sharon saw the intensity in the young woman's eyes. Phoebe Washington was the type of woman Sharon could be friends with. She was a fighter, a woman who drew strength from her adversities rather than be destroyed by them. It was hard to believe she would live in a place so prejudiced against her.

"So you're sticking around to be with your father?" Sharon asked.

Phoebe laughed. "Hell no. I tried to leave. I figured I could make it in Hollywood." Phoebe straightened her back and stuck out her chest, "I was going to be a movie star."

Sharon had no doubts she could have made it. Even though off the top of her head she couldn't name any current black female movie stars, she was sure there must be a role out there for someone as striking as Phoebe Washington. It would be the world's loss not to see her on the silver screen.

"What happened?"

"When I got to the border, they scanned me and found out I was pregnant. I had no idea, honest. I'm probably the only one ever got away with it. I had an interview pre-set for over a month with an agent, and I was only three weeks pregnant. The judge actually believed me. Maybe because my daddy is pretty well known, I don't know. Anyhow, I was fined five thousand dollars for having pre-marital sex, was given five years probation and released. I should have left it at that and waited until after the baby was born, but I was young, and anxious to make it. I decided pregnant or not, I wanted that interview, so the very next day I made arrangements to get smuggled out of the state. And wouldn't you know it, I hired undercover Posse members posing as traders. I was sleeping in Arpaio the next night."

"Your father couldn't help you?"

"He tried, but they wouldn't rehear my case." Phoebe bent down, picked up a small rock and threw it into the stream. "In Arizona, the rules are the rules, and no one breaks the rules." She looked up from where she squatted. "You know we have the lowest crime rate in America."

"I read that somewhere." Sharon felt herself becoming infuriated with the system. Phoebe was the second woman who told her she did not want an abortion, and yet was still incarcerated and denied her baby. "This state of yours seems to put people away regardless of what the situation is. They had no right putting you in jail, Phoebe. You should have fought harder."

Phoebe stood up and shook her head. "We're different here. We're raised knowing what we can and can't do. I should have known better, but I was always too headstrong. My daddy says I got what I asked for. Maybe I did. I've had a lot of time to think about my life since I got out. Hollywood's out of the question now with all these scars, so there's nowhere else for me to go. I guess when it comes down to it, this is my home, and I'll probably stay here the rest of my life."

"You don't have to be a star to enjoy respect and freedom," Sharon said.

Phoebe smiled down at her. "My daddy's told me how blacks are treated in Southern California. You people pretend not to be prejudice, but you really are. At least here I know where I stand. I'm an anomaly. People may look and stare, they may even fear what I represent, but they treat me with respect. They treat me like a rare flower. Afraid to get too close, but always stopping to admire.

"I'm like that woman over there." Phoebe pointed to a woman in a flowered shirt, bicycle pants, and sun hat. She was shading herself with an umbrella and throwing breadcrumbs on the lawn. Dozens of birds flocked at her feet.

"See how closely they watch her? How much they want to see what she has to offer?"

"Yeah," Sharon said. The birds seemed very eager to get close to her, but they would hesitate and wait for her to throw more.

"That woman comes here every day. The birds know her. She's never done anything to them, but feed them. And yet, every time she takes a step, they clear a path for her. It's like they appreciate her being there, but they don't trust her enough to let her join them. They know her, yet they still fear her."

Sharon looked up at Pheobe and half smiled. "Is that how you feel?"

"Kind of."

"Then why don't you leave?"

"Cuz there's no place else to go. Phoebe reached into her skirt's pocket, pulled out the keys to her car and took a step toward the small parking lot.

Sharon started to say something about how wonderful the free states were, but kept her opinion to herself. Phoebe knew what was out there. She just didn't want it.

"Well, thanks for the interview," Sharon said. "I hope everything works out for you."

"Oh it will." Phoebe walked over to her car then turned back around. "I already told you, if you play by the rules, you may never win, but you won't lose either. I learned that lesson the hard way, and I'm passing my experience on to you. So take heed Miss SoCal. There are lots of people out there who aren't going to like what you have to say, so you better be careful who you talk to."

"I will," Sharon said. "If you ever get out to Southern Cali..."

"Yeah, yeah, yeah," Phoebe said, waving her hand at Sharon and laughing before she got in her car and drove away.

Sharon hadn't been able to eat anything when she stopped for lunch. She looked around at the thick crowd busily eating their fast food burgers and fries. From the girl who took her order, to the mentally challenged table washer, everyone, including all the customers were white. A black man had driven by on a motorcycle as she pulled in, but he continued on. It was odd at first. She acknowledged a strange sense of security she wasn't used to in Los Angeles. Then realized it was only illusionary. She was like most people. News and TV had conditioned her to subconsciously believe that whiter meant safer. She looked around the dining room. How many thieves, rapists, drug dealers and wife beaters sat around her disguised as cleaner, whiter, Americans? It was almost creepy, sort of like those Twilight Zone re-runs Thomas loved to watch. Suddenly, Arizona became this ominous entity that she wanted to distance herself from before being swallowed up by it. But she couldn't. She had more interviews to get, and an article to write. She'd have to stay in the lion's mouth a little longer.

She looked down at her watch. It was already one-thirty. Time to shift gears. Her meeting with Reverend Samuels was at three. She took out a fresh disk for her recorder and wads of paper she had collected from pro-life forces in Southern California and began preparing.

7

Martha stared out the window of the black Cadillac that had picked her up from the Living Trust Christian State Home for Children. She had come to terms with her situation while she sat alone in a small room. Four more years of her life were being taken away from her, and she could do nothing about it. Her only hope was that the Sanders were as good as Mrs. Jordan made them out to be.

It was a hot day, and though the air conditioning in the car worked well enough, the heat of the sun baked her face through the glass. She hadn't spent much time in Scottsdale. It was too expensive, too elitist, for her taste. The modern architecture of the medical centers and office buildings lining Scottsdale Road intimidated her for some reason, and her apprehension towards her destination grew.

As they turned down Camelback road, she craned her neck to look up driveways that resembled entrances into housing developments, hoping to catch a glimpse of the homes that sat safely hidden behind their walls. She had always wondered how the rich lived, had even daydreamed about it, but now that she was about to experience it first hand, she feared it.

Camelback Mountain with its rocky surface and occasional cactus, held her attention as they turned up Valle Vista Ave. The driver angled around a large plastic barrier that read "Private Road," and headed higher up the hill.

They turned into a driveway marked by white curved stucco walls with the name Camelback Sands written in large black letters. The car followed the drive for a short way, then turned a sharp corner. In front of her, nestled tightly into the mountain, was the house. Martha's mouth dropped slightly as she looked up at it. It wasn't a house, it seemed more like a museum. The front, a large semi-circle enclosure with white columns separated by floor to ceiling glass panes, jutted out from the earth. Large white concrete pillars supported its weight.

Someone stood at one of the windows looking down at them as they approached. It was a short Hispanic woman in a gray A-lined dress. Martha couldn't make out the expression on her face, but she had a strong feeling it wasn't one of welcome.

The car went under the building, pulling up to one of four garage doors. The door rose by itself, and they drove in. Instead of entering a regular four-car garage, it was like going into a parking structure at a mall. The concrete road lead down two levels ending in a large parking area. There were only three other vehicles in it, one of which was a Posse patrol car. Martha's stomach turned. Her employer was a vigilante.

The driver of the car, who had said nothing during the trip, got out and opened her door. She grabbed her duffel bag and pulled herself out from the back seat. She looked again at the patrol car, and saw the signed name on its driver's door. "Captain Nathan Sanders, Arizona State Posse."

The driver stepped up to a steel door, unlocked it, and ushered her in. She followed him up a curved wooden staircase to a long empty hall and then through a white wooden swinging door into a large square foyer. The floor was laid with white speckled Mexican tile. Abstract art, signed by the artists, covered the white walls. A light blue cement table in the shape of an upside down U held a large sand carved vase supporting an arrangement of fresh flowers. The driver knocked lightly on one of the double wooden doors to her left and a man's voice called for them to enter. The driver opened the door.

Instinct told her to run, but there was nowhere to go. As an indentured ward, she was not allowed to leave the state until after she completed her four years of servitude. Her hand shook as she readjusted the duffel bag on her shoulder. She took a deep breath and walked in to meet her new master.

The room was lined with walls of books. At its center was a large mahogany desk. A tall thin man, his back towards her, was replacing a book on one of the shelves. He turned when the driver closed the door.

Without saying a word, he walked up to her. His eyes scanned her face and body. He put his hand to his chin, and without taking his gaze from her body, walked around her. She kept her mouth shut, her eyes straight ahead, and fought the urge to follow his movement. She felt like merchandise being inspected before the auction.

He stopped in front of her, grabbed her chin with his bony hand and moved her head to the right, then back to the left. "Not bad looking for a Mexican," he said, then withdrew his hand. "What's your name?"

The room was cold, her nerves on edge. She fought to form the words without biting her tongue. "Martha Garcia, sir."

He walked behind his desk and sat down. She quickly glanced around the room looking for a chair – there was none. She stood at attention, her hands at her side, her back straight, eyes focused on an invisible spot directly in front of her.

"Well Martha Garcia, what did Mrs. Jordan tell you about this position?"

Martha tried to recall any specifics about the job, but couldn't. She wasn't sure if she hadn't been paying attention or if it had never been discussed. "Not much sir," she said. "She told me the pay, and the benefits, and that you were a good family to work for."

"Good. I wouldn't want you to start with any false expectations. So let me tell you exactly what this job entails. First off, I want you to know, that even though you are merely a servant here, you are a representative of my family. What you do, whether here or in public, is a direct reflection on my wife and myself. Our reputation is at stake each time you open your mouth, each time you step foot outside this house. You are expected to live up to our standards, to exemplify the high position of the household you serve." He stopped speaking and looked at her as if pondering her ability to understand. "Do you know what type of household you have entered?"

Satan's?

"Do you?" he asked again, then paused.

She had no clue what type of people the Sanders were. Mrs. Jordan hadn't said what work Mr. Sanders was in, only that she liked Mrs. Sanders. She shook her head. "No, sir."

"No, I didn't think you did. Well Martha, this is a house of God. Mrs. Sanders and I are Christians. Everything we do, everything we say is in compliance with the Lord's will. But don't misinterpret that," he said smiling. His teeth were big for his skeletal frame. *All the better to eat you with.*

"Just because we are Godly," he continued, "does not mean we are tolerant and forgiving of sinners. I run a very strict home. There is no profanity, no gossiping, no men."

No breathing.

"You do what you're told, when you're told to do it. I am the head of this household and answer to no one but God. It is by my word that you will live and work. No matter what anyone else says or does, I always have the final word. Is that clear?"

"Yes, sir," she said almost rote. She knew the rules, they were similar to those forced on her the past four months. *'Servants obey in all things your Masters,' Colossians 3.22.* Her mother had taught her to be strong, independent, and self sufficient, but where had it gotten her. Suzanne Garcia was wrong. The only way to live, to survive was to be subservient, humble, to bow down to those who would suppress you.

"You will be paid eight dollars an hour and work forty-eight hours a week. Your shift will be from six in the morning to six at night, four days a week. You will be assigned a day off to take care of your personal needs. Let me emphasize that all your personal business will be taken care of on that day. You will receive no calls or callers here at the house. There will be no excuses for time off during your scheduled workdays. As an added part of our arrangement, you will volunteer your services one day a week to a charity of Mrs. Sanders choosing. You will not be paid for this. Is that clear?"

A whole day to herself? She hadn't equated servitude with privileges. Maybe it wouldn't be so bad after all. "Yes, sir," she said trying to hold back the smile that tempted her mouth.

"Sunday, is the Lords day," he continued. "You will attend morning services with my wife and the rest of the staff here at the house. I am an ordained minister and perform the sermon myself. You will be assigned independent Bible studies that will be turned in prior to the next week's service. If you do not complete the exercises I assign you, you will be fired. I will not have anyone in my employ who does not know and follow the rules of the Lord. Is that clear?"

Clearer than it needed to be. Scripture was something she knew well. Churches ran the only schools available that accepted vouchers as full payment. Bible class was mandatory. To pass a grade you had to memorize scripture and write papers on God's will for your life. Her papers were always too grandiose, too audacious, her Bible teachers told her. She needed to find a more humble purpose to serve the Lord, to remember her place. She should have known back then where her life would lead. *Servants obey in all things your Masters.* Yes, she knew God's rules. They were the same as man's rules, or was it just the opposite? The old, which came first, unanswerable question. But the answer didn't really matter, did it? What mattered was she obey Captain

Nathan Sander's rules. Divine or not, they were the ones to follow.

"Yes, sir," she said.

"You will be paid once a month," Sanders continued. "From your pay I will deduct taxes, room and board charged at four-hundred dollars a month, another four hundred dollars payable to the state to help defer their cost while you were a ward, and a ten percent tithe to the Lord, which I will see is used in His good name. The rest of the money, approximately two hundred and fifty dollars is yours to do with as you please. Is that clear?"

Two hundred and fifty dollars a month wasn't going to go very far, but it was more than she currently had. She had no material needs, so most of it could go into savings. Two-fifty times ten was twenty-five hundred dollars, plus five hundred, gave her three thousand dollars a year. Times that by four years of hell and she'd have twelve thousand dollars. It wasn't much, but it would get Anthony and her out of Arizona. They wouldn't wait around for him to serve his debt to the state.

"Is that clear?" Mr. Sanders asked again.

"Yes, sir," she said.

"Do you have any money?"

Any holdings in your name became property of the state the minute you were made a ward. "No, sir." she replied, not adding how the state had stolen everything she had.

"I didn't think so." Sanders pulled an ID card from his pocket and slid it through a scanner on his desk then punched in numbers on its keypad. "I have just transferred one-hundred dollars to your account. It will come out of your first paycheck."

"Thank you, sir," she said, genuinely grateful.

"Well we can't have you penniless. Tomorrow, Norma will take you to the State Uniform shop. You will need seven uniforms. Norma will put them on our account, but you will have to reimburse us within the first three months you are here. It is required that you wear a uniform while in the house, whether or not you are on duty. On your day off, you can carry a bag with a change of clothing down the mountain with you, but when you return, you are to be in uniform. Is that clear?"

Martha hated dresses, but could live with the bland gray uniform as long as she could change into jeans and a tee shirt, a bright colorful tee shirt, at least once a week.

"Yes, sir," she said.

"You will be allowed to do two loads of laundry each week. I will not tolerate stains, falling hems, wrinkled seams, or anything other than perfection. Your uniform is your responsibility. If you need more, you will purchase more. Is that clear?"

"Yes, sir." Her twelve thousand dollars was dwindling fast.

"Good. You will be given a room of your own, never will you leave that room without it being spotless. The bed will be made, and all clothes put away. The maid's bathroom is communal. You will be allowed a seven-minute shower each morning. If the bathroom so much as has soap scum around the drain, you and all the other servants who share it will be fired. Is that clear?"

"Yes, sir." A seven-minute shower, she was in heaven. And to think there wouldn't be twenty of them sharing the same bathroom. Except for the money, things were looking better with each rule.

"Good." He opened a drawer on the side of his desk, and pulled out a small packet of stapled pages. On the first page, he wrote Martha's name in a blank space, and then his name in another. He flipped to the last page, signed and dated it. He extended his pen towards Martha with one hand and pushed the contract towards her with the other.

"What is it?" she asked, not sure she should sign anything.

"It's your employment contract. It basically states what we have discussed and gives me power of attorney while you are in my employ."

She had never heard the term power of attorney before, and wasn't sure she should sign anything over to him. She was afraid to ask, afraid to speak out of turn, but she was even more afraid of losing the few rights she had.

"I'm sorry sir," she said taking the pen from him. "What exactly does power of attorney mean?"

"Smart girl," he said smiling up at her. "Never sign anything unless you understand what you're doing. Power of attorney means that if anything were to happen to you, I could act in your behalf. Such as an accident. Say you were unconscious and the doctors felt you needed an operation to save your life. You have no family, so the doctors wouldn't be able to operate without your permission. Power of attorney gives me the right to consent to things on your behalf. It's all in your best interest."

Martha wasn't sure she understood it, but nodded her head anyway.

"It does say one other thing that you should know before you sign it. It is a contract. Once you sign it, you're contracted to us for four years. In that time, you agree not to get married, have children, or quit on your own. I still have the option of terminating you if you fail to do your work and abide by the agreement. If that happens, you will be reassigned by the state, and be forced to pay damages for breach of contract."

Martha stared at the packet of papers. Never before had her signature held so much weight. She was confused and afraid. He seemed to grow weary of her hesitancy and pushed the document closer to her.

"If you refuse to sign it, you will be returned to the state and they will find another position for you. As Mrs. Jordan told you, we are a good family. Since all wards must fulfill a four year contract with an employer chosen by the state, you might as well just stay here with us."

Signing the contract meant she was agreeing to four years of servitude, four years of living her life according to the Sanders' desires instead of her own. But what did it matter where she did her penance? One place was a bad as another. Life had betrayed her, well at least her mother had, and now there was no way out. Disparagingly she signed and dated the contract. She didn't look up when she handed Sanders back his pen.

As if on cue, the maid she had seen in the window, walked into the office.

"Norma will show you to your room," Sanders said. "And fill in anything I have forgotten. She is the head housekeeper. If you have any problems or grievances, you are to bring them to Norma, not to Mrs. Sanders or myself. If Norma feels they have merit, she will approach us, not you. Is that clear?"

"Yes, sir." Martha looked over at Norma. The head housekeeper wasn't any older than she was and much shorter. Norma couldn't be more than four foot eight, but still Martha felt as though she was being looked down on.

"Good. Norma, see that she understands all of her duties thoroughly, and that she is given a proper tour of the house. Mrs. Sanders will be in to meet her this evening when she returns from Church."

"Yes, sir," Norma said, then turned to Martha. "This way."

Mr. Sanders had taken out a file from his desk and was flipping through it as Martha turned to follow Norma.

"Martha," he called before she reached the door.

Both she and Norma turned to face him.

"Yes, sir."

"I see in your file you were only a ward of the state for four months."

"That's right. Is that a problem, sir?"

"No. It's just that it wasn't very long, and not knowing your religious background I'm a little concerned with your upbringing. Norma, I want you to make an appointment for her to see Dr. Cartling before her first scheduled day off, and see that she is inoculated. I can't have her getting pregnant while in service here at my home."

Martha went to speak, but Norma grabbed her arm to silence her. "I'll see she gets the shot, sir."

"Very well. You are dismissed."

Martha pulled back as Norma dragged her out of the office. What right did he have to force birth control on her? What right did he have to inoculate her with anything? She pulled her arm free of Norma's grasp and stopped.

"He can't force me use birth control."

Norma's hand met her face fast and hard. "He can make you do anything," she hissed. "Rule number one, don't ever question his authority, or mine. Next time I'll send you for proper punishment. And trust me, Mr. Sanders doesn't use his hand." Norma turned and started back down the hall.

Martha held her hand to her cheek, and stumbled after her. She had been wrong, life here wasn't any better than at Living Trust.

Norma hadn't said much else as she had led Martha to her room and closed the door behind her. Since it was her birthday, she would not be required to work, but should stay in her room and contemplate her gifts from God. Norma would return later and give her a tour of the house and her schedule. Duties started at six o'clock the next morning.

Martha looked around the room. It was small, but comfortable. There were no windows. An empty closet with built in drawers was to the right of the bed. On the other side was a two-drawer desk stocked with paper and pens. A Bible had been placed on her pillow. She picked it up and sat on the bed. God had deserted her months ago, prayers were useless, scripture only lies. She threw the Bible back on the bed.

She took a deep breath and lay down, putting her hands behind her head. Four years was a long time. She missed Anthony, and wanted to go home, but as Mrs. Jordan told her, she had no home. She would have to make the best of it. At least she had her own room, and one day a week, she'd have the privilege of living her own life.

She looked down at the sand colored uniform she was still wearing and remembered her duffel bag. Hopefully, they had given her some civilian clothes. She swept the duffel bag up from its spot on the floor and emptied its contents onto the bed.

The cut up clothing she had worn her first day at Living Trust, was all that fell from it. She picked up the rags and held them to her face. They smelled of freedom, and family. She wanted to cry, sob, but she was afraid Norma would hear. She picked up the bag again and shook it, hoping something, anything, would fall out. But there was nothing. All she had been given to start a new life were the threads of her severed past.

8

Sharon pulled up to the Calvary Baptist Church on Main Street in Mesa. It was a small white building with a simple cross over the front door. The marquee in the front yard read: "Learn of God's plan for a Christian America, Sunday Sermon at 10:00, 11:30 and 6:00." She didn't bother to knock. She didn't think you needed to be invited into a place of worship. Opening the door, she stepped inside.

A man in his mid-forties, slightly overweight, with graying hair, was working on a computer in a corner behind the pulpit. He didn't look up as she entered or as the door behind her clicked shut. She couldn't tell if he was ignoring her, or so engrossed in what he was doing that he was oblivious to her intrusion. Either way, she felt uncomfortable walking down the aisle. She couldn't decide whether she should call out his name, letting her voice echo through the empty room, or wait until she was within whispering range to signal her presence. She had yet to make up her mind when halfway up the aisle, without ever lifting his head from the monitor, or taking his hands off the keyboard, in a loud ebullient voice, he called out to her. "Can I help you, sister?"

"Reverend Samuels?" she asked as she continued towards him.

"Yes," he answered, finally looking up from his work. "Ah, you must be the reporter, Miss Clark, isn't it?"

"Yes. Sharon Clark. I'm with the Los Angeles Sentinel."

"Please come in. I'll only be a minute. I'm still typing my sermon for Sunday's service into the tele-prompter. Marvelous thing," he said as he continued to type. "We have two deaf members, so we bought a special component that adds a computerized translator. Look," he said pointing above where he sat. A large monitor, displaying a man, neatly dressed in a gray suit, his hands held down at his side, flickered. "I type in my sermon, then as I speak he signs. It's voice activated, so it will actually coincide with what I say, but has the sermon to draw from to ensure accurate context. I just love technology."

"I'm always amazed by it," Sharon said, watching and waiting for the man on the screen to come to life.

The reverend rose from his chair, and walked over to the pulpit. "Here, I'll show you." He adjusted the microphone slightly, then pushed a button on the top of the rostrum. "'What does it profit, my brethren, if a man says he has faith but has not works?'" he said, his voice growing louder and deeper as he spoke.

Sharon watched the man on the monitor come to life. His hand artistically signing each word and letter of the scripture the reverend just read. She didn't know sign language, but was impressed with how fluent the computerized interpreter's hand movements were. "Very nice," she said. "James, two fourteen, wasn't it?"

The reverend glanced down at her in mock surprise. "You know scripture. Praise the Lord. A woman of Christ has found her way among Satan's very own. I didn't think there were any Christians left in California."

"Southern California," she reminded him. "And yes, there are still quite a few." Though she was not one of them. What scripture she did know was from the constant bombardment of religious rhetoric broadcast over commercial airwaves in hopes of swaying middle of the road Independents into making a religious and Moral decision at the polls.

"Ah, yes. Southern California. How many years since the split, now?"

"Seven."

"And it's only Northern California that has a moral majority, is that right?"

"Yes," she said. "Central is still primarily an Independent state, but like Southern California, the Moralist party is growing stronger, and more influential, each year."

"Praise be to God. Here, have a seat," he said pointing to the front pew.

Sharon moved up to the front, and took her seat. "Do you mind if

I record our conversation?" she asked as she pulled the recorder from her bag.

"Not at all. As you can see, I'm used to being taped." He pointed to the back of the church. Sharon turned and looked behind her, two video cameras were mounted above the door.

"So I see," she said turning back towards him. "How many of your sermons are broadcast?"

"All of them. I'm one of the twenty or so preachers who make up the Arizona Religious Connection. We're a group of Preachers, Priests, and Rabbis who spread the Word through five-minute commercial breaks between regular programming. We tape our sermons then edit them into small segments for airing."

"That's quite impressive," she said, hiding her disbelief that the public would willingly put up with religious intermissions to their nightly viewing.

"So, what can I do to help your article bring the unrighteous back to the Lord?" he asked, leaning heavily on the pulpit and looking down at her. She felt the obvious intimidation of having someone hover over her while they spoke, but let it pass, acknowledging it as a power play, and knowing any power he thought he had over her was illusionary.

"Well," Sharon said, pulling a notebook created just for him out of her bag. "One of the biggest determents to the Moralists winning in Southern California this election is the debate over women's rights, especially the right to choose. The majority believes that the church and state should be separate and that civil law has no right demanding citizens live under moral standards set by religious leaders. Especially when those leader's religious tenets are much higher than the majority of their constituents."

"Ah, the great debate. We had to win that one here also. Arizona wasn't always a religious state"

"So how'd you do it?" Sharon asked.

"It wasn't easy. It took a lot of prayer, and lobbying before we could convince the legislators and citizens that without living under God's law, there would be no law. But we were able to do it." Samuels paused for a moment as if remembering the great debates that had brought his state to its current belief and political structure, then continued. "We reminded them that our great nation was founded under the grace of God and that the very Constitution that guards our rights, and sets each state up to define their own civil laws, was created under the watchful eye of God Almighty. We made them understand that civil law cannot be detached from moral values. Timothy tells us that it is our right to 'lead a quiet and peaceable life in all god-liness.' Godliness and honesty. We flat out asked our voters how we could do that if society followed laws created by the lawless?"

The lawless? Sharon wanted to laugh, instead she kept up her ruse, playing the part of a crusader trying to find answers. "I'm afraid the majority of Southern Californians don't consider themselves lawless. That's our main problem. We can't get them to see that a life under the Moralists party would bring back the values of the Church and abolish most of the crime."

Samuels watched her as she spoke, his grin growing wider with each phrase, as if laughing at her and her state's infancy in such matters.

"Pro-abortionists," she continued, "are our biggest obstacle. They proselytize that laws are there to protect everyone, not just the religious, and that if those morally opposed to abortions don't want to have one they don't have to, but that they have no right inflicting their beliefs on those who don't hold those ideals to be true."

Samuels leaned over the pulpit and pointed his fingers at her. His voice bellowed. "You should say the same thing right back to them. What right do the immoral have to inflict their murderous laws on the unborn? Who speaks for these children, God's most precious children, whose voices cry to be heard? Would these children opt to die rather than be born?"

"No," Sharon said, as if he really wanted an answer.

"Where are their civil rights? Who protects them?"

"No one," she called out in answer to his fervor.

"We must force morals on the amoral, we must safeguard our brothers and sisters from the very vessels that were meant to give them life. I'm here to tell you, Miss Clark, that the unborn's biggest enemy is its own mother, and if the laws don't protect them we must." His voice lowered. "We must follow Luke, the beloved physician's advice, as told to us in the book of Acts." He banged his fist on the pulpit. "We must obey God not man."

Sharon jumped from the impact of his fist on the wood. She had never been to a Baptist Church before or experienced the fervor of a Baptist minister's elocution, but she had been warned. She caught the breath that had tried to escape her lungs, and gave him her best pity me I'm helpless look. "I know," she almost whined. "But how can we force others to do the same, when the majority of voters disagree?"

Samuels smiled down at her, showing all of his perfectly filed teeth. "By showing them God's grace. By bringing them to the Lord. You, Miss Clark, have the perfect medium to do so. You must show your readers that abortion and euthanasia are against God's law. 'Preach the Word, be urgent in season and out of season, convince, rebuke, and exhort, be unfailing in patience and in teaching.'"

Sharon sat up straighter, and purposely added a note of excitement to her voice. "That's what I'm hoping to accomplish Reverend. That's why I wanted this interview."

"And that's why I agreed to give it. So what are some of the key issues you want to cover?"

Sharon looked down at the notebook in her hand, at the questions she had prepared for him. When she looked up she offered him one of her concerned interviewer grimaces, one she had practiced often before making the trip. "There are horrible rumors about the treatment of women in Arizona imprisoned for attempted abortions, and even worse for those who are successful in obtaining them. Southern Californians aren't ready to charge women with murder over an aborted fetus."

"And why not?" Samuels barked at her. "It is murder! Just like Cain killed his brother Abel, and when rebuked by God, cried out 'Am I my brother's keeper?' so do those who live under Satan's rule. They think it's just to kill their own blood, and for what? Because they do not think they should have to be burdened by God's gift? God tells us in Genesis 9:6, 'Whose sheddeth man's blood, by man shall his blood be shed: for in the image of God made he man.' And don't let them think that doesn't include an unborn child. When the Lord spoke to Jeremiah, he said 'Before I formed thee in the belly I knew thee; and before thou camest forth out of the womb I sanctified thee.'" Samuels voice grew louder as he repeated part of the scripture. "'Before thou camest forth out of the womb I sanctified thee.' Do you hear that? Do you hear what God is saying? He is saying a child is viable from conception."

"But what about..." She looked down at her notes. "Exodus twenty-one, twenty-two?"

Samuels threw his hand in the air and let out a sigh of exacerbation. "One verse, one small verse. The only one pro-abortionists have to throw in our face. I can tell from your eyes, that you too have been seduced by their distortion of this scripture. When God said if a man causes a woman to 'lose her fruit,' he should only be fined, He was talking about an accident. It says, if a man while fighting causes a pregnant woman to miscarry, then he should be fined. That is far different from a willful act of murder. God said 'It is I who bring both death and life.' Regardless of how others want to corrupt the Living Word, we must pay heed to the comman...'"

The door to the church burst open. A Hispanic man in a faded blue tee shirt and jeans came running down the aisle towards the reverend. "Reverend, reverend, you must help me. Hide me," the man pleaded as he ran to the door at the right of the pulpit and tried to open it.

Sharon stood up and edged a little closer to Reverend Samuels. It wasn't fear that made her move, it was instinct. She didn't trust agitated men and though consciously she didn't believe the reverend could protect her if the man meant to attack her, by moving closer she wasn't as obvious a target.

The reverend watched the man with intent interest. "It's locked, my son. Tell me, what are you trying to hide from?"

"The Posse, they're chasing me," he said running over to where Sharon stood and looking up at the reverend. Now, Sharon felt fear. She tried to step away, but couldn't. Her legs wouldn't move.

"The Posse? What have you done?" the reverend asked.

The man showed them a bag of razors, held so tightly in his hand one of them had broken through the wrap. "They say I was going to steal them. But I swear, I was just looking at them when two men in security uniforms came at me. I ran Reverend, I was scared. Now you've got to hide me. If they catch me, they'll never believe I didn't steal them. I'll go to jail. I can't do that. I've got a wife and three kids at home, they need me Reverend. Please help me."

Reverend Samuels didn't move. "Give yourself up, my son. Satan is trapping you into sin. You must redeem yourself, by turning yourself in and letting the law decide your innocence."

The man shook his head. "No, no. They won't believe me."

"God would not allow you to be charged unjustly," Samuels said.

Sirens screamed nearby then passed the Church. The man ran over to another side door.

He wasn't counting on God's divine intervention. *Good for you*, Sharon said to herself, then stepped back. The man's face was getting red. He hit the door with his fist then kicked it. Another blocked escape. He flung himself around and before Sharon could get too far away he grabbed her by the arm. He threw the razors on the floor, then drew a switchblade from his pocket.

Sharon jumped as the knife sprang from its base and its point struck her neck. Her legs went weak. A loud sob escaped her lips, and she involuntarily struggled in his grasp.

"I'll kill her," the man screamed. "Show me where we can hide Reverend."

Sharon fought to push memories of the rape back to the safe chamber in her mind where she usually stored it. She forced herself to refocus. This man meant her no harm, he was only trying to secure his freedom. If she went along with him, she'd be fine. She opened her eyes unaware that she had closed them. The knife was still at her throat, the man still held her. The reverend was calmly telling him to give himself up.

Instead, the frightened man dragged Sharon over to a third door on their left. He kept the knife to her throat, but released her arm as he tried to open it. Sharon looked up at the reverend. With her eyes, she pleaded with him to help the man so she could go free.

"I have the key right here," the reverend said, reaching down below the pulpit.

The sirens grew closer. They stopped somewhere near the church.

"Hurry Reverend," the man said pushing the knife harder against Sharon's neck. She closed her eyes as its sharp edge pierced her skin. The wet warmth of blood trickled down her neck. She could feel her bottom jaw starting to tremble as the fear she had tried to fight overtook her. She felt faint, the room started to blur. She didn't know how much longer her legs would support her.

The reverend slowly stepped down from the stage where he had been standing. "Everything's going to be fine" he said in a gentle voice, then he pulled a gun from behind his back and aimed it at the man's head. "Let go of her!" he ordered.

The sight of the gun shook Sharon from her fear and she was able to lock her knees into place. The man's hand began to shake. She felt the knife's edge nervously scrap the skin of her neck. *Please, God, don't let them kill me.*

The man grabbed her arm again, squeezing it hard. She lifted her chin high and tried to shake her head at the reverend, trying to tell him to put the gun away.

"I'll kill ..."

The gun went off. The man's grip tightened, then released. The knife in his hand sliced the top layer of skin on the right side of Sharon's neck as it fell backwards with him.

Sharon stood still for a moment, her mind not registering what had happened for a full ten seconds. She turned around slowly to see the dead man behind her. Her legs began to shake violently, and she collapsed to the floor.

Reverend Samuels walked up to the man, and laid his hands on his chest. "Forgive him Father," he said, then turned to face Sharon. He grabbed her by the arms and pulled her up. "It's over. You're all right, Miss Clark." He guided her over to the pew where her bag still sat and helped her to sit down.

The front doors burst open and three Posse members, guns drawn, ran down the aisle. "Drop the gun," one of them screamed at Reverend Samuels.

"What the hell," the taller of the three said as he reached the front of the church and looked first at the dead man, then at Sharon.

Reverend Samuels dropped the gun and slowly reached into his shirt pocket. "It's okay," he said, pulling out a badge and holding it up for them to see. "I'm with the Arizona State Posse."

The tall man walked over to the corpse and knelt beside it. The bullet had gone straight through the center of the dead man's forehead and lodged in the door behind him. "Nice shot."

"Who's she," another, much shorter and stockier, man asked while the third, a man barely out of his teens, walked over and knelt in front of her. Normally, Sharon didn't like strangers touching her, but she made an exception and leaned her head so he could examine the wounds. Her nerves were calming, and she was starting to take in what had happened. The reporter in her noted the details surrounding the shooting. She needed pictures.

"A reporter from California," Reverend Samuels answered. "We were just discussing the laws of God when this man ran in and put a knife to her throat. I was afraid he would kill her."

"How is she?" the stocky Posse member asked the boy ministering to Sharon's wounds.

"She'll be okay. They're just surface cuts. I can bandage them." He took her hand in his and placed it over the deeper cut on the side of her neck. "Apply pressure. I'll go get the med kit."

"Thank you, Jesus," the reverend said, raising his hands towards God.

The stocky Posse member walked over to where Sharon's recorder was and picked it up. "I suppose this got everything." Sharon nodded her head. He pulled the disk out. "I'll have to take it ma'am. Evidence. We'll return a copy of it to you in a day or two."

Sharon said nothing as she pulled strands of hair out from under her bloody hand. They would never let her take pictures, that she was sure of, then she remembered Tonja's spy toys.

"Stevens, after Trask gets her fixed up run her ID and if she's not able to drive, have someone take her home."

"Sure thing, Crieghton," Stevens said. He left the body lying where it was and walked over to Sharon. "Can I see your ID, Miss."

Sharon pulled her ID from her bag, catching herself. She got a quick look at the ID number, and exhaled, it was the fake. She handed it to Stevens, then reached back into her bag and pulled out one of the leather headbands. Bending her head forward she scooped the tangled mess of bloodied hair back, making sure the hair on the crown of her head was flat.

Crieghton pulled a gray square device from his belt and walked over to the corpse. He took the dead man's right hand and placed it on the plate of the scanner. Sharon reached over and pulled the stem of her watch. She turned towards Crieghton as he searched her assailant and moved the cross along the chain a little more than an inch.

"Miss Clark," the reverend called to her. "I'm so sorry."

Sharon snapped a few more pictures, before turning her attention to the gun-slinging pastor. "You killed him," she said, looking directly at him, and moving the cross back and forth.

"It's all right," he said. "I'm a member of the Posse. I killed him in self-defense, your defense. They won't press charges."

Trask had returned with a first aid kit and began applying ointment, then bandages to her neck. "He was so scared," she said a little too defiantly. "He didn't mean to hurt me."

"Never," the reverend snarled at her. "Never underestimate the power of Satan."

Trask finished bandaging her neck. "When was your last tetanus shot?" he asked.

She looked up into the boy's kind face, and snapped his picture. "A couple of years ago."

"Good. You might want to have someone check that, but I think you're going to be fine," he said as he picked up her recorder and bag and handed them to her.

Stevens walked up to her and handed back her ID. "We'll be contacting you," he said as she took it and threw it back in her bag. "Are you able to drive? If not we can have someone take you back to your hotel."

"No, I'm fine," she said. "I can drive."

Trask offered her his hand in an attempt to pull her up. "I'm fine," she said, pulling her arm back and standing on her own.

"Well then, I guess you're free to go."

Sharon turned and faced the dead man crouched against the door, blood dripped down his head and across his open eyes. She wondered what his wife would tell their children. *Daddy had a mishap today trying to get a shave.* She moved the cross from one side of the chain to the other, standing as if stymied by the sight, getting as many pictures as she could.

"You can go now," Trask repeated.

Sharon pushed in the stem of her watch, then turned and walked out of the church.

Before the doors closed behind her, Crieghton said, "This would have made number three for him, Reverend. You did him a favor."

The inside of the Jeep was hot and stuffy. Bile worked its way up Sharon's throat, but she swallowed its sour juices, turned the key and pulled away from the curb. Her legs and hands shook as she drove up Power Road and turned onto McDowell. She pulled over next to an empty lot a mile or so up the road, hung her head out the door, and threw up.

"Thomas," she quietly cried as she sat back up and laid her head against the steering wheel. Her right hand searched for the activation button for her car phone, and she pushed it. "Thomas at work," she said out loud. She listened as the number of his work phone beeped through, and waited for the comforting ring.

"We're sorry," a computerized operator told her. "Your carrier is not an Arizona certified vendor. Please use a direct phone line to make your call."

Sharon threw the phone on the passenger seat, and put the Jeep in gear. Her mind was not on the dead man, it was not on Reverend Samuels, all she could think of was Thomas. She needed to hear his voice.

9

Sharon let the phone ring ten times before giving up trying to reach Thomas. She dialed Derek's number at the office. Tonja had the day off, but the temp put her through without much of a hassle. Seeing Derek's face on the monitor broke any semblance of constraint she had, and she started to cry.

"What is it?" Derek asked. "Oh, my God. Is that blood?"

Sharon continued to cry. She had never seen a man killed before and didn't know how to deal with the emotions that were washing through her.

"Sharon, talk to me. What's going on."

"Derek," she said. "I can't reach Thomas."

"Is something wrong? Sharon, what happened? Are you okay?"

"No," she said. "It was. It was unreal. It was horrible. I don't even know if I believe it really happened."

"What, what happened? Damn it Sharon, what the hell is going on over there?"

"He killed him," she said.

"Killed him? Who? Are you all right?"

"Reverend Samuels," she said. He shot..." The monitor became static, the phone clicked, then went dead. "Derek. Derek are you still there?"

The words "Communication Alert," flashed across the monitor in bold red letters. "You have violated Arizona communication code ten forty-three. Your call has been terminated and your phone line temporarily disconnected. Please call 555-1984 to have it reinstated," the same computerized operator that hadn't allowed her to call from her car said.

Sharon stared at the monitor for a full second, then when she realized she had been cut off from the only support she had, she lost it. "Fuck you," she screamed knocking the phone and monitor onto the floor. "Fuck you." Her body went limp and she crumbed to the floor.

It took about ten minutes before she was able to gain control of herself. She pulled the headband off her head and laid it on the bed. Her hand was still crusted with blood and her neck stung. She pulled herself up and ran a hot bath. She was alone, alone in a place where nothing made sense, innocent women went to jail, prisoners became breeders, petty thieves were treated like violent felons, and the clergy wielded guns. No one was safe here, especially a would be journalist spouting lies.

The water in the tub was hot, too hot, but she didn't care. She lowered herself into it, letting it burn away her fears. Within minutes of soaking in the steaming water, she did something she hadn't done since her granddad's death – she cried herself to sleep.

When Sharon awoke, the bath water was cold. Shivering, she pulled herself out of the tub and wrapped a hotel towel around her. She had to get cleaned up and find a phone she could use, somehow she would have to get an encrypted message to either Thomas or Derek. She scrubbed the blood from her hair in the bathroom sink, and with it still dripping rolled it up into a tight bun that she fastened with a hairpin. Dressed in only a towel, she stepped out of the bathroom. A man, his back to her, was sitting on her bed. She jolted back and restrained a scream that was half way up her throat. It was Reverend Samuels.

"I hope you're decent." he said keeping his back towards her.

"What are you doing here?" she asked as she grabbed her suitcase and pulled it into the bathroom. "How did you get in?"

"The maid recognized me from the TV and let me in. I came to make sure you were all right."

"I'm fine," she said closing the bathroom door. "Fuck," she whispered. She leaned up against the door to give herself a second to think, she couldn't. Her thoughts were scattered, her ears rang. She opened the suitcase and pulled out a pair of jeans and a tee shirt, hopping on one foot as she tried to get them over her wet skin.

"I was worried about you," he called from the other room. "Today must have been dreadful."

"I was scared that's all," she said fastening her bra.

"I'm not ashamed to admit I was pretty scared myself."

Scared enough to kill a man. "You didn't show it."

"That's my job. I'm not supposed to show emotion except when it comes to passion for the Lord."

Sharon pulled on her tee shirt, strapped her watch back on her wrist, pulled out its stem and opened the door. He still sat with his back to her. "You can turn around," she said.

Reverend Samuels turned towards her lifting his knee up on the bed. The phone was back on the nightstand. He had her headband in his hand and was running his fingers up and down its arched spine.

"All the fashion these days," he said holding it up to her.

She walked over to where he sat. "I don't know how fashionable they are, but I like them. I can't stand hair in my face," she said taking it from him and putting it down on the nightstand.

"I can see," he said pointing to her tied up hair.

"Yeah," she said half smiling. "It bothers me even more when I'm upset."

"That's just the thing. I knew you'd be upset, so I thought I'd come over and make sure you were okay."

"I'm okay, really. Still in denial I think, but I'll be okay."

"I'm sure you will," he said standing up. He looked down at his watch, and walked over to the TV attached to the wall across from the foot of her bed and turned it on. A Rabbi was talking about having no Gods before the one and only. "The news is next. I was afraid you would sleep through it and I'd have to wake you up."

Sharon shivered at the thought of him seeing her asleep in the tub, but said nothing. She was more interested in the news. "Is the shooting going to be covered?" she asked.

"Yes," the reverend said. "But before it starts I have to explain something to you."

"What, they didn't get my name right?" she said half jokingly.

"It's a little more than that. You see, Miss Clark, I hold a very important position in the state. I'm revered as a holy man, a man of passion, a man of righteousness. It wouldn't fare well with the public to see that their favorite preacher shot and killed a man. I'm afraid the story has been altered to protect my reputation."

Sharon opened her mouth to ask just how, but he held up his hand.

"I know, as a reporter, you believe the truth should be told regardless of the repercussions, but you're not in Southern California. For the sake of peace, we have had to institute a pool system for the media. Only the Posse is allowed to shoot crime video, then we dole it out to the different news stations. It's the only way to protect the people."

"Protect the people?" she asked amazed that any news station would go for such a thing.

"I know it sounds bad. But as soon as your state adopts the Morality platform you'll see that it's for the best. People want to believe everything is well in Arizona. They don't want to see men of the cloth killing anyone, regardless of the man's crime. They want to hear that the bad are punished, and the good prevail, regardless of what the truth is."

That's exactly what Phoebe had said. "How do you justify that?" she asked.

"In the name of the Lord and peace. Arizona is the best place in America to live right now, and that's because we were able to restore law and order. We've learned that the more people know, the more they question, and the more they question the more they resent those of us who formulate the rules they must live under."

Sharon shook her head. "That's not right."

"Maybe not, but it's how it is. And, I'm afraid, it's how you must be. I'm going to have to ask you to put your journalistic principles aside and as a woman in Christ, not report what happened today. If you can't do that, I want you to watch the news tonight and tell it as we have." Reverend Samuels looked at her sternly. "Anything else would go against the will of God, and I know, Miss Clark, you wouldn't want to do that."

Asshole! Fucking asshole. "I'm a reporter, Reverend Samuels," she said. "It goes against everything I believe in to hide the truth."

"The truth," he bellowed. "The truth is the godly protect God. If you let this story be made public, you will be cursing His very name. Everything we've worked for could go up in smoke with one false word. You must promise me, Miss Clark, promise me you will not print what happened in the Church."

Sharon walked over to the window and looked down on the street below. Dozens of cars passed by, people on their way to somewhere, oblivious to what was going on around them. "Are they really better off not knowing?" she asked in compliance with the persona she needed to portray to the reverend.

Reverend Samuels walked up beside her and put his arm around her shoulder. "I know these people. They don't want to know."

Sharon looked over at him and feigned a small smile. "I won't say a thing, Reverend," she said. *At least not until I get home.*

"God will bless you for your decision," he said squeezing her shoulders slightly then removing his arm. "You truly are a godly woman. If I can be of service to you during your visit, please, don't hesitate to ask."

"Actually," Sharon said remembering the flashing red warning across her phone's monitor and the computerized voice of the operator. "I tried to call my boss tonight. When I went to tell him what happened, my call was terminated, and my phone disconnected."

"Yes, I know. Actually that was my doing. I'm sorry to have been so invasive, but I couldn't have you talk to anyone before I had a chance to explain how things must be handled. I'll see that you have phone privileges restored first thing in the morning."

She should have known he was involved. God's law was man's law. If the reverend said it must be done, so shall it. She would be more cautious now that she knew how formidable the religious right had become. Appeasing Reverend Samuels would be her first level of protection. If he believed her, he might also be able to protect her if, at any time, she was caught asking the wrong questions.

"Thank you," she said. "I think I'm beginning to understand. We're still on for Friday, aren't we?"

"If you're still up to it."

"I'll be up to it. Showing Southern California what it would be like to live as you do is the most important thing in my life right now," she said, smiling as she imagined herself accepting the Pulitzer.

The reverend's smile was wider than she had seen it before. "God bless you," he said, giving her one last hug before leaving the room.

"Today at four o'clock, a Hispanic man, Lorenzo Martinez, was gunned down by police after robbing a Smitty's pharmacy in downtown Mesa. Martinez reportedly eluded Posse members and fled into the Calvary Baptist Church where he took a female tourist hostage. When the Posse arrived, Martinez threatened to kill the hostage if he wasn't allowed to escape. Veteran Posse member, Sergeant Bill Crieghton, was trying to barter for the woman's release, when Martinez allegedly started to cut her throat. Crieghton was forced to shoot and kill Martinez to save the woman's life.

Thanks to the fast action of the Mesa Posse, the tourist, whose name has been withheld at her request, is said to have suffered only superficial wounds and after receiving medical care was allowed to return to her hotel, where she is recuperating from the attack. Of special note was the presence of Reverend Isaac Samuels, one of the Religious Connections' most spirited hosts. His life, according to those at the scene was never in jeopardy."

Sharon watched the pictures of Lorenzo Martinez and Reverend Samuels flash on and off the screen as she listened to the monotone voice of the Evening News anchor lie to the public. She didn't blame him. She knew he was just reciting the story fed to him by the state. He droned on about the recent crime wave afflicting the state; three attempted robberies in the past month, five women and two men convicted of possession of a controlled substance, one woman charged with conspiracy to commit murder, and fifty traffic violations. "There is a call for increasing the Posse," the anchor persisted. "Anyone wanting to join the fight against crime is urged to contact the Arizona State Posse Association to see if they qualify for certification."

Sharon turned off the TV. "Just what Arizona needs," she said out loud throwing herself down on the bed. She reached over to the phone to see if there was a dial tone. Nothing. She pushed the red button next to it and reached room service. She would eat, she would review her notes, and she would sleep. Tomorrow she'd figure out a way to get word to Derek and Thomas. The urgency to speak to them had diminished. Now, the events of the day had become only a story to tell. She no longer needed their consolation, instead she wanted answers. How did a state so successfully brainwash a whole society into believing such flagrant lies? And, if they were willing to lie about a justified shooting what other secrets did the Posse conceal from the public?

10

"Daddy," a young boy called from somewhere out in the darkness.

"Daddy, where are you," a little girl's voice echoed.

Sharon stood in the dark, but it was as if her eyes were shielded, blinded by a dark hood. She waited for her eyes to adjust, to see through the black that encased her, but they didn't. She could see nothing. There was a presence, though, an oily smell from somewhere behind her. She put her hands out in front of her, and taking baby steps turned herself around.

A hand grabbed her arm and threw it behind her, yanking her back the way she originally faced.

"Nooo...." Sharon screamed.

"Shut up," a man told her. "I'll cut you."

A bare muscular arm appeared through the darkness. In its hand was a yellowish-orange, hard plastic, disposable razor, it's protective covering still in place. The hand with the razor sprang under her chin. The razor's hard plastic edge poked into her neck.

Reverend Samuels dressed in a long black pastoral robe stepped out of nowhere, his gun drawn. "Release her," he ordered.

"Show me where we can hide," the man pleaded.

"In hell," the reverend screamed as he pulled the trigger.

The bullet left the gun with a long loud bang. Sharon could see it slowly making its way towards them."

"Nooo..." She screamed again. She tried to push the man away, but he *wouldn't budge.*

"Daddy," a boy yelled.

Sharon saw him from the corner of her eyes. She turned her head to look. He was running hard, straight for them.

"Lorenzo, your…" *Sharon screamed.*

The boy ran into Sharon's hip, pushing her directly into the path of the bullet. The small metal casing shined in the darkness, it spun and wobbled as it approached.

"Nooo…," *Sharon screamed again, but it was too late. The tip of the bullet pierced her forehead.*

"Huh." Sharon sat up straight in bed, gulping air. She looked around the darkened room. There was no one there. She reached for the lamp beside her bed and turned on the light. Her hands shook.

"Shit," she said as she pulled herself from the bed and walked into the bathroom. "How many of *those* am I going to have?" She turned on the light and leaned over the sink. She looked like shit. Her hair was down around her shoulders, tangled and stiff from the quick washing she gave it the night before. She pulled the bandages from her neck and examined her wounds, she could still feel the point of the plastic edge of the razor from her dream. "He didn't want to hurt me," she said out loud, then looked closer at the wounds. They still hurt, but were closing and showed no signs of infection.

Sharon replaced the bandages on her neck, making a mental note to pick up new gauze and anti-bacterial cream. She stared at herself a little longer.

"What now?" she asked her reflection.

She thought of the bird in the park, its methodic patience in rendering the poor fish helpless before devouring its flesh, and shuddered. Abortion had only been one break in the state's backbone. Maybe the most obvious, but still only one. There had been numerous others. Somehow she'd have to work that into her article.

She looked down at her watch, it was getting late. She needed to start getting ready. Her first meeting was with an abortionist, then she had three others scheduled for the afternoon. Two of the three women had tried the system and failed. The other, an older woman, had used traders to get out of the state before anyone knew she was pregnant and then had them smuggle her back in the next day. Sharon hoped to make contact with a trader through her.

The phone in her room rang, startling her. "Let it be Thomas," she said as she ran from the bathroom to answer it.

"Sharon. Is that you?" Derek had bags under his eyes, his lips were tense.

"Derek?" she asked, slightly disappointed to see his face instead of Thomas'.

"Yeah. What the hell is going on? I tried calling you back after we were disconnected, but I couldn't get through. Are you all right?"

"I'm fine. I was just a little scared, that's all, and I needed to talk."

"Was that blood I saw all over you last night?"

Sharon opened her mouth to speak then remembered the Arizona Communication Code. Her phone service had been restored, thanks, no doubt, to Reverend Samuels, but they could still be listening. It would be best to recite what she heard on the news, she could always tell him the truth when she got home. "Some guy robbed a pharmacy then ran into the church where I was interviewing Reverend Samuels. He took me hostage for a few minutes before the Posse showed up and killed him."

"No, shit?"

Yes, shit, except it wasn't a Posse member who had done the killing. It was the God blessing, God fucking minister. "It was horrible, Derek. I was pretty scared."

"No doubt. You're okay though? What are those bandages for?"

"A few scratches," she said, rubbing her neck. "But, I'll live."

"Good. Thomas called this morning. He couldn't reach you at the hotel. They told him the phone in your room was out."

"Yeah, they had some problems with their phones. I guess they're fine now. I'll give Thomas a call at work and let him know I'm all right."

"Great." His face relaxed a notch, at least there was some slack in his lips. How's the story coming?"

"Good. My meeting with Reverend Samuels went well until the shooting. My next interview is in a couple of hours." *Get off the phone!* an inner voice screamed. It wasn't safe to discuss the story over the phone, and she didn't know how to tell Derek the call might be monitored without being shut down by some other communications code. She needed to end the conversation and worry later how to communicate effectively. "I really don't have time to talk right now," She said. "I still have to get ready for this morning and give Thomas a call. I'll call you with anything important."

"Okay, Sharon, but you take care of yourself over there. I wouldn't want anything to happen to my new star reporter."

Star reporter. She liked the sound of that and smiled. "I'll be careful," she said. She put the phone back down on its receiver – gently, like an unpinned grenade.

11

Sharon turned up Scottsdale Road and headed for her first interview. She had called Thomas, with a towel hanging around her neck to conceal the bandages, and pretended everything was all right. She didn't like deceiving him, but knew if she began to tell him what happened at the church, she wouldn't have been able to keep the truth from him. Besides, if she did tell him the truth, or even Arizona's version of the truth, he would have insisted she come home. That was something she couldn't do. She owed it to Lorenzo Martinez' children, if not herself, to expose the Godly cover up that supposedly protected Arizonians from themselves.

She pulled up to the Love Me Tender Beauty Salon on one of the side streets in Old Scottsdale. It was a great disguise for an abortion clinic. Women could come and go without being suspected of anything. She smiled as she imagined a would be client. "Take a little off the top, and oh yeah, while you're at it mind if I use those stirrups?"

She got out of her Jeep and locked it. The streets were deserted. She walked up to the beauty parlor and read the sign. "Closed. Open Tuesday through Saturday 11 to 5." She knocked.

A woman wearing a white smock opened the door. She was only about five foot two, but her bouffant hairdo gave her the appearance of being much taller. "We're not open yet," the woman said, chomping loudly on a piece of gum. "You'll have to come back at eleven." The woman went to close the door, but Sharon put her hand on it and held it open.

"I'm Sharon Clark from the Los Angeles Sentinel. I had a nine o'clock appointment with Simon."

The woman looked up and down the street. "Nine, o'clock? That's absurd. Simon doesn't see anyone until after eleven."

"Now, Bonnie," a tall, gray haired, balding man in a white smock said as he opened the door wider. "She's quite right about the time. I wanted to get this silly thing done and over with before any clients showed up."

The woman looked up at him and shook her head. "I told you Simon, this is not a good idea."

"Hush, now. I know what I'm doing. Please, Miss Clark, come in," he said, ushering her past Bonnie and into the shop.

The salon smelled of hair spray and perm solution. There were four stations, each trimmed with aluminum and upholstered in bright red vinyl. Pictures of Elvis decorated the walls, as well as pictures of women in various teased and poufed hairdos like Bonnie's.

"Everything's the late fifties," Simon said as he walked Sharon past the cutting stations and into a small back office. He pointed to a chair and she sat down. "Rumors have it that Elvis lives right here in Scottsdale, you know. I haven't seen him, but reliable sources swear he's been seen hanging around Fashion Square."

Sharon tried not to laugh, but couldn't. "Elvis?" she asked.

"I know what you're thinking," he laughed with her. "But he's good for business. All my women are in love with him. If I had a little more on the top, and the right style, I think I'd look just like him. Don't you think?" he asked showing her his profile then breaking into a large grin.

"A little," Sharon answered, deciding she liked him. She pulled her recorder out of her bag and placed it on the desk. She looked up at him for his approval before turning it on. He nodded his head slightly. "So, tell me about your side job."

Simon's face grew grim. "Business so soon? Well, there's not much to tell. As you already know, I help women in need. I was a doctor once," he said pulling a framed diploma out from under a pile of magazines. "Back before the laws went into effect, I was one of only ten doctors in the state who performed abortions. The moral majority was a powerful force here, and the whole police system..." He shook his head. "They were something else. Moralists, every last one of them, even though they went under the guise of straight Republicans. Anyway, they were all full of themselves and their Agenda for America. They decided they didn't want to wait for the laws to shut me down so they sent in an undercover Posse member. She wasn't even pregnant." He paused as if remembering the woman's face. "Anyway, she accused me of sexually molesting her." He looked back at Sharon. "I never touched her, I swear. It was a complete setup."

"I've heard that one before," Sharon said remembering Dorothy Merrill's accusations toward her boyfriend's father.

"No really. I never stood a chance. The judge ignored everything my nurse said, found me guilty and pulled my license. That's all they wanted," he smiled. "No jail time, no probation, they just wanted to put me out of business."

"So, why didn't you leave the state?" Sharon asked. It was amazing how people who believed their lives had been unjustly interrupted by a state's morals, chose not to move to a place like Southern California where man's law still outweighed God's.

"I wanted to, but my wife wouldn't go. She was born here. Her whole family lives here. There was no way she'd leave. To be honest, it didn't really matter. Without a license to practice medicine, one place was as bad as another."

"Your wife didn't believe the charges?"

"No. No one who knew me believed them. She was very upset at the loss of our lifestyle and standing in the community, though. Unfortunately for her, she was still in love with me back then. Back when she still could have gotten out of the marriage. Now she's stuck. For better or worse, richer or poorer. Till death do us part," he said smiling.

Sharon looked up at a picture above his desk of a woman in her mid-fifties with two grown boys. The woman's smile seemed painted on, not natural. Her hair was frosted and puffed high above her forehead. She seemed hard and unemotional. A woman serving a life sentence in a marriage and life-style she no longer wanted.

Sharon looked back down at the gentle man who sat across from her and wondered if he too would like to be done with the marriage. He had turned and was looking at the picture. It was clear, he didn't see a woman hard and devoid of emotion. He was still in love. This man was no more a molester than Sharon was pro-life.

But he *was* an illegal abortionist.

"So what, you just continued to perform abortions even though they took your license?" Sharon asked, pulling him back into the interview.

Simon turned around. "Not at first I didn't," he said. "I kept my nose clean for about ten years, but our mutual friend convinced me I needed to get back into the business. With her help, I was able to get backing for this place and obtain the necessary instruments I needed."

Sharon wasn't sure who their mutual friend really was, just a female voice over the phone calling herself Helen. She must be an influential woman to have secured backing for an Abortion Clinic and then disguise it as a beauty salon, Sharon thought to herself.

"How long have you been in business?" she asked Simon.

"Nine years. I'll only work with women our friend sends to me, and who can afford it. My prices are high so we can be sure the women who use my services would have too much to lose if anyone found out."

Sharon had expected his fees to be high. He practiced in an upscale neighborhood to wealthy clientele. Helen had already prepared her for that, advising her not to judge them for it. "So, how much is high?"

"Thirty-five thousand dollars."

"Thirty-five thousand dollars?" It didn't come close to paying for a year at college, but it could still buy a stripped down Toyota. "That's a lot of money. I can't believe people are willing to pay that much."

"It's mostly women in their forties. They've already raised a family and don't want to start over. I can't say that I blame them. From what I gather, they're looking for some independence. The kids are getting out of school and they're just starting to realize some freedom. They don't want to be saddled down again. They're thinking more about a career of some sort. Many want to start their own business or get into the arts."

Sharon had started her career straight out of college. She couldn't imagine waiting until she was in her forties before making something of her life or living in a world where housework and children were supposed to be her lifetime achievement. But then she hadn't been raised to take on a subservient role as the women he was dealing with probably had.

"Are these religious women?" she asked.

"Everyone in Arizona's religious, but most aren't fanatics. They accept the rules, follow them, but when push comes to shove, they still want what's best for them. It's a funny thing," he said, his voice taking on a tone of cynicism. "They won't work to help stop what's happened. They won't even say the laws are wrong, but when it's their life being affected, they don't hesitate to dole out the cash and break everyone of them."

"You sound almost bitter."

"Do I? Well maybe. Our friend has risked everything to fight what's happening here, and these women, if they hadn't used her services, would have turned her in long ago. Don't get me wrong," he said, holding up his hand. "I'm no better. If I really cared, I would take more risks myself. But I'm a coward just like the rest of them. I say I do it for the women, but in the end, I know, I'm doing it out of revenge."

Sharon sat back in her chair and studied the doctor. "Very few people are so honest with themselves. You must have a hard time sleeping."

"Who me?" he asked, laughing. "No, not at all. You see, Miss Clark. Once you've done something long enough, you become conditioned to it. I have no moral values assigned to these aborted fetuses, and I have no social obligations towards the women I perform them on. I'm here, I do a job, I'm done with it. When I go home, I'm a lowly hairdresser. When I see women being arrested for attempted abortions, I think, like everyone else, they were stupid, they got caught, and now they have to pay."

"Will you feel the same way if it's you being arrested?"

Simon laughed again. "You get down to it quickly, don't you? I suppose I wouldn't feel the same way then, would I? It's a lot different when it's your life." His laugh lines faded and his eyes looked past her. "If I ever do get caught, I'll be up for murder charges. I'd rather die then spend the rest of my life in prison. That, I do think about." He reached into his pocket and pulled out a small plastic case and handed it to her.

Sharon opened it up and looked down at the one white pill it held. "What is it?"

"Cyanide. I could never go to jail. Unfortunately, I also don't think I have the courage to ever swallow this. I pray to God every night I don't get caught."

Sharon handed him back his case. "If you're so afraid, why do you continue? Why don't you just close up shop and retire?"

Simon looked down at the small pill, closed the case and put it back in his pocket. "I already told you, it's my form of revenge. The money is used to help support our friend's cause. Plus, I get a kickback. A hairdresser doesn't make the same salary as a doctor, so the money helps pay for some small extras that help keep my wife happy." Simon took a small breath then looked past Sharon as if contemplating his actions. "You probably think it's terrible of me to do something like this without real concern for the women."

Sharon hadn't come to judge him, she had come to see how well hidden and proficient his setup was. She decided not to respond to his question. She looked around at the small office walls.

"So where do you do it? Here in the office?"

"No," he said then stood up. "It's quite clever. I have to ask you not to take any pictures, or to even report on how it works, but I'd love to show you."

Sharon turned off the recorder and put it in her bag. "I promise," she said, then followed him back into the shop and through a side door.

"This is the laser room," he told her as she walked into a small cubicle with one station, and a sink. The chair resembled the others in the front of the shop, but instead of having one footrest it had separate ones for each leg. "I use this for removal of inner thigh hair from woman wanting a clean bikini line. Here watch," he said as he flipped a switch.

The chair rose a foot higher and the footrests moved up and apart. He reached behind the chair, pulled a lever and the back reclined.

"The only difference," he continued, "is that instead of using the laser, I use this vacuum."

He pulled a long white ribbed hose with a small flat opening at the top out from under the cabinet below the sink. "Half an hour and they're out of here. I do it during business hours, so nothing seems suspicious. My regulars are quite used to the influx of strangers coming in for the laser treatment, so I'm not really worried."

"Then why the pill?" Sharon asked.

"I said I'm not worried about my regular customers. I am worried about undercover Posse members showing up. I'm not so good with discerning who's real and who's a lie. My wife's much better at it, but she refuses to have anything to do with the beauty parlor. She says it's beneath her."

Sharon looked around the small room. It was quite the disguise. She would never have guessed anything else was going on other than what he stated in his advertising. "So, how many women a year do you see?"

"I knew you'd ask, so I counted them up last night. Twenty-three so far this year."

"That's a lot less than I imagined," Sharon said.

"Well the cost is prohibitive for most. There are a lot more abortions being performed, but in dingy motel rooms by unqualified hacks. I hate to venture how many women die each year in those places," Simon said, looking down at his hands.

"I wish you could guess. Arizona statistics show no women dying from illegal abortions. They say there aren't any."

Simon broke up laughing. "Just like there isn't any adultery going on in our state. The law forbids it so they say it isn't happening. Laws, Ms. Clark, are for the religious and the poor. If you have money and know the right people, you can do as you damn well please."

"I believe that," Sharon said, looking down at her watch, and picking up her bag. It wasn't really all that different where she lived. "I have to get going, Simon. Thanks for all your time. I think I can get a lot out of our interview for the article without giving away your setup."

"I appreciate that. Miss Clark." He grabbed her arm. "Don't let this happen in Southern California. Here the Godly rule in ungodly ways."

"I've noticed," Sharon said looking him in the eyes. "But I've noticed something worse."

"What's that?"

"No one seems to care."

Simon took a deep breath and let go of her arm. "Some people care, they just don't feel powerful enough to stop it."

Sharon gave him half a smile. "That's why we vote," she said in a low voice, then turned and walked out of the room.

Sharon let herself out of the salon and stepped into the hot Arizona air. A young couple, both in jeans and boots, stood arm in arm gazing in the display window of the Western store across the street. An old faded blue pickup truck was parked a few spaces away. As she stepped into her Jeep, the couple turned around and headed for their truck. The boy looked familiar. Sharon stared at him for longer than she thought was polite. He looked liked the young Posse member who had bandaged her neck the day before, but she couldn't be sure. People looked different in civilian clothes. She shrugged her shoulders and turned the ignition. Her next stop was in Phoenix.

She pulled the disk from her recorder and replaced it with a fresh one. Simon's interview was too incriminating to carry around with her. During lunch she would take notes off it, then erase it. She took a few more minutes to dig in her bag for directions to her next interview, then looked up. The truck was still there. The couple was kissing. She thought of Thomas and how they used to kiss in public in those early days of romance and anticipation. Now they were too grown up, too sophisticated to publicly show their affection. She envied the couple's provincial naiveté and took off.

Scottsdale road was slow and busy. She seemed to be two cars too late for each light, and found herself stopped more than moving. A horn blared somewhere close by and she looked into her rear view mirror. The couple's truck was a few cars behind. The young man leaned over the steering wheel, his eyes glued to the traffic ahead. She was sure it was the same man from the church and wondered if he liked what he did, or if it was just a volunteer job to impress his friends. As she turned up McDowell to head into Phoenix, the truck turned with her.

A knot formed in the base of her stomach. Intuition told her that the truck turning with her was no accident. She went through a few lights and checked her rear view mirror. They were still a few cars back. A sign pointed to the Phoenix Zoo. She decided to turn down it. As she made the left turn, she watched them carefully, hoping it had all been a coincidence. Her heart quickened as the truck followed.

"Damn it," she said to no one.

She drove down the street for a while, trying to convince herself that she was over reacting. Either way, she had to know. There was a right turn up ahead. She decided to take it. If they followed her, she would stop and confront them.

The road brought her into a park. At its head were large red clay looking rocks with small cave like pockmarks. These were the same rocks she could see from her hotel. The clerk had called them the Buttes. The road led up to a pagoda sitting on top of a slight hill. Sharon pulled into a side parking area and waited. She thought about Simon Garner and compared him to the man that had aborted her unwanted child. Simon would have warm hands, she was sure of it, but inside he was as cold and uncaring as her doctor. It was all a matter of conditioning, she told herself. They weren't bad men, they just had lost all emotional attachment to the job. She looked at herself in the mirror and ran her hand along the bandage on her neck, letting her eyes scan the road behind her. The truck hadn't followed. The road was deserted.

"You're paranoid," she told herself then leaned her head back on the seat and took a few deep breaths. A good reporter had to become conditioned too, to fear, and uncertainty. She needed to learn to be a better judge of what was going on around her and not fall for delusional conspiracies, although this was Arizona and a small amount of suspicion was warranted.

She looked up the road. It continued deeper into the park and though the rocks were interesting to look at, she had to get back to familiar streets. She started the Jeep and headed back down the way she had come. As she pulled out of the side road, the truck pulled out from the curb where it had been waiting and resumed its chase.

"So much for over-reacting," Sharon said as she pulled over to the curb. The truck pulled up behind her and the young man waved to her. She got out of the car and walked up to their window. "What the hell do you think you're doing?" she demanded.

The young boy, Trask she thought she remembered them calling him at the church, rolled down the window and smiled. "Why, Miss Clark. I thought it was you back there. This is Corrine, my fiancée.

"Hi," the girl said bending forward.

"Hi," Sharon said back. "Trask, why are you following me?"

"I just wanted to make sure you were okay. Who's to tell where that knife had been. I was worried your cuts may have gotten infected. I was just checking up on you."

"Then why didn't you follow me into the park?"

"I didn't know what you were doing. Corrine and I were just discussing if we should go up there or not. You may have been meeting someone, then I wouldn't have wanted to bother you. When we saw you come back down so quick, I decided to follow. I didn't upset you, did I?"

Sharon didn't trust him, or his girlfriend, but she smiled at him anyway. "No, it was just a little scary having someone following me, after what happened yesterday."

"I can understand that. Well, we won't bother you anymore. Have a great day Miss Clark."

"Thanks, and by the way, they're fine."

Trask looked at her a little perplexed. "Who's fine?"

"My wounds, remember? That's why you followed me."

"Oh, yeah. Well that's good to hear. Guess I'm a better medic than I thought. We'll be seeing you, Miss Clark."

"Yeah, maybe so," Sharon said, stepping away from the truck and looking up the road at a black Cadillac waiting patiently against the curb. Must be trade-off time. She got in her Jeep and headed back to the hotel. There would be no more interviews today.

The Cadillac followed her back to the hotel, staying farther back than Trask had. It pulled into the parking lot as she walked into the main lobby. The hotel clerk nodded to her and picked up the phone. "Miss Clark," he said, holding his hand over the receiver. "You have messages."

Sharon walked over to the desk and picked up the two pink slips he had pushed her way. One was from Thomas' earlier attempt to contact her, the other was from Derek. She pocketed both slips and headed for the elevator.

"Just, a minute," a man called from the lounge. "Sharon Clark?"

Sharon turned. A man in his early fifties, slightly overweight, and wearing a light tan suit walked towards her. His face showed signs of wear, or too much sun, she couldn't decide.

"What now?" she asked as he stepped into the elevator with her.

"Miss Clark. I'm Detective Grant with the Maricopa County Sheriff's Department."

"I'm not surprised," she said, looking down at the floor to conceal her nervousness. They had been watching her all day. If they knew the real reason she had come, she could have implicated Simon without even knowing it. "I don't like being followed," she stated in the best authoritative voice she could manage.

"We're real sorry about that, but your involvement in yesterday's shooting has put some folks into a panic. Out of state news reporters aren't looked upon very well here, especially ones from one of the rebel states. We want to be sure you aren't going to print what really happened yesterday."

"Reverend Samuels was here last night. We straightened everything out."

"Yes, ma'am, that's what I've been told. But I was asked to keep an eye on you today, and I'm just doing my job."

The elevator stopped and Sharon stepped out. Detective Grant followed her.

"And how long are you going to follow and eavesdrop on me?" she asked.

"I'm afraid until we're sure you aren't going to jeopardize our peace, ma'am."

Sharon stopped and turned to face him. "Look, Detective Grant. I'm here to get a story. If you and your Posse members are going to follow me around all the time, you'll scare off my informants. I'm on your side, why can't you believe me?"

"Then why were you at Simon Garner's salon today?" Detective Grant asked her, looking directly into her eyes.

"Jesus!" Sharon said, pulling her face away from his inspection, and continuing down the hall.

"Ma'am," the detective said following her.

"I'm sorry. This is getting ridiculous. He was your state's leading abortionist before the abortion laws went into effect, wasn't he?"

"Yes, ma'am."

Sharon stopped and faced him again. "Well doesn't it make sense that I would want to talk to him, to find out what it was like *before* the laws, and correlate it with how Southern California is now?"

Detective Grant paused for a moment, then nodded his head. "It makes sense. So, what did he have to say?"

"Not much I'm afraid. He said it was all in his past and he didn't want to get into it."

"Seems like it took a very long time for him to tell you that. My records show," he said taking a small hand held computer out of his jacket pocket and pushing a few buttons. "You were in with him for almost an hour."

"Yeah. So what? I could have spent all day with him." Sharon squinted her eyes, and slightly extended her head out towards him. "You don't know anything about reporting, do you?"

"No, ma'am."

"Well sometimes, Detective Grant, you have to ease your way into an interview. Make small chat, look at pictures. The most I could get out of him was his rendition of his arrest. It was useless information. Here, look," she said pulling her recorder from her bag and pushing the play button. "Nothing. He wouldn't let me record him, he wouldn't answer any of my questions directly. He's just an old scared man making a living in a job he feels is below him. Now if you don't mind," she said as she walked up to her door and fumbling in her bag for her ID.

"Here, let me," Grant walked up behind her, pulled an ID out of his pocked and slid it through the reader. The door opened.

Sharon looked up at him, trying to hide her shock, but her mouth was hanging open.

The detective smiled. "I have access to everything, Miss Clark. I still need a search warrant, but it doesn't mean I can't get in. I just want you to know things are different here in Arizona. The people want our protection so they have given us special freedoms your police aren't quite ready to handle."

"So, I see," Sharon said slowly. She couldn't tell if the emotions in her brewed through anger or fear, but she knew she couldn't let him see that he intimidated her. "Well, I have nothing to hide," she said walking into the room. She turned to face him, stopping him from entering.

"Make sure it stays that way,"

"I will." Sharon went to close her door.

The detective held it open.

"One last thing Miss Clark," he said. "It's against the law to with-hold any information leading to subversive activities. I realize you're a reporter and you need your space while collecting information. But, before you leave Arizona we want a full accounting of who you spoke to and what they had to say. You promise me that and I'll let you move around without being followed."

Yeah, the next mission to mars maybe. "I promise," she said smiling at the detective. "I'll dump copies of my notes and disks at the sheriff's station before heading out. Is that good enough?"

"That's all we ask. Have a great day, Miss Clark."

"You too," *you bastard.*

Sharon tried one more time to leave the hotel. The black Cadillac, visibly followed her. She found a small café had lunch, then returned to her hotel, the Caddy in tow. There would be no more interviews today.

She left messages for the three women she was to interview, apologizing for her late cancellation, but saying it was unavoidable. She did not want to endanger their lives while she was still being watched. Once the Posse cooled down, she would reschedule, but for now, she would just put together what she had and destroy the disks that would incriminate Dorothy, Phoebe, and Simon.

Detective Grant's access to her room was unsettling. She did have lots to hide, but nowhere to hide it.

"My ID. Shit, if they catch me with that I'm screwed."

Sharon fished in her bag and pulled out both IDs. They were computerized cards coated in hard plastic. Each time you accessed anything, it was recorded in some huge database, and whoever, with proper authorization, was interested, could find out anything and everything they wanted to know about you.

She hadn't understood how the fake one worked, it must somehow plug into the same system and be able to bypass the duplication protectors so widely popularized during the last decade. She flipped the original one over and over in her hand trying to decide what to do with it.

The new plastic was almost indestructible, it was made to withstand high temperatures, hundreds of accidental washings, and sharp objects. The only way to get rid of it would be to lose it, but that would be almost impossible. Everything from napkins to toilet paper was recycled, if she left it in a trash receptacle, it would be filtered out and turned over to the Information Processing Bureau.

She had to do something with it to keep it from falling into the hands of the Posse, but what? Sharon paced around the room, no place seemed safe enough. If Grant wanted her room searched, professionals would do it and they wouldn't leave a drawer unturned. No, it had to be somewhere outside her room.

"The tree," she said, remembering the large potted rubber tree at the end of the hall. It was nearby for easy retrieval, but safely out of her room . Putting the ID in the back pocket of her jeans, she slowly opened her door and looked up and down the hall. It was clear. The tree sat in front of a floor to ceiling window four doors down. Leaving her door open, she walked down to the plant and examined its base. Dirt and roots filled the twenty-gallon bucket.

Looking over her shoulder, Sharon pulled the ID from her pocket and reached down into the soil. She pushed the card down into the roots, knuckle deep.

The bell to the elevator chimed.

She wrenched her hand free of the plant almost knocking over the chair next to it. The chair teetered a little but didn't fall over. She quickly sat down, crossed her legs, hid her dirtied hand between her thighs and turned as if looking out the window.

She watched through the reflection in the glass as two men in suits stepped out of the elevator and turned down an adjoining hall. She waited until she heard their voices trail off then ran back to her room and closed the door.

Her heart pounded slightly as she sat on the bed. She looked around the empty room and realized there wasn't much else to do with the rest of the afternoon. She decided that after she transcribed her notes, she'd go to a movie, dinner and then bed. Tomorrow was her tour of Arpaio Women's Penitentiary and she wanted to be alert. She would be one of only a few reporters ever allowed in, and possibly the only one with a hidden camera. This was a great opportunity to see and show more of Phoebe's version of the system rather than the pool photographs of units like Dorothy's.

Everything was going be great, as long as she stayed sharp, and incognito. Tomorrow would be her chance to win the reverend's – a man who seemed to have more political power than any other minister she had ever met – trust and get him to keep the Posse off her back. The Cadillac could follow all it wanted. She wasn't going anywhere they didn't already know.

12

Sharon met Reverend Samuels outside his church at ten o'clock in the morning. His car was much older than she would have thought. It was an old Wagoner whose tan paint had faded years ago. There were a few scratches and dents, nothing major, just enough to enhance its rustic nostalgia. The seats, covered by a thin green blanket with a pine forest design, were hard and firm, not body conforming like the ones in her Jeep. There was a slight smell of mildew and the air conditioner was noisy, but Sharon didn't care. The Wagoner reminded her of fishing trips she had taken with her grandfather when she was small and the log cabin near his favorite fishing hole up north.

She could almost smell the damp rich soil along the banks of the lake, the pine scented air, and the punk odor of fish guts that permeated the small aluminum fishing boat she had spent so many hours in with her granddad. Those had been the good times, the times away from her mother, away from the city. It was the times with her Granddad she pulled her favorite memories, and many of those started with a long trip in his green Wagoner. *I miss you Granddad*, she said in a short prayer she wasn't sure he'd ever hear.

The Wagoner jolted. Sharon's head almost hit the roof of the car.

"Sorry," the reverend said. "Bad shocks."

Sharon turned to him and smiled. The reverend looked somewhat like her granddad. They were the same size, had the same wind swept hair. They were similar all right – except her grandfather had never killed anyone. Nor, she admitted to herself, had he ever been in a situation where someone had held a knife to her throat. Maybe he would have done the same. But if he had, she decided, he would have admitted his guilt and taken his medicine. Wouldn't he?

The car hesitated as if it were going to stall, then caught again. Sharon laughed. "The engine sounds like it could use some work as well," she yelled over the noise of the motor. "Where do you find gas for this?

"Gasoline? There's no gas available in Arizona. I had to have it converted to natural gas years ago. My wife keeps telling me to get rid of it, but my father gave it to me when I first got my license and I've been in love with it ever since." He looked over at her, his eyes narrowing. "You're not embarrassed to be seen in it are you?"

Sharon laughed. "No, in fact, I rather like it. I've always had a thing for older Jeeps."

"I could tell that about you." He smiled. "Myself, I love backpacking and camping. I used to pack up my children whenever they had weekdays off from school and haul them to the mountains in Payson, or up to Utah. It was a great time. Now I take the youth club out twice a year." He laughed at some inner joke. "It's those kids that make me love my job."

Two days ago he had shot and killed a man, had her phone disconnected, and illegally entered her room. Today he was sentimental towards a car given to him by his father, and every kid's favorite pastor. The contradictory actions in people's lives had always amazed Sharon. Reverend Samuels was just another example. He wasn't a bad person. He wasn't a corrupt man. He was a good man doing what he believed was right. The same as the Nazi soldiers, Palestinian suicide bombers, and every other terrorist who threatened the homeland.

"The kids are lucky to have you," she said, looking out the window at the hills of cactus on either side of them, realizing she didn't have a clue where they were. "I didn't know the prison was so far out."

Reverend Samuels turned his head for an instant to look out her window. "It's beautiful isn't it? This all used to be part of the Salt River Indian Reservation, and that over there," he said pointing across the desert towards some distant mountains, "That was the Tonto National Forest."

"Who owns it now?" Sharon asked, trying to make out the markings on the mountain he had pointed towards.

"The state. After the National Lands Act passed, all unused land on the reservations was returned to the state. Then, remember when the government sold off all its land holdings to balance the budget?"

"Yes," she said, remembering the rush of residents and Hollywood to come up with the funds needed to save the San Bernardino, San Gabrial and Los Padres forests. Some of it made it into private hands, but only small parcels, the rest was set aside as county and state parks.

"We scrounged up the money to buy back all our land. We didn't lose an acre of it to privately owned corporations."

"That's impressive," Sharon said. "We came out okay too, but Northern and Central California weren't so lucky. They lost most of the National Forests to outside interests and now many of the their forests have been leveled either by developers, logging companies, or foreign investors. Northern California has really changed."

"I know. I've seen it. That used to be one of the most beautiful places on Earth, now it's just one big golf course."

Sharon nodded her head as she looked out at the thorny, brush strewn, dry brown earth. What would someone want with so much desert? The Californian forests were beautiful, well worth the effort she and everyone else had put into saving them, but the desert? She just couldn't imagine making the effort to save it.

"So, are you planning to develop out here?" she asked.

Reverend Samuels shook his head and laughed. "Develop it? We aren't going to do anything with it. We treasure our desert. Except for a few state facilities, there'll be nothing done with the land, except to maintain it for future generations."

Sharon shook her head. *Poor kids.* "So where are they now? The Indians, I mean. The Southern Californian Indians got to keep most of their land, but I heard the Arizona tribes were displaced and are holding out in the mountains."

"Unfortunately. You know, we gave them everything. They were given clear title to the land they had built their homes on and any acreage they farmed. But they weren't satisfied. They wanted to maintain complete autonomy from the rest of the state. They refused to fit into our system. They call themselves Native Americans, but there's nothing very American about them. They're still the heathens we found when we first discovered this great country of ours." He paused for a moment and looked over at her.

Sharon didn't maintain his viewpoint on the plight of American Indians. She felt they had more claim to the land than her Scandinavian forefathers, but knew that the majority of people saw them as outsiders. She didn't want to debate Native American rights with him, so she just appeased him by nodding her head in approval.

"They pretended to accept our Savior," he continued. "But they still held their ceremonies, their Pow Wows, and then they had the audacity to take one of our human frailties and turn it against us."

"The casinos?" she smiled. How people hated those casinos. They loved to go to them, they loved to win at them, but they hated that the profits went tax free to a race of people that worked hard to retain independence from the rest of the nation.

"Why we ever gave them permission in the first place, is beyond me. They used their demon gods to tempt mankind into thinking gambling was okay, as long as it was sanctified by the government. Personally, I was glad to see them shut down."

You and the rest of the government, she thought to herself. Capitalism was a grand idea, as long as the profits went to either the government or the rich. God forbid the oppressed ever find a way to make it in America. "So the fact they were making so much money had nothing to do with repealing their sovereignty and taking over the reservations?"

Reverend Samuels turned and smiled at her. "Off the record? he asked.

"Off the record," she smiled back.

"Well, here they did share the profits, it was the only way we let them continue. But they would only give us thirty percent, nothing in the scheme of things. If they hadn't been so greedy, things may have been different. We were already sick of all the perks they had. The fact they had their own government was bad enough, but when they were allowed to make millions off the hardworking people who supported them, it was too much.

The reverend shook his head. They're still a problem though. Pockets of them have moved into the mountains and have just about closed off the Grand Canyon. We're going to have to stop them soon, before someone gets hurt."

She knew who *we* was. Of all the states that had formed Posses back in the twentieth century, Arizona's was the most infamous. They had been credited with ridding the state of drugs, prostitution, and gangs, and now, she supposed, they would clear the renegade Indians off their land. She smiled at him and flashed her eyebrows. "Sounds like a job for the Posse."

"You do learn quickly, Miss Clark. That's exactly what we plan on doing, but not just yet. We're going to wait until after the election. There are still some people who believe Indians should have more rights than real Americans, the ones who sweated blood to make this a great country." He looked straight ahead as he spoke, so he didn't see

Sharon's smile fade. He didn't see the contempt she felt for him as it momentarily flashed across her face. She turned her head toward the window as he continued with his litany. "There are those who think these rebellious Indians are heroes. Right after the election, we'll clean them out. Our Posse is already thirty thousand strong. We plan to recruit another ten thousand to help with the Indian wars."

Sharon found the stories of the Posse raids rather frightening. The Posse would move into a neighborhood a hundred strong and do a sweep, arresting everyone that looked suspicious. Southern California still used academy-trained police, and though the system was far from perfect – LA did have one of the highest crime rates in America – she preferred police to citizen vigilantes. "Forty thousand?" she asked turning back to face him. "Aren't you afraid of becoming a police state?"

"It's not a police state!" the reverend said, too loud, Sharon thought, giving away his fears. "Everyone's able to do whatever they want as long as it doesn't break any laws. You don't see Posse cars patrolling up and down the street. It isn't necessary. With so many people involved in the Posse, just the threat that the person next to you could turn you in or arrest you, makes everyone live a more honest, productive life. We have the lowest crime rate in America."

"So, I've heard."

"We're almost there," the reverend said, his voice calmer as though he was grateful their conversation was over.

Sharon looked out the window at the approaching mountain. She could see razor wire in the distance. "Is that it?" she asked pointing towards the base of the mountain.

"Arpaio Women's Penitentiary."

"Why so far out?" she asked as she tried to see more of it, but couldn't.

"They put it way out here to keep protesters away. In the beginning when they housed these women in the regular women's prison, hundreds of protesters would show up every day. It drove everyone nuts. Now with it so far away from everything, very few people come and those that do don't stay long. The desert gets very hot in the summer. You couldn't live out here for more than a hour without water."

Sharon looked around at the brambles, sagebrush, and cacti that filled the landscape. There were a few low lying trees, but nothing that offered much shade. "Not very hospitable is it?" she asked.

"No, it's not," the reverend said turning onto a long unmarked road.

She was surprised at how hidden it was. No wonder they could get away with many of the things the woman she interviewed had accused them off. Who would ever know? There were no neighborhood watches to see who came and went from such an isolated place. "No, sign?" she asked.

"There's one further up, near the guard's station. Used to be prisons in Arizona were famous. The Maricopa county jails were so close to the street that during the tent city days people used to walk up to the fence and take pictures of inmates dozing in their bunks. It caused a lot of ruckus around the country. When they built this one, they decided they wanted as little fan fare as possible."

"Are they afraid the public won't approve of what they're doing?" Sharon asked thinking again of Phoebe and Dorothy's stories.

"It's not that. It's just this is still a touchy subject. People want these women prevented from killing their children, but no one wants to see a pregnant woman behind bars. It goes against everything they've been trained to respect – motherhood, family, life."

"I see. So, it's another one of those instances where the less they know, the happier they are," she said hoping he wouldn't recognize the sarcasm in her voice.

"You're a quick study, Miss Clark."

Sharon could see the guard station and the Arpaio Women's Penitentiary sign through a stand of saguaro cacti. Behind a twelve-foot tall chain link fence and three feet of razor wire were many single story, sand colored adobe buildings separated by rust colored sand and pavement. Only one had windows.

Reverend Samuels pulled up to the guard gate. "I need your ID," he said to Sharon as he reached in his shirt pocket for his own. Sharon handed him her ID, and he handed both of them to the guard.

"This is Sharon Clark. She's with the Los Angeles Sentinel. The warden knows she's coming."

"Yes, sir," the guard said stooping down to peer into the window past him and scan Sharon's face and body. Sharon faked a smile and waved. The guard pulled the two IDs through a scanner, it beeped twice, then he handed them back to the reverend. "You're all set, drive through," he said.

The reverend handed Sharon back her ID and she put it in her blazer pocket. She adjusted her watch and flattened her hair under her headband. Her stomach tightened, not from fear, but excitement. She loved her spy toys. They gave her a sense of power and self-confidence. The deceit she had maintained for the past three days seemed intact and she felt invincible.

The reverend pulled up to one of the smaller buildings and turned off the car. "This is it," he said pointing to a door to her right. "Make sure you lock the door, and leave your bag in the car. No photographic or recording devices are allowed inside."

Sharon pulled her notebook and pen from her bag, then stowed it under her seat. She got out, locked the door, and waited for the reverend. He took his time to lock the back door of the wagon. "Can't have anyone trying to sneak out with us."

She looked around at the deserted campus. There were very few places to hide. "Have they tried?" she asked, sure no one would be successful.

"Once that I've heard of. A young girl snuck into the truck of a plumber who used to work out here. Thank Jesus, the guards found her before she could get out. The poor fellow, though. I've always felt bad for him. He was given a year's jail time for complicity."

"Even though he didn't know she was in the truck?"

"That's the laws. When you're on prison property, you're responsible for everything you bring onto the property, including your vehicle. If he had locked it, as he was supposed to, she wouldn't have been able to get inside."

"I suppose," Sharon said as they walked up a ramp to a metal door. "It seems a little harsh though."

"I think so too, but who are we to argue with the justice system." Sharon laughed to herself. *Who are we indeed?*

The room they entered took up the whole building. Reverend Samuels showed her to a seat on a stage at the front of the hall and sat down next to her. "I'll introduce you," he said quietly as women proceeded into the room. It was like watching a bubble gum parade. Each woman had on an A shaped bright pink dress. Knee length and sized to fit all stages of pregnancy. She looked down at her ecru tailored suit with its navy trim, felt the security of its tight fabric, and readjusted her skirt, touching it just to be sure it didn't have the look and feel of cotton.

The women were of various height, hair, eye color, and stage of pregnancy. Some didn't look pregnant at all, yet they all had that one remarkable similarity, which Phoebe thought so absent at Arpaio – they were all white

Sharon leaned over to the reverend. "Aren't there any minority women here?" she asked.

The reverend patted her knee in a fatherly fashion. "Sure there are, but they're in a different unit."

"Is that allowed?" she asked, surprised he would be so honest.

"The separation isn't because of race. No, of course not. It's just that we have different types of women here. This is B Group, my congregation. All these women were deemed rehabilitative and have been separated from the rest. We have a special program for them that we hope will bring them back to the Lord and help them to accept their roles as Christian women within our society. Those who show complete remorse for what they attempted are allowed to forgo the mandatory sterilization."

"And no minority women are deemed rehabilitative?" she asked, looking around the room for just one face that wasn't white. She couldn't find one.

"Don't be silly," the reverend said patting her knee once more. "There have been plenty. Just none right now. By next week there'll probably be ten Hispanic women and even a few Blacks. Trust me, there is no racial separation here at Arpaio. You can ask the women yourself."

"I'll get to talk to them?" Sharon asked shocked and excited at the same time.

"Of course. At the end of my sermon, you'll be given time to speak to them directly."

A man, in his early sixties, wearing a sand colored suit, walked up to the stage and greeted the reverend.

"Warden," Reverend Samuels said, reaching out his hand. "Let me introduce you to Sharon Clark, the reporter I was telling you about."

Sharon smiled and stood up.

"Miss Clark, this is Warden Hayden."

"How do you do?" Sharon said, extending her hand.

The warden smiled and took her hand in his. "So you're the young lady hoping to win Southern California over to the cause."

Sharon smiled. "I'm hoping my article will have a major impact on the voting public this upcoming election." It felt good not to lie.

Warden Hayden put his other hand over hers and smiled. "Let's hope you're successful. Anything you need, you come see me. We have nothing to hide here."

Sharon thanked him, then returned to her seat.

"Excuse me. All take your seats now," the warden said as he stepped up to the podium. There was a quick exchange of looks among the prisoners, then in silence, they sat in the metal folding chairs set up in the center of the room. "Reverend Samuels is with us this evening and has brought a guest, Miss Sharon Clark from the Los Angeles Sentinel. She is writing an article that shows how effective our system here at Arpaio has become in hopes to help Southern California voters make a moral choice this next election. After the reverend's message, there will be refreshments brought in and any of you wanting to talk to Miss Clark may do so."

Sharon was surprised at the warden's open invitation to speak with the inmates. When Samuels told her she'd get to talk to some of the inmates, she expected to be given one or two carefully tutored model prisoners that would tell her tales of comfort and well being. She thought she would have to speak to others privately without the reverend or warden knowing about it. This was too easy. She felt in the pocket of her blazer for the folded picture of Bethany Collins. There were going to be more opportunities than she had originally hoped for this evening.

The warden stepped down, and Reverend Samuels walked up to the podium. "Well it's nice to see everyone again. Let us bow our heads to thank the Lord Almighty for bringing us here tonight." The women bowed their heads as the reverend started his prayer. "O Holy Father, be with us this evening and bless..."

Sharon kept her head bowed but looked down at the women who filled the hall, all had their heads tilted downward, their eyes closed. Sharon reached up to the cross and move it across the chain. Her eyes scanned the crowd, looking for prospects to interview. She stopped when she came across a thin woman with a long black braid. As if she could feel Sharon's eyes on her, the woman looked up, saw Sharon was looking at her and quickly closed her eyes. She wasn't sure, but she was almost positive, it was the woman from the border. If she got nothing else tonight, at least she'd get the satisfaction of knowing why the couple had been arrested.

"...Amen," The reverend said.

"Amen," the women in the congregation repeated.

"I'm here tonight because I want to speak to you about life, the sanctity of life. I know many of you were misled, misguided into thinking that a child would harm you, would prevent you from living a life yourself and others had drawn out for you. But you must realize that life is a precious thing, and you, as women, are nature's, God's, chosen vessel to bring forth new life into this world.

"I want to tell you what Jesus says is our obligation to one another in the Lord. And as women, what your place is in God's great design. Is it to have careers? No. Is it to wander freely, promiscuously through life? No. God created woman to be man's helpmeet. Man's helpmeet. He gave her a womb, so that she could be fruitful and multiply. He gave her life and the ability to harbor life within her." Reverend Samuels voice boomed throughout the hall. It would be hard not to fall into the fire of his message, Sharon realized, as she watched the inmates gaze at him in respect and awe.

"Life is a gift from God. No man, or woman, or doctor, or lawman has the right to deny life to one that God has granted it. What of those of you who cry, 'I was raped,' 'it's my father's child,' 'it's deformed.' I ask you this. Does God care where the seed came from? No. Will he punish the child because of its parentage? No. God gives life, let no man or woman take it away."

Not a subject Sharon wanted to get into. She purposely blocked out the words of the message. The last thing she wanted to do was break down and repent for her own abortion. This man had great power; no wonder so many believed the message was God's not man's.

Reverend Samuels bellowed his litany for almost an hour, taking only a few sips of water and deep breaths to exhale loud epithets towards the women. He accused them of traipsing on God's gifts, of neglecting their motherly instincts, of being too self possessed to see the light. Then he calmly led them away from the viciousness of their intended sin and spoke encouraging words for them to hold onto while beginning their journey with Christ. He told them of the great blessing in store for them for embracing God's most perfect design for women and accepting their place within society and a Christian home.

He ended his sermon by asking God to bless each and every one of them with a loving husband, financial security, and many children. He asked God that they might walk in the light, and that through their years of suffering, they might become stronger daughters to "Him who gives life and taketh it away."

The women clapped as Reverend Samuels stepped down from the podium. "Praise Jesus," many called out. "Forgive me father," others cried.

Warden Hayden took the podium briefly to thank the reverend and to indicate there would be an extra hour of refreshments and talk so that Sharon would have time to speak to a few of the inmates.

"Now she doesn't have time for sob stories," the warden warned the women. "She's more interested in how you're treated and what changes have been made in your attitudes towards life and children since you came here. Be as honest as you like. As I've already told Miss Clark, we are proud of what we do here and have nothing to hide."

Sharon pulled the stem of her watch to turn on the recorder and stepped down from the stage. She was leery of heading straight for the woman she had made eye contact with earlier. She knew the woman was new, and it might look suspicious, so first she walked over to an attractive red headed woman who had stayed in her seat when the rest had moved towards the back of the hall for refreshments.

"Hi," Sharon said as she sat down next to her. "I'm Sharon Clark." She stuck her hand out towards the woman. The woman didn't offer hers back.

"Allison Taylor."

Sharon looked at her and smiled. "Well Allison, if you don't mind, I have a few questions I'd like to ask you?"

Allison looked over at Sharon, her face remained flat. "I don't have anything to say."

"But," Sharon looked at her, fumbling for a second. She hadn't realized that the women she would want to talk to, would be the ones least likely to want to talk to her after hearing she was writing a piece that supported the system they probably hated. "At least tell me how long you've been here."

"Three weeks, or something like that." Allison looked back towards the front of the building.

"Do you feel you were wrongly incarcerated?"

"Look," Allison said, turning back towards Sharon. "I don't give a damn about you or your article. I'm not going to give you any great quotes, so leave me alone. Find someone else to tell you lies." Allison got up and walked away.

"Having a problem?" the warden asked from the edge of the aisle.

"No. She just wasn't very interested in being interviewed."

"Try someone else," he said, giving Sharon a quick wink. "There are many who would love to talk. Don't believe everything they say though. We really do run a tight ship."

Sharon smiled back at him, got up and walked towards the refreshment table. She nodded her head at many of the women and edged her way towards the woman with the long black braid.

"Hi," she said, sticking out her hand. "Can we talk?"

The woman looked past Sharon towards the warden. Sharon turned and followed her gaze.

"It's all right," Sharon said. "He's given me permission to talk to whomever I want."

Sharon and the woman walked up to an empty section of chairs far from the guards who stood sentry at each door, the reverend, and the warden.

"I'm Madison Courtney," the woman said as she sat down next to Sharon.

"How long have you been here, Madison?" Sharon asked, wanting to confirm it was the same woman at the border.

"Two days."

Sharon leaned a little closer to her and lowered her voice. "I think I saw you the day you were arrested. At the border between Southern California and Arizona, right?"

"Yeah. Were you there?"

Sharon nodded her head, smiled, and sat back up. "So, were you trying to leave the state to obtain an abortion, or did you get caught unaware of your pregnancy?"

"Neither," Madison said, looking into Sharon's eyes as if wondering if she could be trusted. "I'm not pregnant."

"Not pregnant?" Sharon leaned closer towards the woman. "What?"

"I can't be. I haven't had sex in over six months, ever since I broke up with my boyfriend."

Sharon looked down at Madison's abdomen, it was flat. "Did you tell the judge that?"

"Of course I did. He ordered a blood test, and supposedly that came back positive too."

"I don't get it. If you weren't pregnant, why would they say you were?"

Madison looked around the room again, then in a hushed voice said, "To get me off the street. That was my brother with me. I haven't heard what they charged him with, but I'm sure he's in jail too. They didn't like what we were teaching in our after school program out in Apache Junction."

Sharon kept herself from gazing around the room. She knew that even if they weren't outwardly watching them, they had an eye on them. "Stop looking around as if you're hiding something," she whispered to Madison.

"I'm sorry. I'm just very nervous. I don't know that I should trust you, and I know I sure as hell don't trust any of them."

"It's okay, you can trust me." Sharon said. "I'm not really doing the article I told them I was. I'm trying to expose the system here in Arizona to help show Southern Californians that we don't want the same type of religious dictatorship in our own state."

Madison shook her head and smiled. "You've got guts. If they catch you, we could be sharing a cell."

"I know. So tell me. What's really going on?"

"I don't know much. The women who have been here for a long time seem to tolerate it well and don't complain much. The pregnant ones are not so compliant with the guards and the rules, but then they are being faced with unwanted pregnancies. Those who are just getting to the point where they are starting to accept and nurture the child within them are scared and bitter towards the eventual adopting out of their babies. I guess it takes a while to get over that and move on."

"Anyone mention additional pregnancies?"

Madison drew back and raised an eyebrow. "Has someone mentioned them to you?"

"Yeah, but I'm not sure she wasn't dreaming."

"Well, I'll be honest. I'm expecting them to do something to me. How else are they going to explain my being here. I stay awake every night, afraid they're going to impregnate me or give me something to make me hemorrhage."

"That would be good, wouldn't it? I read that if a woman miscarries, then she's automatically released because it was God's will that the child didn't live."

"Maybe. Maybe this is just a scare tactic. They want me to leave the state and not come back, or else close down my school. Right now, with the Constitution the way it is, they can't prevent me from teaching what I want to anyone who wants to hear."

"So what exactly were you teaching?"

"Self-respect, self-pride, women's rights, autonomy?"

"You *were* living dangerously. I didn't think those words were allowed to be spoken in Arizona," Sharon said half joking.

The look on Madison's face made Sharon realized Madison didn't take any of it as a joke.

"Someone's got to do it," Madison said. "Girls are being raised as subservient domesticated chattel. In a few generations there won't be anyone left who remembers women's rights. It will be rewritten in the history books as a time when crazy women rebelled against mankind and almost destroyed America."

Sharon laughed. "I wouldn't put it past them."

Madison's face was still grave. *Make fun,* Sharon admonished herself. *This woman's afraid for her life and you make fun.* Sharon thought for a moment of how she could help the woman, but quickly decided there was nothing she could do while still in Arizona or she'd blow her cover.

"Once I get back to Southern California, I'll see what I can do. A friend of mine has a lot of connections here in Arizona. Lots of old college chums. Maybe between him, and me mentioning you in my article, we can help get you out."

"Thanks," Madison said. "If I do get out, I'll look you up. My brother and I have plenty of stories to tell. We've just never found anyone interested in hearing them.

"I'm interested," Sharon said. "The truth has to come out, if not," she said looking around the room, "this could be the future for all of us."

Sharon stood up, she had spent too much time with Madison, and shook the woman's hand. "Thanks for the interview. I'll do whatever I can once I get back to Southern California."

Madison stood up and smiled. "Thanks. Would you mind doing me a favor though while you're still in Arizona?"

"I'll try."

"Check on my brother. His name is Daniel Courtney. We were arrested on May fifteenth. If he's out, would you get a message to him that I'm okay?"

"Daniel Courtney. I'll do my best," Sharon said then headed towards the refreshment table to recruit more informants.

The next few women Sharon talked to had little to say. They missed their families and friends. The one's who had given birth were remorseful towards the loss of their child, and the pregnant ones cried about the injustices of the Arizona laws. No one remembered any minority women in the unit and no one remembered seeing the girl in the picture she had been showing.

As she walked up to another woman to ask her if she would mind talking, she saw the woman she had just finished interviewing and showing Bethany's picture talking to the warden. *Shit.*

"Reverend," the warden called out across the room, interrupting the small prayer group that had formed, and signaled for the reverend to join him.

Reverend Samuels walked over to the warden and they started to talk quietly. Sharon could feel both of their gazes on the back of her neck as she reached over and picked up a glass of punch. She kept herself from looking as she listened to the woman's story of how her husband forced her into attempting an abortion. From the corner of her eye, Sharon watched the warden and Reverend leave the hall through a side door. She tried not to panic. She focused her attention on the woman talking, but could feel herself tensing up.

A few minutes later a side door opened and a female guard entered the room. Sharon tried hard not to watch her, but felt the dread of approaching confrontation. The guard stepped up behind her. Sharon could feel the woman's breath on her neck, then a heavy hand landed on her shoulder, and though Sharon thought she had been prepared, she jumped.

"Miss Clark," the guard said, "Warden Hayden and Reverend Samuels would like to speak to you, in private."

The punch in Sharon's hand almost spilled as she shakily laid her glass on the table, and stood up to accompany the guard. She smiled at the woman she was interviewing, Loren something, and followed the guard. Her legs trembled so fiercely she wasn't sure she'd be able to lift them to step over the threshold of the building.

The guard led Sharon out of the hall across a short expanse of pave-

ment and into a larger building. The hallway was empty and silent.
They stopped at an unmarked door on the left and the guard knocked.

"Come in," the warden called.

The guard held Sharon's arm firmly as she escorted her into the
room. Reverend Samuels, his back towards Sharon, stood looking out
a barred window. Warden Hayden sat in front of a long metal table,
empty except for a quart sized light blue plastic bowl.

"Is something wrong?" Sharon asked, trying to appear innocent,
knowing she wasn't. Showing Bethany's picture to the inmates had
been a disastrous mistake.

"I'm afraid so, Miss Clark," the warden said, reaching out and
taking Sharon's notebook from her hand. He leafed through some of
the pages then nodded to the guard. The guard reached over to the
lapel of Sharon's blazer and pulled it back towards her shoulder.

"Disrobe," the woman ordered.

"What?" Sharon looked at the guard then back to the warden.

"Do as she says, Miss Clark," Reverend Samuels said without
turning.

"Prison policy, I'm afraid. You've been accused of bringing propaganda onto the premises with the intention of stirring up descent.
Don't make this harder on yourself then you have to Miss Clark," the
warden said. "Take off all your clothing and jewelry and hand it over
to the guard."

Sharon froze for a second. They would never get away with
arresting her for bringing Bethany's picture into the meeting and
showing it around, but if they found the watch and headband...

"Now!" the guard demand.

"I don't understand," Sharon said as she fumbled with her blazer.
"What did I do?"

"You were showing a picture of a young woman to the inmates and
asking them if they knew the woman. Is that correct?" the warden
asked.

The guard took her blazer and searched every pocket. She handed
the warden Sharon's ID and the picture of Bethany, put her pen in the
plastic bowl, then ran her hands up and down the blazer's lining.

"Yes." Sharon stopped unbuttoning her blouse and watched as the
guard tore a section of lining and reached inside one of the sleeves of
her blazer. "I didn't realize there would be a problem with that," she
said.

"Well, unfortunately for you, Miss Clark, you didn't think at all.
Reverend Samuels tells me he told you to leave your possessions in his
car, and that you couldn't bring anything inside the prison but your

notebook and pen.

"I thought he meant video and recording equipment."

The guard pushed the blazer over to one side of the table. "Hurry up," she said reaching for Sharon's blouse. Sharon pushed her hand away, finished unbuttoning, took it off and handed it to the guard. "The skirt too," the guard said as she turned the blouse inside out and threw it on the table next to the blazer.

Sharon did as she was told. She tried not to cover herself with her hands as she stood before the warden in only her bra, slip, and panty-hose. The guard tore the hem of her skirt, then using a knife cut open the waistband. She picked up Sharon's shoes, pulled out the inner soles and ran her knife through them then pried off the heals. "Nothing," she said to the warden.

Sharon could feel her eyes well as the guard came back for more. She cursed herself for letting them break her, but couldn't stop the first of her tears from falling down her face.

"Everything," the guard ordered.

It was over. She was caught. There was nothing else she could do. She handed over her watch making sure to push in the stem before doing so, then gave the guard her headband and the cross. The guard placed them in the bowl with Sharon's pen then turned back towards her and waited for the rest.

Slowly, Sharon unfastened her bra. Reverend Samuels did not turn around. The warden did not look away. Sharon tried to cover her breasts as they fell from the cups of her bra, but had to release them to remove her slip, pantyhose and panties. She stood naked looking down at the floor, letting her hair cover her face, her shame, and her tears.

The guard cut the silk padding of the bra and the crotch of Sharon's panties. She removed a hand held scanner from her back pocket then pulled the plastic bowl that held Sharon's camouflaged camera and recorder towards her. The scanner ticked as the guard slowly ran it over each individual piece.

Sharon held her breath. The scanner passed the pen, then the cross. It beeped. The guard's hand stopped. Sharon stiffened. The warden looked down at the items in the bowl. The guard moved the scanner a second time over the cross and waited. It was silent. She picked up the headband and ran the scanner up and down its spine. Nothing. She dropped it back in the bowl. The watch was next, the guard picked it up, then holding it from its leather strap she ran the scanner up and down it length. She turned the watch over in her hand and held the scanner firmly against its back.

"Nothing," the guard said throwing the watch back in the bowl. "Must have been a malfunction."

Sharon swallowed hard instead of letting the deep breath she had been holding escape. The guard put the scanner back in her pocket and left the room.

"You can get dressed now," Warden Hayden said pushing Sharon's clothes towards her.

Sharon grabbed her clothes and hurriedly put them back on. The bra and panties were ruined. She held them for a moment staring at them, wondering what to do with them, then balled them up and threw them in a waste basked next to the door. She hurried to put on the rest of her clothing and her heelless shoes.

Her skirt was backwards and she had misbuttoned the blouse, but she didn't care. Being completely exposed had sent a horrible sense of vulnerability through her, one that she had only felt once before in her life. She put back on her watch and headband. Her hands were almost convulsive in how fast they were shaking. There would be no way to clasp the cross' chain. Instead she held it tightly in her hand. She tried, but couldn't manage to discretely pull the stem of her watch back out. Her jaw trembled as if she had been caught in a blizzard while dressed for the beach.

"She's decent," the warden said, but the reverend didn't turn around.

Warden Hayden picked up the picture of Bethany Collins and examined it. "Is this the girl you were looking for?" he asked turning the picture around and holding it up for Sharon to examine.

"Yes," she said, looking at the picture of the young girl. She nodded her head too fast and too many times. *Calm down!* She screamed at herself.

"Who is she? A friend of yours, a coconspirator?" The warden demanded.

"No. No," Sharon said trying to think of exactly who the girl was. Her mind raced with lies and excuses, then it clicked. *Be as honest as you can, then beg for forgiveness.* Sharon consciously willed herself to speak without stuttering or biting her tongue and to stop the tears that were running down her cheeks. "The daughter of my boss's friend. He ordered me to show it around and find out if anyone had seen her. I told him I didn't want to, but he threatened me with my job. I'm so sorry, Warden, Reverend Samuels," she said, looking at each of them hoping the fear and humiliation she felt would register as remorse.

"Why didn't the father ask the courts directly?" the reverend asked, turning around to face her. "Why did your boss feel it was necessary to use deceit to find his friend's daughter."

"I don't know. Really. I was just doing what I was told to. I'm sorry if I've caused any problems for either of you."

Warden Hayden stood up and leaned on the table towards her. "You should have just asked me, not showed it to the women as if you were trying to get away with something behind my back. I'm very disappointed in you Miss Clark. The reverend here tells me you're pro-life, that you're a Christian woman seeking to lead the stray sheep of Southern California back to the Lord, but yet, here you are infiltrating our hospitality with your deceits."

Deceit, that's what she needed, a great deceit, and knew the only one they would fall for. Sharon wiped the tears from her face. "I guess I blew it," she said. "I should have let them send Walter. Men are so much better at this, but I wanted to be the one to show my state how great your system works, how great our own system could work if we just brought in the right people to guide us."

The reverend walked up to her and put his arm around her shoulders. "You should never have acted on your own. You should have asked me, I would have helped you. Why they would send a woman is beyond me," he said, looking over at the warden. "I'm so sorry, Joe. I should have known better."

"Well, no harm was done," the warden said relaxing and sitting back down. "Maybe, Miss Clark, this will teach you that your place is in the home, not gallivanting all over the country playing at a man's job."

Fucker. Sharon bowed her head and looked down at the floor. "I know. I just thought the Lord wanted me to do this one last thing before I got married this Fall and started a family."

"And maybe he does," the reverend said. "But from here on out, while you're in Arizona, I expect you to let me know before you do anything else that might jeopardize your article or your freedom."

"I promise," Sharon said, still feeling violated, but not as scared. They had bought her story and she was safe. The reverend now saw her as incompetent and stupid. Maybe that was for the best. The assignment was more dangerous than she had ever imagined. She may need Reverend Samuels to bail her out again before she was done. The more helpless he thought she was, the more help he might be if she was in trouble.

Warden Hayden picked up Sharon's ID and hesitantly handed it back to her. "You're lucky Isaac has so much faith in you, Miss Clark. I'm not going to charge you with anything. I'm going to let you leave with the reverend, but we'll be watching you. We have your ID number, and I will be marking your profile. One more slip up and you'll be getting a tour from the inside. Is that understood?"

"Yes," Sharon said, taking back her ID. She reached into the pocket of her blazer, but it had no bottom, so she held it. Its sharp plastic edges cut into her hand.

"I'm afraid I'm going to have to ask you to leave now. You won't be allowed to see or speak to any more of my girls. I hope you had ample time to get the information you were looking for," he said, pushing her notebook towards her. "The tour, of course, is off. You'll have to do your research at the library, I'm afraid."

Reverend Samuels walked up to the warden and offered his hand. "I'm real sorry Joe. I never would have brought her if I thought she would do something like this."

"I know you wouldn't," the warden said, taking the reverend's hand in his. "No harm done. Like I told Miss Clark, we have nothing to hide. And for this," he said picking up the picture of Bethany Collins, "I would have remembered someone so young and pretty. I'm afraid her father will have to search somewhere else. She's never been here."

"He'll be glad to hear that," Sharon said, picking up her notebook and pen. Reverend Samuels took her arm and pulled her towards the door. She stopped him and faced the warden, he was looking down at the picture of Bethany. "I'll be more careful in the future," she said.

The warden looked up at her and smiled. "I'm sure you will Miss Clark." Sharon turned to leave. "By the way," he continued. Sharon stopped and turned to face him. "I saw you talking to Madison Courtney. I'm sure she told you she wasn't pregnant."

Sharon nodded her head. "That's what she said."

"Did you believe her?"

Sharon didn't know how to answer, he obviously knew what each woman was going to say to her. "I don't know. It's hard to believe she'd be here if she wasn't."

"Good answer. She didn't happen to tell you who we think the father is, did she?"

"No. She just said she wasn't pregnant."

"It will be interesting to hear her say that in a month or two when she starts to show, now won't it. Anyhow, we won't have proof until we've done some genetic testing, but we're pretty sure it's her brother."

Sharon let her eyes open in wide surprise. "Her brother?" she asked.

"I'm afraid so. He's been released pending the test results, but I'm sure we'll be picking him up shortly on charges of incest. You think about that before you print anything about our Miss Courtney. She isn't as good as she seems."

"I'll do that. Thank you," Sharon said as she turned back and let Reverend Samuels guide her out of the door. She could feel her body shivering under the warmth of her torn blazer. She turned back for one last look at the warden before Reverend Samuels closed the door. He had picked up the picture of Bethany Collins and was crumbling it in his hand.

As she stepped out into the hot afternoon sun, she felt over-whelming relief. The headband, cross and watch had held their secrets and she had maintained her freedom – something for the first time in her life, she wasn't taking for granted.

The drive back from the prison had been in silence. Sharon stared out the window, her mind reliving the past hour of her life over and over. The strip search had been an exercise of intimidation. She knew that, but still it had been degrading. The humiliation she felt was nothing compared to the fear that consumed her thoughts and kept her staring in the side mirror of the Wagoner. She watched and waited for lights and sirens to appear, for the warden to pull them over. *Sorry Reverend, we made a mistake. The guard misread the data. Miss Clark did indeed bring illegal recording devices into the prison and will now have to go to prison for the rest of her life.*

No cars followed them, no cruisers pulled out from behind a clump of cactus. She had made it out, she was free, but it had been close. The fear she felt while being searched had almost crippled her. She had worried less for her safety when Lorenzo Martinez had held his knife to her throat than she had when the guard ran the electronic scanner over her jewelry. Did she subconsciously believe Simon Garner? Was freedom more important than life? *At least once you're dead it is.* A life-time of confinement with no privileges, no visitors, and no telling what physical and mental abuse inflicted by a prison system without any outside monitoring was scarier than a desperate frightened man with a twitching knife. She now understood Simon's little white pill.

The arms of the cross that should have been hanging from her neck pushed against her palm, and she loosened her grip. She opened her hand and looked down at the small shutter. Why didn't the jewelry set off the scanner? It wasn't luck. Derek must have known she would eventually fumble and had planned for it. She turned the cross over in her hand. What kind of connections did he have to provide her with equipment that even Arizona's detectors couldn't sniff out? Her mind wandered for a moment, then she decided she didn't want to know. She was safer not knowing. *Thanks*, she silently told him. *Thanks for having enough doubt in me to protect my ass.*

She put the chain around her neck and fumbled with the clasp a few minutes before finally getting it hooked. The cross felt good against her chest, it was her amulet, her security. Not because of its religious symbolism – Christ hadn't helped her, Derek had. The cross stood for freedom – her freedom, and the nation's. It had kept her secrets and would hopefully expose Arizona's. Her hand was automatically drawn to it, and just as Tonja had instructed she played it back and forth against the chain, except the fidgeting this time was real.

She stared out the window, chastising herself. *How could you have been so cocky? How did you allow yourself to get sloppy like that?*

Don't let this destroy you, a softer inner voice warned. It was right. She had a story to write. But did she have it in her to get it? She thought she was prepared for this assignment. She thought she understood the risks, but she had been wrong. One last tear fell down her cheek.

She pulled her ruined blazer tight, wrapped her hands around her chest and rested her head on the window. A picture of Thomas appeared in her mind and she managed a smile. What would Thomas do if he found out what had happened? He would drive up to the prison, demand to see Warden Hayden, and before the warden could say a word, Thomas would punch him in the mouth. He would defend her, he would stand up for her rights, and then he would be carted off to jail. Good thing he wasn't there.

She missed Thomas. She wanted to melt into his embrace and stay there forever. Life was too difficult and she had lost her strength. But she wouldn't call him, wouldn't let him pacify her fears. "Count on no one but yourself," Granddad had told her when she was small. "Mothers, aunts, husbands, lovers, and even grandfathers are no substitute for a strong will. When it comes down to it most people put themselves first, so take care my little one, and force yourself to be strong." Words she knew she would live by, but not necessarily the ones she wanted to hear right now. Self-pity was a much bigger lure.

They pulled up to the Church. Reverend Samuels stayed in the car. His hands in the ten and two o'clock position on the wheel.

"I don't want to diminish the seriousness of what you've done, Miss Clark," he said not looking at her. "But, I'm sorry for how you were treated."

Sharon didn't turn to face him. "I'll get over it," she said. She opened the door, placed one foot out, and stopped. She owed him more. "I'm sorry too, for betraying your trust."

Her foot slipped a little when she went to stand. She had forgotten her shoes had no heels. The torn hem of her skirt angled in at her knee. She bent down to brush at it and found herself trying to fold it up. It wouldn't stay. She turned and pulled her bag from under the seat.

The reverend turned and looked at her. "You know, I lied to you back there."

Sharon looked up at him. His face was heavily lined, his cheeks sagged, his eyes were dull. The events at the prison had caused him pain also, though he probably wouldn't be having nightmares about it the rest of his life as she undoubtedly would. "About what?"

"About there being minority women. I've never seen one. Warden Hayden told me they're housed in a different unit, and that he has other preachers minister to them."

No big surprise. "Segregation's illegal isn't it?" she asked, not really caring. Today her main concerns weren't racism, radicalism, or anyone's rights but her own. The only thing she could concentrate on was getting back to her hotel room, curling up in a ball, and crying herself to sleep. Pity me mode was becoming a habit.

"I imagine segregation's illegal," the reverend said. But I'm sure they have their reasons. It could be as the warden says. Those types of women feel differently about their reasons for wanting to abort their children. Their upbringing makes it almost impossible to rehabilitate them. The women you saw tonight are going to be given a second chance. The warden said it would be unfair to give the others a sense of hope when there was none."

"Oh," Sharon said. She didn't know why he was telling her this. He had to know that a racist element in the treatment of women would be detrimental to their supposed cause. "I'm sure they're able to justify their reasons."

"Yes," the reverend said turning away from her and staring back out the window. "Yes, I'm sure they are."

Sharon pulled herself free of the car. Not knowing what to say, she turned and left. She didn't worry about not saying goodbye.

13

The black Cadillac that had followed Sharon the day before sat in the hotel's parking lot when she returned from Reverend Samuels' Church.

"I quit," she said out loud placing her head on the steering wheel.

She sat in her Jeep for a few minutes staring at the polished exterior of the car. The morning had weakened her, and she was tired, tired of them all. It was time to give up and go home. To do just what they wanted. Let Americans believe a world where religion ruled and women were diminished to the roles of motherhood and wives was a better, gentler, place. Let people like Madison Courtney be imprisoned for teaching ideas contrary to biblical dictum, and let men like Simon Garner commit suicide for giving women power over their lives.

She looked at the Cadillac. In her mind she saw the rapist, felt his need for dominance and control, felt his hands on her body tearing away her autonomous shroud and gutting her sense of self-reliance. The face she saw and identified as her rapist morphed into Lorenzo Martinez, then Reverend Samuels, finally formalizing as Warden Hayden.

"Fuckers," she said out loud. "Fuckers," she yelled louder banging her fist against the steering wheel. "God damn mother fucking son of a bitch," she barely whispered lowering her head once again on the wheel.

An image of Madison Courtney flickered in her mind. Madison

teaching a group of young girls, Madison being escorted to prison, Madison defying all those that would try and break her, Madison at the stake, fire all around her, screaming for women's rights. Well, she wasn't Madison, would never be Madison. Madison Courtney had courage and passion for what she believed in. Sharon believed in only one thing, herself. She would fight to protect only one thing, herself, and possibly her story. Move ahead, move on, and push aside all obstacles. Get the story and get out. Her mother would be proud. *Check your emotions at the door.*

She brushed away the tears that covered her face and stared again at the Cadillac. There would be no story if the tail didn't disappear. "So, get your ass in gear and go see what the fuckers want," she ordered herself.

Sharon took a deep breath, adjusted her headband, pulled out the stem of her watch, opened the door to the Jeep and stepped out onto the pavement. When she reached the Cadillac, she banged the tinted driver's side window with the side of her fist.

The window electronically lowered, and a young Hispanic man in a chauffeur's hat smiled up at her. "Hi, Miss Clark. I wasn't expecting you back so soon," he said. He looked down at her misbuttoned blouse, then down at her shoes. "Is everything all right?"

Sharon closed her blazer and leaned into the window. "Detective Grant said he was going to send you home, so why are you still following me?"

"Detective Grant?" The boy shrugged his shoulders. "I don't know him. I'm just supposed to give you this message." He reached over to the passenger side of the car, picked up a small lavender envelope and handed it to her.

Sharon took the envelope with her name printed neatly on it then looked down at the driver. He was a young kid with a nice face, but she still didn't trust him. "Then why were you following me yesterday? Why didn't you just stop and give me the damn thing then?"

"I was told to make sure you were alone before speaking to you and yesterday I was sure that truck was following you. Later I couldn't tell if a blue sedan was following you or not, so I stayed back."

Sharon calmed down, of course. *The truck.* Why would there have been two of them at the same place? If Trask had been following her and was caught, the pick-up tag wouldn't have made himself so obvious. Another Sharon Clark folly.

"You're not a Posse member, are you?"

The young man shook his head. "No. I'm a chauffeur. I'm just doing what I was told, Miss Clark. I didn't mean to upset you."

Sharon looked up towards the sky and shook her head. "It's okay. I've had a bad day, that's all."

The chauffeur looked again at her torn suit. "Looks like. Are you sure you're okay?"

"I'm sure," Sharon said, looking back down at the envelope in her hand. "Who's this from?"

"I'm not to say. If you're sure you're all right, I should go."

"I'm sure. Thanks," she said stepping away from the car.

The chauffeur gave her a quick nod of his head, his window slowly rose, and the Cadillac backed out of its parking space.

Sharon stood outside her hotel in her torn suit with its navy blue trim dangling from her collar and pockets, jamming the toe of her heelless shoe on the ground. She watched the Cadillac pull out of the parking lot then turned her attention back to the envelope. *All he wanted to do was deliver a Goddamn envelope.* She had canceled the previous day's appointments because of him, she had almost given up because of him. Whoever wanted to contact her had better have a damn good reason for causing her so many problems. She tore the envelope open and removed a small lavender flowered note from it.

> *Dear Miss Clark:*
> *Please meet me at four o'clock this afternoon at the park*
> *you visited yesterday. Go to the pagoda at the top of the*
> *road and wait for me. I have valuable information for you.*
> *Helen*

Sharon looked down at her watch, it was already three o'clock. "Derek's classmate," she said out loud putting the letter back in the envelope, and smiling. Maybe there was still a way to salvage this story and get word back to Derek regarding her *tour* of the penitentiary. She had been told not to contact Helen while in Arizona, she would have to go it alone. But Helen had contacted her, an ally, someone to confide in, to trust. Her body, tense since the day she had arrived, relaxed one notch.

The small lot in the park where Sharon parked the day before was empty. Even though she had changed her clothes and taken time to eat a sandwich in the dining room of the hotel, she arrived over fifteen minutes early for her meeting with Helen. She parked her Jeep and walked up to the covered sitting area.

Elliot's Pagoda, a small sign read as she walked up the back path and took in the view. The buttes were beautiful. Small paths wound around the hilly desert area leading up to the red smooth rocks marred by time and weather with deep pockmarks. She looked for lizards, snakes, any life whatsoever, but saw nothing. Except for the muffled distant echoing of a PA system she was all alone. Helen had chosen well.

It was another ten minutes before she heard the Cadillac make its way towards her. As it parked, an older white woman and a young Hispanic girl got out of the back seat and headed up the hill towards her. The woman had that air of sophistication and grace Sharon always admired in the elite. She was tall and fit, her back was straight, her white hair neatly coifed in a high bun. The young girl had a darker beauty about her. She was about five four, heavy chested and slim. She wore a bright turquoise blouse neatly tucked into white jeans. Her hair was unevenly cut, her posture unnaturally rigid.

"Sharon Clark," the older woman called as they walked up to the pagoda.

"Yes," Sharon answered. "You must be Helen."

The woman smiled and offered her hand. "Nice to finally meet you in person. This is," she said, looking at the girl for a moment as if trying to remember her name. "This is Alicia."

Alicia smiled at Helen and then looked back at Sharon. "Hi," she said.

"Alicia's mother worked with us up until her arrest this past winter," Helen said as she motioned for Sharon and Alicia to sit down. "Alicia was forced to spend four months as a ward of the state and has some valuable insight for you on the conditions of the state homes."

Sharon looked over at the girl and smiled. The state homes were a huge area of concern for the rest of the nation. The boys who graduated from them usually joined the Army, the girls got state jobs and rarely spoke out against the treatment they received.

Sharon took her recorder out of her bag, turned it on then turned and faced Alicia.

"So, what would you like California to know about Arizona's Foster Home program?"

The girl hesitated for a moment, and looked at Helen. Helen nodded her head.

"Go on, Alicia. Tell her what you told me. Tell her how they stripped searched you." Helen's shoulders drew up. Her voice grew louder. "Tell her how they beat you, humiliated you. Tell Sharon how they tried to destroy your soul and make you into a mindless drone."

Alicia drew further back on the bench.

Sharon held up her hand. "Whoa. Helen, I think you're scaring her."

Helen looked at Alicia. The girl was on the verge of tears. "I'm sorry," Helen said. She put her hands on the girl's shoulders and knelt in front of her. "I'm just so furious about what happened to you."

"It's okay, I'll tell her. What she said is true," Alicia said turning to Sharon. Helen stood up and took a few steps back. She wrung her hands as Alicia told Sharon her story. "Their first goal is to break you down, to make you afraid to stand up for yourself or your rights. Their next goal is to make you believe you are worthless, that the only reason you're alive is to serve God, the State of Arizona, and any one else they deem worthy."

"How?" Sharon asked, already knowing the answer.

"By taking away our dignity."

"Tell her about the strip search," Helen said.

Alicia looked up at Helen and nodded her head. When she began to speak, to tell Sharon the tale, Sharon envisioned herself as a ward, or was it prisoner of the state. Alicia talked for almost half an hour with tales of abuse and intimidation. There was nothing godly about the treatment this girl had received, or the servitude she was being forced into to repay her debt to the state.

When Alicia finished, Sharon was emotionally exhausted. *Don't become involved in other people's problems,* her mother's voice warned, but it was too late. Alicia had struck a chord, a chord Sharon hadn't known existed.

Sharon turned off the recorder and gave Alicia a hug. "I don't know how things got so bad here," she said to Helen. "Yesterday a man was killed in front of me for stealing a package of razors."

"I heard about that. Was that you? You were the tourist?" Helen asked.

Sharon nodded her head, then lifted her neck to show Helen the bandages. "He was so scared. I don't think he would have hurt me, but he didn't have a chance. Reverend Samuels, do you know him?"

"Isaac Samuels?" Helen asked.

"Yeah. He shot the man. It wasn't Crieghton like the news said. It was the reverend."

"Poor Isaac," Helen said, putting her hand to her chest.

"What?" Sharon looked over at her own version of African Violet in disbelief. "How can you say that? He was more concerned with his reputation as a religious leader than he was about the man he killed. He had my phones tapped and then when I tried to tell Derek what had happened, he had them disconnected."

Helen walked over and put her hand on Sharon's shoulder. "I'm sorry. It's just Isaac is an old friend, and a true Christian. I'm sure he didn't want to kill that man. He must have honestly believed your life was in danger. You know, not all people of faith are bad, Sharon."

"You could have fooled me."

"Reverend Ames was bad," Alicia said.

Helen smiled. "Reverend Ames *is* a bad man, but he's just one man. Remember, both of you, it's religion as politics we're after, not personal faith."

"In truth," Sharon said. "I just want to get my story, and get the hell out of Dodge, before I end up in jail."

"Jail? I don't see why…"

"I almost got caught today doing Derek a personal favor," Sharon said. "It was my own fault, but still…"

"What happened?" Helen asked.

Sharon looked at both Helen and Alicia. She started at the beginning with Madison Courtney being arrested at the border crossing, and ended with meeting Helen's chauffeur. Then with her head down, she apologized for jeopardizing Simon Garner's operation.

"It's all right. We knew the risks. I'm just sorry you've had to endure so much since coming here," Helen said. "I didn't mean to put you in any danger when I asked Derek to send you."

Sharon looked up. "It was your idea for the article?"

"I'm afraid so. I figured we could use some outside help in our fight against the fanatics that run our state. We thought if some of the free states stood behind us, and a few of the religious states that teeter between Independent and Moralist governments could be swayed before the election, then Arizonians might take a closer look at what's going on here and start working for change."

"They'll never change," Alicia said. "The only way out is across the border."

"And how long do you think it will be before there are no more Free states?" Helen asked rather forcefully. "You can't run, Alicia. Neither can you Sharon. What's happening here is happening all over the country. It's like a plague, infecting everyone with a kind of moral passion, corrupted from the power it yields. Soon America will have its own inquisition, people will be forced to hide, or lie about their personal faith. No one will be free. It's up to us to stop it."

Sharon shook her head. Helen was seeming a little fanatical. But then wasn't it the extremists who got things done. *Well, I'm not an extremist, I'm a journalist.* Tonja warned her about religious fervor, now she'd take the same advice towards anti-religious fervor.

"You know the Moralists are almost at the three-quarter state mark. Once they start ratifying the Constitution, it's over for America."

"I know," Sharon said. "That's why I'm here." *Liar.*

"I have it from reliable sources that their first action once reaching the majority will be to institute a polling exam and revoke the nineteenth amendment."

Sharon wanted to laugh. Propaganda was an extremist's and politician's favorite weapon. An arsenal Sharon never put much stock in. "That's ridiculous. The first thing they've promised to do for decades is give the fetus human rights, nationally. Which I'm not saying is good, but I find it hard to believe they would focus more on taking voting rights away from women and the illiterate. Plus, once rights are established, it's almost impossible to take them away."

It was Helen's turn to laugh, and she did. It was a gentle light laugh, but a laugh all the same. "Don't be so naïve," she said. "Throughout history, nations have gone between democracy and dictatorship. Rights and freedoms come and go. We tend to forget how young we are as a country. We have no real history to judge ourselves. But, if you look at other countries' histories, the pattern will become clear enough."

"Maybe so, but I find it hard to believe enough states would vote for such things," Sharon said, looking first at Helen then at Alicia. Alicia was staring longingly across the desert at Phoenix.

"Regardless," Helen said. "We still need to do our best to prevent any more Moralists states, agreed?"

Sharon smiled at the activist. "Agreed. Just don't ask me to go back inside your prison system."

"I won't. But, I'm afraid I won't be able to meet with you again, it's too dangerous. I really shouldn't have done it today, but I thought Alicia's story was too important for you not to meet her. From now on all of our communication will go through her, is that all right with you?"

"That's fine," Sharon said. The girl was a little peculiar, but that was to be expected. Sharon looked at the girl for a few moments. Alicia appeared lost and it didn't seem like she'd be finding the path to happiness any time soon.

"Well then," Helen said putting her hand on Alicia's back and prompting the girl to stand. If there's nothing else, we best be going."

"Oh," Sharon said, remembering the phones. "I was wondering if you could do me a favor and get word to Derek. He doesn't know what's been happening to me out here. I'm afraid to tell him anything over the phone.

"I'll do better than that. Here." Helen reached into her pocket and pulled out a plastic ID card with no picture on it. She handed it to Sharon. "You can use this to make any calls you want. They're untraceable, unless they know exactly what phone you used. So make all your calls from card phones. Gas stations are good. So far none of our numbers have been flagged for random tapping, so you'll be able to speak freely."

"Great," Sharon said, putting the card in the back pocket of her shorts. It was time to talk to Thomas, she knew she wouldn't tell him everything that had happened to her, and even though she wanted to remain strong, more than anything, she wanted to hear his voice.

"We only use each card for a week at a time. After that it may arouse suspicion by the Communications Securities Foundation. I'll send Alicia over with a new one next week."

"That'll be great," Sharon said smiling at Alicia.

"Alicia will be your contact with me," Helen continued. "You can't call me, and please don't send her home with any written notes. Anything you want to convey to me while you're here, must be done on a verbal basis only. No one will recognize Alicia because she's new, so no one will know where she works. It should be safe enough for the time you're here as long as she's careful not to arouse too much suspicion," Helen said, raising an eyebrow at Alicia.

"I'm pretty good at keeping a low profile," Alicia responded.

"I know you are, dear," Helen put her arm around the young girl and gave her a quick hug. "Alicia's mother smuggled medicinal herbs to her community for years before getting caught. We believe someone turned her in, or else she'd be free today and poor Alicia wouldn't have had to live through the last four months of hell like she did."

"You must be proud of your mother," Sharon said, thinking how embarrassed she had been of her own mother, and wondering what it would have been like raised by a woman of courage and compassion.

Alicia didn't answer, instead she turned around and faced Phoenix. Sharon refocused on the girl, there was no such thing as retrospect.

She could no more change who raised her, than Alicia could change what had happened to her. In the end, maybe it was Sharon who had gotten the better deal. At least she knew what she wanted in life – to be the best, to be independent, and to stay strong. Alicia seemed lost.

"Are you from Phoenix?" Sharon asked.

"Yeah. We grew up there. I miss it."

"Nonsense," Helen said. "You miss your family. She has a brother still in the ward system that she's been pining over for the past four months."

"Will you be able to get him out?" Sharon asked.

Alicia turned towards Helen, her eyes full of hope.

"I'm afraid not," Helen said shaking her head slowly at the young girl. "He's too old for the adoption program, and I'm afraid the state has very strict rules about the dispensation of state wards."

They have strict rules about everything," Sharon said.

"I know," Helen sighed. "Alicia has to understand that once a child's put into the system, it's impossible to get them out. Even if a relative tried, they would fail."

Alicia's shoulders slumped and she turned back towards her home.

"Isn't there anything you can do?" Sharon asked.

"We'll try to get him assigned to us on his eighteenth birthday. I already told you that, Alicia."

"I know and I'm grateful. I'm just homesick, that's all."

Me too, Sharon thought to herself.

"You'll get through it, my dear. I'm here and I'll make sure you have a good life while you live with us."

Alicia didn't respond. Sharon didn't blame her. What kind of life was the girl going to have as a servant? What did it matter if her mistress was a good woman. A slave was a slave no matter who their master was. The war between religion and freedom was nothing more than a fool's parody of right and wrong. The good, the bad, they were the same. People fought for what *they* wanted, heedless to the individuals' rights or freedom. Even Helen. She took dangerous risks to fight for what she believed in, yet had no qualms in denying Alicia and her brother's right to live how they wanted. What a crux.

"You know," Sharon said, "Alicia could go home with…"

"What do we have here?" a young man's venomous voice interrupted. Sharon turned around. Three teen-age boys, their head's shaven, their bare chests scarred with swastikas, were walking up the path towards her and her companions. Sharon's knees had that weak feeling again. Her heart raced.

"Go away," Helen told them, taking a step forward. "We don't want any trouble."

"Trouble, lady? Looks to me like you're the ones causing trouble. Don't you know it's not permitted for a group of women to congregate outside the home?"

"And lookie here," another of the boys said, walking up to Alicia and putting his hand on her shoulders to turn her around to the other boys. "A Mexican."

Sharon's fear turned to anger, and she took a step forward. "Let go..."

The boy holding Alicia took out a knife and pointed it at Sharon. "Step back," he said. Sharon stood her ground.

"What are you white women doing with this Mexican bitch?" the older boy demanded.

"If you don't leave, I'm going to have to turn you into the Posse," Helen said.

"The Posse. Did you hear that Michael. She's going to turn us into the Posse."

"Ohh, I'm scared," Michael answered, shaking his hands about himself in an exaggerated shake.

"The Posse has no control over what we do. We follow God's law, not man's law. And God says keep with your own kind," the older boy said, taking the palm of his hand and hitting Helen on her forehead knocking her backwards.

Sharon jumped to catch her before her head hit the ground. "Get the hell out of here," she screamed at them.

The older boy pointed his finger at Sharon, his face turned beat red, the tendons in his neck straining with his anger. "Watch your mouth, bitch and learn your place. God created man above women, do you get that?" he screamed pointing his finger in her face. "Above women." He reeled his foot back to kick her, when the one called Michael pulled him back.

"Watch it man," Michael told him. "We don't need to be beating up on our own kind. You got something to get out, take it out on the wetback," he said, turning the boy around towards Alicia.

"Run," Helen screamed. "Martha, run."

Alicia didn't move. The boy holding her grinned. He took the knife and cut open the buttons of her shirt. "Here you go Dylan," he said as he sliced through the front of her bra and exposed her breasts. "Nice brown tittie for the taking."

Sharon jumped to her feet. Michael grabbed her and held her. "Let go of me," she screamed as she struggled against his embrace.

At first Alicia's face seemed emotionless, tilted to the side just a little, her eyes glazed over as if she had temporarily departed her body, then as the boy took his hand and cupped it under her left breast Sharon saw fire. Mount Rainier all over again. Without giving any notice, Alicia stomped the heel of her shoe on her keeper's instep then jammed her elbow into his stomach. The boy let go and Alicia took off down the hill.

"You'll regret that, bitch," the boy screamed as he straightened and hobbled after her.

Alicia was half way down the embankment. The driver's side door of the Cadillac opened. The chauffeur, six foot three and at least two hundred fifty pounds stepped out. It was the boy who had given Sharon Helen's note.

Michael's arms loosened around Sharon. The boy chasing Alicia fell as he tried to stop himself from making it down the rest of the hill. Without saying a word, the chauffeur opened the back door of the Cadillac for Alicia, then after she scrambled in, he locked and closed it.

"I'm sorry I let this get out of hand, Ma'am," he called up the hill to Helen. "I wasn't paying attention like I should've. I've called the police, though. They should be here any minute."

"Billy," Michael screamed. "Get your ass up here."

Michael had let go of Sharon altogether and had backed away. Dylan was jumping nervously back and forth, his anger still flushed in his face. He pulled a jackknife from his back pocket and pulled out its blade. "Come on, come on," he beckoned to the chauffeur.

The chauffeur smiled up at the enraged boy then turned back to the car. Reaching into the front seat of the Cadillac, he pulled out a handgun and pointed it up the hill as he slowly walked towards the three skinheads.

Billy, the boy who had chased Alicia down the hill, scooted backwards from where he had landed in the dirt. "Let's get out of here," he screamed, then turned and ran towards the path where they had first entered.

Dylan faltered. He took a few steps towards the chauffeur, looked back over his shoulder at Michael, then turned and followed his friend. He stopped before disappearing over the hill and pointed his finger at Helen. "You'll pay for this," he screamed, then turned and ran. The chauffeur continued up the hill, slowly, methodically, menacingly.

Michael let out a small nervous laugh then turned towards the picnic table and grabbed Sharon's bag. "Wouldn't want it to be a total waste," he said as he followed the path of his friends. Sharon dove after him.

"No," she screamed reaching out for her bag then tripping over a rock. She landed on her knees. "Fuck," she screamed as she watched them run down the street to a parked white van.

Michael jumped into the open side door of the van. He turned and waved at her then laughed as the van pulled off and sped down the street towards what Sharon thought was a golf course.

Helen appeared at her side and offered to help Sharon to the table. "Are you all right?"

"I'm fine," Sharon said brushing the sand and rocks from her bloodied knees.

"Thank God. Sharon, I'm sorry. We shouldn't have met in such a secluded place. Here you were telling me of all the horrible things that have happened to you since your arrival and I inadvertently arranged for more."

"I'm becoming used to it," Sharon smiled back to her. "I can't believe they took my bag, though. All my notes were in it."

Helen helped Sharon back to the Pagoda. "There's nothing we can do about it I'm afraid. If we call the police we'll jeopardize our cover. You're just going to have to recreate them from memory."

"I thought he already called the police." Sharon looked at the Chauffeur.

The boy looked down at the ground and kicked dirt. "I lied," he said, then looked up and smiled at her. Sharon smiled back.

The only notes and tapes in the bag were from her adventure at Arpaio, they were safe enough if the wrong person got hold of them. But her fake ID had been in it too. No one would be able to use it to get her money, not without her thumbprint, but now she would have to use her real one and that could mean getting caught. The recorder with Alicia's story had been left behind on the picnic table, that was one good thing.

"I had my fake ID in the bag," she told Helen. "I still have my real one, but I'm afraid to use it here."

"It will be all right for now. I'll get you a copy of the fake one. Just don't do anything where you have to show your real one to an official. It will only take a couple of days. I'll have Alicia bring it to you."

There wasn't much Sharon could do about it, so she just nodded her head. Her brief encounter of courage and anger had quickly dissipated back into self-pity mode. She sat on the bench and lowered her head. "I think I'm jinxed, Helen. I don't think I've ever had such a string of bad luck before in my life. I'm beginning to wonder if this article is meant to be."

"Don't even think such a thing. This article is too important," Helen said kneeling in front of her and taking Sharon's hands in hers. "You can't give up, no matter how difficult it gets. Too many of us have worked too hard for you to give up. Think of the women you've talked to. Think of Alicia down there, and poor Madison Courtney. So many of us have risked our freedom to get the word out."

"I know, but..."

"What about our country, Sharon? How would you like to live in a country where everyone was forced to believe and to live by one set religion, where religious morals outweighed what was right and fair? Where women are nothing more than wombs and house-maids? Think of it Sharon, and see if that's the life you want for your children and your grandchildren. Then you tell me if you want to give up."

"I don't want to give up," she told Helen. "It's just everything's going wrong. I can't seem to take one step without falling flat on my face."

Helen lifted Sharon's chin with her hand and smiled into her eyes. "That's how revolutions are won. One step at a time. Whether or not you fall, you've moved on. All you have to do is keep getting up and taking that next step. Derek believed you were the most tenacious of all his reporters. He told me that if anyone could work through this assignment it was you. We've put a lot of hope in you Sharon. Don't let us down."

Helen removed her hand from Sharon's chin and pulled her to her feet. "Go back to your hotel. Clean up that knee and take a shower. There's still a lot of work ahead of you."

Sharon nodded her head. "I sound pitiful, don't I?"

"Not at all, you sound like someone who is very tired. You've been through a lot since you got here, and you'll probably go through a lot more before you're done. You just need to keep your focus on how important this assignment is. I have no doubts you'll pull through it."

Sharon's strength reserves were low, but somehow Helen made them appear so much fuller. "I'll be alright," she said smiling back at Helen. "I imagine things can't get much worse."

"Good girl," Helen said, clearly pleased.

I acquiesce well.

"What else can I do for you?" Helen asked as she brushed dirt off her sleeve.

Sharon had the phone card which would offer her the link she needed with Derek and Thomas. She could get back a copy of her interview list from them and have Thomas find the copy of her schedule she had put on the computer at home. She was pretty well set with everything but the name of a trader, something she had hoped to get from one of her canceled interviews.

"I need the name of a reputable trader. One of the women I interviewed had hired undercover Posse members. I don't want to make the same mistake."

"Done. I know the best, but you can't tell him you're writing an article. He'll have nothing to do with that. Tell him you're pregnant and need to go home. Robert," she said turning to the chauffeur, "go get me a pen and a piece of paper, would you?"

As Robert turned and ran down the hill, Helen continued. "I'll give you the number to call. Use the card I gave you. He'll set up a meeting with you."

Robert returned with the pen and paper and Helen wrote down a phone number and handed it to Sharon.

"Derek said he set you up with enough money to hire them, so do it. Set it up for the first of next month. You should be done with your research by then. The trip across the border will give you the final feel for what it's like living under religious rule where you have to steal out of your own state to be able to take charge of your life."

Sharon stepped up and took the paper from Helen's hands. "I'll call him tonight and set everything up."

"Good." Helen took a deep breath and brushed her hair back. "I'm sure things will go smoother. Just don't give up, Sharon. People need to know, and you're the one who's going to tell them. My life, your life, they're nothing compared to the future of our daughters and of our country."

Sharon didn't have a daughter, as for her country she wasn't sure it was worth saving. All she cared about right now was her own ass. "I'm all for working to stop them, Helen, but I'm not willing to risk my life or my freedom for future generations. I'm here for my story and whatever good I can do for California, but don't expect me to be a hero. Joan of Arc I'm not."

"We'll see," Helen said, then turned and headed down the hill with her chauffeur.

"Helen," Sharon called down to her.

Helen stopped and turned.

"Why not let Alicia go home with me. Maybe Derek can pull some strings and get her brother released."

Helen shook her head. "She's needed here."

"But she wants her freedom."

"Personal freedom is an illusion, Sharon. No one's free until all are." Helen turned and continued to the car. Robert opened the front passenger door and she got in.

Sharon wanted to stop her, to argue with her, but didn't know how.

14

Martha sat in the back seat of the Cadillac clutching her blouse. Not out of modesty, though she didn't like the feeling of being exposed, but as a means of self-defiance. Robert might have saved her from the racists, but that didn't give him the right to see what was privately hers. No one had that right. From now on, she would decide who saw what, and when.

The soft leather seats seemed to embrace her, and she sank deeper into them as she relived the scene at the park. A small smile played on her lips, but she pushed it aside, not wanting anyone to notice the pleasure she took from what happened. Mrs. Sanders needed to think that she had let her ward be defiled, that she had exposed Martha to unwarranted danger, that she owed Martha. But the truth was the incident had been exhilarating. It had been a gift.

At first she had responded through fear, no habit. She had collapsed back into the docile creature the state system had created, but then something clicked. Had she heard her mother or grandmother screaming at her to act, or was it herself who had kick started the self-defense mechanism that had lay dormant for the past four months, the one the state system had worked so hard to destroy?

She could feel herself, her strengths, re-filling the void that had become her soul. Things would be different now. She would still have to act as a submissive servant, obedient to her employer's will, but that's all it would be, an act. Something done for self-preservation while she was bound to the state, while Anthony was still a ward. But her behavior would be by choice. She would be like her friend Sara, a player. Someone who knows how to bluff and leave the game unscathed.

"You were pretty assertive back there," Mrs. Sanders said reaching over and putting her arm around Martha. "Did your mother teach you that move?"

"My brother," Martha said, looking up at the woman. Mrs. Sanders was a powerful woman, as powerful as a woman could be in Arizona. She had been able to manipulate the system to get Martha placed in her household, not just anybody could have done that. There had been no other choices on that list Mrs. Jordan had pulled out from under her blotter, anything she might have thought she saw had been nothing more than props. Barbara Sanders had planned on taking Martha in the day her mother had been arrested.

"There is no such thing as coincidence," Mrs. Sanders had told her that first night in the Sanders' house. "When fighting a war you must calculate, plan, and then have the patience to wait it out." Martha was grateful, but she couldn't help feeling she had been just another pawn in Mrs. Sanders crusade. A crusade Suzanne Garcia may have supported, but not Martha.

Martha was smarter than the other state drones. She wasn't falling for Mrs. Sanders prolific babble on human rights. There were only two humans whose rights she would fight for – Anthony's and her own. But she understood Mrs. Sanders' words, about how to fight a war. She too would calculate and plan, and then make herself have the patience to wait it out. She would use her position in the Sanders' household to make connections and save money, and then it would be she who would secure freedom, not for the nation, but for the Garcias. Everyone except Suzanne. She could rot in hell as far as Martha was concerned.

"We better stop and get you fixed up," Mrs. Sanders was saying. "You can't go back to the house braless and with torn clothing. Norma would be too suspicious and might mention it to Mr. Sanders."

"Thank you," Martha said, not sure how Norma would even know except by going through her things, which wouldn't be too out of place for that house. In the few days she had been there she had learned a lot. The Sanders didn't share a bedroom or for that matter much of a life. She suspected that Norma was more than a house-keeper to Mr. Sanders, but didn't dare ask anyone or take the initiative to investigate. There were three other housekeepers, young women not too long out of the state home. They kept to themselves.

There was no camaraderie between any of them. They had the rigid stance and expressionless faces of properly raised state wards.

"Well, we have to take care of each other, now don't we?" Mrs. Sanders said giving Martha a quick hug, then withdrawing her arm. "Robert pull over to the WalMart over there, will you? I need to run in and get a few things for our brave girl."

"Yes, Ma'am," Robert said as he guided the car into the parking lot and pulled up to the front entrance.

"I'll only be a minute," Mrs. Sanders said jumping out of the car. "Thirty-two C?" she asked Martha with a smile. "Size eight blouse?"

Martha was impressed, "Yes," she said. "How'd you know?"

"I was about your size when I was young, it was a good guess that's all."

Martha smiled, it was a forced smile, a calculated smile. Mrs. Sanders pulled herself from the car and entered the store. Robert parked the car and sat vigil waiting for his mistress to emerge.

Robert didn't talk much to Martha or the other servants, but he seemed quite close to Mrs. Sanders. He obviously knew of her outside activities and was trusted by her. Martha pulled her shirt tighter and leaned forward towards the front seat. "How long have you worked for the Sanders?" she asked.

Robert turned and faced her. He frowned slightly. Martha waited to be told to mind her own business, but then his frown turned to a quick smile. "Three and a half years," he said, turning and putting his arm over the back of the seat.

"Wow, so you're almost done," Martha said, jealous of his impending freedom.

"Done? Oh you mean my contract. Yeah, I guess I am, but I've decided to stay on. There's nowhere else for me to go. I figure I can do more good working with Mrs. Sanders than I can on my own."

Martha's guard went up. He obviously had been seduced, converted, to Barbara Sander's cause. Martha didn't want to say anything that could jeopardize her standings with the woman, but still, she was curious. How could he, a young Hispanic man, be so willing to take on a cause that invariably was out to help white women regain the freedoms they had recently lost?

"You know," he said, turning even further in his seat. "Our mothers knew each other."

Martha wasn't surprised. Another Sanders connection. "They did?" Martha asked, relaxing a little when she realized he wanted to talk. He could be an invaluable source on how to survive the Sanders' household, if not just someone to consider a friend. No, there could be no friends, she reminded herself. Robert was a loyalist, and though he had a gentleness about him that she had never seen before in a man, he couldn't be trusted. Or could he? There was something about him. Martha felt drawn to him, she could almost feel his embrace around her shoulders, feel the safety of his arms.

"Yeah, your mother saved my little sister's life with some concoction she brewed. We didn't have any medical insurance and my sister got real sick. She had a fever of over a hundred and three, couldn't eat, could barely drink. We didn't think she was going to make it. Then Mrs. Sanders shows up with your mother and a bundle of herbs. Within hours the fever broke. Two days later Thina was well enough to start eating. Your mother saved her life."

"Yeah, my mother had her way with herbs," Martha said turning back towards the windows, the mere mention of her mother drew her back to reality. "Until they finally caught her. Now, she's in jail for life, and you know, for all those people's lives she saved, there's not one person trying to get her out."

"I know," Robert said. "I was with Mrs. Sanders when she heard. She was devastated. It's real hard for her sometimes to look at the whole picture and not concentrate on each individual. She would have done anything for your mother, most of the women in the network would've, but if they exposed themselves the whole movement could've gone under."

"Damn the movement," Martha said, feeling her anger growing. "It's okay for my mother to rot in jail as long as they don't get caught."

"I know it sounds unfair, but they need to keep their anonymity so they can continue with their work. Most of them are prominent women in the church and most of their husbands are pretty high up politically. It's what gives them the edge. They have to be willing to make sacrifices to keep it all together and moving forward."

"You sound like a convert," Martha told him without looking over at him. "What do you care about women's rights? Obviously Mrs. Sanders' group didn't do anything to help your mother, or you never would have ended up as a state ward."

Robert turned slightly in his seat and looked out the passenger side window. "My mother killed herself two weeks before my eighteenth birthday," he said. "There was nothing they could have done to prevent it."

Martha looked at Robert. *Insert foot.* She had a lot to learn about placing her anger and keeping her mouth shut. The healing process was going to be harder than she first thought. The pre-state, pre-slave, Martha never would have said something without first knowing the whole situation. This Martha was still at the edge, teetering. She'd have to be more careful, more guarded. "I'm sorry," she said. "I didn't know."

"It's not your fault," Robert said, turning back towards her, his face a little flush. "It's the state's fault and all the new rulings that are being passed against women, especially single women. I'll never forgive them for what they did to my mother, and that's why I'll work with Mrs. Sanders as long as I can. There are certain things that are just wrong. Regardless of the circumstances. Regardless of what's deemed best by the state."

Martha didn't interject. She could sense his anger building and that he was about to tell her the whole story, a story she wasn't sure she really wanted to know.

"My mother didn't have a chance," Robert continued. "She worked two jobs so I could stay in school, but neither paid over minimum wage or offered any benefits."

"Where was your father?" Martha asked.

"Gone. He paid his obligatory child payments, but they were nothing. After my Mother died, he said he couldn't take me, not even for two weeks, that's how I ended up as a ward of the state. Never even made it into a home, but on paper I was legally theirs and bound to the four year contract."

"I know that story," Martha said.

Robert nodded. An acknowledgment that seemed more requisite than concurring, Martha decided. He was too into his story to be diverted.

"My sister is twelve years younger than me. Luckily my mother was able to get around the Nurturing Law or else the state would have stepped in and taken both of us away when she was born."

Martha remembered her mother's scramble to get their grand-mother certified as competent to care for Anthony and her when their father died. The Nurturing Laws were strict. Any woman deemed incapable of supporting her children, lost them. Constant child super-vision was mandatory until a child reached the age of twelve. Luckily, Martha had been old enough when their grandmother died to be cer-tified to watch over Anthony, or else he would have been a ward of the state a long time ago.

"Maybe," Robert said, looking past Martha and out the back window. "Maybe that would have been better. My mother might still be alive."

There is nothing worse than being in the state system, not even death, Martha wanted to scream. Maybe it would have been better for his mother, but then it would have been him or his sister that would have taken their lives.

"Trust me," Martha said in a calmer voice than she thought possible. "Nothing is worse than being turned over to the state."

Robert jerked his gaze back at Martha. "No? What about losing your daughter to the man that had raped and impregnated you," he almost yelled. "It could have been a hell of a lot better. At least, she would've had a chance with the state."

"Raped?" Martha responded.

"Unbelievable, isn't it? But that's what happened. A convicted rapist was granted full custody of my sister and given permission to take her to Alabama. My mother was stripped of all rights and given no visitation."

Martha shook her head. "How could that be? What kind of judge would do such a thing?"

"You don't get it Martha, do you? Single women are nothing here, especially minority women. This guy convinced the courts he had been reformed, said he found Christ while in prison. He walks into court wearing an expensive suit, a new wife at his side, and proof of financial stability. His lawyer argues that since Thina is of mixed blood she's better off with her white family since they can provide better for her and open more doors."

Martha remembered Mrs. Jordan and how nicely she had phrased it. "Your kind…is best suited for service jobs or assembly manufacturing." It was a known fact. The results of some biased study, giving the white man answers he wanted. There was only one race, their race, and it was the only one with doors that could be opened. Martha started to say something to this effect, to tell him maybe the courts were right, his sister would have a better future branded as white. There were no such things as careers for Hispanics, not with the whites running things. She wanted to tell him that if Thina had stayed with him and their mother, her only opportunities would have been servile or as a wife to a laborer. Any dreams they had had for careers, wealth and fame were fantasies compared to the reality of life as a minority in religious America.

"You know," Martha said then closed her mouth. He didn't need to hear this. He had lost his sister, and in his mind, like most of *their kind*, love was more important than fame and wealth. The truth was ugly and bitter. She could taste the bile of her hatred towards her oppressors. It would do no good to pass on such an infection to Robert, at least not right now. His anger was focused on the courts, the rapist – he wouldn't be able to see past it. "It's hard to believe a rapist could win out over anyone," she said instead, even though she didn't find it surprising at all.

Robert made a guttural half laugh. "That's what we thought in the beginning. We didn't think he even had a case. We were shocked when his lawyer was the one that brought up the rape first. He said how it never would have happened if my mother had been home where she belonged instead of working at a bar. He said this guy was as much a victim as my mother and that regardless of how my sister was conceived he was still her biological father and had rights."

"White rights," Martha said.

Robert looked at her a moment, then continued. "My mother didn't have a chance. Within two weeks Thina was gone. We weren't given a forwarding address. Nothing. It was like we were supposed to pretend she never existed."

"So your mother killed herself?"

"A month later. I don't blame her, though. It was like being raped a second time." Robert turned his gaze back towards the window. "Did you know that when a woman is raped she's kept in the hospital with constant supervision for three days so they can check for pregnancy?"

"No, I didn't know that," Martha said a little surprised a Hispanic woman could get into any hospital.

"Yeah. They make it almost impossible for rape victims to get by the system. They say they're the most susceptible to abortion and therefore hold the largest risk. It's bullshit, but it gives the state control, I guess."

"That's what they're into," Martha agreed.

Again, it was as if Robert wasn't hearing her remarks. He was so lost in his memories, he couldn't or wouldn't look at the truth. All this didn't happen because his mother was raped; it was because she was Mexican. Martha wanted to take him by the shoulders and shake him, to make him realize what was really happening, but she could tell by the watery film that glazed his eyes, it would do no good.

Robert's voice quieted as he continued. "You know, she didn't want to keep the baby, but she'd been tagged. It was either have it or go to jail. She said she couldn't stand the thought of my ending up in a state home, so she went through with the pregnancy and with plans to put the baby up for adoption."

Robert brushed the back of the seat with his hand as if trying to whisk away the layer of emotions that came with the past. "She was depressed the whole nine months. The only thing that kept her going was that at some point the pregnancy would end and she'd be able to get on with her life."

Martha's anger quelled, as Robert spoke. His soft voice and emotions touched the spot in her heart that longed for her brother. It was as if their individual pain were intertwined, meshed as one. They had both lost everything. Been ripped from their families and exiled into servitude. Martha felt a bond with the boy in the front seat. She leaned back in the seat, let the shadows cover her face as she put away her anger and allowed the tears in her eyes to run freely.

Robert took a deep breath. "When my mother was about six months along, the social worker told her that they would have a hard time finding anyone willing to take a mixed child conceived through rape. That the state would more than likely take the baby on as a ward. My mother couldn't bear that, so finally, near the end of her pregnancy, she came to terms with it and decided regardless of who the father was, she would embrace the child and give her a loving home. And she did," he said, looking up and smiling. "For six years. You never knew a child more loved. It was like Thina made the hurt go away. She was the sweetest, most beautiful little girl you ever saw."

Robert's eyes filled with tears and he looked away. "I miss them both, Martha. They were all I had, and this fucking state stole them from me."

"I'm so sorry," Martha said, brushing the tears from her face.

They sat in silence for a few minutes. Martha pushed the tears away. An image of her mother, lecturing her on the malfunctioning of the state and the corner it had backed them into, slowly appeared. Martha pushed the memory aside.

"I had heard of men automatically being given custody after a divorce and knew women were being jailed for adultery," Martha said. "But, a rapist being considered a fit parent? That's too hard to believe."

"Well believe it. It's not getting any better, either. Each year more and more laws are passed that strip women of their basic rights. Soon you'll be nothing more than wombs to continue the race."

"Not our race," Martha said "If there are any Mexican wombs left, they'll only be used to produce servants."

Robert smiled, making light of her comment, taking it as a joke, she suspected. But Martha wasn't joking. "I'm serious," she said. "My mother told me that anti-abortion laws had nothing to do with promoting life of minorities. That they were there to make sure white women kept their babies and didn't let the preeminent whites slip into minority status. Did you know minority children in America have the highest mortality rate in the world?"

Robert shook his head.

"They do. And many of the ones that survive are taken away by the state the minute someone can prove the children are receiving inadequate care. So even in a world where women are nothing more than wombs, there would still be minority wombs producing minority children. Whites need someone to exploit, without minorities they'd have to feed off each other."

"Maybe," Robert said. "But that's not the point. This isn't a race issue, Martha."

"What?" Martha was sure he had been blinded by Mrs. Sanders' rhetoric. "That's all it is, Robert, and if you don't see it, maybe you need to re-evaluate how you feel about what happened to your family. I know it must be hard, seeing as a white woman took you in and all, but open your eyes. Don't you think it's strange every one of the Sanders' servants is a minority?"

Robert shook his head. "You're wrong. Sure the state's bigoted as hell, but not Mrs. Sanders. Not the women in her network. This is a human rights issue, Martha. Everyone's affected. And now, you should be grateful you're in a position to help."

"Help who?" Martha asked. "Help women like your mother or my mother? I doubt it. These are white women Robert. What do they care about our rights? They're fighting for their own rights. And you know damn well whatever they accomplish isn't going to trickle down to us."

"You just don't get it, Martha. Mrs. Sanders is fighting for everyone's rights, even men. She doesn't care if you're white, Mexican, or Chinese for that matter. She's fighting to abolish religious rule in this state and to return equal standing to women, all women and that includes you."

"Yeah, she's done a great job for me and my mother so far," Martha said, looking back at the entrance to the store. Mrs. Sanders was at the bag checker having her purchases examined. "There she is," she said, not looking at Robert.

Robert turned back in his seat and started the car. "She made sure you had a good home to go to," he said as he backed up. "And she's giving you something better to do with your life than just clean someone's house, so you better be appreciative."

"I am," Martha said. "And because it's my job, I'll do what I'm told. But I can tell you right now, Robert, I would never do it willingly."

"I said the same thing in the beginning," Robert said as he pulled up to the curb. "Just keep your anger focused on the real culprits and don't blame Mrs. Sanders for what happened to your family."

"I don't blame her. I just blame *her kind*."

Robert smiled and shook his head. "You're something else."

Martha smiled back at him, so wasn't he. Maybe their politics were different, but their histories, their future, were too similar not to consider him a friend, and she could tell he felt the same way.

Robert got out of the car, ran around to the passenger side, and opened the door for Mrs. Sanders.

Martha sat up straight and smiled at the woman. "Thank you," she said as Mrs. Sanders handed her the bag of new clothing.

"Hope you like the blouse," Mrs. Sanders said. "I tried to match it up to the one you had bought yourself."

Martha pulled a bright turquoise blouse out of the bag and held it up, it was very close to the one she was wearing. Norma wouldn't be able to tell the difference. "Thank you," she said.

"You're very welcome. Robert, go find a park somewhere so she can change and safely throw out these ruined things before we go home."

"Yes, ma'am," Robert said as they pulled out of the parking lot. "I know just the place she should change."

15

Martha had put back on her uniform and placed her blouse and jeans back into her daypack. They threw away all evidence of the attack at Papago Park and came up with a cover story of where they had been all day – something Mrs. Sanders said they would do each evening before going home. All stories needed to coincide perfectly to prevent Mr. Sanders and Norma from becoming suspicious.

Mr. Sanders wasn't home when they got there. Martha was glad. Whenever he was gone, a large amount of the tension at the house was gone with him. It was hard to figure out what had brought the Sanders together. Mrs. Sanders was calm and loving, where Mr. Sanders was abrasive and cold. Whenever Mrs. Sanders touched her husband, a shiver ran down Martha's spine. She kept herself from imagining them intimate with each other and prayed for Mrs. Sanders' sake, they never were. That was Norma's duty after all, wasn't it?

The evening went smoothly. Robert and Martha ate their dinner in silence in the kitchen with the rest of the help. Martha was careful not to look up too often at Robert or show any signs of affection or friendship towards him, even though she could sense a bond had been made. A secret bond, but one that would make the stay at the Sanders home more bearable.

When Martha returned to her room she found a note on her bed with a pair of her underwear folded in threes. Martha picked up the note. It was from Norma. The head housekeeper had gone through Martha's drawers and discovered two pair of her underwear had not been folded properly. Martha sat down on the bed, and stared at the note. It was going to be a very long four years living under Norma's scrutiny with or without Robert. Since Martha arrived, the woman had found fault with everything she did. When she polished the silver, Norma said they didn't shine enough. When she ironed Mr. Sanders' shirts, Norma said they weren't starched enough. When she hand mopped the kitchen floor, Norma made her redo the grout with a toothbrush. Now she was displeased with how Martha kept her belongings. It was so absurd, it was almost funny, except for the fact that Norma ran the house, and if her rules were not followed, the offender was punished. Martha didn't know how severe those punishments were yet, but she was determined not to find out. She had already felt enough pain and humiliation for one lifetime.

Martha picked up the slightly rumpled misfolded underwear Norma had been so appalled by and got up to put them away when someone knocked on her door. *Please don't let it be Norma*, she silently prayed. *I don't have the energy to deal with her tonight.* She put down the underwear and quickly opened the door. Any type of hesitancy would be a sign of defiance.

It was Lupe, another product of Living Trust.

"Mr. Sanders wants to see you in his study," Lupe said without any hint of emotion. There was no telltale sign of impending doom or elated surprise. The woman wore a mask as plain and dull as a lobotomized zombie.

In silence, Martha followed Lupe down the hall to Mr. Sanders study. Martha felt like a convict being led to her parole hearing. What would it be, exoneration or incarceration? Was she to be reprimanded for slovenly folded underwear, or had they tapped into her mind and found out she thought of Robert as a friend? Worse, did they have a hidden recorder in the Cadillac? Had she and Robert's conversation been heard? If that were the case, Mrs. Sanders would be in trouble too. No, Martha decided, Mrs. Sanders was too smart to get caught. It had to be something else. Maybe she had made eye contact one too many times with Robert over dinner.

The door to the study was opened. Lupe stepped aside. Martha hesitated for a moment. Mr. Sanders scared her, but her heart quickly calmed when she saw Mrs. Sanders and a balding man in a brown crumpled suit.

"Martha," Mrs. Sanders said, walking over to her and putting her arm around Martha's shoulder. "This is Detective Leonard. He has some distressing news, I'm afraid, and needs to speak to you."

Mr. Sanders turned and looked out the large bay window. This was not good. Martha looked first at Mrs. Sanders, then at the detective. "What is it? Is it my mother? Is she okay?"

"It's not your mother," Detective Leonard said. "It's your brother. He ran away while out on a work detail. We thought he may have tried to contact you."

"He wouldn't have even know where she was," Mr. Sanders said, turning around. "Really detective, he's not here and I'm sure Martha has no idea where he is. Isn't that right, Martha?"

Martha looked over at Mr. Sanders. Had Anthony called today and no one told her? Was it possible he had found out where she had been sent? She didn't know. It didn't matter. If he had escaped, there was a chance she could find him, and if she could, then she would do whatever it took to get the two of them out of Arizona.

Martha tried hard not to smile, not to show any elation in her brother's escape. "I haven't heard from him," she told the detective in a flat even tone.

"Well, Martha. You have to understand that once someone is turned over to the state, it is illegal for them to leave the state home. Anthony is a fugitive from the law right now and if you do anything at all to help him, you'll be considered an accessory. You would go to jail, Martha. Do you understand that?"

"Yes, sir," she said. *Fuck you*, she thought.

"Well then, here's my card." The detective stepped over to her and handed her his business card. "If you hear anything, make sure you do the right thing and call me. It's a dangerous place out there for a thirteen-year-old boy. You'll be doing him a big favor."

"Yes, sir," she said looking down at the card, not actually seeing it. She was too busy sorting out the possible places Anthony could be hiding and where she'd go first to find him. Freedom was only a few escape routes away.

Detective Leonard shook Mr. Sanders' hand and thanked them all for their time. Lupe reappeared and showed the detective out.

"Will that be all?" Martha asked Mr. Sanders. Every nerve ending in her body was firing. This was it, it was almost over. Anthony was free and very shortly she would be too. All she had to do was get out of the room and then the house. She'd work out a plan to get out of the State later, after she regained her power, after she found her brother.

Mr. Sanders turned towards her. His eyes narrowed. He was displeased. "Mrs. Jordan warned me about your brother. She said he was no good and that the state home was having a hard time with him. I took you anyway, sure that he couldn't be a burden to us while you were here. So, let me get this clear with you. If I so much as hear you whisper your brother's name while you're here, I'll turn you in myself. Norma," Mr. Sander's yelled.

Norma appeared from somewhere beyond the study's door. "Yes sir."

"Norma, I want you to put a cot up in your room tonight. Martha will be sleeping in there with you. I want you to keep your eye on her. If she gets up to go to the bathroom, I want you to go with her. Is that clear?"

"Yes, sir," Norma said, looking rather disdainfully at Martha.

"Darling, I don't think that's necessary. I'm sure if Martha gives you her word she won't try and go after her brother, then that will be sufficient. Wouldn't it dear?" Mrs. Sanders asked.

"Yes, ma'am," Martha said, hoping Mr. Sanders would buy it.

"She's new here, Barbara. How much faith do you really put in her word? No, I don't trust her at all. According to Mrs. Jordan, her brother is all she could talk about during her exit interview. I'm not taking any chances. Can you imagine what it would look like in the papers? 'Nathan Sanders' maid indicted on charges of aiding and abetting.' What will people think? If I can't control my own household, how can they trust me to protect theirs? I'm sorry, but I'm not going to take that chance. She's not to leave Norma's sight until after the boy's caught. You'll have to take Lupe or Rosa down the hill with you if you need them to help at the church."

"But I just got Martha trained," Mrs. Sanders protested. "Neither of those two girls is smart enough to handle the phones and marketing for the fundraising."

Mr. Sanders held up his hand. "I've made up my mind. Discussion closed. Martha, gather your things together and move into Norma's room, tonight."

Martha looked down at the floor. She knew Mrs. Sanders was looking at her apologetically, but she didn't want to acknowledge any type of allegiance to the woman. Tonight, somehow, even if it meant knocking Norma unconscious, she would escape. Mr. Sanders would be proven correct. She wasn't to be trusted, not when it came to choosing between family and enslavement.

16

Sharon called Thomas before returning to her hotel room. She told him the truth about Arizona's communication codes, but little else. His voice was calm and comforting, exactly what she needed. He was a respite, an oasis in a desert bereft of sanctities and freedoms. She wasn't about to ruin that by telling him the truth. She'd let Derek do all the worrying. He had sent her here, he could be the one losing sleep over her safety. Besides, if she told Thomas, there would be a war, a war she knew she would not lose. She was in this assignment too deep to back down now, no matter what Thomas would say or want.

It wasn't the first time she had lied to him to keep peace, to prevent confrontation. She had never told him about the rape. Not telling wasn't exactly a lie, just the omission of an event. A very traumatic event, one that had affected her life completely, but still just two single days in her life's history.

Thomas wouldn't understand. He loved her, she knew that, but would he love her if he knew she had had an abortion? She wasn't sure. He was pro-choice, he respected a woman's right to make decisions regarding her own body, but he didn't believe in abortion. He had been one of ten raised by a woman who in his opinion should have been sainted. If his mother could do it, anyone could. He had said that often enough when debating the issue. No, he wouldn't understand her need to abort a rapist's child. He would have loved the child no matter whose it was. And he would have expected the same from her. She had kept her secret to keep him. Someday it would probably backfire, but for now everything was safe and she could count on him being there when she returned.

Now, back at the hotel, she wondered if she had made the right decision. It bothered her to think she didn't trust his love to test it. Someday, she'd tell him the truth and see what happened. The worst would be he'd leave her. Well, she had been left before, and though never from someone she cared about as much as Thomas, she knew if she had to go it on her own again she could. If Arizona was doing anything for her, it was making her stronger.

Sharon sat on her bed, the TV on, but muted. A young boy's face flashed across the screen as well as a phone number. She got up to raise the volume when someone knocked on her door.

"Miss Clark," a man's voice called through the door.

"I'm coming," she called back. She didn't recognize the voice and was hesitant to let anyone in. "Who is it?"

"Detective Paul Matthews. I'm with the Maricopa County Sheriff's Department. I think we found your purse."

Sharon's heart stopped for a brief second. If the police had gone through it, who knew what assumptions they would have made or how deeply they would have looked into her profile. She knew she had to let them in, and she knew if the purse were hers, she had to acknowledge it, but still, she hesitated. She thought she had used up her supply of fear and apprehension in the past few hours, but obviously she was wrong. Her knees shook as she reached for the door.

"Miss Clark. Did you hear me? I said I think we found your purse."

"I'm sorry," she said as she opened the door . "I wasn't expecting any…"

She stopped in mid-sentence as Detective Paul Matthews stepped into her hotel room. He had dark short curly hair, deep blue eyes, and the beginning of a five o-clock shadow. He was about six two and built more like a beach volleyball player than a Sheriff's detective. In his hand was her purse. He held it out to her.

"Is this yours?"

His was a face she knew, one she had fantasized of often. The blue-eyed Italian that would whisk her away from daily troubles into a seductive love affair where all that mattered was passion and romance, gondolas and roses. He was a Harlequin hero, and he was standing only two feet away.

"Miss Clark?"

She had been caught staring. She reached out and took the bag from him.

"I think so," she said, looking up at him and smiling. "Where did you find it?"

"One of our Posse members pulled some boys over for speeding this afternoon. After they left, one of the volunteers noticed it on the side of the street. We figure they threw it out when they were stopped. Do you want to go through it and see if anything's missing?"

Sharon walked over to the bed and opened the bag. She went through each item. All of her watch cells were there as well as her notepad and headband. The only thing gone was her ID. "Everything seems to be here," she said turning back towards him and smiling. He was without a doubt the most handsome man she had ever met. Wasn't he? Or was it some weird pheromone thing? She wondered if he felt it too.

"Everything except this," he said holding up her fake ID.

"Right, how did I forget about that?" she asked with a nervous laugh, then reached out for it. He drew his hand back and walked over to the chair by the window.

"Why don't you tell me what you're doing here in Phoenix, Miss Clark. I flipped through some of your notes, and I must admit I'm a little concerned."

Reality check. He was a cop, a cop who had gone through her belongings and now needed to interrogate her. His feelings were strictly official. *Only the facts, Ma'am.*

Sharon didn't know how else to explain what her notes held except by telling the truth. The same truth, at least, that she told Reverend Samuels and Warden Hayden. She explained she was a journalist and writing a piece on criminalizing abortion in Southern California. She told him about some of her interviews and that she had toured the prison. Knowing he had already checked her profile, she told him about being caught showing Bethany's picture and the treatment she received.

He listened intently without interjecting, letting her finish. She ended her story by showing him the torn suit in her trash bin and letting a small tear fall down her face.

"That sounds tough," Matthews said, "and it explains the notes. So now why don't you explain how those boys got your purse."

Sharon looked past him and out the window. This was going to be trickier. She knew if she veered too far from the truth she would risk getting caught. "I had a meeting with someone who is pro-abortion over at Papago Park. We were attacked by skinheads while we were there and they stole my bag."

"Pro-abortionist, in Arizona?" Detective Matthews smiled as he pulled out his own notepad and pen. "Do you mind telling me who it was?"

His smile was magnetic, she felt drawn to him, charmed into trusting him. *He's a seductor reeling you in for the kill,* a small inner voice warned. She stepped back. No matter how physically she was attracted to him, she had to remember, he was the enemy.

"I'm not at liberty to say." Sharon picked up her bag and pretended to go through it again. "That's why I didn't call in the theft. If I'm to write a good article, I have to have viewpoints from both sides. It took me a long time to find someone to bad mouth the system, so I'm not about to compromise my promise of anonymity."

"If you're as anti-abortion as you say, what do you care what happens to the contact?"

His left eyebrow rose. It was thick and dark like black velvet. Sharon wanted to put a comb through it, to touch it, to let her finger outline his cheekbone and... *Stop it! He's a cop for God's sake.*

"Look detective. I'm a reporter," she said rather flatly. "Sources are my lifeblood, don't ask me to put my career on the line so you can arrest some misguided fanatic."

Detective Matthews held up his hand. "And I'm only trying to do my job. Look at it from my point of view. First, we find a threesome of skinheads with a stolen purse. Then inside the purse I find notes talking about people wrongly jailed and insinuating a conspiracy in the judicial system. Now you tell me you personally know of a pro-abortionist actively working against the system. I have to tell you, Miss Clark. I'm a little concerned."

"I can see that," Sharon said smiling. "But you don't need to be. I'm already working with a Detective Grant. I'm sure if you contact him..."

"Grant, I know him. What's he got to do with this?"

"He came to visit me after the shooting?"

"Shooting, what shooting?"

Sharon put the bag down. The shooting which seemed so scary at the time was barely a memory. It seemed one of the minor events of her stay. She felt no hesitancy in telling the comely detective. Besides, another story might keep him around longer. She'd have to go to confession afterwards. Ten Hail Mary's ought to do it for lusting after a man she couldn't have especially when she already had another packed safely away at home. *Good thing I'm not Catholic,* she laughed to herself before telling him the true version of what had happened at

Reverend Samuels' church and about the interrupted phone call, the lies she heard on the news, and the tail Detective Grant put on her the following day. "So you see," she said at the end, "the police are very aware of my actions."

"I guess they are. I should have checked your profile further. All I looked for was an address."

She had said too much, as usual. Now that she had bored him with her daily crises, she should let him go. "I didn't realize deputies had enough free time to hand deliver stolen purses. I'm grateful."

"We don't usually, but it was on my way home and I personally wanted to ask you about those notes."

Sharon walked over to where he stood and pulled her ID from his hand. "Well, I can assure you, Detective Matthews, everything is above board. I've already arranged with Detective Grant to leave him copies of my notes and my contacts before I leave. We kind of have an understanding."

Detective Matthews took her hand in his as if to shake it and held it for a minute. Sharon's whole body tingled. This wasn't good.

"I'm sorry if I've disrupted your evening, Miss Clark."

"Call me Sharon," she said looking up into his eyes, they were evening sky blue. The color you could only see in SoCal if you went up to the mountains after a good rainstorm.

"Sharon," he said placing his other hand over hers. Her chest, then her face flushed. "Tell me, do you know many people here in Phoenix?"

She shook her head, hoping the blush didn't materialize as dark strawberry across her neck and face. "Just those I've interviewed."

"Well," he said, smiling down at her, "if it wouldn't seem too improper, I was wondering if you'd like to have dinner with me tomorrow evening. I get off at seven. We could meet here at say, eight?"

Sharon smiled. She knew she should say no, but it wasn't about to come out of her mouth. "I'd love to," she said.

"Great. Then I'll be going." He let go of her hand and walked towards the door.

She tried to think of something intelligent to say, some witticism, or memorable remark, but there was nothing. "Don't you need my bag as evidence?" she blurted out like a schoolgirl trying not to let the football player pass her desk without acknowledging her.

He rested his hand on the doorknob and turned back towards her. "No, I'm sorry to say, we won't be prosecuting the boys. I shouldn't be telling you this, but the driver is the nephew of someone pretty high up in the Sheriff's department. It was decided it would be best just to give you back the bag and drop it. I'm sorry, Sharon. Hey," he said smiling at her, "look at it this way. If we did prosecute, you wouldn't get your bag back for some time. This works out best for everyone."

"You're right. I'm just as happy things turned out the way they did. This was much better."

"I think so too," Detective Matthews said smiling. "See you tomorrow at eight?" he asked as he opened the door.

"Eight," she agreed.

"Great," he said then turned and left her room.

Sharon followed him out and watched him walk down the hall. His ass was tight and his shoulders broad. She imagined her fingers combing through sweat covered hair on his chest and back. There was a tightening in her groin. "Behave," she said to herself as the elevator doors closed. There'd be plenty of time for that tomorrow at eight. She kissed her ID and took a small skip.

As she readied herself for bed she wondered who would fill her nighttime fantasies, Thomas or Detective Matthews. Either way, she was in for a night of otherworldly passions. Finally, something pleasurable. The best part was that no matter who she made love to while sleeping, she was guiltless. There was no penalty, no accountability for dreamscape affairs.

17

Martha waited until she could hear the steady breathing of her jailer. She had waited hours for Norma to fall asleep, and during that time devised her escape. She would head off to the kitchen in her pajamas. If she was caught she would say she couldn't sleep and had come in for a glass of milk. They would buy that, no one would imagine she would go out looking for her brother in her pajamas. She had left her daypack under the back seat of the Cadillac. She could change once she got to the garage. She wasn't sure if the garage door would open from the inside without an alarm going off, but she had to chance it. Anthony was alone and probably afraid. She had to get to him. She figured it would take her all night to walk there, but she didn't care. He would give her the strength to get them both out of Arizona, and she knew just the person who could help them.

She slowly climbed off her cot and waited, watching closely the rhythmic movement of Norma's chest. She stepped over to the door and quietly turned the knob. Norma didn't respond. She opened the door. Nothing. Norma was a deeper sleeper than she dared hope. She turned and held the door as she closed it, minimizing the click as best she could. If she were to get caught it would be right now, but again, nothing. Norma hadn't heard her. She was almost free.

There were no lights, no insomniac roaming the halls. Her foot-steps on the carpeted hall went unheard, and she safely reached the kitchen. Her heart pounded in her ears as she reached for the handle to the door that led down to the garage. It was unlocked and opened easily. She slid behind it and held it as it closed. She leaned against the door, anticipating something, anything. It had been too easy she thought for a moment, but then quickly she assigned her fears to paranoia and forgot them.

Slowly, one step at a time, down the darkened stairway, she made it to the third level where the Cadillac was kept. There was a small yellow light on above the car and she headed towards it. "Almost there," she whispered to herself as she approached the back door of the car. She pulled on its handle, but it didn't open.

"It's locked," a voice called from beyond the Cadillac. Martha's heart stopped and she jumped. The shadows played tricks with her eyes. She couldn't see anyone.

"Robert," she asked catching her breath "Is that you?"

"Who else would be lurking in the garage?" he asked as he stood up from his hiding place and walked over to her. "Where do you think you're going?"

"My brother escaped. I've got to find him. I've got to get us out of Arizona or he'll be sent back to the state school. You don't know what they do to the kids in there. By the time he's eighteen there won't be any Anthony left in him. He'll just be another one of those robots the schools put out. He'll be like Lupe or Rosa. I can't bear to think of it. Please, just let me get my clothes and leave. No one has to know you saw me."

"I don't know," Robert said pulling a cell phone from his pocket and dialing.

"Please, Robert," she begged.

"She's here," he said into the phone then closed it and put it back in his pocket. He reached over to the door she had tried to open and unlocked it. "Get your stuff," he said.

Martha looked up at him confused. "You mean, you're..."

"Of course we are. Mrs. Sanders gave Norma a sleeping pill before she went to bed tonight and I've arranged for a car to meet you at the bottom of the driveway. If she had more time, Mrs. Sanders would have gotten you a fake ID and some credit on account, but she knew you wouldn't wait. This is the best she can do."

"I don't know what to say." Tears of gratitude ran down her face.

Robert reached over and wiped the tears from her face. "I had hoped we would become friends," he said then bent down and kissed her on the lips. Martha reached her hand up to his face and kissed him back. It was her first kiss, it tasted like the sweet nectar of a ripened peach.

"I'm sorry," she said as she pulled away. "He's my brother."

"I know," Robert said brushing hair from her face. "If it was my sister, I'd go."

"Come with me then. After we get Anthony out, we can go find Thina."

Robert shook his head. "I can do more good here, than I could by kidnapping Thina. It's been so long she probably doesn't even remember me."

"I'm sure that's not true. She…"

"No," Robert said as he opened the door. "I can't go with you, Martha, and after you walk out of this garage, you can't turn back. Don't try to contact Mrs. Sanders or me. If you get caught, you're not to mention we helped you. You'll need to take all the responsibility yourself."

"I will," Martha said.

Robert reached down and kissed her quick and hard, then turned and walked away. Martha watched his back as it receded into the shadows. She touched her lips and felt the moist warmth he had left behind. He would have been her first love, she realized. And even though it would never happen, she would always remember him as if it had. He would always be the love she had left for her brother and freedom.

Martha grabbed her daypack from under the back seat of the car and ran up the ramps to the garage door. The alarm was off and the door opened as quietly as all the others.

At the bottom of the drive, a small dark blue Toyota waited. She turned and looked once more up at the white-pillared mansion, then opened the car door and pulled herself in. She would change on the way.

Martha walked around the abandoned church softly calling her brother's name. There was no answer. She was sure this was where he would have gone, where he knew she could find him. This had been the secret place of their childhood. The place they had disappeared to when upset, bored, or when they just needed to be alone. No one knew about it. Not their friends, not their neighbors, not even their mother. There was no way the Posse would know to look here. It was the only place Anthony would hide.

She walked around in the darkened hall searching each corner with the small flashlight the driver had given her. Maybe it was too early, maybe he hadn't had enough time to get here, she thought to herself. The detective hadn't said where Anthony had been housed, or how long he had been missing. She called his name one last time, then turned to return to the car, to tell the driver to go on without her, to leave her. She was going to wait for her brother to show up.

"Martha," a small whisper cried.

Martha stopped, not sure she had heard her name. "Anthony," she called back louder.

"Martha, is that you?"

"Anthony, where are you?" she asked as she frantically let the light search the building.

"Up here," he called back to her. "I'm in the balcony."

Martha shined the light up and saw her brother's small round face peering over the edge of the balcony. Even with the flashlight shining on him, his dark eyes seemed dim. "I'm hurt," he said as his head slowly disappeared below the edge of the balcony.

"Stay there," she yelled. "I'm coming." Martha ran up broken stairs and found her brother lying on the floor curled up like an unborn fetus. She ran over to him and cradled him in her arms. He was hot, too hot.

"Oh, my God," she said as she rocked him back and forth. "What's wrong with you?"

Anthony didn't answer. He just laid there, his hand tightly holding his sister's arm.

"Did you find him?" a woman's voice called into the church. "We have to go before someone calls us in."

"I found him," Martha called down to the woman who had driven her there. "He's hurt, can you help me?"

The woman made her way up the stairs and together they carried Anthony down to the car. His fever was intense. Martha was scared. She couldn't lose him, not now, not when they had risked so much to be together. She had to get him some help.

"It's too risky to take him to a doctor," the woman told her. "I can drop you off somewhere, but that's all I can do. I have to get the car back before it's missed."

"Okay, I know," Martha said, not knowing what she would do at all. "Will you make a call for me?"

"A call, I don't know. Calls are traceable," the woman said.

"I'll be discreet. The woman I want to call doesn't even know me by my real name. No one will ever know."

The woman relented and pulled up to a phone booth at a closed gas station. Martha first called information to get the number of the

Desert Suites, then dialed the hotel, insisting that they ring Sharon Clark's room.

"Hello," a groggy Sharon answered.

"Sharon, this is Alicia from this afternoon. Remember me?"

"Alicia, Alicia. Oh, yeah. What's going on? What time is it?"

"I don't know, late. I'm sorry to bother you, but I need you to meet me at the picnic table. It's an emergency."

"An emergency? What kind of emergency?"

"An emergency, that's all. Please, you're the only one I can trust."

"At the picnic table?"

"Yeah, you know which one I mean?"

"I think so. I'll be there in about fifteen minutes."

"Thank you," Martha said then hung up the phone. She looked over at the car. Her brother's head leaned lifelessly against the side window. "If you're up there, God," she said raising her gaze skyward. "Please, help us."

18

Sharon looked at the clock after hanging up the phone. It was only three o'clock. "Jesus," she said as she pulled herself together and got dressed. "This had better be one big fucking emergency."

Still sleepy, she took the elevator to the lobby. The doorman sat by the front door, his cap halfway down around his eyes. Sharon quietly walked by the lobby to a side exit and let herself out. The night air was warm, but still. A single car drove by, it's lights quickly fading in the dark. It posed no threat.

It was dangerous going out at night. If her Jeep was being monitored, a flag would definitely be raised if it was moved this late. She sat staring out the window for a moment or two, debating whether or not to take the chance when she remembered Tonja's penlight. A smile slipped slowly across her face as she found the light, and flicked it on. If the thing worked, no one would know she was gone.

She watched her rear view mirror as she pulled out of the parking lot onto McDowell. When she reached the top of the pass that ran between the buttes, she let out the small breath she had been holding. She was alone. No car pulled out to follow.

The road leading into the park was dark. It seemed longer than she remembered, and for a short moment she worried she had taken the wrong street. But then, she saw it – the shadows of the lone pagoda standing sentinel in the night. She parked in the same small lot she had used twice before. Using the flashlight she always kept in her glove compartment, she found her way up to the pagoda. "Alicia," she called out quietly, "Alicia."

"Over here," a small voice called back to her as the young woman stood up from behind one of the benches. "We're over here."

"We, who's we?" Sharon asked as she walked over to where the woman stood.

Lying on one of the benches was a young boy. Alicia knelt down beside him and firmly held his hand.

"He's sick," Alicia said. "His fever's way out of control. I need your help."

Sharon went over to the boy and laid her hand on his head then quickly drew it away. He was on fire. Whatever was wrong with him, was not something she could cure. "He needs a doctor," she said, standing upright then stepping back.

"I can't take him to a doctor. He's escaped from the state school. If I take him to a doctor, they'll report him," Alicia cried.

The girl seemed pretty upset, Sharon envisioned her on the brink of a total emotional breakdown, but the girl and the brother weren't Sharon's concern. They couldn't be. Just being here jeopardized Sharon's cover. If they were caught, any chance of getting her story would be lost, any chance of staying in Arizona would be gone, that was if they let her leave Arizona at all. *You're over dramatizing,* she told herself. He's was a runaway, not a criminal. What harm could it be to help the girl? *More than you can afford,* a small inner voice warned.

She wished the girl hadn't called her, hadn't known where to find her, but it was too late. She was already here and already involved. She let out a sigh of resignation, then looked back at the sick boy and his devoted sister. "What do you want me to do?"

"I don't know," Alicia said looking up at her, tears escaping and running down her face. "He's all I've got."

"I'm not a doctor," Sharon told her. "Wasn't your mother some kind of healer? What would she have done?"

Alicia took a deep breath. "She would have made up some kind of poultice I guess. But I don't know out of what. I never paid much attention," she said leaning over and putting her cheek against him. "Stay strong," she whispered. "We'll get you well, I promise."

That was not a promise Sharon intended to make. She didn't know much about children or medicine, and was pretty sure her best wasn't going to be good enough. The boy needed medical care. Sharon looked around at the night sky. There were a few planes coming in from the East, the passing of a car in the distance, and some lights from the city, but nothing else. There was no one they could call, no place they could go. Whatever was going to be done for the boy was going to come from them. She needed to think. What had her mother done for her when she was sick? Not much, it had always been Granddad, and he would have given her some form of aspirin. That was something she did have.

"I'll be right back," she told Alicia then turned and ran down to the Jeep. She hadn't rummaged through her earthquake kit in years, but that didn't mean her medical supplies wouldn't be good. She found the bottle of generic aspirin and a packet of water. They would have to do for now.

Sharon ran back up to the bench where the boy lay. "I've got aspirin. It might bring down the fever," she said pulling off the bottle's cap and dumping three of them out. "Sit him up."

Alicia put her hands on her brother's back to lift him up. He jerked and cried out.

"What's wrong with him?" Sharon asked as she put the aspirin in this mouth then poured a quarter of the water pack in behind them.

"Look." Alicia lifted his shirt and aimed her flashlight on his back. Greenish yellow pus mixed with blood oozed from a mishmash of open wounds.

"Oh my God," Sharon said, looking up at Alicia. "What the hell happened?"

"I don't know. He's barely been conscious since we found him."

"We?" Sharon asked looking around. "Is there someone else here?"

"No. Some friend of Mrs. San... I mean Helen took me to find him then dropped us off here. What am I going to do?" the girl pleaded.

Sharon stood up, away from the boy and his agony. She turned to the night lights of Phoenix and brushed back hair from her face. She didn't know what to do. Obviously Helen was out of the question or Alicia would have taken him back to her. What about Simon? He was a doctor, he could at least tell them what to do.

"Look," Sharon said turning back towards Alicia. "I know someone who might be willing to help, but we won't be able to contact him until tomorrow morning. For now, we've got to get your brother somewhere and clean out those wounds."

"Your hotel?" Alicia asked.

"No, we can't take him there, I'm watched too closely. Let's get him into the Jeep. We'll have to find a motel or something. Someplace where they won't ask too many questions."

"Van Buren. That's the best place," Alicia said, smiling up at her.

"They pretend like it's been cleaned out, but it's still full of prostitutes. No one will care who we are."

"Great," Sharon said, not really believing anywhere in Arizona was free from telling eyes. She pulled her headband to her brow, and hoped all the gadgets she had brought with her weren't fakes. She looked down at the boy. He was young, maybe thirteen or fourteen, but still he was quite large, larger than she expected either of them could handle without help. "Can he walk?"

Alicia looked down at her brother. "Barely." With the back of her hand she gently rubbed his cheek. "Anthony, Anthony," she whispered. "We have to go." Anthony's eyes slowly opened. "You have to help us. Get up. Try and stand up." Anthony closed his eyes then slowly he lowered one leg, then the other to the ground. "That's it," Alicia told him. "Take it slow. We'll help you."

Alicia wrapped his arm around her neck and pulled him to his feet. Sharon stepped over and grabbed his other arm before he fell back down to the bench and together they half walked, half carried the ailing boy to the Jeep. Lifting him into the car was harder than Sharon had realized. The Jeep was high off the ground and Anthony had little if no energy left to help them. Alicia pulled from the driver's side as Sharon hoisted him up into the seat. The boy's fever had taken him beyond his pain and though they were being rougher than was good for him, she knew, he felt nothing.

Sharon looked over at Alicia and saw where the pain had gone. The girl's face was ashen, her eyes dulled by fear. Sharon prayed to whoever was listening that the boy would survive, but in her heart she worried it was too late.

They found a small motel on Van Buren with lights still on in the office and a neon vacancy sign blinking wildly. Sharon didn't want to stay in the one floor stucco building, sure it was infested with more than a few roaches and bed bugs, but Alicia had insisted. The proprietor was a small bent over women with wiry gray hair. She didn't look up at Sharon as she ran her ID through the scanner, obviously she didn't care if Sharon was the owner of the ID or not. After the word "APPROVED" flashed on the readout, the woman handed her a keycard. "Room 12, be out by noon," the woman said then turned and walked through a curtained door.

The room was surprisingly clean, though the bedding was old and the tub and toilet stained with years of use. Together, almost silently, Sharon and Alicia removed Anthony's soiled clothing and put him in the bed. Alicia filled the ice bucket with warm water and using a face cloth, gingerly washed his wounds clean. Sharon was amazed at how the girl didn't turn away from the rank purulence. She, however, refrained from looking and instead returned to her Jeep to collect some of the first aid items from her earthquake kit. Hydrogen peroxide, Neosporin, bandages, tape, and clean clothing. When she returned to the room she saw that Alicia had stopped washing her brother, the girl's hands lay motionless on her brother's back. Tears ran down her face.

"Have you two always been so close?" Sharon asked after realizing she was staring.

"My mother wasn't around much. Once my grandmother died, I kind of took over watching out for him, and at times, him for me. We're all each other has now."

Sharon walked over and put her hand on the girl's shoulder. "Here," she said handing her the hydrogen peroxide. "Wash those down with this then we'll put on some Neosporin and bandage him up."

"It's not going to do much good," the girl said, setting the bottle on the nightstand. "He's too hot. The aspirin didn't bring down the fever very much."

Sharon placed her hand on the young boy's back. He was as hot, if not hotter, than he had been at the park. "I have an idea," she said, taking the ice bucket out of Alicia's hand and dumping the sullied water into the bathroom sink. "I saw this on TV once. No guarantees, but it might work," she said as she reached over and turned on the cold water in the tub. "Help me get him in the tub, then we'll bring the water temperature down even further with ice. That just might be what we need to keep the fever down so he can fight this off himself."

"Are you sure?" Alicia asked.

Sharon stood up from the tub and looked at the frightened girl. "I'm not sure of anything," she honestly told her, "but at this point it's better than nothing. So what do you say? Do we give it a try?"

Alicia looked down at her brother then back at Sharon and nodded her head. "Let's try."

Sharon grabbed Anthony under his arms. Alicia picked him up at his knees, and they carried him to the tub, lowering him quickly into the cold running water before they dropped him.

Anthony's eyes popped open and his arms flailed. Sharon was knocked backwards. She reached out and grabbed the shower curtain to catch herself, but it pulled free from its restraints and fell down on top of her.

Alicia grabbed her brother around his shoulders and rocked him. "It's all right," she told him. "It's all right. This will help you. We're trying to help you." The boy went limp in her arms.

Sharon untangled herself from the curtain and pulled herself off the floor.

"Are you all right?" Alicia asked.

"I'll be okay. Here," Sharon said, pulling a towel from the rack behind her. "Put this against his wounds, then let's lower him down into the tub." Alicia took the towel, wet it, then plastered it onto his back. Sharon pulled his knees up as Alicia slowly lowered his back into the water. "Okay," she said, more out of breath that she thought she should be. "I'll go get ice. Watch him. The fever should start going down quickly if this is going to work."

Alicia nodded her head. Sharon grabbed the ice bucket and ran out of the room. The ice machine was three rooms down and full. She made many trips through the early morning. In the beginning the ice had melted fast as the heat from Anthony's body warmed the surrounding water, but as his fever subsided the water retained its cooling properties longer and longer.

Alicia told Sharon that her real name was Martha, something Sharon had already guessed from their previous meeting, and that Helen and the chauffeur had helped her escape. Sharon admired the girl's determination and courage, but felt Martha had been foolish to take such a risk. If she hadn't, Sharon reminded herself, the boy would probably be dead.

They were good kids, but Sharon didn't know how she'd be able to help them. Hiding them might be the only thing she could do. She would be careful not to make any promises she might have to break. Martha didn't look like she could handle any more let downs. The girl had been through enough.

The cold bath worked. Anthony came to a little after sunrise, and though still very sick, he helped Sharon and Martha get him out of the tub and back to the bed.

Martha pulled his wet underwear down and off him, and started to dry him off while Sharon supported him under the arms. He was heavy and limp, Sharon didn't know how long she could hold him up and prompted Martha to hurry.

"I'm almost done," Martha said as she bent down by his feet and began to dry his legs. Half way up, she gasped. "Oh, my God," she cried as the towel fell from her hands.

Sharon looked down at the girl. "What? What's wrong?"

"He's, he's..." Martha stammered as she lifted his penis. "His balls are gone," she whispered.

Anthony moaned, his right hand tried to reach down and brush his sister's hand away.

"What?" Sharon said almost dropping him.

Martha looked up at her. "They cut off his balls."

Sharon moved Anthony over the bed and lowered him down to it. Martha, still kneeling on the floor stared at her brother's groin. "Why?" she asked.

Sharon pulled Anthony's legs up onto the bed, and though she didn't look as closely as Martha, she could tell he was no longer whole. "I don't know," she said, quickly covering him with the blankets. Martha stood up and reached to pull the blanket back. Sharon grabbed her arm. "Leave it alone," she said. "You can ask him in the morning."

Martha stared up at Sharon, her eyes misted and wide. "I'll kill them," she said. "I'll kill them all."

Sharon pulled the girl into her and held her. Martha didn't sob, she didn't cry. She stood stiff in Sharon's embrace. Why anyone would castrate a thirteen-year-old boy was beyond Sharon's grasp, but she knew no legitimate answer would be found. She walked the girl to the other side of the bed and sat her down next to her brother. "He's going to be fine," Sharon said, not really sure it was true. "He'll be able to tell us everything, but for right now, you need to be strong. You still have a long way to go before you're safe, Martha."

Martha made no response. She lay on the bed staring up at the ceiling. Sharon sat down in the armchair next to the bed and wondered, of the two, who would take the longer to heal.

"Housekeeping," a woman's voice called through the door after a heavy knock. "Are you folks still in there?"

Sharon had fallen asleep and woke with a start. "Just a minute." She looked down at her watch, it was ten-thirty. She had missed her first interview of the morning. "Damn," she said as she got up to answer the door.

A young girl in cut offs and a crop top, her arms laden with towels and linens, stood smiling at the door. "Housekeeping," she said through a mouth full of gum.

"I'll do it." Sharon took the items from the girls' hands. "My brother's still sleeping. We're going to stay another night, so I'll do this myself, all right?"

The girl tried to look around Sharon into the room, but Sharon closed the door slightly to obstruct her view. "I guess so," the girl said. "You want me to add it to your bill?"

"That would be great," Sharon said, smiling at the girl. "We may be staying for a few nights. We're on vacation and this place seems central to where we want to visit. Tell your mother to keep the bill open, would you?"

"My grandmother," the girl said. "So what, you don't want me cleaning the room while you're here?"

"It's just that it's a bad time for us. My brother likes to sleep late. Just leave the towels and stuff outside the room. I can change them. If you give me some bags, I'll put the soiled ones in it and you don't have to worry about anything."

"Fine with me," the girl said. "Just don't tell my grandmother. She's got this thing about how the rooms are supposed to be cleaned."

Sharon assured her that the grandmother would never know and closed the door before the girl had any time to argue further.

"How long do you think we'll be safe here?" Martha asked.

"A few days, I suppose. I've got a meeting this afternoon. You need to lay low, stay here with Anthony. I'll check in after my meeting, but I have another appointment tonight. I'll bring back some food, and more bandages. Anything else you think will help?"

Martha looked over at her sleeping brother and placed her hand on his forehead. "Fever's down. I guess we're fine for now. I'll clean his back again and reapply the Neosporin. But what about, you know," she said looking over at her brother's body.

"There's nothing you can do. It's done. He can't get them back. The most important thing now is getting you two out of Arizona. Think about that while I'm gone. And for God's sake, if he wakes up, don't start questioning him about it. He needs his rest."

Martha took a deep breath and lay back down on the bed. "I won't. I'll wait till he's better, but someday," she said as a tear ran down the side of her face, "someday I'm going to come back here, and I'm going to make them pay."

"I believe that," Sharon said picking up her bag and throwing it over her shoulder. "If he was my brother, I would do the same. But for right now, leaving Arizona is more important than revenge. I want you to promise me you won't leave this room. They've probably already reported you missing and the Posse will be looking for you."

"I'm not going anywhere," the girl said, still staring up at the ceiling.

Sharon looked down at Martha and then over at the boy. If this was the work of God, Arizona could keep Him.

After bringing Martha and Anthony breakfast, Sharon called Simon. Though she thought Anthony was better, she wanted Simon to take a look at him. Simon refused her call.

"Please don't call back here," the receptionist pleaded. "You've caused enough trouble already."

The receptionist did not elaborate on the *troubles* Sharon had caused. She had been rather rude and hung up before Sharon had been given the chance to apologize for whatever problems her visit had prompted. It didn't matter too much anyway. Anthony was her major concern, not Simon Garner. Simon had taken on the risks of what he did all by himself. Anthony's situation had been forced on him. So, if she had to choose whom she would worry about, it would be Anthony. Unfortunately, he was out a doctor. But in truth, it wasn't Anthony's health Sharon was preoccupied with, it was his safety.

His had been the young face she had seen plastered across the TV screen the previous evening. Every Arizonian was a potential informant. There would be no safe haven, no commiserate family to take in the boy while he healed. Who could blame them? She had yet to figure out why she was risking so much to help them. Maybe it was because they were so young, maybe it was because although her mother hadn't abandoned her, she might as well have. There was a connection there, something about Martha and Anthony that made her see herself. She understood their loss, their fear. She had suffered at the hands of Arizona law, but only briefly. These two kids had dealt with so much more, and yet they hadn't given up, they only grew stronger. Maybe in the long run, she envied them, maybe not, but it was something, and she was sure it wasn't pity. Regardless, she knew she was going to help them, even though every ounce of instinct told her not to.

But how? They would have to find outside help, and there was only one outside source she trusted. She pulled the phone card through the reader and dialed Derek's number.

"I just don't have the money to help them." Derek told her after she finished the story of Martha calling her the night before and telling him how sick the boy was. "The best I can do is get Helen to get them some new ID's. They'll have to make it across the border on their own."

"On their own? They're just kids," Sharon protested. "The boy's picture is already being flashed across the TV screen. They'll never make it."

"Look, Sharon. I'm sorry. But they aren't your concern. You're a reporter, not the goddamn Red Cross. Don't lose sight of your assignment. The stakes are a lot bigger than two runaways."

"Yeah," Sharon said. "But I'm not harboring the entire state of California in a motel room. These kids have nowhere to go, Derek. I'm not going to abandon them."

"Look, Sharon," Derek said. "I didn't send you there to rescue people, I sent you there to get a story, possibly the biggest story of your career. Try and stay focused. Don't get so involved with the individual cases that you lose track of the larger picture."

"It's too late. But don't worry," she said sarcastically. "I won't let it jeopardize my story."

"All right, you win," Derek said. "I'll see what I can do from this end. It will take me a few days to get up the money. Then you're going to have to find traders willing to get them across the border. I'll take care of them once they reach Southern California."

"I knew I could count on you," Sharon told him.

"Yeah, more like you knew you could manipulate me," Derek said. "This is risky, Sharon. If you get caught, they won't let you come home."

"I know, but you'd have to see this boy's scars. It's something else. Did I mention, they castrated him as well?"

Derek was silent for a few minutes. Probably calculating the impact Anthony would have on her story. Finally after what seemed minutes, he spoke. "Sharon?"

"What?"

"Be careful."

Sharon laughed. "I'm trying, but the state's just not cooperating."

Sharon hung up the phone, returned to her hotel, and re-engaged the GPS tracking on the Jeep. A small vase holding three long stem roses waited for her at the front desk. It was from Paul Matthews, a sweet reminder of their date. It had been years since anyone had sent her flowers, especially roses. Though Thomas was a romantic, he bought her expensive jewelry that she never seemed to wear and naughty nighties from Fasinations that often times ended up being more of a gift for himself. Not that she complained, of the two of them she had always been the horny one, the aggressor. Thomas liked to be seduced, he liked to be the one to say no. But once he said yes, watch out. He was great in bed, almost addictive. It was what she missed most since she left Southern California. It was what she thought of as she smelled the roses and remembered the curve of Paul Matthew's ass.

This was not the time for illicit love affairs, though. No matter how badly Paul Matthews enticed her. She had bigger business. Derek was right, she needed to keep her mind focused on the story, and on Anthony. His story could overshadow the abortion issue. She would make a bigger impact on the voters and those on the committee to choose next year's Pulitzer winner by focusing on the side effects of a nation gone insane over the right to life and enforced installation of family values. She had come to show the abuse of the women, but to hell with the women. People would be more interested in the children. They wouldn't have much sympathy for the Phoebe Washington's of the world, but they would for the children. The thousands of children taken from their parents in the name of social responsibility.

If she could showcase the little lives that were being abused and brainwashed inside the state system, she could wrap it back to the abortion issue and make a bigger statement, a statement that would spark emotions in everyone who read it, even the right-to-lifers.

She knew the story already. In her mind, she could see it in print. A teen-age girl is forced into servitude for four years to repay four months of state care. A boy is castrated and beaten when he refuses to be altered into a state clone and then declared a criminal when he flees his tormentors. It would be perfect. People may not care too much about women trying to abort their babies, but they sure as hell would care if those babies were being abused by the very people so intent on protecting their right to life. *Well, maybe not life,* she thought to herself, *maybe they were only protecting their existence.* Because life, as she understood it, was supposed to be about liberty and the pursuit of happiness.

Her interview with Senator Listner suddenly became something to look forward to. He had been one of the key people in setting up the ward system almost twenty years ago. He even had a few schools named after him like the Listner School for Girls in Sedona and Listner Academy in Flagstaff. If anyone knew what was happening to these children, it would be him. Now all she needed to do was find a way to manipulate him during the interview into slipping with a quotation or two about the state's true reasoning behind the treatment of the children it swore to protect.

As she showered and dressed for the interview she couldn't help but smile. She really was a reporter. She stretched her neck and shoulders and inadvertently rubbed the scars that were already forming from the knife wounds. She could feel the story. It was brewing. All she needed now were some missing ingredients before she set it to boil.

19

Sharon sat, her hands in her lap, in a plush blue chair across from Senator Listner's secretary's desk. She had dressed professionally for this interview. "If you want to be taken seriously," Granddad had taught her, "appearance makes the difference. Never let them think you're beneath them." This was advice she had heeded. She smoothed down the skirt of her camel linen suit, and brushed back the small strand of blonde hair that had eased its way loose from her French twist.

The secretary, Byron Wilson according to his name plate, a man in his mid-twenties wearing an expensive double breasted gray suit, informed the senator that she had arrived. He offered her coffee which she eagerly accepted and handed it to her in a black mug with the words "Listner, He Knows What You Want!" stenciled in gold. She read it out loud to the secretary and smiled up at him. "That's good to know," she said.

The secretary smiled back then returned to his desk where he had busied himself with the computer and phone. The coffee was too hot to drink, so she placed it on the table next to her chair and looked around the room. The walls were decorated with pictures of Senator Listner shaking hands with various men, a few whom she recognized as CEOs of some of the biggest companies in American, the last two presidents, and one with Governor Duke, the reigning asshole of Arizona.

"Quite the showcase," she said, picking up the mug.

The secretary looked up from his work at a few of the pictures on the wall. "The senator's a very influential man, highly regarded in the world of politics."

"And finance," Sharon added.

"And finance," the secretary concurred.

"Will he be making a bid for the White House?" Sharon asked as she brought the cup up to drink. The aroma was strong, too strong. It made her queasy. A small amount of bile shot up her throat and she pulled back. She could feel her eyes water.

"We're all hoping... Are you all right, Miss Clark?"

Sharon put the mug back down on the table, took a deep breath and coughed. "Yeah, I guess it's a little stronger than I'm used to."

"Are you sure? Can I get you anything?"

"No, really." Sharon held up her hand. "I'm fine." She looked back down at the coffee and shook her head. She couldn't remember ever reacting so strongly to coffee. *It must be the stress,* she thought, *those kids are getting to me.*

The computer beeped. Sharon looked over at the secretary as he read whatever message came through.

"You can go in now, Miss Clark," the secretary said as he stood and opened the door to Senator Listner's office.

"Well, well. So you're the young reporter I've been hearing so much about. Miss Clark, it's nice to finally meet you," a tall, athletic looking man said. He was dressed in a navy blue double-breasted suit. His hair was stiffly combed back with a slight pouf at his forehead, his white teeth sparkled as if freshly painted.

Sharon was startled for a moment by his comment and hesitantly shook his hand. "What exactly have you heard?" she asked.

"I'm a senator, my dear," he said, pointing to a chair for her to sit down. "I know everything. All your misadventures have read like one of Shakespeare's comedies. It seems you can't stay out of your own way."

Sharon disliked him immediately. His dark blue eyes reminded her of the deep water off the coast, the exact depth and color that concealed the great whites. One foot over the edge and it was gone. She put on her most gregarious smile and produced a short laugh. "I guess you could say that. All I can hope for now is a happy ending."

"That remains to be seen," he said, walking behind his desk and sitting down without once taking his gaze from her. "So, what is it I can do for you?"

Sharon kept the lift in her smile as she spoke to him, telling him the details of her article. She let her eyes widen a little as she told him of her intent to make an impact in the next election, to make sure that the baby killers were finally stopped. Not just in her state, but all across America.

"It's a sin, Senator," she said leaning forward. "How people see it as anything else is beyond me. I think the majority of voters are scared. Morally, they believe abortion is wrong, but they're afraid of what will happen. They think that if one right can be taken away, so can others."

Senator Listner brought his intertwined hands up near his face and slowly ran his knuckles back and forth against his chin, studying her, or so she thought.

"So, Miss Clark," he said after a moment's hesitation. "Where do you stand on women's rights? You have a career. You've made a choice. Aren't you afraid of losing *your* rights?"

Sharon expected this. She looked up at him and smiled. "I have all the rights I need. I chose to have a career first, to get a taste for what it's like to be on my own, but I know what my heart wants. I want what all woman want, to be a mother and wife, and fulfill my duty to God. As a matter of fact, this is my last assignment. That's why it's so important." Sharon sat back in her chair, looked down at the floor for a quick moment, then looked back up at the senator. "I'm going to get married this Fall."

"Well, I guess congratulations are in order. I'm sure you'll make a fine wife. I hope your future husband is as fair as you. I hate to see pure genes such as yours corrupted, like mine," he said, laughing as he pointed to his dusty brown hair.

No, Thomas didn't have her blonde hair and blue eyes. He didn't even have her white skin. And though Sharon wasn't about to tell Listner her boyfriend was black, she wasn't going to give him the satisfaction of thinking her Germanic genes were going to be passed on either.

"I had always hoped to," she said. "But I'm afraid Thomas has dark hair and dark eyes."

"What a shame," the senator said, unfolding his hands and leaning back in his chair. "So, tell me, what can I do to help your article along?"

Sharon reached down into her bag and pulled out her disk recorder. "Do you mind?" she asked.

"No, of course not."

Sharon turned the recorder on and placed it on his desk. "First of all Senator, I've been told you have a ninety percent approval rating.

Do you think this is in direct relation to your work in pushing for nationwide fetal rights?"

"Well," the senator said, smiling. "The abortion issue is only one of the things I've worked hard for, not necessarily the most important. I think the reason the voters have given me such a high approval rating is because of my earlier fights in Congress to amend Arizona's constitution and the enforcement of individual responsibility on citizens for a safer community. I also set up the State Posse system and developed a workable social welfare program."

"I've heard that," Sharon said as she looked down at the notes she had prepared for the interview. According to that list, he could be credited with many of the atrocities that were going on in this state.

"Now I'm fighting to reintroduce many of the issues that were given back to the states in the early part of the century and create National laws that uphold the majority of American's moral values."

"Such as personhood for the unborn child."

"Exactly. The abortion issue used to be just an individual cause. Fundamentalists fighting for the rights of the unborn. Now it's a state issue, or rather a National issue. How can we continue to survive as a unified country, Miss Clark, if we allow rebel states to allow legalized murder?"

Sharon shook her head as if absorbed in his litany.

"We can't," the senator continued. "The rift between the so called Free states and states like Arizona that follow an ethical moral code is growing wider each year. Free states harbor moral criminals at an alarming rate. Flocks of minorities and social and sexual degenerates have migrated to states like yours causing an unfair burden on each of your citizens. We need federal extradition laws so our enforcement officers can go into any state and bring back criminals to stand trial."

That was one of the things Southern Californians were fighting hardest against. They didn't want to give Religious states any rights within SoCal's borders. Twice Congress had tried to pass a similar bill, and both times it had been shot down, but the margin was narrowing with each election.

Sharon smiled uneasily. "Do you think that will pass Congress next time?"

Listner beamed. "If I have anything to do about it, it will. Even some of the Independents are seeing the need for us to join again as a nation and put a stop to the separatism.

"Not all laws need to be national, do they? Constitutionally the states are suppose to make their own decisions regarding many of the issues you want to take Nationally."

"That will be for the Supreme Court to decide. But I'm sure they'll see things our way. We desperately need National abortion laws to stop the illegal crossing of our borders for the purpose of killing children. And, we need a Federal ward system that will make sure all unwanted or uncared for children are maintained and raised in an environment that will guarantee the end of poverty and crime. Gratefully, people are beginning to see this and they're starting to come around."

"Southern Californians are hard headed when it comes to giving up their freedoms, Senator. I don't think they're going to readily support National laws on issues they've fought so hard to keep out of state law."

Listner smiled. "Take my word for it," he said. "By the next Presidential election, Americans will make the right choice. The Independent Party will be ousted and fall away just like the Republican Party. All that will be left are Moralists."

He leaned forward. "We may have to break our party into two separate factions, just to keep the country democratic for a while, but in the end we will accept only one form of rule, and I guarantee you Miss Clark, it will be God's rule."

"Praise Jesus," Sharon said with a smile.

"Indeed," the senator responded narrowing his eyes, and shaking his head slightly as if in disdain for her fanaticism.

Sharon wanted to laugh at is hypocrisy. He was nothing more than a political con artist who saw religion as the perfect harness. Control and conquer. Isn't that what religion had been used for throughout history? He was a smart man this Senator Listner, he knew manipulating the courts wasn't good enough, he needed to have complete control over the voters. And what better medium was there than their faith. A man like him could unite the country, and then just as easily destroy it.

"The Moralist party was an offshoot of the Republican party wasn't it?" Sharon asked.

"Yes," Listner said, sitting back up in his chair.

"Well, didn't the Republican party stand for small government, not big government? And didn't the Moralist party start out in that same venue?"

"Yes, we did."

"Then, why are you changing now?"

"Because we have to." Listner stood up and walked over to a large window. "We hate it, of course. We always have. But there are some things that can't be trusted to the individual states, not if we care about our fellow Americans. As a young girl, did you ever hear anyone speak of the AIDS internment camps?"

Sharon had. Her mother's older brother died in one of those camps, and though Sharon never met him, she had heard tearful stories about him from Granddad. "Isn't that where they rounded up all the people with the AIDS virus and put them in quarantined camps out in Wyoming?"

"Yes. Now some people," he said turning around towards her. "Some people called them death camps. And I guess that's what they were. But it couldn't be helped. There was no cure, and it was contagious. We tried setting up state systems, but they failed. They failed because some of the states that like to call themselves free are really bastions for the ungodly. Southern California is notorious for its leniency towards homosexuals and drug users. The only way we were going to combat the AIDS epidemic, is if we did it on a national level. I don't mind telling you, Miss Clark, that that was one of the mightiest movements seen in Congress and the Senate. Thank God, we had, by that time, acquired a Republican majority in both the House and the Senate to work with our President or we would still be in crisis today. By instituting mandatory AIDS testing, and the internment of anyone who tested positive for the HIV antibody, we were able to abolish the disease here in America almost completely in fifteen years. With aggressive testing at the borders, we have kept every American citizen safe. Quite the accomplishment, don't you think."

Sharon forced a small smile in acknowledgement. "So you think encamping women who threaten to abort their children will work like the AIDS internment camps. That it will wipe out abortion?"

Senator Listner smiled. "It's working too. Each year less and less women attempt abortions here in Arizona and fewer and fewer unmarried teen-age girls are getting pregnant. I'm the first to admit we're not one hundred percent yet, but we're getting there. Women are starting to take responsibility for their own lives, they are beginning to see the important role they play in society as mother and nurturer. We're very proud of what we're doing here. We've proven that it works. Now it's time to take our methods nationally. It's time to instill our moral ethics in those states who would rather trample on life than defend it."

"Even where the majority of voters are against it?"

Senator Listner walked over to the flag that hung on a tall brass pole and swept his hands down its fold. "Do they teach you the Pledge of Allegiance in Southern California schools?"

"Yes."

"I'm amazed. Do you know the words?"

"Yes," Sharon said, letting the short prose work its way through her memories. It had been a long time since she had said it, but she was sure she could recite it. "I pledge allegiance to the flag of the United States of American and to the Republic for which it stands, one nation under God…"

"There," he said turning around and pointing his finger at her. "One nation under God. One nation, not half a nation. We can't have only half our nation living under God's rule. Our country was founded under the Christian god, and I'll be damned if I'm going to let a few renegade states destroy us, regardless of what the majority wants. You, Miss Clark, you must take up the cause. Southern Californians must vote Moralist this November if our plan for a unified nation is to see fruition.

"If we want to remain the world leader our forefathers fought so hard to become, we must come to terms with who we are and what we are. To survive we must once again become *one* nation under God."

One nation under God? A phrase that hadn't been added to the Pledge Of Allegiance until the nineteen fifties. God had been an afterthought, not an originating ideal. Sharon doubted Listner knew this, and if he did, he probably wouldn't admit it.

"One nation, indivisible," Sharon repeated in what she hoped was a dreamy voice. "It's going to be a hard fight."

"All worthwhile battles are," Listner said.

"I believe if we trust God's words to guide us, we'll win," Sharon said.

"That's the attitude." Senator Listner's stance seemed to relax. "The country needs more women like you, Miss Clark. I think they're out there too. I think most women understand the necessity for these laws and though they don't support their loss of rights, in their hearts they're anxious for the decision to be taken from them. Only then will they be free to return to their natural duties."

Sharon smiled up at him, hoping her fangs weren't showing. *Change the subject*, she warned herself.

"Another big issue is the children, she said. "Southern Californians don't like the idea of a state ward system. We've heard terrible rumors of the mental state of the children who graduate from your state schools. Some, we've heard, have been forced to undergo involuntary sterilization." Sharon watched his face for signs of acknowledgment. If he knew this was happening, he'd be as much to blame as the ones doing it. He oversaw these schools, that gave him culpability.

Senator Listner laughed and returned to his desk. "Our state homes offer excellent care and career training to all the children we take under our wing. And don't forget these are unwanted children. Children whose parents couldn't or wouldn't care for them. Some states, when the welfare systems shut down, abandoned these kids. Not us. We understood who would be our future. We knew who would guide us into the middle of the century. We've put an awful lot of money into providing for these kids. You tell your readers, Miss Clark, that the minute Southern California can claim there are no children dying in their streets, no runaway girls prostituting themselves, and no gangs replacing the family unit, then they can come and criticize our system. But until then, we offer no apology for how we run them. Besides, talk to any child whose been raised by the system. They'll tell you they thank God for the state. They love the state, and there isn't anything they wouldn't do for it."

Good little soldiers. "But what about the sterilization? How do you justify that?"

Senator Listner walked away from her and returned to the window. "Sterilization is used in only a few rare cases. We do enforce hormone treatment for the boys to lower their levels of testosterone. But we do that for their own good. We're not like some states who believe you can keep a lid on premarital sex. Sure we have our laws, but we don't actually believe we can enforce them, so we safeguard our children until they are old enough, mature enough, to make appropriate decisions."

Sharon didn't say anything. She kept her pen poised over her notebook.

Listner turned and looked at her. He sighed and sat back down behind his desk.

"As for actual sterilization, that is a form of punishment. Punishment for women who have tried to kill their unborn children and for men who can't seem to control their lusts and perpetually force themselves on women. We've had a few cases in the schools where we've had to that that, but they are very rare. And let me point out before you even ask, we're not out to use sterilization, as many of our critics have claimed, to wipe out any race. We see a place for everyone in our society and look toward a future of continued ethnic diversity."

Sharon hadn't expected such honesty. She thought he would have denied it, but then he did cover his bases. He admitted to it, just in case she had some proof, and then he justified it. He was good.

"Is mandatory birth control something else you hope to take nationally?" She asked.

"Yes. Though we think our ward system is one of the greatest in the country, we would much rather have children raised by loving, caring parents. In the beginning we believed that abstinence training was the way to go, but that proved a huge failure. Nothing personal, but girls give in too easy. So, to protect them from their own weaknesses, we're proposing legislature that would require all women be put on birth control at the onset of menses and to remain on it until they are married and can show financial stability. It is then, when a man and a woman can financially and emotionally support their children before having them, that we'll be able to abolish poverty and return the raising of children to the family where it belongs."

"Sounds a little utopian, don't you think?" Sharon asked.

Listner leaned forward. There was that smile again. The one she couldn't tell if it meant she were giving away her true feelings or if he thought she was stupid.

"No, not at all. Texas instituted a similar program two years ago and is having great success. What we need to do is raise America's consciousness to the importance of controlled propagation. We need everyone to understand that if we're going to continue to be the world leader, economically, that we need to stop wasting money on reactionary social programs and put it, instead, into building a financially secure American empire."

With you as dictator? "What about the Constitution?" She asked. There are rumors the Moralists want to ratify the 19th..."

The computer on the senator's desk beeped. He held up his hand to silence her as he read his incoming message.

"I'm afraid we'll have to end here, Miss Clark. My next appointment has arrived. If you have more questions, you'll have to schedule another visit with my secretary."

Though Sharon wanted to hear him deny Moralists wanted to take the right to vote away from women, she was glad to end the interview. Politicians were too hard to break. They practiced their speeches, debated their ideas, and honed their interview skills, giving nothing away. She thought that if she let him continue, he would have her agreeing with him on many issues. But that was his job, wasn't it? Hers was to manipulate his words in a way not to promote his views, but to use them to instill fear in Southern California voters. To show them what he saw as positive action on the part of the state was detrimental to personal freedom and what she, in her short life had decided was the backbone of American society. But he didn't need to know that. He needed to think she was on his side, more now that she decided to help Anthony and Martha. She smiled at him.

"I think I've got enough for now. You're a very ambitious man," she said. "I wish we had someone like you fighting for us in Southern California."

"You could," Senator Listner, said walking over to the door. "I know both Baxter and Montgomery. They're men with similar visions. All you have to do is get people out to vote.

"Well," Sharon said reaching over, turning off her recorder, and putting it back in her bag. "I'll do my best, sir."

"I'm sure you will. Now if you'll excuse me. I have someone waiting."

Sharon shook the senator's hand and thanked him for his time before stepping out of his office. A tall lanky man, stood with his back towards her.

"Nathan, how good to see you," the senator said as she left the office.

20

Sharon returned, with another bag of groceries and a few magazines, to the motel where Martha and Anthony were hiding. She had not engaged the GPS inhibitor. If they were watching her, they would know she had rented a room at the hotel. She would have to come up with an excuse why she needed another room, but it was safer to let them think they knew what she was up to, then to let them find inconsistencies in her banking and movements.

Anthony still had a fever, but it was mild compared to the night before. Martha had cleaned his wounds and changed the bandages twice during the day. She seemed very attentive. When the boy woke up, he'd have his sister to thank for saving his life.

Martha hovered over her brother, adjusting his covers again and again. Every few seconds she'd look up at the muted TV. Sharon sat in the side chair and watched the girl. Martha's hands were shaking.

"Is something wrong?" Sharon finally asked.

Martha looked over at her. She didn't say anything. She picked Anthony's already folded clothes up off the foot of the bed and refolded them. Sharon remembered the day of her grandfather's funeral, and how she had to hold back the tears and be strong when all she wanted was for someone to hold her, to console her. She stood up and walked over to Martha. Gently she turned the girl around and pulled her into her chest.

"Martha. If something's wrong, you need to tell me. We're in this together, you know."

"I know," Martha said in a low voice.

"Then what is it?" Sharon pushed the girl away a few inches and took her hands into her own.

Martha opened her mouth to speak then pulled away quickly. "There," she said pointing at the TV. Sharon turned and looked. The screen was split in two. On one half there was a picture of Martha, on the other, one of Anthony. Below their ID photo's was an eight hundred number for people to call. Sharon reached up and raised the volume.

"The Garcia children are still thought to be in the Phoenix/Scottsdale area. If anyone has any information to their whereabouts, please call Child Services. Do not try and apprehend them yourselves. The boy, Anthony Garcia, is considered dangerous." A man's voice-over said.

Sharon turned the TV off and looked down at the sleeping boy. He didn't look dangerous. "You knew this would happen. Didn't you?" she asked Martha.

Martha sat on the bed. "Yeah, I suppose I did. But, I didn't think they would make us out to be criminals. We'll never get out now. No one will help us."

"I'm working on that," Sharon told her. "My boss is making arrangements for IDs. Once we get them, we'll smuggle you out, somehow. There's got to be a way."

"You don't know how they are here," Martha said. "If anyone sees us, they'll call that number."

"I know," Sharon said. She was worried too. IDs weren't going to do much good when the kids' faces were so well known. Everyone would be looking for a brother and sister, they would be caught the minute they stepped out of the motel room.

"That's it," Sharon said.

Martha didn't respond.

Sharon smiled, she loved it when she had an idea. "What if we turn Anthony into a girl?"

Martha looked at Sharon. "A girl? I don't get it. What good will that do?"

"Don't you see? They'll be looking for a sister and brother, not two girls. We'll get a couple of wigs, so you each look different from the photos they're showing, and then get new ID pictures taken. You'll be able to drive out of the state. All we'll have to do is rent a car, and out you go. Piece of cake."

"Do you think it will work?" Martha asked.

Sharon bent down and gave the girl another hug. "Why not? You're just runaways. They aren't going to be combing the streets for you. That ad is probably just routine.."

Martha nodded her head in quick multi-movements as if the truth to all life's questions had just been absorbed. Then her shoulders fell and her smile disappeared. "What about your friend Madison?" she asked.

Sharon stood up and laughed. Nothing got by this girl. "You're not pregnant are you?" she asked.

Martha's eyes narrowed. "No," she said, harshly.

Sharon heard the contempt behind Martha's answer and decided to ignore it. There was so much more to this girl than Sharon had seen previously. There was bitterness and hate that Martha would have to learn to get over or at least control if she was ever to find peace in her life. Sharon could only do so much, though. She'd help the kids get out of the state, then they were on their own. Foster mother, she wasn't. Sharon smiled and let out a short chuckle as if making a joke.

"And I don't expect your brother is, so there's no problem." The tension in Martha's face relaxed. Sharon picked up the pace of her voice, hoping her enthusiasm would be contagious. "I'm telling you Martha, the ID they got for me has passed each time. These are quality fakes. It will work. All we have to do is keep you two hidden until the cards are ready."

Martha looked up at the blank TV screen, then at Anthony. Sharon could tell she wasn't sold on the idea, but it was the only plan they had and it would have to do for now.

"Well?" Sharon asked after a few minutes of silence.

Martha lay down on the bed next to her brother and closed her eyes. "I'll do whatever it takes," she said.

21

Sharon left Martha and Anthony alone to go back to her hotel to get ready for her date with Paul Matthews. She couldn't get the picture of Anthony and Martha's faces on the television out of her mind. She tried to put herself in the girl's shoes and imagine what it had been like living under the conditions at the state home, then finding your brother half dead and having no where to take him. Being a fugitive was just added angst. Martha was holding up pretty well, even if she hadn't given Sharon a thumbs up for her idea on getting them out of the state.

Sharon pulled up to a gas station and called Derek with the changes she wanted to make to the IDs. He said he'd do the best he could, but made no promises about getting new pictures taken or when she'd have them. It wasn't exactly what she wanted to hear, but it was better than no.

At the hotel, there were no new messages. Thomas hadn't tried to reach her. Paul hadn't called to cancel. She didn't know how she felt about that, but she wasn't disappointed. It was best not to talk to Thomas, and though she knew she shouldn't be going out on dates, she hadn't wanted Paul to cancel. She thought about the two of them, comparing them, as she took the elevator up to her floor and fished for her ID to unlock the door.

It felt good to be back in her room. She plopped herself down on the bed and stretched out. What she really could use was some sleep, or some other type of relaxing exertion. She couldn't help wonder what it would be like to have Paul Matthews between her legs. She closed her legs, and pushed the thought aside.

She had never cheated on Thomas, had never even considered cheating on Thomas, but then she'd never met a man like Paul Matthews before, not outside her fantasies, that was.

"I should cancel," she said out loud, but to herself. "Too late for that," she laughed back. "Okay, but no funny business.

"No," she said more sternly. "I respect Thomas too much for that.

"Okay, then," she continued. "Go, have a good time, and come home."

It was settled. She would explain to Paul that she was planning on returning to Southern California and that any future relationship was out of the question. But, she would save that little speech for the end of the evening. No use spoiling the only good time she might have while stuck in Arizona.

She had brought the perfect black dress with her, just in case. Not that she expected to be asked out, or invited to a party, but you never knew, and she didn't want to be caught off guard. She took the dress from her suitcase and steamed out the wrinkles. It was made of a silky lycra fabric that felt like satin, fit tightly, and moved with her.

Standing in front of the mirror in her bra and underwear, she checked her profile. Her stomach seemed a little bloated. She redid her hair neatly in a French twist then turned sideways again. Using her hand she pushed in her stomach. It was only a slight pooch, Paul would never notice, but she did. Too much fast food. She'd have to hit the gym when she got home.

She put on the dress and checked her stomach. It was rounded, not flat like she preferred, but she didn't mind. It gave her figure a fuller, sexier look. Besides, the ruby necklace and bracelet Thomas had given her for her last birthday would draw attention away from her bloated belly and back up to her neck and face.

There was a knock on the door at exactly eight. She opened the door and blushed. Paul was wearing black trousers and a white shirt unbuttoned at the neck. She had overdressed, over estimated the date.

"I'm so embarrassed," she said trying to hide the disappointment. "Give me a minute, and I'll change."

"Nonsense," Paul said taking her arms and drawing them up. "You look beautiful. I didn't know what you would expect, so I came prepared. My coat and tie are in the car."

He was a man who thought ahead, a man who presumed nothing.

He was becoming more perfect with each meeting.

Paul took her to a quiet restaurant in Old Scottsdale. It was in the center of what seemed like a miniature mall catering to high priced specialty shops. The maitre'd showed them to a table in the back of the dining area. Waiters, dressed in coat tails, took their order. A three-piece orchestra played on a small stage. The prices were high, the wine aged.

"This is lovely," Sharon said looking around at the old Spanish style architecture. "Do you come here often?"

"On my salary, are you kidding? No. I save this for special occasions, when I really want to impress someone."

"Oh," Sharon smiled. "Trying to impress me are you?"

"Thought I'd give it a shot." Paul reached over and took her hands in his. "Is it working?"

A shot of electricity swept through Sharon's body along with an urge to tear off all her clothing. "Well," she said. "it's not a bad start. But you realize, I'm going back home in a week or two. This may turn out to be a waste of money."

Paul smiled. "I don't think so."

Though the knot in her groin never diminished, she was able to tell Paul her Arizona version of the truth, about who she was and what she was doing in his state. He told her that his parents had come from Massachusetts when he was a teenager and that he had never gotten used to the religious slant of Arizona law. He wasn't very political, had no stand on abortion rights, and hoped one day to return to Massachusetts. But for now, he liked his job. Posse members were a little hard to control at times, he explained. They liked to take the law into their own hands when in reality their jobs were to assist deputies and to help with surveillance.

He was easy to talk to and enjoyable to be with. If she were ever to leave Thomas for another man, this would be him. He was handsome, articulate, and yet had a sense of vulnerability about him that endeared her to him. She felt bad that so much of what she told him about herself were lies, but she couldn't help it. Even though her body and heart wanted to deny it, her mind couldn't – he was a cop, an Arizona cop. She'd be a fool to trust him.

After dinner they went to a nightclub in an office building.

"It's Arizona's version of a speak easy," Paul told her. "Though wine is still legal and they can't keep the opposite sexes apart, one of the Posse's duties is to harass legal establishments enough to discourage them. Many of the hottest spots have taken to moving from one week to the next. Kind of like the old Rave parties."

Sharon nodded her head. Her mother had been to plenty of those Rave parties. That's where she had picked up many of her addictions. This place seemed to be at a higher class than the outdoor events her mother had described.

The club was packed. There were no tables to sit at, no empty bar stools. Paul got them each a glass of wine and they stood by a metal support beam watching the sexual innuendo's being exchanged by the hoards of sweaty, sexy men and women hoping to break the law and not go home alone.

"Is it too loud?" Paul asked.

"What," she yelled into his ear. She couldn't hear anything. The music, the cacophony of voices and laughter absorbed his words.

"Is it too loud?" he yelled back. "Do you want to go somewhere else?"

No, she didn't want to go anywhere else, this was perfect. She took his glass of wine, put it on a small ledge along with her own and dragged him to the dance floor.

At first he shook his head, then he gave himself over to the music and they swayed in unison. The wine had loosened her. The music seduced her. She was caught up in the evening and being with him. All she could think of was touching and being touched. Thomas became a vague memory.

She pulled the pins that held up her hair and suggestively shook it out so it fell to her shoulders. Rubbing her body against Paul's, she reached up and put her hands around his neck. He pulled her close, and they danced as one. She wanted his hands to climb from her hips to work up towards her chest, but she did nothing to prompt him. The music slowed and he pulled her closer. She put her head on his shoulder, his left hand dipped and rested at the bottom curve of her ass. She could feel him getting hot, but didn't pull away. He lifted her head by her chin and kissed her. It was a kiss she would never forget. She thought she would come right there on the dance floor if the music didn't end, but it did.

"I think I should take you home," he whispered in her ear.

She kissed him again. "I think you better."

The drive back to her hotel room gave her time to cool down. Paul kept his hands to himself, and she was able to put things back into perspective. She had never wanted anyone as bad as she did Paul Matthews, but she couldn't ask him to join her in her room. Maybe she needed to re-evaluate her relationship with Thomas, but until then, she would not betray him.

Paul held her hand tightly as he walked her to her room. When they reached her door, he reached over and kissed her again. She was about to tell him about Thomas, to apologize for how she had acted when he said, "I need to go."

Relieved, she kissed him back. "I know."

"How about brunch tomorrow morning? I could pick you up at ten."

No, her inner voice demanded. "Brunch" she said accepting his invitation.

Sharon pulled her ID from her small clutch bag and opened her door, her hand shook. Paul put his hand over hers and helped her slide the card through. He kissed her neck as she opened the door.

"Tomorrow?" he asked.

"Tomorrow," she agreed.

He stepped her into her room and kissed her again. His hands worked their way up from her waist to her chest. One hand moved under her arm to the small of her back and pulled her against his body. His other hand rested on her breast slightly beneath the edge of her dress, one finger brushed her nipple. Sharon could feel moisture forming between her thighs, she pushed her groin tighter in against his erection, her hand found the waist of his pants. Paul pulled away.

"I'll see you at ten," he said then backed up and closed the door.

Sharon just about collapsed to the floor.

She pulled off her dress and under things, threw them in a chair, and fell back, naked, on her bed. It was too big for one person. She pulled the extra pillow towards her and cuddled up to it. She could still feel Paul's hand moving up her body, his warm lips on hers. Sexually she was on fire. She reached down and let her fingers massage and prolong the feelings Paul had initiated, but the man in her fantasy, the man whose name she called out when she came was Thomas'.

22

Martha lay on the bed next to her brother. His breathing was easy and steady. The fever had broken, and she had got a few hours sleep. Throughout the night, she gently nudged him from dreams that caused him to whimper. Once, she was woken by his screams. She held him and rocked him, and though he didn't wake, he held on to her.

Sharon hadn't come back. She had explained her date to Martha and made no promises of when she would return. Martha didn't doubt she would. Sharon may be no better than Barbara Sanders, she had a mission to fulfill and was not about to jeopardize it for them, but like Barbara she seemed to genuinely care. Yes, Martha decided, Sharon could be trusted.

Martha wasn't sure Sharon's plan for their escape would work. It seemed too risky to be seen in public, even with disguises, but Martha didn't have a better idea. They couldn't stay in the hotel room forever. She looked over at her brother, he deserved to be free. He had fought to hard for his freedom. She owed it to him to get him out of the state. She'd go along with Sharon and try for the border. Maybe it would work. Anthony didn't really have any distinguishing characteristics that couldn't be softened with makeup. He'd be able to pass for a girl, and with a wig, she might be able to alter her looks enough that a white Posse member wouldn't be able to tell her from any other young

Mexican woman. For once in her life, racial stereotypes were going to work in her favor.

Anthony stirred, and rolled over towards her. She brushed his hair from his eyes. He was beautiful. His skin was a light brown without blemish, his eyes and hair almost black. Long lashes accented the prepubescent roundness of his face and the fullness of his lips. Her mother had always said he had kissable lips. Martha had never noticed before, but now she saw it. They seemed pouty. She reached over and kissed him gently. "Get well," she said then lay down on her side of the bed.

She thought of the wounds that scarred his back and wondered what he could have done to merit such punishment. They were new. Had they been the reason he had run? Or, had he received them for trying to escape earlier? And what about his testicles? What could have happened to cause them to take such severe action against him? Sara, her friend at Living Trust, had told her about some of the other wards who had been "fixed," but they were problem kids, kids who masturbated or had been caught alone with a member of the opposite sex. Anthony wouldn't have fallen into either of those categories, would he?

Anthony slowly opened his eyes and looked over at his sister's face. "Martha," he said.

"I'm here. You're safe now." She sat up and kissed him on the forehead.

"Martha," he cried. He reached up for her and wrapped his arms around her. "Martha, I was so scared."

"I know. I know. But we're safe now. You're going to be okay, and we're safe." Martha pried her brother from her. "You still need to rest though. Go back to sleep."

Anthony tried to pull himself up, winced at the pain in his back and lay back down. "My back's bad, isn't it?"

Martha nodded her head. "We stopped the infection, but the cuts are still raw. What happened?"

Anthony looked around the room. "Is there someone else here?"

"No. There's a woman helping us, but she's not here right now. She'll be back later. She's going to help us get out of Arizona."

Anthony grabbed Martha's arm. "They can't find us, Martha. I can't go back there."

"I know," she said pulling his hand off her arm. "We'll be safe as long as we stay in this room and wait for Sharon. No one's seen us."

The boy relaxed and stared up at the ceiling. "How long have we been here?"

"Not long. This is our second night. You were pretty sick when I found you. Do you remember anything?"

"Running," he said. "I remember running, but that's it. How'd you find me?"

"You went to the church. The woman I worked for had someone drive me there after we found out you escaped. You were hiding in the balcony."

"They told me I'd never see you again," he said. Tears ran down the side of his face. "They told me you could have come and gotten me, but you didn't want to. I never believed them Martha, I never believed them."

"I know," she said reaching over and brushing the tears away. "They told me horrible things too, but it's over Anthony, it's over. We found each other, and they're not going to separate us again."

"But if they find us?"

"They aren't going to find us. Now go back to sleep. You need to rest."

Anthony closed his eyes, squinting away the tears. "I have to pee," he whispered.

Martha reached over to the nightstand and grabbed a wide mouth bottle that had held ice tea and handed it to him. "Here, use this," she said, not telling him that she had helped him pee in it a few times when she had seen him clutching himself in his sleep.

Anthony took the bottle from her and dragged it under the covers. Martha looked away as the first splash of urine hit the glass. A few seconds later the flow stopped and she turned back around to take the warm spillage to the bathroom and dump it. When she returned Anthony was crying again.

"It's all right," she said. "Everything's all right."

"Where are my clothes?" he asked.

"They were filthy, Anthony, we had to take them off. You were so sick, and your fever was too high. We gave you an ice bath to cool you down. Don't worry about it."

"Did you see?"

Martha knew what he was talking about and nodded her head. "It's okay. It's not that big a deal."

Anthony turned his head. "They said I didn't need them. They said boys were better off without them." Anthony turned back toward her. "That's not true, is it Martha? Boy's are suppose to have them, aren't they?"

Martha couldn't help the tears that ran down her face. "Yes," she said nodding her head. "Boys are supposed to have them, but you can still be a man without them."

Anthony looked away again. "I ain't going to live long enough to be a man. That's what the guards told me. They said boys like me end up dead before they're sixteen."

Don't say things like that," Martha yelled at him. "We're going to get out of here, Anthony. You aren't going to go back there, I promise. I promise."

"I can't go back," he whispered then closed his eyes.

Martha didn't think he was really asleep, but knew he wanted to be left alone. She would find out about the beating later. She moved over to the armchair and picked up one of the magazines. She fought the scream that ached to be released and brushed away the tears.

23

Paul picked Sharon up at ten-thirty. She had dressed casually for this date, shorts and light green tank top. Her hair was pulled back with one of the headbands, not because she assumed she'd be taking pictures of Paul, but because they were a part of her expected wardrobe. She had come to terms with her relationship with Paul. Brunch would be their last date. It had to be, she was too drawn him. He was a nice man, but her attraction to him seemed more sexual, lustful, than it did intellectual. She didn't know him and she didn't have time to get to know him. Her love for Thomas came from mutual admiration and respect built over the years. She did not intend to jeopardize that for a good night of sex.

Paul took her to a small restaurant at the far east side of McDowell road. It was in the center of an orange grove, with a small duck pond. They took a table out on the verandah closest to the pond. Mist floated down from the lattice of pipes on the roof, cooling the air. At first, the strong scent of orange blossoms was overwhelming, but it didn't take long for Sharon to grow accustomed to the heavy perfume and enjoy it. The rustling of duck feathers caught her attention, and she turned to watch a mother duck with seven ducklings stepping out of the water and onto the bank of the pond.

The waitress brought champagne and took their order. Paul ordered eggs, toast, and sausages, Sharon opted for the small stack of strawberry topped pancakes. She was about to tell Paul how beautiful the morning was when he asked if she'd had a good time the night before.

"A great time," she responded with a slight conspiratorial smile. "And you?"

He reached over and took her hands in his. The butterflies that overtook her stomach were less than they had been the night before, but they were still there. Sharon didn't really believe she'd ever get over Paul Matthews. Once she went home, he'd turn from a life long fantasy into *a could have been* longing. Life didn't seem fair.

"It was wonderful," Paul said. "Do you think we can do it again, while you're here, maybe next Friday night?"

Sharon wanted to say no. She had planned on saying no, but instead she blushed and said, "I'd love to."

Paul squeezed her hand in his. "I'm so glad those kids stole your purse," he said. "Meeting you has been... Well, I mean..." Now it was Paul's turn to blush. His face turned a crimson red. "I'm sorry, it's just I haven't met a woman like you before. I mean... I don't know what I mean, I just know I want to see more of you."

Sharon couldn't help becoming caught up in his amorous stuttering. "I know what you mean," she said. "I feel the same the way, but Paul, this can't go any further. I'm going back to California. I can't stay here."

"I know," he said rubbing the top of her hand. "I'd go with you, but..."

"No, let's just have a nice time together today and then say goodbye. I can't get caught up in a relationship right now. I've got a story to get and..." She wanted to tell him, but she couldn't. She looked at him. He was gorgeous and wonderful, but she'd leave it at no. "I have commitments I can't get out of," she said.

"Oh." Paul pulled his hands away. "I understand. Friends then, we'll keep it at that."

"Friends," Sharon agreed, grateful she wouldn't be in Arizona too long. A platonic friendship with Paul Matthews wasn't something she believed possible.

Paul looked down at his watch. "Well then, as friends, I was wondering if you'd mind if I stopped by tomorrow or Tuesday. I have something I want to talk to you about."

That was odd. Sharon cocked her head to the side, not much, just enough to show her confusion. "Sure you can stop by, but why not ask me now?"

"No, I don't want to spoil the morning."

Sharon smiled. Nothing could spoil the morning. "You won't. Ask."

Paul straightened in his seat. "Are you sure?"

Sharon nodded her head. Maybe he was married, or involved with someone. But now that they had decided to keep their relationship at a friendship level, why would he feel compelled to tell her?

"I went through your notes, remember?"

"Yeah," she said. Her heart sped up. He had read her notes. Had there been something incriminating in them that he was willing to overlook while he thought they might be more than friends, but now he wanted explanations? "That's what you told me," she said. Her previous smile turned downward. There was a small quake in her voice. How easily relationships twist.

"Well, something in them really bothered me. I know one of the women you met at the prison. She's an old girlfriend."

That was not what she expected him to say. "Really, who?" A lover, a wife, that would be understandable, but an old girlfriend. Why would he care about an old girlfriend? Sharon's heart sank. Was he the father of one of those unwanted babies?

"Madison Courtney," he said.

"Madison Courtney?" Sharon pushed back her chair almost falling backwards. Of all the women at the prison, how could he be connected to Madison Courtney? The only woman there that Sharon cared the least bit about.

"You remember her then?"

Sharon's guard went up. Had the fantasy been a scam? Had she and Madison been set up from the start? Maybe it hadn't been chance that she had seen Madison being arrested. Hell, for as far as Sharon knew, Madison could have been a set up too. Sharon felt foolish. She didn't know who to trust, but she could play this game too. She could feed into his story and dig out what she needed at the same time. Right now what she needed was answers.

"Madison said she had broken up with her boyfriend over six months ago. Was that you?"

Paul looked down at the table. "Yeah. I guess it was about then. We had been dating for a few months when all of a sudden, out of nowhere, she tells me she can't see me anymore."

Sharon took a sip of her champagne, looking at him over the glass, pretending she wasn't as interested as she really was. "Did she say why?"

"No. I tried asking her brother, but he said he didn't understand it either."

Sharon put down the glass. "Well, she said she was conducting classes and that the state wasn't too pleased with her. Maybe she was afraid of getting you in trouble." *Or you turning her in to the Posse.*

"I thought of that, even convinced myself of that, but deep down, I've always felt it was more."

"Did you love her?" Sharon asked.

Paul smiled. "No. Infatuated, maybe. You met her, she's beautiful and very confident. She intrigued me more than anything. I'm over it now," he said reaching for Sharon's hand again and smiling. Sharon wanted to pull her hand away but didn't.

"It's just that I was surprised to see her name in your notes," he continued. "It had the words, not pregnant next to it. What does that mean, Sharon? She has to be pregnant or why else would she be there?"

His interest seemed genuine. It felt good to know he hadn't loved Madison, and to think that maybe he had known the woman. Sharon's entrapment theories were nothing more than paranoia. But if he didn't love Madison, besides just curiosity, why was he was so interested, unless it was to confirm his belief in the judicial system. Obviously he couldn't handle thinking that Madison had been imprisoned unfairly. He was looking for validation. He didn't want to believe the people he worked for were corrupt. Well he was wrong, and Sharon decided he should know it.

"She said she was set up. You knew her. Would she lie?"

Paul hesitated for a moment. "Not the Madison I knew. She believed strongly in people taking responsibility for their own actions. But it doesn't make any sense. Why would they set her up?"

"You tell me. She said she ran some kind of school that taught self-empowerment to young girls. I can see how that would land her in prison."

Paul shook his head. "Maybe," he said, but not Arpaio. That place is strictly for women who try to abort their fetuses. I may have only known Madison for a short time, but I know she wouldn't have done that. She loved kids, her life was dedicated to helping them."

Sharon could feel herself believing him, believing in him. Maybe he could help Madison, pull some strings to get at the truth. "She was positive she wasn't pregnant. She said she hadn't been with anyone since her last boyfriend, which I guess was you. She figures they are either going to induce some kind of hemorrhaging and say she miscarried or impregnate her."

"That's impossible. That's not how it works," Paul said too loud. He stopped for a minute and looked around the verandah. Sharon looked with him. No one seemed interested in their conversation. "The prisons are for women who try to abort babies," he said in a softer voice. "They would never get away with something like that."

Sharon wanted to laugh. How little he knew about his state. "No?" Well that's not all, Paul. The warden told me they think her brother's the father. They want to do a paternity test. So as I see it, they're probably going to cause some kind of hemorrhaging and then discredit her by claiming it was her brother's baby."

"No," Paul said. "That's not the way it works." He looked out over the duck pond.

He was still in love with Madison. *He used me to find out about her.* It was all right though. Sharon had used him too. It was time to leave. She covered her food with her napkin and looked around for their waitress so she could get their check and go home.

"I don't know what to say," Paul finally said looking back at her. "I've heard things, but I never wanted to believe them. I don't know what I can do to help her. I'm county. She's in a state facility."

"Well," Sharon said waving the waitress down. "She did want me to get word to her brother that she was okay. Maybe you can do that."

"Sure. I'll go over there. I haven't seen him in a while, but we were always friendly."

"Check, please," she said to the waitress, then turned her attention back to Paul. "Well, he may not be at home. The warden said that he had been released, but that they planned on charging him with incest as soon as the tests were done. If he knows about it, for his sake, I hope he fled the state."

"This gets worse by the moment," Paul said. He looked at her while the waitress summed the ticket and Sharon handed the waitress her ID card. "I'll get that," Paul said.

"No, it's my turn," she said picking up her bag.

Paul looked down at his watch, then back at her. "You're mad at me, aren't you? I told you I wanted this to wait. Sharon, you have to believe me when I say my feelings towards you have nothing to do with Madison. In the few months I was with her, I never felt the way I do with you. Damn! I'm sorry."

Sharon's anger faded, but not her suspicion. "It's all right, really. I just need to get going. I have interviews set up for today. I think you should take me back to my hotel."

"I will. Just give me a chance to make this up to you. Waitress." Paul held up his hand. "More champagne, please." The waitress gave him a quick almost irritated glance then brought over the bottle and filled their glasses. "Tell me more about you. You don't act like a zealot. Why are you so adamant about the abortion issue?"

Sharon took a sip of her champagne and relaxed. What would a few moments or a few more lies matter. "Well," she said. "You don't have to be a Fundamentalist to believe abortion is wrong. Personally, I believe in birth control. I think that a fetus has rights at the time of conception and aborting it is murder, pure and simple. I'm not on a religious crusade, though I admit I put it on thick when I'm with religious people as a means of getting them to open up to me."

"Kind of a ruse, huh?"

"Kind of, but it's not like it's a total lie. I believe in God and I uphold Christian morals, most of them at least," she said offering him a sly suggestive smile.

"I guess I'm about the same," he said smiling back at her. "Except, I like strong women. I don't think I could ever love a woman whose only ambition was to stay home to cook and clean. The monotony of her life would drive me crazy."

He was a single rose in a tangle of thorns. She couldn't help wanting him, but the risks were too high. "I think we should go now," she said in a soft voice, pushing her champagne off to the side.

Paul looked down at his watch again. "Yeah, I guess maybe we should."

Sharon tried not to think of Paul as they drove home. Instead she went over the things she needed to buy for Anthony and Martha. New clothes, wigs, more bandages, purses, makeup. She remembered the small wig shop she had seen in Old Scottsdale by Simon's beauty parlor. She would go there.

She looked out the window at the barren street. It was odd that such a large stretch of road between Apache Junction and Scottsdale would be left undeveloped. There was dirt, a few low thorny looking bushes, and trash. Halfway between the restaurant and the first sign of civilization, she saw smoke. "What's that?" she asked pointing to what looked like a car burning in a ditch up ahead.

"I don't know," Paul said. He sped up and stopped thirty feet behind the car – a black Cadillac. Pulling the trunk release, Paul quickly opened his door. "Call for help, then grab a blanket and the fire extinguisher out of the trunk. But don't come too close, it could blow."

Sharon pushed the phone activation button and ordered 911. The phone rang and a dispatcher quickly answered. "911, is there an emergency?"

"Yes," Sharon said watching Paul as he ran up to the car. The day had already reached at least one hundred degrees, and the flames seemed disjointed as she looked through the rippling haze of heat. "There's a car on fire, possibly people inside. We're on the north side of McDowell, a few miles west of Power Road. Detective Paul Matthews of the Maricopa Sheriff's Department is at the scene."

"Fire engine and ambulance is on the way, Ma'am, could I please have your ID…"

Sharon didn't listen for more. She could see Paul pulling someone out of the back seat of the car. Quickly she got out and grabbed the blanket and fire extinguisher from the trunk. The Cadillac looked familiar, but it couldn't be. She ran harder. When she reached Paul and looked down fear seized her. It was Helen. Blood flowed from the her stomach and left shoulder. Sharon started to call her by name, then stopped herself, she wouldn't be able to explain knowing the woman, instead Sharon put down the extinguisher and took Helen from him.

"Get her to my car. I'm going back for the driver." Paul picked up the fire extinguisher and ran back towards the burning vehicle. Sharon was half carrying half dragging Helen as fast as she could. Paul looked back. "Put pressure on the wounds and get that blanket around her," he yelled.

Flames shot up from the hood of the car. Paul reached for the door handle then jerked his hand away. He pulled off his shirt and used it to hold on to the door handle, then he disappeared inside the car.

"Be careful," Sharon called to him. She lowered Helen to the ground next to Paul's car. The wounds weren't clean, they seemed as though they had been singed. Helen coughed, her eyes stayed closed. "Helen, Helen," Sharon called to the woman, keeping one eye on Paul the other on the dying woman.

Helen reached up and grabbed Sharon by the shirt. "Sharon?"

"It's me. We found your car. What happened?"

"I don't know. We were coming back from. Ugh." Her hand reached down and covered her stomach. "an errand my husband had sent me on. A white van pulled up and started shooting." Her eyes went wide. "Robert, is Robert okay?"

"I don't know," Sharon said. "Paul's getting him now." Sharon saw Paul pull the body of the chauffeur a few feet from the car and drop it. He grabbed the extinguisher, aimed it at the hood of the car, and sprayed. The flames diminished after a few seconds, but Sharon knew they were probably still alive beneath the hood. Paul threw the extinguisher onto the ground, and went back to Robert. He picked him up under the shoulders and dragged him back to where Helen and Sharon waited then lay him down on the ground in front of the car, outside Helen's view. Paul bent over the boy for a few minutes, then looked up at Sharon and shook his head. Robert was dead.

"How's she?" Paul asked as he walked over and knelt down beside Helen. He pulled back Sharon's hands and examined the wounds.

"It's bad," Sharon told him. "Help is on the way."

"Good. Mrs. Sanders, Mrs. Sanders can you hear me?"

Helen turned her gaze from Sharon to Paul and nodded her head. "An ambulance is on the way. You're going to be okay." He took Sharon's hands and placed them back over the bullet holes. "Keep pressure on these. I'll be right back." Paul ran to the back of his car and came back with a first aid kit. "I don't know what good this stuff will do, but we've got to control the bleeding until the ambulance arrives. He took bandages and gauze and put them under Sharon's hands. "Lie still," he told the woman, then sat down on the ground next to them.

"You know her?" Sharon asked.

"Shit, yeah? Barbara Sanders, Nathan Sander's wife. He's one of the richest men in the state, inherited everything from his father. He's big in politics too, never held his own position, but puts big money behind men like Senator Listner. She's pretty famous herself," he said nodding towards the bleeding woman. "She's on just about every charity board in the county."

"Who'd do something like this?" Sharon asked looking over at Robert's body.

"I don't know. Maybe it was a case of mistaken identity. These black Caddies are pretty plentiful out here. Maybe they thought they were getting someone else, or maybe the chauffeur cut some lunatic off. One thing I am sure of, they didn't intend for anyone to get out of that car alive. The driver's side is riddled with bullet holes."

The sounds of flames catching air, caught their attention and they looked back at the car. The hood buckled and flames burst from under it.

"Drive by shooting? Sharon asked. "I thought you didn't have that type of crime out here?"

"We don't have much petty crime," he said. "But where there's big money, there's big criminals. We've been getting a different element moving into the area. It's kept under wraps for the most part, but it's growing each year."

Something popped over at the car, the acrid smoke of burning rubber blew towards them and stung Sharon's nose. She thought the car might blow, and that they should move Helen farther away. As she was about to suggest it to Paul, they heard the oncoming sound of an ambulance, or a fire truck, maybe both, she wasn't sure.

Paul stood up and walked out to the middle of the road to wave them down. Helen reached up for Sharon again. "Don't let them kill me," she said.

Sharon let go of the woman's shoulder and pried her hand from her shirt. "Take it easy. No one's going to kill you. Help's almost here."

"He knows," Helen said then closed her eyes.

The fire was extinguished quickly. Paramedics took vital signs and hooked Helen up to an IV. Sharon couldn't help wondering who "he" was and what it was he knew. Helen, or was it Barbara, was afraid. She had been shot, her chauffeur had been killed. The worst had happened, and yet, she was still full of fear. What was going on?

Sharon thought back to the shooting at the Church and decided not to let the Posse pool have the only evidence of the scene. She reached down into the dirt by the side of the road and wiped her hands in it. The dirt turned red and stuck to her palms. She vigorously rubbed her hands together to dislodge the last of the dirt then wiped whatever was left on her shorts. She stood above the paramedics, pulled her hair back tight under the headband, and moved the cross slowly back and forth against the chain. She pulled out the stem of her watch.

"Where are you taking her?"

"Scottsdale Baptist," one of the EMTs responded. Sharon took his picture when he looked up. Robert still lay on the ground where Paul had left him, the coroner was on his way. Sharon took a few photos. Robert's head had been hit so many times she wouldn't have recognized him except for his size. His chest was mangled and two fingers were missing from his left hand. Her stomach lurched, and she backed away.

She walked over to the ambulance, snapped a picture of its license plate and company name, then walked down to the burnt Cadillac where Paul and a fireman were pointing to the numerous holes in its side. Sharon stepped out from the curb to get a good view of the car and let her hidden camera record what she knew no one else would see.

Two cruisers, their lights flashing, and sirens screaming were racing towards them. Paul walked Sharon away from the Cadillac and halfway back towards his car. "Go back to the car and wait," he said. "We're probably going to be a while."

Sharon did as she was told, but stopped at the back of the ambulance. "Is she going to make it?" she asked.

"I don't know," the EMT said, then jumped in the back with Barbara Sanders. The other attendant closed the door behind them, ignoring Sharon altogether, and ran to the front. The ambulance took off just as the two police cars came to a stop along side the Cadillac.

Sharon watched from the passenger seat of Paul's car as the police got out of their vehicles. The drivers were both in Posse uniforms, but the passenger of one of the cars was dressed in plainclothes. It was detective Grant.

Grant walked over to Paul, and they started talking. One of the Posse members headed towards Sharon. More questions. The volunteer cop looked at her through the front window, smiling as he got closer. He didn't come to the passenger window, instead he stooped down by Robert. Sharon leaned towards the front of the car to see what he was doing, but the hood blocked her view. She turned her gaze back towards Paul.

Grant was kneeling in front of the burnt Cadillac and running his hands along its side door. He looked up at Paul. Paul said something looking her way, then the officer looked over at her too. She leaned back. Paul waved for her to join them.

As she got out of the car, the man that had been examining Robert stood up. "Sorry, Ma'am. I'm going to have to ask you…"

"It's all right," Grant yelled from behind them. "Miss Clark could you please come here."

Sharon walked slowly towards them. "Detective Grant," she said as she approached.

"Miss Clark, what a surprise. Seems you just keep popping up at all our shootings."

"Ah, but this time you don't have to warn me. I already know the drill," she said. "Don't tell anyone, and if I do, make sure I repeat what I heard on the news, and not what I've seen."

Grant smiled. "If all reporters had been so easy to work with, we wouldn't have had to institute the pool. Detective Matthews tells me he thought he saw you talking to Mrs. Sanders. Did she see who did this?"

Sharon didn't know how much she should tell. She decided to keep the part of Barbara Sanders being afraid of being killed to herself. She would investigate that further on her own. She wasn't sure who Barbara was talking about when she said 'He knows.' Was it Paul? Or was it someone else.

"She said they were on their way home from running an errand when a white van pulled up beside them and started shooting."

"A white van?" Paul said eyeing Sharon suspiciously.

Damn it, why hadn't she put it together sooner. The skinheads had been driving a white van, and Paul knew it. Sharon gave him her best, don't say a word or I'll kill you look. Paul seemed to get the message and dropped the subject.

"I don't suppose she got a license plate?" Grant asked.

"What?" Sharon asked, not sure she had heard the question.

"A license plate. Did she mention if she got the number?"

How absurd. Sharon curled her lip. "She didn't say. She seemed more concerned about Robert than she did about who did this."

"Robert?"

Sharon froze. Had Barbara Sanders said the name Robert? She couldn't remember.

"The chauffeur," Paul said.

Grant looked at Sharon and squinted his eyes. "How'd you know his name, Miss Clark? Were you acquainted with Mrs. Sanders?"

"No. She asked for him by name."

"There you have it," Paul said quickly as if relieved. "If that's all for now, I should take Miss Clark back to her hotel. I'm already late for my shift."

"Yeah, all right. We still have lots of work to do here. Miss Clark, I assume you're still at the same hotel."

Sharon told him she was, then followed Paul back to the car.

"You don't like him too much, do you?" Paul asked as they left the scene.

Sharon looked over her shoulder at the detective. He was headed towards Robert. "Let's just say, I don't like how the public is always fed half truths."

"I don't see why that bothers you. You're a reporter aren't you? You don't seem to have any problem telling half truths, even to me." Paul looked over at her, a smile played on his lips. "It was Barbara Sanders you were with when your purse was snatched, wasn't it? That's why you didn't want me to bring up more about the white van."

Sharon looked down at her blood stained hands and clothes and shook her head. "No, the white van is just a coincidence. I just didn't want Grant to hear about another one of my mishaps."

"I see," was all Paul said.

24

Sharon sat on the bed in her hotel room, naked and clean, staring at the three messages from Thomas. She wanted to call him, she wanted to hear his voice, but something inside kept her from picking up the phone. It would be too easy. His sweet talk would make her forget all about Paul, Helen, the white van, Martha and Anthony. He would give her the reassurance, the verbal hug, which would make her think everything was fine, life was okay. But it wasn't, and she didn't know if it ever would be again.

So much had happened since she arrived in Phoenix. She was intertwined in so many lives. She felt entangled, snared. If she could shake some of those tethers, she could go back to being herself. She could look at her story as the penetrating factor in her life, write it, and go home. But they weren't going to let her do that. Martha and Anthony needed her.

She thought of the two kids cooped up in the little motel room. She felt responsible for them. In the few hours she spent with them they had become more than a story. The pain and suffering they had been through in just four short months of being part of the State Foster Care program was overwhelming. Sharon had had a pleasant, uneventful life, compared to their last four months, and she had been raped. *Yeah, but I was only raped by one man, one sick man, not a whole state.*

On the floor were her blood stained clothes. *More trash.* She reached up to feel the scars on her neck, they were almost gone. Superficial cuts from an insignificant man whose life's worth had been measured by the price of disposable razors. There had been so much blood since she arrived, there was so much wrong, but she was only one woman. She couldn't save the world. Her article might be able to stop a few voters from making the wrong choice at the poll, but it wouldn't stop what was happening. The country was in a spiraling dive. The small breeze she might cause wouldn't even divert it, never mind stop it. People like Senator Listner were too powerful and the general public too brainwashed. If she were going to make a difference, it would be in the individual lives, the lives of Martha and Anthony, Madison Courtney, and Barbara Sanders. She would gear her efforts towards them, and then, whatever she was able to pull out of it for her article, she would.

She fished in her suitcase and pulled out a clean tee shirt and a pair of jeans then looked at her watch. It was already two o'clock, she needed to get going. There were still errands she needed to do before going back to the motel.

First the bathroom, then she would go. As she got up, the phone rang. It was Thomas.

"Hi babe, where have you been? I've been trying all morning." His smiling face lit up the monitor.

Sharon couldn't tell if seeing his face and hearing his voice was a relief. She had purposely not returned his call. Thomas was from another world, a safe haven she couldn't afford to be drawn into. A sense of security made you careless, and she'd already been careless enough.

She smiled back at him, hoping to pacify him. "I had interviews this morning," she lied.

"Is everything going okay? You look tired. What's that on your neck?"

Sharon's hand darted to her neck, she had forgotten about the cuts. "I'm fine. I tripped and landed in some cactus. They're only scratches. I'm getting some good stuff for my article." She drew her hand away from her neck and smiled.

"That's great," he said. "I miss you, babe."

"I miss you too," she said in a flat voice. *But not right at this moment.* And it wasn't like he really missed her, he just didn't like being left alone. He could have cared less about her article. He never understood her passion to work, to investigate, he never came right out and said it, but he would be been just as happy if she quit the paper, married him, and stayed home raising a large family. Their ideals of a future happiness always came between them, always would. Maybe Paul *was* a better suitor.

"You know, I stayed home last night," he continued. "I thought you'd call."

"I'm sorry," she said, sarcastically. "I should have put my story on hold just so I could call you." She was being selfish and she knew it. Thomas loved her, he loved her more than anyone except her granddad.

Thomas' face grew larger on the screen. "What's wrong?"

"Nothing's wrong," she said looking away from the monitor. "I'm busy, that's all."

"What you mean is, you don't have time for me, isn't that it?"

"That's not what I said, and you know it."

"No, I guess it's not, anyway, I forgive you," he said as if he hadn't caught the tone in her voice, or the sour grimace that had spread across her face. "But from now on, I want to hear from you every day."

"I'll try," she said. Anything to get him off the phone.

"That doesn't sound too promising." He smiled again, all those shiny white teeth coming across the screen ready to consume her.

Sharon backed away from the monitor. He was right, it wasn't a promise. She had no plans to stop whatever she was doing and make sure she called Thomas, but why she was lying? "Just appease her," Granddad used to say. "Say you'll do whatever she wants. She'll forget soon enough and you avoid fighting." Smart words and they had worked well, but that was with Mother. Thomas didn't forget so easily.

"Look Thomas," she said. "I'm pretty busy here. The article is taking on a life of it's own. I have a meeting in half an hour. I really can't make any promises about when I'll call. I have to go."

"Jeez, I didn't mean to get in the way." His face pulled back. He was pouting. The urge to hang up, to move on, was great, but she didn't do it. Instead she did as she had been taught and sought to pacify him. Yes, it was wrong, but so what. She had things to do. "You're not in the way, I'm just headed out that's all. I'll call you soon, I promise."

"Tonight?"

"I don't know. I'll try."

"You'll try!" He was mad. His angry face filled the screen. Why hadn't she just told him she'd call and hang up? "God, Sharon, if I had known you'd forget all about me the minute you left, I wouldn't have allowed you to go."

That was it. There were some things in life she couldn't tolerate, and having someone think they controlled her life was one of them. She had warned him early on in the relationship never to take that stance, never to expect her to cow to his authority.

"Allow me to go? You mother fucker. Who the hell do you think you are?" she asked, not really wanting a response.

"That's not what I meant and you know it. I..."

The phone went dead. "Thoma..."

"You have violated Arizona communication code 10189." The Arizona watch angel said in her nasal voice. "Your call has been terminated and your phone line temporarily disconnected. Please call 555-1984 to have it reinstated."

Sharon burst out laughing. She had done it again, broken one of Arizona's codes of ethics. *Obscenities not allowed.* "Good. Now I have an excuse not to talk to you until I feel damn good and ready." There was a skip in her step. Maybe what she had hoped for all along was to have a fight, to free herself from the guilt of lusting after Paul Matthews.

She grabbed her clothes off the bed and headed for the bathroom. She was still laughing, but underneath that laugh was a piece of anger so large she knew it wouldn't go away. She would have to deal with her feelings towards Thomas, re-evaluate their relationship, and see if it was something she wanted to continue. But for now she had shopping to do. And while she was at it, she'd pick up something new for herself.

Sharon's face had disappeared from the monitor before Thomas heard the dial tone. It took a few seconds to realize they had been cut off. Had she hung up on him? "No," he said out loud. "She wouldn't dare." But something had happened. He called her hotel room, but the clerk wouldn't put him through.

"I'm sorry, sir. Her account has been disconnected."

"Disconnected? What for?"

"I really couldn't say, sir. The state communications system is very touchy though. Out of staters usually violate at least one of the codes while they're here and their phone privileges are pulled. I'm sure she will contact the authorities and get her access back shortly. Shall I leave her a message you called?"

Thomas asked him to do just that, then hung up the phone, more annoyed than angry. What could be going on? Sharon had never blown up at him like that. Maybe he shouldn't have said the thing about not letting her go, but he was mad. He didn't like her being away, especially on a weekend. How could she not know that? How could she not know that she was the most important thing in his life, the only thing he really cared about?

There was more going on than she was telling him, he could feel it. Damn, he hadn't wanted her to go in the first place. What if she was in trouble? What if she thought he wouldn't be able to handle it, like the rape she had never told him about or the abortion. Well he wasn't going to wait around to hear it from her mother at some drunken party. Not this time. This time he was going to make her confide in him, trust him not to over-react. He went over his schedule for the next week in his mind. Monday and Tuesday he had meetings with vendors, meetings too important to miss, but the rest of the week was clear. He picked up the phone, called Southwest Airlines and made reservations for Tuesday evening to Phoenix.

25

Martha got up from her chair and started to pace around the room. Anthony was asleep. His fever had broken completely, and the wounds on his back were starting to heal. He was going to be fine. That was one thing she didn't have to worry about.

Sharon hadn't returned yet. The waiting was starting to work on Martha's nerves. She knew that much of it came from her feeling of entrapment. She didn't dare open the curtains, afraid someone would see her. The darkened room had a sense of dread to it, the smell of sickness permeated the air. The drone of the swamp cooler and its heavy moisture became an oppressing presence that made her think she would explode. She had taken a shower and washed her hair, but it hadn't been enough. She needed to get out of the motel room, to stretch her legs, to see the sun and let the hot dry air cleanse her.

She was sick of TV, sick of reading, but she had to have something to keep her mind off her discomfort. Maybe she could find an exercise station, something that would help her get her limbs moving. She turned on the TV and started flipping through the channels.

Barbara Sander's face filled the screen. The remote fell from Martha's hand. Picking it up quickly, she raised the volume to hear what was being said.

"Earlier this afternoon, Barbara Sanders, the wife of billionaire Nathan Sanders was run off the road. Mrs. Sander's car apparently rolled over in a

ditch along side McDowell road and caught fire. Her chauffeur, Robert Her-
nadez was declared dead at the scene. Mrs. Sanders was rushed to Scottsdale
Baptist hospital and is in critical condition."

Martha's mouth dropped. She stared at the picture of the woman
who had rescued her. Robert was dead. It couldn't be true, it must be
a means of flushing them out, she decided. Robert couldn't be dead.
She touched her lips where he had kissed her. Tears fell down her face.
It just couldn't be true. Martha looked back up at the TV screen and
listened intently as the newscaster related all the charity work Barbara
Sanders had done, and how the Posse was looking for a white van they
believe was involved in the accident.

It had to be true. They wouldn't have gone through so much
trouble to find a couple of runaways. Robert was dead. Mrs. Sander's
hospitalized. Martha backed up to the armchair and fell into it. All
hope was now lost. There would be no IDs, there would be no escape.

The doorknob turned. Martha jumped, then dropped the remote
and threw herself on the floor, rolling under the bed.

"Martha?" Sharon called.

Martha peeked out from under the bedspread. The door was still
open, Sharon's arms were full of shopping bags.

"What are you doing under there?" Sharon asked as she kicked the
door shut with her foot.

"I didn't know if it was you." Martha pulled herself out from under
the bed and wiped the tears from her face. "Did you hear about Mrs.
Sanders and Robert? Did you watch the news?"

Sharon looked up at the TV screen, and looked back at Martha. "I
know. I was there. But it was no car crash, they were shot."

Martha stood up. "What? No, I just watched the news. They said
they were driven off the road by a white van."

"Don't believe everything you hear on the news," Sharon said.
"I've had first hand experience with how the reporting is done here,
and it's never the truth. I was with Helen, or I guess Barbara, before
the ambulance took her away. She had been shot twice. She's pretty
bad."

Martha didn't understand. Why would anyone shoot Mrs. Sanders?
Why would they kill Robert? And why had the news lied? Martha
looked at Sharon. "Were you meeting her about something?"

"No. I was coming home from a brunch date with that man I went
out with last night. We just happened to be coming down the road
minutes after the shooting. It was strange. Something's going on,
Martha. I feel like I was supposed to see that accident."

"You? Why?" Martha asked, confused as to Sharon's role in everything that was happening. She was looking at the incident from her viewpoint, not Sharon's, or Robert's for that matter. She had forgotten about Mrs. Sander's cause. She hadn't seen it as dangerous, not even after the attack by the skinheads. She had been wrong. This wasn't about two runaway teenagers. It was retribution for trying to help others. Mrs. Sanders and Robert had been set up, just like Martha's mother. Helping people only accomplished two things, death or jail.

"I'm sorry, Martha," Sharon said putting the bags on the bed next to Anthony. "I don't understand it either. Those jerks who attacked us yesterday were driving a white van. I'm pretty sure they were the ones doing the shooting. Why they would want me to witness it? I don't know. Maybe they know it was Barbara who I met with yesterday. Maybe they want to scare me off my assignment."

"Did she say anything," Martha asked. "Did she tell you who had done it?"

"No," Sharon said. "But, I'm going to get into her hospital room tonight and find out who's behind it. Then when I get proof, I'm going to broadcast it all over the... Oh, my God," Sharon said then reached for the remote and turned the volume of the TV up higher.

Martha turned. The face of a balding man in his fifties was being shown.

"In other news today, the body of Dr. Simon Garner was found in the back office of the Love Me Tender beauty salon in Old Scottsdale. Authorities are calling it a suicide. Dr. Garner, as you may remember, a noted gynecologist in the Scottsdale area had his license revoked over ten years ago after accusations of sexual molestation. Friends close to the family say that he had been distraught ever since and that they are not very surprised..."

"What's going on?" Anthony said waking up and pulling himself up in the bed.

"Take it easy," Martha said trying to reach over and help him. "Your back."

"I know him," Sharon said.

"Who are you?" Anthony asked.

"This is the woman I was telling you about," Martha said then turned her attention back to the TV. They were showing the front of a beauty parlor. Sharon's sat, her eyes fixed on the screen.

"Who was he?" Martha asked.

"An abortionist. He worked closely with Barbara Sanders. They must know. Come on," Sharon said, springing from the bed and pulling clothes, make-up, wigs, and other items from the bags. "Get dressed, both of you. We have to get out of here."

Martha watched the woman frantically tearing tags off the clothing.

"What's going on?" she asked.

"Look," Sharon said, putting down a pair of jeans she held in her hands. "I went to see him the other day. They followed me, but when I was questioned about him, I lied. I said he didn't have any information. But somehow they got to him."

"He committed suicide," Martha said, louder than she meant to.

"No. He told me that before he would let them take him, he'd kill himself. He showed me a cyanide pill that he carried with him all the time. If he's dead, it means they were about to arrest him. If they've got him, and they shot Barbara Sanders, and they set me up to see it, they know what I'm really here for. And they're probably watching me closer than I thought. You two have to get out of here and find somewhere safe to hide until I can get you out."

"I know where," Anthony said.

Martha turned towards her brother. "Where?

Anthony looked at both Martha and Sharon. "The Superstitions. There are caves, old abandoned shacks and mine shafts all through it. We can hide out there."

"Caves! We can't hide out in caves. You're too sick," Martha said. She turned to Sharon. She could tell by the hesitation in Sharon's eyes that she was contemplating it. "Sharon. He needs rest. He can't be traipsing through the mountains looking for caves."

"Glad to see you're better, Anthony," Sharon said with half a smile. "Tell me more about these caves. Do you know how to get to them?"

"Sharon!" Martha said, angry that she would go along with it.

Anthony perked up. "Yeah. Actually there's this old cabin near the opening of a cave my mother used to store her dried herbs. The cabin's not in very good condition, but it's well hidden. She used it to brew her medicine. You remember it, Martha. We've been there many times. There are supplies and everything. It's where I'd planned on going if I couldn't find you. They'll never find us there."

Martha remembered the place all right. She remembered the day they had walked in to find two rattlesnakes going at it in the middle of the floor. It was too dangerous. The place was always infested with scorpions, centipedes, and red ants.

"No," Martha said. "Sharon, he's a kid, he thinks it's an adventure. I've been there, it's a horrible place. My mother used to have to go in for an hour or so just to make it safe."

"Get dressed," Sharon said, throwing a package of underwear and a pair of jeans at Anthony. "Martha, we don't have many choices. They could be on their way here at any moment. If they check my account, they'll know I've stayed here. If they come looking..."

Martha wasn't paying any attention to Sharon. Barbara Sander's face was once again up on the screen, below it were both hers and Anthony's. "Look," she said, pointing at the TV. Sharon and Anthony looked back at the TV.

"This report just in. Sources say that the two runaways we've been airing for the past couple of days have been linked to a white van that fits the description of the vehicle that allegedly ran Mrs. Nathan Sanders' car off the road this morning. The girl, Martha Garcia, was in the employ of the Sanders and disappeared early Saturday morning from their home presumably to meet up with her runaway brother. If anyone has any information regarding the whereabouts of these two teenagers, you are requested to call the tip hotline at 555-TELL."

"No. That's not true," Martha said. "We had nothing to do with it."

"It doesn't matter," Sharon said pulling two wigs from another bag. She threw a long black one at Anthony, and a red teased bob at Martha. "You've got to get these on, and get dressed. It's not safe here any more. Now move it."

Anthony picked up the wig and held it out in front of him as if it was some soiled laundry. "You don't think I'm going to wear this, do you?"

"Look, Anthony," Sharon said picking up a white frilly blouse and holding it up for him. "They're looking for a girl and a boy, not two girls. It's a disguise that's all."

Anthony bobbed his head up and down for a minute. "A disguise? Sure, I can do that."

Martha looked at Sharon, the wig, then back at the news. The newscasters were discussing the ward systems.

"It seems to me, Mike, that there's a real problem in the way the state is handling these wards. It was designed to raise these kids to uphold our morals and laws."

"Well, according to the information we have on the Garcias, Gregg, they've only been in the system for four months. I don't think it's a matter of what they're able to teach them this time, I think it has more to do with the amount of time they had them. If anything, maybe they should look into a mandatory guidance period. Last year, Senator Listner addressed this very issue, but folks were afraid to institute a minimum two year program for all children regardless of their age."

"I'm sure we'll be hearing more from the senator on this one, Mike. In other news..."

Sharon raised the red wig into Martha's face. "You don't have much say here, Martha. I don't know where to take you, and you can't trust anyone you know. Anthony's plan is the best we have, now get this thing on and let's get out of here. We'll deal with whatever is living in that shack when we get there."

Martha took the wig from Sharon, and headed for the bathroom.

"It'll be okay, sis," Anthony said. "I don't think I'll make a very believable girl though." Anthony took his wig and placed it on his head, stuffing his hair underneath it.

"You'll do fine," Sharon said. She got up and followed Martha into the bathroom. Martha could see her in the mirror, but averted her gaze. She didn't even know if she could trust Sharon, but she had been right, she didn't know anyone else she could trust either. Sharon was their only hope. If it meant living in a shack for a few days, she'd do it. If not for herself, than for Anthony.

"Here," Sharon said, putting a small bag down on the sink. "I got you some make-up. When you're done, put some on Anthony. I'm going to pack up the medicine and stuff."

"Sharon," Martha said, turning around and facing her. "I'm scared."

Sharon wrapped her arms around the girl and pulled her close. "I'm scared too. So is Barbara Sanders. I'll find out what's going on then I'll come back and get you. I promise. I won't let them find you."

Martha pulled away and looked up at her. The scars on Sharon's neck were barely visible. She had been through her own ordeals since coming to Arizona, but she was a reporter, she was here for a story. "Why are you helping us?" she finally asked.

Sharon let out a small sigh. "It's the right thing to do. Of course when I get you back to California it will be one hell of a story. I won't lie to you about that, but for right now I think I'm just more interested in the truth. And the truth is, you and your brother had nothing to do with Barbara Sander's accident, and I'm not about to let them put you in prison for it. Plus, and maybe this is the biggest reason, I'm not too sure myself, but if they catch you and find out I've helped you, I go to jail. And I have no intention of rotting away in one of Arizona's hell holes."

It was a good enough reason for Martha. She sensed Sharon was telling the truth, and even if she wasn't, there was no one else to turn to. She would have to trust Sharon, and she would have to trust herself to keep her brother safe until they escaped.

"How do I look?" Anthony asked standing in the doorway. He had on the black wig, jeans and the blouse. Martha wouldn't have recognized him herself if she bumped into her at the mall. He seemed to have back his strength.

"Great," Sharon said, handing him a brush. "I'm going to remake the bed. Martha get him ready, but hurry. I have a bad feeling about this place."

Martha did as she was told, brushing out Anthony's wig and putting make-up on him. He seemed much better, maybe the thought of getting outdoors, or the excitement of hiding out in the Superstitions did more good for him than the hours she had sat over and watched him. He had been abused. Maybe, finally, he felt like he was taking back some of himself. She cleaned the sink area of the stray hairs from the wigs, and checked the tub for any signs of Anthony's first bath. There were none, the bathroom seemed clean enough, yet there were an awful lot of dirty towels. "What should I do with all these towels?" she yelled out to Sharon.

Sharon stepped into the bathroom and looked at them for a moment. "Take them with us. Leave the two we got this morning, but take the rest. The housekeeper won't say anything, she doesn't want to get in trouble for not cleaning the room."

Martha grabbed her old clothes, and the towels and went back out into the main part of the room. Anthony was admiring himself in the mirror and making exaggerated feminine poses. Martha found this amusing, a frivolity in the midst of so much upheaval. It made her laugh.

"Okay, Angie, I think you've had enough of yourself."

He turned around and frowned. "Tell anyone and I'll kill you."

"Just every girlfriend you ever have," Martha said in an attempt at humor. She turned back towards Sharon. "Well. I guess we're ready."

26

Maybe Martha was ready, but Sharon wasn't sure she was. She wanted to seem confident in front of the kids, but inside she was as scared, maybe even more than they were. Her Aunt Theresa told her years ago that the reason they discontinued using cash as a means of commerce was that it was easier for "them", people she always referred to as "Big Brother," to keep tabs on your every movement. Granddad had laughed at Theresa, calling her a paranoid doomsday sayer. Sharon had always laughed with him, but now she understood. Everything she purchased, the wigs, the make-up, everything had been recorded. If Grant or anyone else suspected her of helping these kids, then they would check her recent purchases, and would use the missing merchandise as proof of her complicity.

Things were becoming complicated fast. If she were smart, she would head right out of Arizona tonight. Get out before there was too much suspicion. But she couldn't, she still needed IDs for the kids and there was only one woman who could help her get them. She had to see Barbara Sanders, and not just for the IDs. She had to find out who knew about their meeting, who arranged the shooting. It was becoming an obsession. Simon's death had been the clincher. She didn't believe he had the courage to kill himself. He was a weak man by his own admission. He wouldn't have popped that cyanide tablet easily, and if he had, it would only have been at the last minute. The

Posse had to have been there with an arrest warrant. And if they knew about him, they could know about everything and everyone Barbara Sanders touched. No, it would be a few more days before she could safely try to get herself and the kids out of the state. For now, Anthony's idea of hiding in a shack somewhere in the Superstitions was the best idea any of them had.

First, she'd need to get them supplies and she needed to do it in either Phoenix or Scottsdale. She couldn't afford to make any purchases close to where they were going. She'd leave the jeeps position at a mall in town and then take them to the mountains. When she left them, she'd take the wigs with her. They could be her fatal flaw. She could convince anyone that she bought the clothes for herself, but wigs they might want to see. She would take them back and show them to Paul. He'd be her alibi, just in case.

Martha found the path that led up to the shack easier than any of them expected. They drove through a tangle of dirt access roads that branched and seemingly disappeared more often than Sharon had thought possible. Martha jumped out at each turn and marked stones and cactus with red and pink nail polish. Pink for Sharon's trip back to town and red so she could find her way back. The spots were so small that Sharon wasn't sure she would find them, but she knew she needed something and the marks were the only idea she could come up with. Anything else would be too dangerous. They had stopped off and picked up two gallon water jugs, candles and more food. Martha had wanted insect repellent, but Sharon was too afraid to have it register on her account. They would have to kill any desert marauders the old fashion way, by stomping on them.

Using the word *shack* to describe the wooden structure was being kind. There were boards missing and the roof had a hole in it. Sharon had taken a flashlight and two emergency blankets from her earthquake kit and a small pan for heating water. As they stood outside the dilapidated building staring at it, Sharon was grateful she wasn't the one being forced to spend the night in it. "You might be better off sleeping under the stars," she told them, but Anthony, who seemed completely recovered, brushed her off. He took the flashlight from her hand and walked over to the door. It almost came off in his hands.

"There's probably plenty of black widows in here," he told them. "I'll get them."

Martha stepped towards him, but Sharon grabbed her arm stopping her from following him. "Let him alone," she said. "He seems to know what he's doing."

Sharon and Martha stood outside the cabin listening to Anthony whoop and holler as he killed various vermin inside the wooden structure. Sharon looked around the barren land and up at the large boulder Anthony said hid the entrance to the cave. It was hot, very hot. Sharon couldn't imagine their mother coming here to work. The towns had vanished behind them. There was rock, there was desert, a few jackrabbits and some roadrunners, but there was no civilization anywhere to be seen. "Your mother would come out here all by herself?" she asked Martha.

"Mostly. Sometimes she made us come with her, but not when she was going to spend the night. It's spooky out here at night," Martha said, wrapping her arms around herself.

Sharon worried that maybe she was making a mistake taking them out here, leaving them on their own against nature. As if reading her mind, Martha turned to her and smiled. "Well, at least they won't be able to find us." Reaching over, Martha put her hand on Sharon's arm. "We'll be okay. If my mother could do it, we can."

"All clear," Anthony said, sticking his head out the door. "There still might be a few hidden spiders and stuff, but that will give us something to do this afternoon. And look," he said stepping out from the structure. He held up two tightly rolled sleeping bags. "Warmth."

"You better air those things out," Sharon said not wanting to touch them. "I can only imagine what's been living in them."

"There's more," Anthony said, throwing the bags at Martha. She backed away so they didn't hit her, but ran quickly to grab them before they rolled into cactus. Anthony ducked back into the shack and came out with a duffel bag. Carefully he opened its' top and turned it upside down. He held the bag as far from his legs as he could, keeping its top close to the ground as he shook it. Pots and pans clashed against each other, their handles spilling from the bag's canvas. Anthony stepped back, pulling the bag away from the utensils and shook some more. A snake kit, some bug spray, matches and a knife fell to the ground.

Sharon looked at the gallon of bug spray and hoped it had enough in it to get the kids through the next couple of days. She was about to stoop and pick it up when the bag jerked.

"Whoa." Anthony dropped the bag and stepped back. All three of them stood staring at the bag as the head of a rattlesnake peered out from the canvas, it's split black tongue darting outward. Within the confines of the bag, they could hear a muffled rattle warning them of a strike. Sharon put her arm up across Martha's chest and took a slow step backward. Martha took one with her. The snake sprang, missing them by a foot. They jumped back. Martha stumbled and started to fall, Sharon reached out for her, trying desperately to keep one eye on the snake. It was completely out of the bag and coiled. Its tail rattled frantically. Its open mouth aimed at Anthony. He seemed paralyzed.

"Move," Sharon whispered to him.

He slowly shook his head. "I can't," he said, so softly Sharon barely heard him. There wouldn't be enough time to sidestep the frightened snake. Sharon looked around for something to throw at it, to divert its attention so Anthony could get away. Something rushed by her side. It was Martha holding a board. Her mouth was open. As she swung the board a loud hysterical scream pierced the air. The rattler sprang, its head hit the board with a loud snap and was thrown backwards. Martha moved again, the scream still pouring from her lungs, and hit the snake's startled head with the board's edge. Anthony was moving, he was headed towards his sister. "Martha, no," he cried. Sharon stepped forward and grabbed him, holding him back from interfering with his sister. Martha took a short breath and continued her scream, beating the snake again and again until parts of its body were no more than mashed meat. Finally Martha's screams turned to sobs. The snake was dead, her arms grew weaker, her pounding slower.

Sharon let go of Anthony. His body was limp, his eyes fixed on his sister. Sharon reached for the board to stop Martha, but the girl fought loose for one last strike.

"I, I think you killed it," Anthony said.

Martha turned around and stared at him. The board dropped from her hand. She was shaking. Sharon stepped in and held her. "It's okay," she told the girl.

Martha cried in her arms for a few seconds then pulled herself away. "I thought it was going to bite him," she said stepping over to Anthony and taking him in her arms. "I won't let anything happen to you."

"Guess not," he said pulling away. "Just next time, you don't have to go so berserk, okay."

"Okay, okay, but..." Martha sat on the ground, covered her face with her hands, and cried.

Sharon stared at the girl for a long moment, wondering just how close to the edge she was and how much more any of them were going to be able to take.

Anthony found a small broom in the shack and started cleaning. Martha had yet to go inside, but Sharon forced herself to take a look.

There was a stone circle beneath the hole in the roof with charred ashes in it, two cots, some empty glass canning jars and nothing else. She still couldn't picture their mother working in such a place but realized people would do what they had to do when they believed strongly enough in their objective. She admired the woman and wished she had known her, but realized, before now, she wouldn't have been able to appreciate her. She would have thought she was some strung out fanatic and have stayed clear.

The sun was hanging low in the sky. There would only be an hour or so of sunlight left. Martha picked up the supplies that came from the duffel bag and arranged them in a pile in front of the door.

"You have to come inside sometime," Anthony told her.

"I will," she said, poking her head in the door.

The girl was still shaken from the incident with the snake. Bringing them here had been a mistake, Sharon decided. "Maybe this is a bad idea. We could find another place."

"No," Martha told her. "I'll be fine. Look," she said stepping into the shack and looking around. "I'm in. It'll be okay, I swear."

Martha walked over to where the canning jars were and picked one up, turning it in her hand. "She sure went through lots of these. I wonder how many of them are scattered around the old neighborhood."

Anthony sat on one of the cots. He looked over at the jars himself, but said nothing. Sharon knew he was thinking of his mother. "Maybe when we get back to California we can try to get her sentence reduced," she said.

Anthony looked up at her, his mouth opened into a wide smile. "You think?"

Martha shook her head. "It's no use. Even if she did get out, she'd just do the same thing all over again." Martha put the jar back with the others and looked over at Sharon. "It's getting late, you should go or you won't be able to find your way back. "We'll be all right. We can take care of ourselves."

Sharon looked at both of them. There wasn't much more she could do, not tonight. She needed to get in to see Barbara Sanders and she still needed to find a way to get them IDs. Babying them wasn't going to do anything for their situation except pacify her guilt for having brought them. Somewhere in the distance a coyote howled. Neither of the kids flinched. "Okay," she finally said. "You're right. I have to go. But keep the door closed and make yourself a fire for the night."

"We know what to do," Anthony said.

"When will you be back?" Martha asked.

"Tomorrow, Tuesday at the latest. You have enough food and water for a couple of days."

"What should we do if you don't come back?" Anthony asked.

Sharon hadn't considered not coming back, and was a little hurt that he thought she might not return. She would be back, and she would get them out. If she was unsure about anything, it wasn't helping them escape. She would do whatever it took.

Life wasn't about her anymore. It wasn't about Thomas or her mother. It was about doing what was right. Self doubt, self pity, were luxuries she no longer had. But Anthony didn't know that, his experience with adults was worse than her own when she was his age. She hadn't trusted anyone but her granddad. Not even Thomas. Why would Anthony put his faith in a woman he didn't even know? His misgivings were understandable, and she didn't take them personally. She stepped over to the boy and rustled his hair. "I won't desert you."

"What if you have no choice?" Martha asked, then got up and walked out of the cabin.

27

Sharon found her way back to the mall. She had missed the pink nail polish markers a few times coming out of the desert, but was able to back track and pick up the trail without too much trouble. By the time she reached Mesa to reset her GPS position it was already seven o'clock and dark. The children she had left behind, worried her, but she forced herself to put them out of her mind for a while. Barbara Sanders was her current assignment.

A radio broadcast stated Barbara had undergone four hours of surgery and was expected to recover. She was listed in serious but stable condition. Which meant she'd still be in ICU and it wouldn't be an easy task getting in to see her. Sharon thought about waiting, giving it a day or two, but she had to get going on the IDs. Every day Martha and Anthony were in Arizona they were at risk of being found, and though the shack seemed remote enough, Sharon wasn't sure how safe it really was. They had no idea who else knew about the shack or if their mother had told the police where it was. From what little she knew of Suzanne Garcia, Sharon didn't think she would have told them anything, but she couldn't be sure. She needed to get Martha and Anthony out of there as soon as possible.

Sharon found the hospital and parked her Jeep in the visitor parking area. The plan she had come up with didn't seem very sound, but it was the best she could do. She would pretend to be a relative, and, if the

Fates were with her, there wouldn't be anyone around to disprove it. Sharon brushed her hair back with her headband, readjusted her bag on her shoulder, got directions to ICU and headed for it. The wide corridors, waiting gurneys, and spotless floors reminded her of the last time she had been in a hospital – the last time she had seen Granddad alive. Memories of tubes and hoses, IV drips, beeping monitors and dirty bed pans surrounding a frail, diminished man, nauseated her, and she stopped for a second to calm her nerves. She tried to bring up a memory of the healthy, husky, man that she had done so much with as a child, but she couldn't do it. Hospitals were for the dying and to remind the living that they too would someday be a cadaver on cold steel, their only link to the living, a tag tied to their toe.

Sharon swallowed back the bile that forced its way up her throat, and continued down the hall. ICU was up ahead. She stopped an orderly, got directions for the waiting area, and went there. Hopefully, she would be able to pick out any family waiting to see Barbara then hide out until they were all gone. It might take all night, but she was determined to get answers regarding what had happened, and who was trying to kill her informant.

There were two groups of people huddled in the room. One was a family, parents, grandparents and two children. The mother, a woman in her early thirties, sat apart from the rest rocking in her chair, her face swollen from tears and fear. The two kids slept on their father's arms. The grandfather paced. The grandmother stared at the crying mother, signs of accusations registering so sharply that Sharon wanted to scream for her to stop. Whatever had happened, the mother was already putting the blame on herself.

Two women, one in her eighties, the other in her sixties, sat silently next to each other, their hands tightly interwoven. Sharon sensed their agony, their feelings of mortality. This was a cold, horrible place to be while waiting for someone you loved to die.

At least, Barbara wasn't going to die. The reports had said as much, but she was still here, surrounded by death, and watched very closely. There could be someone in with her. A woman like Barbara Sanders would probably have lots of family and friends. Sharon felt she was being foolish to think she could just walk in without anyone questioning her. She thought about finding a laundry room and stealing a set of scrubs, impersonating a doctor or orderly, but realized it was only in movies someone would get away with that. The nurses would know who belonged in their ward and who didn't. She would be stopped and questioned immediately. No, the best way was the direct approach, but, first, she would take some precautions.

She returned to the main lobby of the hospital. It fluttered with activity. People were busy waiting. Some sat in hard black plastic seats, most milled around, talking, laughing, flirting. These were the people who knew life was safe. Their loved ones would be coming down the elevators to go home or were getting some type of routine exam and would be leaving. They weren't afraid of death, not yet. Those people were safely locked away in waiting rooms of the various wards through out the hospital. There was no place for the anguished mother waiting outside ICU in this lobby. It was for the showcase people, the life goes on people. Sharon found herself hating them as she pushed her way to the information desk.

She got the number for the ICU ward and went directly to the wall of phones. Of the seven phones, only two were being used. Sharon found the one most isolated and called upstairs.

"Hi," she said in a dry serious voice. "I'm looking for Nathan Sanders."

"Nathan Sanders?" a man's voice asked. Sharon prayed she had remembered his name correctly.

"Yes, that's right," she said. "Nathan Sanders. Is he still there with his wife?"

"Oh, right. No. I'm sorry," a man's voice responded. "Mr. Sanders left about half an hour ago. He said he was going home."

"Is there any other family members there that I could speak to?" Sharon asked.

"I don't think so. Let me check." The nurse put her on hold for a moment and then came back. "Sorry, there's no one here."

Sharon thanked the nurse, bought a cup of coffee from a vending machine and headed for the ICU ward. She didn't enter the ward though, instead, she found a waiting area close to the elevators outside the ICU ward and sat in a chair by the door, watching to see who came and went. She would wait fifteen minutes, then she'd go make her claim as Barbara Sanders' favorite niece.

As she watched nurses and doctors pass by her she couldn't help wonder how so many people were involved in keeping the truth of what happened to Barbara a secret. Nurses would know, doctors would know. You didn't get a gunshot wound from rolling your car. Maybe Reverend Samuels and Paul had been right. Could it be they just didn't want to deal with the truth? Studies suggested that if the public didn't see violence, didn't watch it on TV or at the movies, there would be less of it. Southern California hadn't bought into that yet. They still wanted to see the truth as it happened, and though no more violent movies were made, there was plenty of it on the news each night. Of course, as the religious states were so often pointing out, there was still a lot of crime on the streets. But that didn't matter to Sharon. She decided she would rather live in a world where the darker side of humanity still threateningly loomed than in a septic bubble where the truth was doled out in lies.

A nurse who had passed by three or four times smiled at her as he pushed a man in a wheel chair down the corridor. Sharon checked her watch. It was time. She hadn't seen anyone who looked liked visiting family come off the elevator so she assumed she was safe. Of course she could never be sure, but it was as safe as she was going to get. She picked up her bag and headed for the ICU nurse's station inside.

Two nurses, both men, sat in a u-shaped booth. Lights blinked on a screen behind them. "Hi," Sharon said in a very soft voice as she approached them. "I'm looking for Barbara Sanders."

"Are you family?" one of the nurses asked her.

"Yes," she said somberly. "I'm her niece."

"I'm sorry," he said looking down at one of his charts. "Only immediate family is allowed in."

"Look," Sharon said, bending down so she could look in his face. "My Uncle Nathan called me and asked me to come. I was up in Flagstaff. I'm sure if you tell him I'm here, he'll agree I should be allowed to see her."

The nurse shook his head. "Your uncle left about an hour ago. We're not expecting him back until morning."

"Please," Sharon said, allowing her eyes to water. "She just about raised me. I have to see her. She'll want to see me. I promise I won't upset her."

The nurse stood up and looked at her, then at the other man. "What do you think, Mark?"

"If she's awake."

"All right. Come with me. But if she's not awake, you'll have to wait until morning."

Sharon nodded her head and wiped her eyes. "Thanks," she said, then followed the nurse to the fifth small room. Barbara Sanders lay in her bed, a sheet pulled up to her waist. Her hair was tangled in a knot above her. An IV solution dripped into her veins. Oxygen was being fed to her through plastic hosing clipped to her nose. Four separate monitors were attached to her by cables and wires. Two were just blue boxes with dials on them. Another had two rows of lights that intermittently blinked. The last was above her head, showing the rhythm of her heart in blue and green lines while a white one monitored her oxygen.

She didn't look well. Her skin was pasty and more wrinkled than Sharon remembered. Her eyes open and wet. She had been crying.

"Ten minutes," the nurse told Sharon then stepped away.

Barbara turned her head, her eyes were glassy. Sharon couldn't tell if it was from drugs or tears. "It's me Sharon," she said. "I told them I was your niece." Barbara made a weak smile and held up her right hand.

"Sharon," she whispered.

Sharon went to the side of the bed and took the woman's hand. "Barbara. I know I should have waited to come, but I need your help. It's Martha. I have to get her out of the state. They're accusing her of doing this to you."

Barbara turned her head slowly from side to side. "Martha," she whispered.

This was a waste of time. Barbara was still drugged. She probably didn't even know who Martha was.

"Why would they say that? Martha wasn't there." Barbara's gaze fixed on Sharon's face.

So, she was there. *Get the information and get the hell out before someone who doesn't recognize you comes in*, her inner voice warned. Sharon chose not to listen. Barbara was hurting and it showed. She needed to be compassionate and was slightly saddened by the thought that she had to remind herself to be so. She lifted Barbara's hand and rubbed her arm. "I don't know. Someone to blame. They aren't telling anyone you were shot. They're saying you were run off the road."

Barbara squinted her eyes as if trying to adjust them. "Run off the road. Oh, my poor Martha. Is she okay?"

"I have her and her brother hidden right now. I hate to bother you with this when you're so sick, but I need to get in contact with the person who makes the IDs. I have to get IDs for them if I'm going to get them out of the state."

Barbara nodded her head. "Deitrich, Stan Deitrich. Works at the Desert Nursery in Mesa. I already contacted him, he's expecting you tomorrow." Barbara's grip loosened. "Tell Martha I'm sorry. I didn't mean for her to get hurt."

"I will," Sharon said. More tears formed in Barbara's eyes. "It's all right. The doctor's said you're going to recover."

Barbara shook her head. "He'll never let me live. Not now."

Sharon pulled a steel chair closer to the bed, not letting go of Barbara's hand. This was the other reason she had come. The skinheads, more than likely, did the shooting, but at the accident Barbara had alluded to there being someone else behind it.

"Who, Barbara. Who won't let you live?"

Barbara looked away for a moment, then turned her head back towards Sharon. "My husband. He found out, I'm sure of it. I think he arranged the shooting. It was him who sent me down that road. Normally I would have been home by then." Barbara paused and looked up at the ceiling. "He'll be back to finish me. He never leaves things unfinished."

This made no sense. Sharon could understand Barbara's husband losing his temper when he found out his wife had been working to further the cause to reclaim women's rights, but killing her was a little too hard to believe. "Why," she finally asked. "Why would your husband want you dead?"

"Out of fear. I know too much."

Sharon leaned over the bed. She pulled the stem of her watch. "What do you know, Barbara? Tell me. I'll have him arrested."

Barbara let out a small laugh, it came out more like a cough. "It's too big, even for you. And you'd never be able to prove it."

"Prove what?"

"The babies," Barbara said. And then as if reliving some memory, her voice lowered. "All the babies."

"What babies?" Sharon asked.

"The ones taken away from the women. Since they criminalized pre-marital sex there's a been a shortage of adoptable babies, especially white ones. The market's huge. Nathan and Listner are making a fortune. They list the babies as stillbirths and then sell them to the highest bidder. And not just here in America," she whispered. "Some are sent overseas, especially the girls."

Sharon couldn't believe what she was hearing. Senator Listner, a man many projected as the next president, was in the baby racket. Sharon could smell the Pulitzer. "Do you have any proof?" she asked.

"Norma," Barbara said. "Our housekeeper. She was one of the first taken. We didn't actually pay for her, but that's only because Nathan and Senator Listner are partners."

Sharon let loose of Barbara's hand and sat back in the chair. "Your housekeeper? I thought you were talking about black market adoptions."

"Most," Barbara said. "But some, primarily the minority children, are sold into servitude. You get them as babies, have a housekeeper raise them. By the time they're eight or nine, they've been taught their position and end up staying with you for life, out of gratitude. Here in the states you have to accept the possibility of them wanting to leave when they're adults, but you have their whole life to work with them, like Nathan did Norma. She wouldn't leave him, not ever. She works for room and board and a small spending allowance. When she has a baby, it will be his, too, then the cycle will continue."

"Does she know?"

"No. She thinks we kept her after her mother abandoned her. My husband," Barbara said reaching out for Sharon's hand. "He sleeps with her."

Sharon pulled her hand away. Barbara Sanders, the woman who chaired so many charity organizations was a slave owner. It was as simple as that. She fought for everyone else's rights and yet stood by while in her own home people were nothing more than possessions.

"I know what you're thinking," Barbara said. "I'm ashamed. But hers was only one life, Sharon. If I did anything to prevent it, he would have been suspicious. People in his position buy and sell human life without any consideration for the individual. Money and power are what our class is all about. And without that money and power I wouldn't have been able to do all the things I've done for the past twenty years."

All that money and power seemed wasted to Sharon. Arizona hadn't come around. Barbara hadn't worked to change laws or politicians. Maybe she had formed a network of people like herself, but that was it.

"I don't see it," Sharon said.

"A revolution isn't fought in a day. It takes years of planning. You have to build an army before you can topple a regime."

Sharon shook her head. "We have an election coming up. If I can get proof of what you're saying then we can stop it now, by keeping Independents in office."

"Slow it down, maybe," Barbara said. "But you can't stop it. There's a momentum crippling our minds and seducing our souls, Sharon, and the only thing that can stop it is an all out revolution. Religion or freedom, soon everyone's going to have to make their choice."

Sharon made her choice a long time ago. She believed in a higher power, but hated organized religion and the way its followers thrust their beliefs on others. She'd do her part to stop religious rule, but a revolution? No, Barbara was wrong, only democracy had the power to heal their fractured country. Democracy and journalism. Barbara had valuable information, information Sharon would disperse willingly.

"What if we could get him to acknowledge the baby market?" Sharon asked. "What if we got it on disk. I could take him and Listner down. He wouldn't dare hurt you then."

"It will be too late by then," Barbara said. "I expect he's planning it now. He won't let me live. I did the one thing he'll never be able to forgive."

"What's that," Sharon asked.

Barbara smiled. "I disobeyed him."

Sharon looked at the woman's eyes and realized she was serious. She had married a mad man and had probably known it from the start. Barbara Sanders had never doubted her fate, she had just wondered when it would play out. Sharon admired her. She envied her. She had never been that brave.

"So," Barbara asked. "What's this about getting it on disk?"

Sharon explained her plan. She would hide her recorder somewhere where Barbara could reach it, then when Mr. Sanders returned Barbara would have to bait him into reveling what he and Listner had done. Barbara said she expected her husband in the morning, and already knew how to get him talking. "I'll even get him to admit trying to kill me. That should make for a good story."

Sharon smiled back at the woman. It certainly would. "Don't do anything to endanger yourself. As soon as I have the disk, I'll release it. He'll be too afraid to hurt you."

Barbara patted Sharon's hand. "I'm not afraid of him."

The nurse popped his head in the door. "A few more minutes," he said, "then you're going to have to leave." Sharon nodded her head and he left.

"I'm glad," Sharon said, feeling released of the responsibility. "Now, let's find a place to hide this recorder." Barbara dropped her good arm down along side the edge of the bed and stuck it under the frame.

"Under here," she said. "You can jam it in the frame."

"An old pro at this, are you?" Sharon asked. Barbara didn't answer. Sharon knelt down by the side of the bed and looked up and under it. She took the recorder and wedged it in the bed frame, buttons pointing to the center so Barbara could work it. She turned it on. "Say something," she told Barbara.

"Welcome to my web, said the spider to the fly."

Sharon looked up at her and smiled, then rewound the recorder and played it back.

"Welcome to my web, said the spider to the fly."

"Perfect," Sharon said. Not rewinding it this time, she thought it would make a good opening for the recording. "Okay, now you try to turn it on. Reach down and feel for the tallest button and see if you can push it in."

Barbara reached her hand down, easily reaching the recorder and its buttons. Her fingers fumbled for a moment on each button, then she located the right one and pushed.

"Great," Sharon said, turning it off. "One more time." This time Barbara found the button quickly and turned it on. It would work. Maybe by tomorrow, she'd have the story of a lifetime.

"What are you doing?" the nurse asked as he stepped into the room. Sharon reached under the bed and turned the recorder off.

"Praying," she said. "We were just praying together."

"Well, I'm going to have to ask you to leave now. Mrs. Sanders needs her rest."

Sharon nodded her head and stood up. The room spun around, she closed her eyes and shook her head. She reached out for the bed railing, but it was too late. She was already falling.

28

Sharon came to in a hospital room of her own. She was still dressed, her shoes and socks were off, her jeans unbuttoned. She pulled herself up in a sitting position, still a little woozy.

"You're awake," someone to her right said. She looked up and saw Detective Grant sitting in a chair.

"What are you doing here?" she asked rubbing a sore spot on the side of her neck. "What happened."

"Seems you fainted while visiting your aunt. A Mrs. Barbara Sanders, the doctor told me. Funny, seems you might have mentioned that at the scene."

Sharon ignored him. She was still a little light headed. She had never fainted before. She tried to remember what had happened. She was talking to Barbara, the nurse came in, and then... She remembered the vertigo and the sense of plunging into space, but nothing else. She looked over at Grant. "That doesn't explain what you're doing here."

"Well, since you can't seem to stay away from danger, I had your ID monitored so I'd be notified if you were in any type of mishap. And what do you know, first day and I get a call."

"Who tagged my ID?" she asked, buttoning her pants and pushing her legs over the side of the bed.

Grant raised his hands. "Not me. I was only watching. It's the hospital that's added a tag onto it. Seems you've got yourself into another predicament."

"So what. I lied to get in to see Mrs. Sanders. I'm a reporter, it's my job."

Grant nodded his head and made a forced frown. "I'll give you that. I especially liked the niece story. You'll be happy to know, I didn't even bother telling them you're not her niece. I'm here because I wanted to be the one to break the news."

"What news?" Sharon asked as she put on her socks.

"Well. You fainted here in the hospital. Even hit your head on a bed railing. The hospital had to protect itself, so they ran a few tests."

Sharon stopped pulling on her sock and looked over at him. She didn't like the idea of things being done to her when she was unconscious. For all she knew, they could have given her a lobotomy. It was creepy. People had handled her without her knowing it. She couldn't stop the anger washing through her. "What kind of tests?" she demanded.

"Let me be the first to congratulate you, Miss Clark. You're pregnant. About six weeks they think."

"Pregnant?" Sharon said. "That's impossible." Wasn't it? She used birth control, had been using it most her adult life. Religiously even, since the abortion. The last thing she had ever wanted was another unplanned pregnancy. Sharon thought back. When was her last period? She couldn't remember. Had she been so excited about her assignment that she hadn't noticed she missed it?

"Well, as impossible as it may seem, it's true. And so I just thought I'd be the one to tell you and to let you know that you won't be able to leave the state until your eighth month."

Sharon was busy contemplating the idea of being pregnant when Grant's words struck her. "Eight months! I'm not staying in Arizona for eight months."

Grant stood up, his grin more of a laugh than a smile. "Those are the laws, so I guess you should call your paper and whoever else might give a damn and tell them you'll be on hiatus. I guess your reporting days are just about over, Miss Clark. I suggest you wrap up your story and send it off. We don't have much need for female snoops here."

"Go to hell," Sharon said.

"Now, now, watch your mouth. You're supposed to be a Christian, or so I'm told. Oh, and by the way. I took the liberty of telling your new beau."

"What?"

"Detective Matthews. He's on his way down to get you now. I thought he'd be mad, you kissing up to him when you're obviously involved with someone else, but he took it well. I think he likes the idea of having you around for a while longer. He might even be willing to sponsor your stay for a few favors.

"You son of a..."

"There goes that mouth of yours again. If I were a betting man, I'd say you're not quite the Godly women you hoped we'd all think you were." Grant walked over to the door.

"I'm not staying here," Sharon told him.

He turned back towards her. "You will or you'll end up in jail and that baby of yours will end up on the adoption block."

"I'll fight it!" Sharon screamed at him as he walked out of the room.

"You do that, Miss Clark" he yelled back to her then started to laugh. She could still hear him chuckling as he walked down the hall.

Sharon finished putting on her socks and shoes. She grabbed her bag, checked for her ID. It was there, nothing else seemed to have been touched. Her headband and watch were on the nightstand. She put them on, got off the bed and headed for her Jeep. She didn't want to see Paul. She needed time to think, to be alone. She'd get another test, that's what she'd do. A test by someone who didn't know her, a test she could use in court to prove they were wrong. She wouldn't be another Madison Courtney. They weren't going to lock her up to shut her up. No one was going to stop her, not even a baby she may or may not be having.

29

Barbara Sanders lay in her hospital bed. She was scared. As the bustle of morning activity got underway, she knew that everything was coming to a close. She had worked hard for twenty years to see the revolution put into place, and now, at its threshold, she would be stopped from entering into it. She thought about Moses and how God had kept him from entering Canaan and wondered to what purpose. Had her sins against Norma, Martha's mother, and the multitude of others she let be taken, finally caught up with her? Had all the other women she helped, even against the advice of the others, amounted for nothing in the eyes of whomever or whatever controlled the events of the living? Maybe not.

She preached against reactionary movements, against public displays of civil disobedience. She wanted them to go unknown until it was time to move. It was the only way. Take them while their guard was down. But yet, she couldn't stand by and watch as women were being chattelled. That had been her mistake. If she had taken her own advice and stayed away from the Women's Network, she could have gone on indefinitely. She could have seen her hard planned revolution take fruit.

It was too late now. Nathan knew. No one else would have planned her execution.

"How are you feeling this morning?" Doctor Lambert asked as he stepped into the room.

She looked up at the man that tried so hard to save her life and pitied his wasted effort. "A little sore, but otherwise fine," she said offering him a congenial smile while he studied her chart. It wasn't his fault. He was no more to blame for her fate than Martha was. They were just cogs, pawns in the greater scope of world politics.

He lifted the sheet that covered her and pulled up her nightgown to look at her abdomen. Carefully he pulled back the bandaging. "Still a little swollen," he said pushing at the wound. It hurt. Barbara winced from the pain, but said nothing. "Still tender, I see. Well it's healing nicely, but I still don't want you sitting up on your own or even coughing for that matter. It was a mess in there. I had to do a lot of cutting to repair the damage done to your intestines."

"I'll be careful," she said.

"I'm sure you will." He replaced the bandages and sheet then pulled down the sleeve of her nightgown and examined the shoulder wound. "You were lucky," he said.

Lucky? She wanted to laugh. Luck would have been if the bullet had hit her a few inches to the right and punctured her heart. At least it would all be over.

"How's she doing, Doctor Lambert?" Nathan Sanders said as he stepped into the room. Barbara's quick intake of breath made the doctor pull his hand away from her shoulder.

"Sorry," he told her then looked up at Nathan as he covered the wound. "Better than we expected. As soon as a room becomes available, I'm going to move her upstairs."

"To a private room, of course?" Nathan asked, looking right into Barbara's eyes.

"No promises," the doctor said. "An apartment complex burned down last night. We admitted over thirty patients. The hospital's pretty full. I'll do what I can."

"That's all anyone can ask." Nathan said.

"Well, Mrs. Sanders. I think you're on your way to a full recovery. Just mind me about those stomach muscles. The slightest effort could cause a tear and internal bleeding. Now I think I'll leave you two alone and finish my rounds."

Nathan thanked Doctor Lambert and shook his hand. "You've done a great job, doctor. I don't know what I would have done if I had lost her."

Doctor Lambert nodded his head and left. Nathan followed him to the door and closed it. It was time, time to undo the monster that she allowed to destroy so many lives. Barbara reached under her bed and turned on the recorder, wishing she had had the courage to destroy him years before.

"Well, a full recovery. What do you know about that? Yesterday I thought you were headed for judgment."

Nathan walked over to Barbara's bed, his tall thin body menacingly hovered above her. She had never thought about it before, but she had always been afraid of him. Maybe he was the reason behind everything she did, the instigator of her rebellion. She was forced to marry him, but she never loved him, not for a moment. She secretly defied him throughout the marriage, and now, finally, she would get to do it openly.

"I thought judgment had already been passed," she said.

Nathan grinned, only showing his top row of unevenly spaced teeth. "And so it has," he said.

"And you've been made my executioner? Why?"

Nathan put both his hands on her bed rail, threw his head back and let out a short low laugh. "I always underestimated you Barbara. All those years I thought I knew you. The do-gooder. The chaste pious woman. I think back on all the things I've told you. All the trust I placed in your being the perfect vassal. Loyalty, allegiance, that's all I ever asked of you."

"Loyalty to what?" Barbara asked. "To your black market baby business, to your desires to be the puppeteer of a world leader? Oh, I know all about you and Listner. You think if you can get him into the presidency, you can rule, you can force your brutish ways on the world."

"God's ways," he yelled leaning over her, his face only inches from her own. His hot breath intermingled with the pure oxygen being fed to her through plastic tubing.

She looked him straight in the eyes. She didn't back away or avoid his gaze. "So you did try to have me killed."

Nathan pulled back. "I do whatever I need to keep the Lord's word."

"Whatever happened to 'Thou shalt not kill?'"

"Murderers have always been put down. God justifies the death of a life taker. And that's exactly what you are. How many deaths have you orchestrated? How many of God's children have you helped destroy?"

"How many have you sold?"

Nathan pointed his finger at her and took on his preacher stance, legs set apart, his body angled so the finger was an extension of the whole body. "Let you who among us hast not sinned cast the first stone. I may have profited from the selling of a few lives, but you my dear, you took it upon yourself to play God and take them. You are the sinner among us. The unrighteous one. The one condemned by God."

"God?" Barbara said in a humorous tone. "What do you know about God?"

"I know everything," he hissed. He walked to the foot of the bed and held on to its footboard. "Everything I do is for the Lord. No one, not even you, can condemn me for it. Those babies, they wouldn't have been born if it wasn't for my work here. I saved them. Is that clear?" The bed shook as he yelled in hushed tones. Barbara worried about the recorder, but there was nothing she could do about it, so she rode out the storm with only a little discomfort. The bed stopped and it seemed as though his anger subsided. He let go of the footboard. "I saved their miserable little lives and they pay me back by contributing to the continual sowing of the Lord's seed. Without that money we wouldn't have been able to hire the men we need to do God's work."

"Like hiring white supremacist assassins to shoot ungrateful wives and their chauffeurs?"

Nathan Smiled. "That was an unforeseen expense. We have many others. Growth takes money Barbara. We do what we must to get it."

"You have tons of money Nathan. You sell those babies because you enjoy owning people and having people be owned. Look at the pleasure you get from mounting your own little concubine. What do you think Norma will do when she finds out the truth, that you bought and paid for her? Do you think she'll jump in your bed so easily then?"

"Shut up," Nathan said. "I will not listen to you speak of such things."

"Oh, so now you want to deny it?"

"I deny nothing. What I do is none of your business. You're the one being charged here. You're the one who has defiled God."

Now she really wanted to laugh, but didn't. "If it's your God you're talking about, there's no one to defile, Nathan. The God you worship isn't the creator of mankind, he's the creation of your own selfish lusts."

Nathan's hand came quick and hard. It pressed against her neck and she could barely breathe. "Never, never blaspheme the name of the Lord." Barbara used her good arm to grab his, to try and pry away his long deadly fingers. The machine monitoring her heart and oxygen started to scream. Nathan released his hand and stepped back. The machine went silent. He reached up and turned off the alarm.

Barbara started to cough. She tried to hold it back, but couldn't catch her breath. Her abdomen squeeze tight as she pulled up coughing long and hard. The stitches pulled. She reached her hand down to cover the tearing wound and felt the oncoming moisture of warm blood.

"Look what you've done," Nathan said pulling the sheet down and exposing the red stained bandage beneath her nightgown. "I suppose I should call the nurse."

"Yes, do that," Barbara said hoarsely as she lay back down on the bed. The pain was growing worse.

"Not quite yet. You see Barbara. I'm afraid I can't let you live. Now that you know I know what you've been doing behind my back, I can't really trust you to keep my secrets. Can I?"

No. "I won't tell anyone. I promise."

"Too late for promises," he said pulling the sheet over her wound. "It's time to pay for your sins." He put one hand over her mouth. "Oh, by the way. How is our dear niece Sharon doing? Did she recover from her fainting spell?"

Barbara tried to talk under his hand, but he held it too tight. She tried to tell him Sharon knew nothing. Only mumbling came out. She could taste the salt of his sweaty hands, smell his hatred. His free hand reached inside his suit coat and he pulled out a picture. A picture of her, Martha and Sharon at the Elliot Pagoda at Papago Park.

"You see, I've known for a while. I would have let you continue for a few more months if that nosy reporter hadn't shown up. We couldn't have you helping her anymore, so we had to put an end to it. Like we put an end to your baby killer friend, Dr. Garner."

Barbara relaxed under her husband's hold. Simon was dead and she was next. There was no use fighting. She would let the hidden recorder do it for her. Nathan put the picture back in his pocket and placed his hand over the bleeding wound. "Oh, and did they tell you, Miss Clark is pregnant," he said as he jabbed his hand down hard on her stomach. "I guess that means one more baby for me."

Barbara could feel her insides burst. Hot pain tore through her. She tried to scream, but his hand stifled it. The pain quickly subsided. All she felt was warmth. It was a pleasant sort of feeling and she felt her body relax into it. His hand left her mouth. She knew she would die, but there would be no pleading, no crying. Just pity. Pity for a man who had lost his soul to religion and the world that would have to fight against him.

"They'll stop you," she said. "The people will wake up and see you for what you are. You can't fool them forever."

Nathan bent over her and kissed her forehead. "I'm not afraid of them. As a wise man once noted, when an opponent declares 'I will not come over to your side', I calmly say. Your child belongs to us already. In a short time, your descendants will know nothing else but this new community.'"

She knew who his mentor was. She had always known. It was relief to finally hear him admit it. "You're as insane as he was," she whispered as the warmth overtook her. She smiled at that thought. People like him, dictators, degenerates wanting power to consume and destroy, were always undone in time. Maybe not soon enough to save millions of lives, but long before they could destroy the world. It was a comfort she could take with her as she moved away from her life and her death.

"But unlike my illustrious mentor, we're not trying to extinguish a whole race," Nathan said from a far enough distance that his words held no meaning. "Just trying to put the nation back in its proper order."

30

Sharon woke from a dreamless sleep at the motel on Van Buren, She had been afraid Paul, not finding her at the hospital, would have gone to her hotel, so she opted for the privacy the motel would offer. Sleep did not come easy, she was plagued by rambling thoughts of the possibility and consequences of being pregnant. Around two o'clock in the morning exhaustion finally overtook her and she fell asleep, curled up in a ball, cradling her pillow like a frightened child.

She came to terms with the fact that she could be pregnant. The nausea she experienced throughout her stay in Arizona was evidence of sorts, but the coincidence of it happening now was suspicious. She would get a second opinion, but not right away. She didn't have the time for her own problems and decided she would have to put it out of her mind. She had too many things she still had to do before she could start thinking about the problems a pregnancy would present when she tried to go home, or what Thomas would say when he found out he was going to be a father. After she was given positive proof and Martha and Anthony were safe, she'd take the time to sort out her life and the life of her baby.

It was already nine o'clock. She got up, took a shower and put back on the clothes she had worn the day before. It was too early to try and retrieve the recorder from Barbara, so she decided to get Martha and Anthony and take them to get their IDs. With that out of the way, she could concentrate on her personal problems and find a doctor to perform the pregnancy test. Thomas and Paul would have to wait.

Sharon tried to call her hotel to find out if there were any messages, but was reminded by the now familiar operator's voice that her account was still suspended. She never called to have it restored. She didn't want to take the risk of them finding out about her fake phone card, so she decided to take the chance and return to her hotel. It would give her the opportunity to change, and pack up her notes and tapes. She didn't know how things were going to unfold, but she didn't think it would be wise to be unprepared. She needed to be ready to move on a minute's notice. If they were setting her up, things would happen fast. She didn't want to chance the information she had already accumulated being lost.

At the hotel there were four messages waiting for her. One from Derek, two from Thomas and a fourth with no name. The clerk told her the anonymous message had come in this morning and that it was from a woman. It would be the first she returned, but not from here. She'd find a private phone and use the untraceable card Barbara had given her. As she took the elevator to her room, she thought about Paul. Why hadn't he left a message?

Her question was answered as she opened her door and found him waiting inside. Great, now, she'd have to spend her morning answering his questions – something she didn't want to do.

"Where the hell have you been?" he asked, standing up from the armchair she supposed he had slept in while waiting for her to return.

"Don't you have to work?" she asked, putting her bag on the bed.

"Not till this afternoon. Sharon, I've been worried about you. Where did you go?"

It was none of his business, but she knew if she didn't tell him, he would probably find out for himself. "I rented a room in a motel. I didn't want to see you last night. I wasn't ready to be interrogated."

"I don't blame you," he said, walking up to her, putting his arms around her, and pulling him into her. "I don't care whose baby it is. I don't ever have to know. Just promise me you won't try and leave. Promise me you'll stay here and let me take care of you."

Sharon pulled away. The last thing she needed was a cop taking care of her. "I'm not even sure I'm pregnant."

"What? But the results at the hospital?"

Sharon looked at the sadness in his eyes. If she didn't believe it, he certainly did. He was just as much a victim of his society as the rest of them. "If they could do it to Madison Courtney, what makes you think they wouldn't do it to me?"

"That's ridiculous. Why would they do that to you?"

It was time to tell him the truth. How he reacted would indicate how much she could trust him. "Because I lied,' she said. "I'm not pro-life. I'm pro-choice and the article I'm writing is against this blasted state of yours, and they know it."

Paul sat on the bed. "I can't say I'm surprised. But it's still not a good enough reason. Whoever you think this great conspirator is can't have the whole state working for him. You had doctors examine you, unbiased professionals, unconcerned with your motivations for being here."

"How do you know, Paul? Detective Grant was there when I woke up. He monitors my profile. He watches everything I do. I fainted, okay, I admit that, but what if they used that as an excuse? What if the tests were just another way for them to repress my article?"

"I think you're taking yourself way too seriously, Sharon. No offense, but you're a novice reporter working for a second rate paper. You're just not a big enough threat to them."

Sharon opened her mouth to retaliate, to tell him just how much she knew, minus the connection with Martha and Anthony, when he held up his hand. "Look, Grant talked to me yesterday. He said you were a pest, that's all. He didn't like how you were showing up at every corner and told me to keep you out of his hair. He could care less about your article. He just doesn't like you."

Sharon sat on the bed beside him. If he were right, if Grant didn't care, then the truth was she really could be pregnant. If she was pregnant, she would be trapped within the state or forced to risk everything by trying to escape. "I can't stay here, Paul," she said in a defeated tone. "I have a life in Southern California, a career and a home. I would kill someone if I were forced to stay here. I've lived in Los Angeles my whole life, I need to be in the midst of people who are alive and living each day, fully aware of what's going on around them. The way you people live is too safeguarded and subdued."

"It's not that bad here. I tell you what, after the baby's born, I'll take you to Boston, Los Angeles, New York, anywhere you want to go. Just don't do anything stupid."

Too late for that. "Paul, you don't understand."

"Yes I do. It's you who doesn't understand. It's either eight months here or it's five years in prison and the loss of your child."

She thought about the child for a minute. Thomas' child. If she was pregnant and she was caught trying to get out of the state, they would take it away. Paul was right, it was a big risk, one she wasn't sure she would be willing to take if her next test came back positive. She lay back on the bed and sighed. She would have to stay. "What about my article?"

"What about it? No one said you can't still work on it. They said you can't leave the state. That doesn't mean you can't continue working on it or send things to your paper."

He was right, of course, but it didn't make it any easier. "I don't know Paul. It's all happening too fast."

Paul lay down beside her, pulled her over to him and kissed her. He put his hand on her thigh and pressed upwards, his fingers gently brushing her crotch. She felt the familiar tingle of lust and kissed him back. She needed this.

Paul's hand migrated upward and slid under her shirt, beneath her bra. She grabbed the cloth of his shirt, pulled it free from his pants, and placed both hands on his stomach. Her fingers found a path of hair leading both ways. She rubbed downward from the waist of his jeans, applying pressure as her fingers felt his hardness. He moved, raised one leg over her and knelt above her. She reached for the button of his pants, then stopped. Something was wrong.

Sharon removed her hands from Paul's waist and pulled down her shirt.

"What's the matter?" he asked, pulling himself off her and falling hard back on the bed.

Sharon turned over on her side and looked at him. "Why doesn't it bother you I'm pregnant with someone else's child?"

Paul didn't turn towards her, he stared up at the ceiling. "Because that was in the past, it was before you met me. I'm not going to judge you on what you did before we met."

"But it was only six weeks ago," she said sitting up. Actually it was only a few day's ago since I was with another man. That should bother you."

Paul pulled himself up and sat next to her. He lifted her chin with his hand and kissed her gently. "I know it should, but it doesn't. All I know is..." He hesitated, then in a hushed voice said, "I'm falling in love with you. Nothing else matters, not the baby or its father."

Sharon looked at Paul for a moment. He always seemed so sincere, and that alone made her suspicious. "What if I said I loved him?"

"Do you?" Paul asked staring into her eyes. "Or are you having doubts now that we've met?"

Sharon looked away. She was so attracted to Paul physically that she couldn't stay focused when he was around. Just last night she thought he had purposely driven her by Barbara Sanders' accident and now she almost threw herself at him. She would have to be stronger.

"I don't know. But if I'm pregnant, he's the father. I need time to sort all this out."

"Sure," Paul said standing up, adjusting his jeans. "Take all the time you need. But when you make up your mind, I'll be here."

Sharon smiled. How she wanted to believe that. She pulled herself off the bed and put her arms around his waist. "Thanks," she said, kissing him softly on the lips. "Now go before I change my mind.'

"If you're going to change your mind, I'd rather stay."

Sharon tucked his shirt back into his pants, turned him towards the door, and pushed.

"All right, I can take a hint," he said, taking a few extra steps. He opened the door and stepped partially through it. "Can I come by tonight after I get off work?"

"I don't know," Sharon said.

"I promise to behave."

A piece of her didn't want to lose him, it wanted him to be who he said he was, but another piece screamed for her to be leery of Trojan soldiers with hard bodies. She didn't know which to trust, her longings or her instincts. Either way, she would be a fool not to meet with him again.

"It's not you I'm worried about," she said then agreed to meet him.

31

Martha sat staring out at the desert. She had climbed on a rock near the shack at sunrise and stayed there. Anthony woke up an hour later and went to their mother's cave to see what she had left behind. It was peaceful in the desert. She hadn't seen any more snakes, but there were lizards and roadrunners moving among the low-lying cacti and rocky dirt.

Anthony had told her about his life as a ward as they lay on their cots the night before, the darkness invaded only by the dying embers of their fire. He hadn't surrendered to them, no matter how many times they had beat him. Youth impeded his judgment, he had no doubts in their mother and held on to every lesson she had taught them about fighting for what was right. During every beating, he would clench his fists and lock his jaw. He would picture their mother in jail and his determination to survive would strengthen. Each day, he told himself that on the fifteenth of May, Martha would show up to claim him, to take him home.

"But the fifteenth came and you weren't there," he said. "I went to see a counselor and asked when you would be coming to get me. He put his arm around my shoulder and told me that they had contacted you and that you didn't want me. But I didn't believe him."

Martha hadn't asked him any questions. She knew he had been stronger than she had and she was proud of him. She felt guilt for having given in so easily and then hatred towards their mother for having abandoned them. Neither of them deserved what had happened, no one did. She was about to tell him this, to make him put the blame where it belonged, when he slowly told her about his last beating.

"It was the day after your birthday. I was sent out on a work detail to clean up some horse stalls at a ranch in Gilbert. The guardian that was supervising us was this big white guy who gave me most of my beatings. He hated me. Well, at least, I think he did. It was so hard to tell what any of them were thinking. Anyway, I was always looking for a way to escape and was doing just that when he showed up behind me.

"'Get to work, Garcia,' he screamed not two inches from my face. Then he pushed me down in a pile of horseshit. I don't know what made me do it, but I picked up a handful of the stuff and threw it in his face. That's what started it. He grabbed me by my shirt and pulled me to my feet. Straw and shit stuck to his face, but I could still see how red it was. He pulled back his fist. I closed my eyes and cringed backward but the blow never came. When I opened my eyes he was smiling. It was the scariest smile I ever saw. He had two broken teeth. His tongue was rubbing one of them and his upper lip started to curl. I knew then it would have been better if he had hit me. Instead he threw me back down into the pile and walked away. I heard him order everyone out of the barn and to wait out front. I pulled myself up and was just about to go myself when he stepped in front of me and put his hand on my chest.

"'Not you,' he said. Then he pulled a short black rod from behind his back. I knew I was in big trouble. His grin came back. He picked up some horse shit and rubbed it on the rod. 'We don't want you forgetting this too soon. Now turn it over boy,' he yelled.

"I didn't move. At the school they have to beat you with a strap. But this thing was like wire. He grabbed me again, flung me around, jammed me into the side of the stall and pulled my shirt up over my head. Then he beat me. At first it wasn't so bad, but then he got into it. I tried to think of Mama. I tried to be strong, but I couldn't do it. I was so scared and it hurt so bad. Finally I couldn't stand anymore and I fell to the ground. But it didn't stop him. He just beat me some more. My shirt had fallen down and I could kind of see the ground. Everything was blurry, but I could tell my hand was only inches away from a metal meal bucket. I don't know where I got the strength, but before he could hit me one more time, I rolled over, grabbed the bucket and hit him in the head.

"I don't know if I killed him or what, but his head was bleeding. That's when I decided I had to run. It didn't matter how much pain I was in, I knew if I didn't run I'd be dead. So I took off. I found my way to the old Indian reservation and headed for South Mountain. It took me that night and all the next day to make it to the church. I don't remember much of it, I saw a few Posse cars, and hid in alleys a few times, but other than that all I remember is getting to the church. I don't even remember finding the stairs to the balcony or you finding me."

Martha hadn't said anything when he finished. She turned over, put her back to him, and cried. After a few minutes, he moved over to her cot and lay down beside her. Putting his arm over her he whispered, "Don't cry. They can't hurt us anymore."

Martha sat on the rock, tears once again falling down her face. Not because he had been beaten, not because of what he went through when he ran away, but because he still had hope.

32

Sharon dug her real ID out of the dirt at the base of the rubber plant at the end of the hall, gathered all of her disks, headbands, recorder cells and notes and packed them in her small tote bag with her makeup and jewelry. She wasn't taking chances on leaving anything behind if things started to get too hot. It was better to keep these things with her, just in case. She didn't know what she expected to go wrong or when and if it would, but she felt better knowing she was prepared. She took the tote with her to the Jeep and stashed it under her seat. Just knowing it was there made her feel better, made her feel like she was in control.

She decided her first stop of the day should be the nursery where Barbara's friend worked. She would set a time to bring Martha and Anthony in to have their IDs taken then find a doctor to reissue a pregnancy test. Barbara and the recorder would have to wait, which was just as well, since she had no idea how long it would take Barbara to get her husband to talk. She didn't want to reappear prematurely, risk being caught, and then find out there was nothing incriminating on the recorder.

As she found the address of the nursery from a phone book at a nearby gas station she remembered the anonymous message she had been given by the hotel clerk. She didn't know who the caller was, but assumed it was someone from Barbara Sanders' organization. A women's voice answered the phone. Sharon identified herself and said she had been asked to call. The woman was silent for a moment.

"Hello," Sharon said. "Are you still there?"

"Yes," the woman said tentatively, slowly.

Sharon didn't like playing games with people. Sure she could lie with the best of them to get what she wanted, or to safeguard herself, but even then she was always direct and to the point. The hesitancy from this woman was starting to grate on her nerves. That was one of the things she hated about her job, being forced to show patience and compassion to time consuming idiots. "Is there something you want?"

"I, I, want to meet with you. I have something I want to show you."

She speaks. "Can you tell me what that is?"

"No, not over the phone. Meet me at twelve thirty at the food court in the Kachina Mall. It's on the Beeline, two exits past Fountain Valley."

"What's this..." The phone went dead.

Sharon hung up more annoyed than curious, but she knew she'd go. There had been fear in the woman's voice and that was a good sign. People were only afraid when passing along information that was incriminating. She didn't know where Fountain Valley was or what the Beeline was, but she would find them. She fueled her car then went inside and asked for directions to Fountain Valley. The attendant pulled out a map similar to the one she had in her glove compartment and showed her the best route to take from where they were. She thanked him and headed back to the Jeep. It was already eleven o'clock, but it didn't look like it was going to take long to get there. She still had time to go see Stan Deitrich and make arrangements for Martha and Anthony's IDs.

She had no problem finding the nursery. She was beginning to know the area quite well. The streets ran two directions, north and south, east and west. They seemed perfectly straight and set apart at consistent intervals. The street names carried from one town to the next, not that she could tell when she left one town and moved into another. Everything looked the same, housing complexes, trailer parks, apartment buildings, and strip malls. There was a gas station or convenience store at every corner. Sharon was once again amazed at the orderliness of things. "What these people need are a few curves in their lives," she said out loud as she pulled into the nursery parking lot,

The Desert Nursery yard was littered with cacti, bougainvillea, and various other plants Sharon didn't recognize or like. Desert plants had a different kind of texture and look about them. Everything seemed to come to a sharp point and had hard ridges. Even though most of Southern California had been desert as well, the fauna had a greener, more natural look to it. She could never go for desert landscaping – it was too stark and uninviting.

The parking lot was empty except for an old beat up maroon Toyota hatchback and a flat bed truck. She assumed these belonged to the owner, and headed into the main building.

"Can I help you?" a tall overly tanned, overly blond man with a pony tail asked her.

"I'm looking for Stan Deitrich."

"Found him," the man said lifting a large plastic roll and walking it out the door. He rested it against the side of the building, brushed his hands off and turned to face her. "What will it be today?"

Sharon looked around to make sure there were no prying eyes or ears then took a step closer. "My name is Sharon Clark. Barbara Sanders told me you'd be expecting me."

The man glanced around the yard and back through the opening of the building, then signaled for her to follow him. He walked into an area crowded with rows of saplings. "Most of these trees are a year or two old already and should transplant very well." He stooped down at a six-foot ironwood. She stooped with him. He pointed to the roots as if showing her their high quality or perhaps instructing her on proper care. "I can't believe she's dead," he said picking up some loose soil and letting it fall back into the pot."

Sharon looked over at him. "Dead? She's not dead. I saw her last night. They expect her to make a full recovery."

"Guess you haven't been listening to the radio then. She died this morning. Doctor said she suffered some kind of rupture." The man stood up and pulled some branches from the base of the tree. "Look here," he said.

Sharon stood up, her legs weakened by the news. Barbara had foreseen her death, had even accused her would be assassin. And though Sharon believed her, it hadn't seemed real. With everything Sharon had been through, she still found it hard to believe that a man could kill his wife in the middle of a hospital and not get caught. Maybe he didn't worry about being caught. Knowing Listner would protect him and the hospital would cover up for him, had he stepped into Barbara's room fearless? If that was the case, no one was safe. Why couldn't they wake up and see it? What's wrong with everybody, she wanted to scream, but didn't.

Calm down, she warned herself. Barbara could have died from her wounds. She had been hit pretty bad. There was no telling what had happened overnight. Or was there? She thought about the recorder stuck beneath the bed frame. Had Barbara had time to turn it on? If she did, then Sharon would have proof, and if it proved that Sanders had killed his wife, she would make sure the whole God damn state knew it.

"I can do the kids this afternoon," Stan said drawing her out of her reverie.

"What?" she asked.

"The kids. I've already designed new IDs for them, all I need is their pictures, thumb prints, and face specs. Bring them to the Artisan Print and Portrait shop on the corner of Alma School and Baseline. It's in a strip mall, so be careful. Tell them Helen sent you to have your pictures taken."

Sharon nodded her head. She'd be careful. Now more than ever. With Barbara Sanders dead, Martha would now be accused of two murders. People may not care too much about one Hispanic boy, but they would care when one of their leading citizens was killed. People would be watching for Martha. Everyone would be a potential informant.

"How soon after the pictures will the IDs be ready? I need to get them out of the state immediately," she asked him.

"Half an hour. They'll give them to you there."

"Great," she said. She would have Derek rent them a car and she'd send them on their way tonight. Two less lives to worry about. Sharon knew no money could be exchanged for Stan's services. Accounts were too easy to trace, but usually in situations like these there was some sort of exchange. "How do you want me to pay you?" she asked.

"Don't worry about it. Barbara took care of everything yesterday morning."

Of course Barbara had taken care of it. She had taken care of everything since Sharon first heard about this assignment. It was going to be hard to go on, knowing she wouldn't be there in the background watching out for her.

Sharon thanked the man and turned to leave. "Look," he said. "I know you're some kind of reporter. There are a lot of us who didn't like the idea of Barbara helping you the way she did, but we respected her and did what we were told. I just want you to know that if anyone finds out about us, we'll go to jail for life. And everything we've worked for, that Barbara's worked for will be destroyed."

Sharon looked at the man with his long hair and leathery face. He wasn't part of the Women's Network. He was involved with Barbara Sander's other project, her so called revolution. There had always been radical organizations in America working towards its political downfall. But they never did much. The occasional kidnapping or bombing or military standoff, would disrupt the world for a day or two, but nothing in over twenty years had made an impact. How could there have been, these groups were always small pockets of misfits led by extremists. With homeland security so tight, gatherings of more than five were scrutinized so closely that subversive groups were shutdown before they ever formed. Sharon didn't believe that was the case with Barbara's group. Sharon didn't think Barbara would have wasted her time and given her life for something unorganized and ineffective. She would be behind a movement, one that Sharon doubted was made up of only a four or five Arizonians. When she got back to Southern California, she'd do some research and find out if there were any other branches in her state.

But first, she'd see what was waiting for her at the Kachina Mall, get proof how Barbara died, and get Martha and Anthony out of the state.

The mall was smaller than she was used to, but still busy enough so no one would pay attention to two women having lunch. A great cover. The smell of various types of food being offered from dozens of concessions made Sharon hungry. She walked up to the China Express counter. A woman with chin length straight black hair got in line behind her. Sharon ordered pork fried rice, two egg rolls, and a Coke. The small Asian woman behind the counter dished out her food, took her ID and ran it through the register.

Sharon found a table in the middle of the court next to a planter, surrounded by empty tables, and sat down. She looked around the room. Who was the woman that wanted to meet her, and how was she supposed to recognize her? There was a young girl at the Wendys' stand who seemed nervous. The girl had looked over her shoulder numerous times and seemed to be in a hurry when she grabbed her bagged lunch and headed for the tables. She stopped at the edge of the sitting area and scanned the diners. Sharon was about to stand up, make herself more visible, when the woman who had been behind her at the China Express sat down across from her.

"Eat," the woman said.

Sharon picked up her fork and put it into her rice. The woman picked up a piece of sweet and sour pork and plopped it into her mouth. Her other hand slid an envelope over to Sharon. There was a disk in it Sharon suspected was undeveloped film. Sharon took it and put it into her bag."

"Who are you?"

"I work at the penitentiary," the woman said in a low but steady voice. "That woman you were looking for, she's there. I got pictures." Sharon rubbed the band of her watch, pulling out the stem as she did so.

"Is she all right?"

"The pictures will show you. She tried to escape but got hurt. We took her baby right there in the desert, but it didn't make it." The woman took another bite of food.

Sharon followed her lead, and as she sipped Coke from her straw she said, "So. Where's the crime in that?"

"Right now she's five months pregnant."

Sharon kept herself from spitting out the drink she just took and slowly put down the cup. Dorothy Miller had been right. "I've heard this before," she said. "Have there been other multiple births?"

The dark haired woman nodded her head. "There's a whole section of breeders. They get three, sometimes four babies out of some of the woman. They keep them drugged while they're there. It keeps the mothers disoriented, but doesn't hurt the babies. The women think they're always dealing with the same pregnancy."

"Are there pictures of that?"

The woman shook her head.

A custodian walked up to the empty table beside them and cleared off the dishes.

"So what do you think of this?" the woman said reaching into her bag and pulling out a shirt. It was a sleeveless chartreuse silk shirt with a cowl neck. Sharon thought it was hideous. But said she liked it. The custodian finished washing down the table and stepped away. The woman put the shirt back in her bag.

"So what do they do with all those babies?" Sharon asked.

"I don't know. We're not allowed to record them. We don't even keep them for the first ten days like we do the rest. They're picked up the day they're born."

Sharon remembered what Barbara had told her about her husband's and Senator Listner's side business. "Have you ever seen Senator Listner or Nathan Sanders at the prison?"

"No. But," the woman looked around the room and then quickly back to her food. "The doctor is the senator's sister."

Sharon had taken another bite of food and almost choked on it. She coughed into her napkin. "What a set up," she whispered. "Listner and Sanders are in the black market baby business."

"I figured something like that. But I don't really care about the babies. I'm sure they go to good homes. It's her," she said looking down at Sharon's bag. "It's what they're doing to her that scares me. They're planning on transporting her to a new facility they've built sometime this week. They plan on keeping her like that the rest of her life."

"Like what?"

"Pregnant."

Sharon looked into the woman's eyes. Her skin had a deep rich color to it that seemed natural, not the result of weathering from Arizona's sun. Her eyes were honest, yet tinted with a shade of fear. The same shade Sharon saw in Barbara Sanders eyes the last time she had seen her. This woman was doing something beyond her inner level of courage. She was taking chances she thought would come back on her. There was no reason not to believe her.

"That other woman's next," she said.

"What other woman?"

"The one you spent so much time with when you visited. Madison Courtney. Doctor Listner ordered genetic testing done on her. If it comes back clean they'll impregnate her. I heard the warden tell the doctor she's to be shipped off with the Collins girl."

Sharon leaned over the table. For some reason she felt a bond with Madison, maybe because of Paul, she wasn't sure. More likely it was because of her admiration for what the woman had done with her life. She regarded her with as much respect as she did Barbara Sanders and Suzanne Garcia. She couldn't let them imprison her for life, using her as a living incubator.

"Do you know where this facility is, where they'll take her?"

The woman picked up her bag and shook her head. "I obtained a copy of Madison's pregnancy test and the order for her genetic testing. It's dated with the infirmary's stamp. It's in the envelope. I go on vacation next week. I'm planning on leaving the state. Please wait before you do anything with what I've given you. If they find out what I did they'll kill me." She pushed her lunch away and stood up. "Please don't call me again."

"I won't," Sharon said, looking up at her. "You've done the right thing."

"I know," she said then walked away.

Sharon stayed and finished her lunch. *Breeders.* The woman had used the word easily. It was no new idea. Sharon wondered just how many women had been used and what type of facility they were building for them. She pictured Madison Courtney strapped to a life of child bearing, lost in a haze. Then a shiver ran through her body. In her mind the image of Madison changed. It was her own reflection, life-less and pregnant that looked back.

Before she did anything else she would go the hospital to reclaim her recorder. With Barbara dead, it was too risky leaving it jammed in the bed frame. Martha and Anthony would have to wait.

She entered the hospital feeling relatively safe. If Barbara was dead, there would be no one to dispute her relationship with the Sanders. She would tell the nurses she had lost an earring when she fell and needed to look for it, they wouldn't be able to deny her that. Unless, of course, a new patient had already been moved into Barbara's room. Mentally, she crossed her fingers as she got off the elevator and headed towards ICU.

The waiting room was empty. That was a good sign. Anyone recently admitted would have family waiting. She thought about the alienated mother who had been waiting the night before and what happened to the child. Hopefully, the mother wasn't being arraigned for child endangerment. The woman was suffering enough. Sharon had seen it on the woman's face. She felt responsible and would pay, emotionally, for the rest of her life. Sharon looked away, saddened by the woman's ordeal and her own fear of motherhood. The laws were too strict. Children too precarious. One lapse off attention, one slip of the hand, and they were gone, and with them not only their mother's heart, but the rest of her children, her husband, her family, and her freedom. Motherhood was too much of a risk. Why would anyone purposely impose it on themselves? Could children really bring enough joy to outweigh the responsibility? Sharon though of Thomas and smiled. He would think so, and maybe she did too. Having Thomas' baby might just be the most wonderful thing that ever happened. She would be a better mom than the one that raised her. She would give it the love and...

"Stop it," Sharon scolded herself. She didn't have time to dwell on unplanned pregnancies or imaginary children. Until she knew for sure she was pregnant, she wouldn't waste her time thinking about it. There were other things, more important things to do right now. She had to get the recorder. Like Martha and Anthony, her baby would have to wait.

The man at the nurse's station wasn't the same one she spoke to the previous night. This one wasn't concerned with the loss of her earring.

"If it were there," he told her, "housekeeping would have found it and left it with us, but they didn't. I suggest you look elsewhere." He moved a few feet, picked up a chart and started to write in it.

"Please," Sharon begged. "Those earrings were a gift from my aunt. I have to find them."

The nurse didn't look at her. "I told you they aren't here. You need to be going now."

Fucker. "Look," Sharon said using her most assertive voice. "I am not leaving until you let me search the room. My uncle will be devastated if I don't wear those earrings to the funeral."

Sharon paused, waited for a response. There was none.

"Fine," she said putting her bag on the shelf that separated them. "I'll just call my uncle, tell him what happened, and have *him* get me permission to search the room." The nurse looked up, his face flush with anger. Sharon didn't care. What right did he have to keep her from searching an unoccupied room? "You do know who my uncle is, don't you?" she asked.

"Search your heart out lady," the nurse said. Picking up the chart, he turned his back to her and moved to a different desk behind the station. Sharon thought she heard him mumbling something, but didn't care enough to listen. Instead she hurried down the small hall before he changed his mind.

The room was empty. The equipment lifeless. The bed had been changed, the sheets tightly folded waiting for their next victim. The butterflies that beat their wings so often on her stomach lining were in a frenzied panic. What if he had found the recorder? What if Barbara hadn't been able to activate it? Sharon knelt down next to the bed and reached under it. The recorder was there, she could feel its warm plastic against the steel frame of the bed. One down, one to go. Tentatively, she ran her hands along the buttons. The tallest one, the record button, had been pushed in, firmly, snugly. If there were goods to get, Barbara had gotten them.

Sharon smiled as she dislodged the recorder from the frame. Hopefully, there was enough on the recorder to indict both Sanders and Listner. And maybe, if justice would for once take off that damn blind, there would be enough evidence to prove Barbara's husband had ordered the shooting that caused her death.

"I won't let you down," Sharon said in a whisper, hoping Barbara, wherever she was, was listening.

Soft plodding of rubber souls moved down the hall. Sharon put the recorder in her bag and pulled out the ruby earring she had brought with her. She grabbed the bed railing to pull herself up into a standing position. The memory of waking up in a hospital bed after fainting, slowed her down. She didn't need a repeat performance. Sharon

Clark, down for the count. Scene two.

"Found it," she said as the nurse walked into the room.

"Good for you, now get out. We need the bed."

Sharon looked at the nurse with great distaste, but he was right. It was time to go. She put the earring back in her bag and brushed past him. "My uncle will be pleased," she said.

"Yeah, yeah. Tell him to credit my account," he said as he walked over to the night table, opened its small draw and took inventory of its contents.

Sharon shook her head. Congeniality wasn't this man's strongest suit. He was an ass. He had no right working with ICU patients and, she decided, someone needed to let him know. But, what good would that do? He wouldn't just up and quit because she thought he needed a career change. So why waste the effort? She pulled her bag close to her side. Besides, if she was going to let loose her venom, she had bigger game, more lethal opponents to destroy.

33

Anthony found the stash of herbs and two battery operated lanterns his mother had hidden in the cave and showed Martha where they were. Martha stayed deep inside the earth's cool walls to get out of the desert heat, and to be among her mother's belongings. Anthony left to explore a smaller cave he had found a few hundred feet from their mother's hold.

The lantern's bright glow reflected off the mineral rich cavern walls showing the entrances to two tunnels Anthony had already explored. One led to a smaller chamber that was empty. The other was a long tunnel leading back outside, away from the camp. A prickly pear bush blocked its entrance. Small vials of herbal oil were neatly stacked on a three tiered bookshelf evened out on the rocky floor with slivers of wood. Dried herbs in resealable plastic bags filled a large woven basket stained with dried mildew. Mason jars with herbs, suspended in an oily substance, were lined up against one of the walls.

Martha took a vial labeled eucalyptus oil and sat down among her mother's things. Everything was neatly marked. Everything had been meticulously packaged. Her mother dedicated her life to this. And for what? Martha opened the vial of eucalyptus and ran it under her nose. Its menthol aroma was strong and stung her nostrils, but she didn't pull it away.

"This is you, Mama," she said. "This is all you've left for us. This is all you ever cared about." Martha inhaled the pungent herb, its powerful tincture filled her lungs and made her gag. She pulled back. Her eyes watered. "Well, you can have it," she screamed as she flung the small bottle against the cave's wall and jumped to her feet. "You can have it all!"

Martha ran over to the bookshelf and began knocking its contents onto the floor. First the top shelf, then the middle. She threw herself on the ground and yanked each bottle from the bottom shelf, smashing them against the stone floor. The oils mixed in a puddle of glass. Their perfumes saturated the dry air. Martha didn't notice. A low hysterical scream worked its way up her chest. She pulled herself up, flew into the basket of dried herbs and started ripping them open, handfuls at a time.

"What's going on?" Anthony yelled from a few feet behind her.

Martha stopped and looked over at her brother, then down at the plastic bag held tightly in her hand. She didn't know what was happening. She opened her hand and let the bag fall to the floor. Anthony stared at the mess. Martha followed his gaze. She had destroyed everything. She looked down at herself, she was covered in dried leaves.

"You're insane," Anthony yelled, then turned and ran out of the cave.

Martha sat down in the pile of scattered herbs and put her hands over her face. He was right. She was losing it. First the snake, now this. The rage that had festered in her for the past four months had finally taken control. She took a few deep breaths, and coughed.

"Focus on Anthony," she told herself. "He's the important one. Get him out of Arizona, then you can go insane." She wouldn't be like her mother. She'd show Anthony that family really did come first. They had each other, that was all that counted. To hell with her mother. Suzanne Garcia could rot in jail, just as fast as her precious herbs would now that they were exposed to the Arizona heat.

Martha coughed again. Her eyes stung. The tang of the room overcame her. She could barely breathe. She stood up, brushed herself off and headed out to apologize to her brother and make promises that she would force herself to keep.

As she approached the opening of the cave she heard voices. Sharon must have returned and Anthony was telling her about what had happened. Now Sharon would know she was crazy. But it didn't matter, with or without Sharon she was going to get her brother out of Arizona. She stopped for a minute to let her tears dry and her hands stop shaking.

"Help me tie him up," a male voice ordered. "Then I'll look for the other one while you go get the police."

Martha's heart leapt. They had been caught. She moved outside the cave and hid behind the rock that concealed it.

"Leave me alone," Anthony hollered.

"No way, murder boy," another voice said. "We thought we saw lights up here last night. But no way did we think we'd be lucky enough to find you."

"You're going to bring us a handsome reward. Now tell me where your sister is."

Martha peered around the edge of the boulder. Anthony was lying on his belly, his feet pulled up behind him, his hands behind his back. The boy that held him looked about fourteen. The other one, much bigger than his friend, was probably older. She couldn't be sure. He was wrapping what looked like the string to their sleeping bags around Anthony's hands and feet.

"I don't have a sister," Anthony sneered at them.

"I'll find her," the bigger one said. "She's around here somewhere." He used a second cord to tie Anthony's hands to his feet. "There," he said standing up. The younger boy stepped away and the bigger one used his foot to roll Anthony over. "That ought to hold him. Now go get the police, and don't get lost getting out of here," he ordered the younger one.

"I won't." The younger puffed out his chest. "I know this ground better than you. Well almost," he said, then turned and ran down the path.

"Be quick," the older boy yelled as he bent down and picked up Anthony's flashlight. He turned around and looked up at the base of the mountain. Martha ducked behind the boulder. "Now, where could she be hiding?" he asked. Anthony didn't answer.

A motor started somewhere down the path. The younger boy was leaving to get help. She didn't have much time. Martha got back on her feet and ran into her mother's keep.

34

Sharon played the disk as she drove towards the mountain. "Bingo," she said when it reached the part where Nathan admitted trying to kill his wife. "You did it, Barbara! Now, with the disk, not only will I be able to bring Sanders down, I'll be able to clear Martha and Anthony of murder charges," Sharon said with confidence.

The end of the recording was harder to listen to. Barbara's coughing and apparent pain hit Sharon as if it had been her lying on that hospital bed. The scratchy voice asking for help was too much to listen to. Sharon turned off the recorder. She was nauseous again. She pulled off the freeway and pulled the Jeep into a Basha's shopping center.

She put her head on the steering wheel and caught her breath. The nauseousness faded. Without looking up she clicked on the play button of the recorder and listened to the final words of a dying martyr. When she reached over to turn it off, she lifted her head and wiped away the tears that covered her face. "I'll get him," she whispered. "And I'll get everyone who helped him."

She looked out her window at the people walking in and out of the store. They were all clueless of what was happening around them. The nation's communication blackout had done its job. People were no longer allowed free access to Internet service or independent cable shows. Communications laws had stymied the rampant exchange of ideas and news across the country. Only the government had access to any new technology, the general public was forced to remain ignorant. She'd change that, she promised herself. If it took broadcasting the disk illegally over pirated airwaves, she'd do it.

Sharon found a public phone and called Derek at home. He was shocked and saddened by his friend's death and told her to get a copy of the disk to him as soon as possible. "Don't trust anyone," he said. "Make a back up copy and tell no one about it. I'll make arrangements for a rental car for those kids then I want you to contact the traders Barbara told you about and get the hell out of there. You've got your story. Bagging those two will cause such an uproar around the country that no one will make a moral choice for the next decade."

Sharon smiled at the thought and hung up the phone. Things were going well. Unfortunately it had taken Barbara Sander's death to bring it altogether.

She turned on her penlight to mark her position, put a new cell in her watch and pulled out the stem. Then she turned the recorder on and listened to her friend die. With that copy made, she replaced the cell with a new one and made a duplicate recording. She wasn't taking any chances. This had to get out, but first she had one stop to make, one promise to keep.

35

Martha grabbed both of the lanterns. They had large battery cases and sturdy metal fittings for the light. She turned one off and set it by the entrance to the tunnel Anthony said lead out of the mountain. She used the other to guide her to the tunnel's other side. She didn't know how far from the shack its entrance was, but hoped the tunnel angled well enough to be in the boy's sight or at least his hearing range.

The tunnel was longer than she anticipated, but seemed to be heading in the right direction. There was a section that was only a few feet high. She crawled through it scanning the floor in front of her. There were a few foot deep dips and slanted stones. They could be a problem on the way back.

She reached the end of the tunnel and examined the prickly pear bush that blocked its entrance. The cactus' base was thick, but not so thick she wouldn't be able to break it. She tried to look out past the large, green, tear dropped branches, but couldn't see much. What she did make out of the view seemed similar to the one she had while she sat contemplating Anthony's struggles earlier in the morning.

Loose gravel fell somewhere off to her distant right. He was close. She sat on the ground, placed her feet on the prickly pear's base and pushed. She didn't want to break it, she just wanted it to look as if it had been pushed aside wide enough for a person to enter.

She pushed as hard as she could, but the cactus didn't move. She stopped and caught her breath. There was more movement, but it was fainter, more distant. Had he turned and gone the other way? Pulling her legs back, she gave the bush one, sharp kick. The plant's spine broke. Its massive branches toppled, hitting the ground hard and loud.

"Shit," she said, scrambling to get back on her feet.

"I've got you now," the boy yelled.

She turned and ran, making sure to keep the light on the path and watching her footing. She jumped two dips but on the second her foot caught on a small ledge and she fell to her knees. The lantern flew out of her hand. Glass shattered and the tunnel was consumed by a thick heavy blackness.

The boy was behind her; she could hear him. She looked over her shoulder. The small beam from his light dimly flashed above her head. *Keep going*, she told herself. *Feel your way through*. She got back on her feet and walked faster than she knew was safe. She put her hands along the wall of the cave to guide her, but still fumbled. He was gaining ground; she could hear his footsteps only yards behind her. It was time to run.

She lost her footing and tripped over the slanted rock. Picking herself up, she edged her way around the rock. The ground went out from under her. Her knee hit the edge of the dip and she involuntarily cried out from the pain

"Look sister," the boy yelled. "It's dangerous in here. There's no way out, so save us both a lot of trouble and just give yourself up."

"Go to hell," she yelled back as she pulled herself out of the hole. Her knee hurt. She ignored it. She needed to watch her head. There had been a dip right after she had made her way through the shallow section of the cave. She put her hands out in front of her and kept going.

The roof slanted down at a better angle on this end than it had coming through the other side. She got down on her knees. Pain shot through her injured leg as she crawled through the shallow passageway. She didn't know how long it was, so every few feet, she raised her hand above her head to feel if the ceiling was still close.

The boy's light flashed on her and then ahead of her, she thought she felt his hand brush the back of her foot. She crawled faster. The beam of his flashlight bounced off the ceiling in front of her. She was almost out. She didn't remember seeing any other dips before she had entered the shallow tunnels and, whether it was safe or not, she decided to run. The entrance to her mother's make shift apothecary wasn't too much farther. She could smell the spilled oils. The boy's light illuminated the area ahead of her and she was able to run faster.

One more turn.

As she reached the turn, she lost the light from the boy's beam. She almost tripped again, but was able to keep her momentum going. The air temperature dropped and though she couldn't see, she was sure she had made it to the larger chamber. She spread her arms out to the sides. No walls. She came to an abrupt stop and used her feet to feel around the opening. She nudged the waiting lantern, stooped down, and grabbed it.

"Jesus, what's that smell?" the boy said. "How far does this fucking thing go?"

Don't give up yet, she silently prodded him.

Martha stepped to the side of the entrance and braced herself against the rock wall. A bright beam of light broke through the dark. She waited, raising the lantern above her head and to the right with both hands. First the flashlight, then his hand slowly emerged from the tunnel. His breathing was heavy. Martha swung the lantern in an arch, down then back toward his head. Rage added strength as the metal base hit its mark.

Bones cracked on impact. The boy let out a loud but short scream. Martha watched her hands, still holding tightly to the lantern, bounce back, as if in slow motion. The boy's flashlight flew from his hand. Metal clanged on the rocks somewhere toward the front of the cave as the shadow of the boy's body collapsed to the floor with a hard singular thud.

Martha leaned back against the wall, inching away from him. Her hands were wet. She fumbled for the switch on the lantern and turned it on. The boy lay face down, half in the chamber, half in the tunnel. A pool of blood shadowed his face.

She kept her light on him, ready to bolt at the slightest moment. He didn't move. She stepped closer and kicked at his hand. Nothing. Holding the lantern out to her side, prepared to pounce again if she had too, she knelt beside him and felt for a pulse. There was none. She put the light down and rolled him over. His nose was gone, flattened against his face, his mouth caved in, his wide eyes staring, but seeing nothing. He was dead. She had killed him.

"I didn't mean to..." she started to say, but stopped. It was exactly what she meant to do, and she had known it all along. She stared down at the boy and smiled, a tight flat smile. Everything would be different now. She had the courage to kill. No matter what happened from this point on, the coward who had given away her brother's whereabouts the day her mother was arrested was gone.

36

Mark Bolton rode his dirt bike as fast as he could through the desert landscape that lay between the mountains and his home. He knew the area well. His best friend, Sean, and he had been riding through it all spring on the dirt bikes they received from their parents at Christmas. Neither of them were rock climbers or cave enthusiasts, so they had kept their exploration at ground level, but last night when they escaped to the desert to drink the wine Sean stole from his dad's liquor cabinet, they saw light reflecting off the mountain's edge. Sean thought it might be some old miner's camp. They decided to play sick in the morning to get out of school, and when their mother's left for their volunteer jobs down at the hospital, they would scope it out.

"Never know what valuables he might have lying around," Sean said as they headed home last night. Though they weren't really thieves – it was too easy to get caught – they didn't mind snatching up things they didn't think would be missed.

Mark knew from experience that if they found the miner's camp, Sean wouldn't take much, a knife maybe or even some tools. Nothing that would get them in serious trouble. Sean's older brother was already a ward of the state and Sean had no intentions on following him. Mark also knew that if the miner was there, Sean might just decide to sit and visit with him. One adventure was a good as another.

"Maybe he'll share some of his gold," Sean had teased as they set out in the morning.

They left their bikes at numerous paths at the base of the mountain and hiked up looking for the camp. None showed any signs of someone recently being there, until they found the one that led to the shack. They gave each other the high five when they stepped inside and found two unrolled sleeping bags, clothes and groceries. They were going through a pile of pots and pans and other junk when the door opened and the boy walked through it. What a find. The bounty on the boy and his sister would buy more knives than either of them could possibly every use. The only problem was finding someone who would believe him and help carry the murderers to the police.

Their neighbor, Roy Boggs, was a Posse member. He was around thirty, out of work, and loved playing cop. Roy didn't like either Mark or Sean, but Mark thought his constant need to be the tough guy, the one in charge, would induce him to check the story out with his four wheeler.

Mark looked over his shoulder at the expanse of desert behind him as he pulled out onto a paved road. It all looked so similar. If he wasn't able to find his way back to the shack, he knew, Roy would leave him in the desert to die.

"No problem," he said as he pulled up to Roy's house and knocked on the door.

37

Sharon pulled up to the path that led to Suzanne Garcia's shack. A dirt bike was at its foot. She got out of the Jeep and walked around it. There were two sets of tire prints. "Fuck," she said. Quietly, she headed up the path.

As she crested the hill, she slowed down. There was one turn left before she'd be in the open area surrounding the dilapidated building. She stopped before taking the turn and peered around a large rock. Anthony was lying on his side facing her, his hands and feet were bound. No one else was around. She stepped out from behind the rock and put her finger to her mouth. Anthony saw her and nodded his head, "Where's Martha?" she mouthed to the boy.

He shook his head.

Sharon looked again. Everything was quiet. She ran out to Anthony and quickly undid the knots that bound him. Just as she finished untying his hands, they heard the crunch of gravel ahead of them and looked up.

Martha stepped out from behind the boulder that concealed the cave. Her clothes were torn and wet, her knee cut, her hands covered in blood. Anthony worked hard at freeing his feet as Sharon stood up. The two of them stared at Martha as she slowly made her way towards them.

"What happened?" Anthony asked when she stopped in front of them.

"He caught me. I had to defend myself. I killed him," she said in a monotone voice.

Sharon looked up at the boulder that obstructed her view of the cave. "Is he in there?" she asked.

Martha nodded her head.

"I'll go see."

"No," Martha said, slowly reaching out for Sharon's arm. "We don't have time. He sent the other one for help. We have to go."

Sharon looked over at Anthony for confirmation. "It's true," he said. "They should be here soon."

Sharon grabbed Martha by the shoulders, careful not to let any blood get on her clothing. "Are you sure he's dead."

Martha held up her hands, blood dripped on the ground. "I'm positive."

Sharon didn't know what to do. If he was dead, there was nothing she could do for him, except waste time so his friend could come back and they could all go to jail. If he wasn't dead, but only hurt, she would have to suffer with the consequences later. She ran into the shack and came back out with one of the sleeping bags, an unopened bottle of water, and their clothes. She threw the sleeping bag to Anthony, put her arm on Martha's back and gave her a little shove. "Let's go."

Drops of blood stained the ground where Martha stood. Sharon ground the blood into the dirt, took the sleeping bag from Anthony and handed it to Martha. "Here," she said. Wipe your hands. You're leaving a trail,"

Martha did as she was told, but didn't do a thorough job. There was still blood on the girl's hands. Sharon wondered if Martha had left it there on purpose. Remnants of the kill. *You're over dramatizing*, Sharon warned herself as she pushed the thought from her mind. Martha only did what she had to, protect herself and her brother. The girl wasn't taking trophies. Sharon searched the rest of the area for other signs of struggle, but found none. Eventually the cave and the boy would be found, but hopefully not before they were all safely out of the state.

"We should get rid of that," Martha said, pointing to the dirt bike when they reached the bottom of the trail. Her voice was cold and dry. "There are hundreds of paths that lead into the mountain. Without the bike as a marker it will be harder for them to find him."

There was no remorse in that voice, no fear, no guilt. The words were stated very matter of factly. *This is what we need to do*. Martha had finally cracked. It took killing a man, but it had happened. Maybe that was for the best. It would take steady nerves to get them across the border. Without feelings or emotions, Martha might just be able to do it.

Anthony jumped on the bike and started it up. "See that pile of rocks up ahead?" he said, pointing to a cluster of tall rocks to their far left. "I'll hide it in there." Before Sharon could tell him otherwise, the bike was spitting dirt at them and he was on his way. Sharon took the sleeping bag from Martha's hands and wrapped it around the girl.

"Keep the blood off the Jeep," Sharon said.

Martha nodded her head, wrapped herself tightly in the bag, even though it was over a hundred degrees, and got into the passenger side of the Jeep. Sharon jumped in beside her and headed off in the direction Anthony had gone.

Martha didn't say anything else as Sharon pulled the Jeep up near the rocks and Anthony ran over to the car. Sharon didn't know what to say either. Things were bad now. Even if the kids were able to get out of the state, Martha could be sent back once the body was found. They could pull her fingerprints off the shack and whatever she had used to kill the boy inside the cave. Southern California no longer extradited people to religious states, but Sharon doubted they would hold back on a murder charge.

It was self-defense, Sharon reminded herself as she drove out of the desert, and if it wasn't, she didn't want to know, nor, she suddenly realized, did she care. The state made Martha who she was now, the girl didn't choose the events that had occurred and when Sharon got home, she'd make sure the nation knew it.

Right now though, she needed to get Martha cleaned up and get them into their disguises. She pulled the Jeep into a dried up wash and headed down it, stopping a few yards after a sharp bend. They were far enough away from the shack that anyone searching wouldn't see them. It was a risk, she knew it, but not as risky as riding around with them in the back of her Jeep where people could identify them.

Martha got out of the Jeep and using the water they had brought started cleaning herself. Sharon pulled the wigs and makeup from the back and helped Anthony get dressed. His clothes were dusty and brushed off easily. She stepped back and admired her work, it was amazing how easily he had been transformed. If she hadn't known his real identity she would swear he was a girl.

Martha didn't bother finding cover to change. She stripped her clothes off and hosed herself down with the water. She put on clean clothes, her wig and makeup as if nothing had happened. Anthony hadn't said much to her before, but he walked up to her when she was completely dressed and wrapped his arms around her. "I'm glad you did it," he said.

Martha kissed the top of his head. "No one's ever going to hurt you again."

"Hurry up," Sharon said, hoping to rush them and get as far away from the mountains as possible.

Tires bore through hard dirt and the roar of a truck's engine reverberated through the heat. Anthony climbed the embankment, popped his head up over its edge then jumped back down. "Big truck," he whispered as he ran back to where Sharon and Martha stood.

Sharon looked around. There was no place to hide. Either the truck would find them or it wouldn't. Sharon could hear her heart pounding as the truck moved closer. Anthony ran down to the turn. A dead bush jutted out from its side, and he hid behind it.

"Get back here," Martha said, running towards him. He flattened his body against the embankment and waved for her to stay back. She did as she was told. Sharon could hear tires crash against desert soil and held her breath while the sound went from in front of her to behind. Anthony ran back to where his sister stood. "They crossed over," he told her.

"Good," Sharon said. She grabbed Martha's soiled clothes, wrapped them in the sleeping bag and piled rocks on top of them. "Anthony, make sure they can't see us," she told the boy, then stepped in front of Martha. "Look," she said. "You've been through a lot and you still have a lot more to get through. So you have to put what happened back there behind you."

Martha's lips formed a straight line across her face. No teeth showed. It was the smile of a maniac. Sharon stepped back.

Slowly, the edges of Martha's mouth lifted on either side. The girl looked Sharon straight in the eye and said, "I already have."

38

Roy Boggs sat in the idling truck waiting for the kid to return from yet another path he was positive led to the shack where his friend was holding the Garcia boy. The truck's radiator was running hot and he had to turn off the air conditioner. The heat worked its way into his brain. He could feel himself beginning to simmer. "That's it," he said turning off the engine and getting out of the truck.

He climbed into the bed and grabbed the kid's dirt bike. Why had he agreed to come? He knew all along the kid was full of shit and this was probably some kind of joke he and his piss ant buddy were trying to pull.

"I found... Hey, what are you doing?" Mark yelled as he ran down the path.

"Getting rid of excess baggage," Roy said throwing the bike at a saguaro cactus. It hit the center of the cactus and hung for a moment before falling to the ground.

Mark stared at it for a moment, then looked up at Roy. "You son of a bitch."

"Yeah, well make something of it," Roy said as he jumped from the cab, landing a few feet from the bike. The back tire had a spine sticking out of it and was going down fast. Roy caught movement out of his left eye and swung just as Mark jumped him.

Mark was thrown by the punch and hit the side of the cab. As he slid down its side, Roy saw the dent the kid's body made. "Mother-fucker." Roy pushed the kid aside with his foot, then ran his hand down along the dent. Mark moaned but he ignored him. "You'll pay for this fairy boy," Roy said, bending down and picking Mark up by his shirt.

Mark raised his hands in front of his face. "I'm sorry, I'm sorry. I'll get if fixed I promise."

"You bet your sweet ass, you will." Roy threw the boy against the cab again. He had had enough. He was going home. "Have a nice hike," he said as he climbed into his truck and slammed the door shut.

"No wait," Mark screamed at him. "This is it. I found it. The cabin's in a clearing at the top of the trail."

Roy rested his hand on his keys. Bringing the Garcias in would be a great boost to his image in the Posse. It might even help qualify him for the force. He leaned his head out the window. "Your friends still up there?"

Mark dusted off his clothing. "Well, no. But Sean said he was gonna go look for the sister. He probably made the boy go with him."

"Fuck you," Roy said. "I'm outta here." He started the truck and threw it in gear.

"No wait," the kid yelled. Somehow Mark managed to pull himself up on the door. His face inches from Roy's.

"Get off the truck," Roy warned him. The boy didn't move. "Get off the truck," he said again. He could feel the rage building. If the kid didn't move, he'd have to get nasty.

"You can't just leave me out here," the kid said, sticking his arm through the window and reaching for the steering wheel.

"That's it." Roy grabbed the kid's hand with his left, pulled him further into the truck, and with his right fist pelted him in the face. Once, then again and again. The rage boiled. Roy kept hitting the kid until it worked its way out. By the time he had finished, the boy's arm had gone limp. His head lopped to the side, blood trickled from his nose and eyes. Roy let go of him and the kid dropped to the ground.

Roy watched for movement. The kid lay in a heap where he had fallen, his arm unnaturally bent behind his back. "Holy shit." Roy jumped out of the truck, his hands shaking. He picked the kid up by his shirt collar. "Wake up kid. I didn't mean to hit you so hard." Mark didn't move. He couldn't. He was dead.

Roy jerked himself away from the body and inched up to the truck. "Motherfucker, what am I going to do now?" He stared at the corpse, then his eyes caught the beginning of the trail. He knew exactly what he would do. He'd take the kid up to the shack and when his friend found him, he'd think the girl had done it.

"That's it," he said. "She's killed before. Everyone'd buy that." He picked up Mark's body and threw it over his shoulder. He could feel the kid's blood soaking his shirt. *No big deal* he said to himself. *I'll burn it.*

The trail was long and steep and though the kid was small for his age he was getting heavy. Roy shifted him onto the other shoulder and continued. Turning a bend, he saw the clearing. "Cabin, my ass," he said as he took in the shack and its surrounding. It seemed deserted. Like a pellet from a BB gun, a thought hit him. What if it had been a set up? What if that other kid was hiding out and they had planned to bushwhack him? He dropped the kid on the ground. "Hey, Sean," he called out. "You here?"

There was no sound. He listened for the tell tale noise of rolling stones, but nothing happened. He had an odd sense of being alone. Headed up towards the mountain, he called Sean's name again. No one answered. Roy was about to turn back, stash the body and the bike and take off when he saw a red stain on the side of a rock. He walked over and rubbed his hand against it. It was still wet. His eyes scanned the rest of the area. There was more blood on some other rocks up ahead. He followed the trail Martha had left up to the mouth of the cave. A foul odor stung his nose as he stuck his head inside it. "Mother..."

He turned and ran down the path of rocks, past Mark's body and back to his truck. What if it was some kind of meth lab. Pay dirt. He'd hide the body somewhere else, stake out the area and turn their drug making asses in. He grabbed the flashlight from the glove compartment of the truck and ran back to the clearing. Red ants had already made their way to the kid's body. Even though he had killed the kid, leaving him for the ants seemed callous, he'd have to get the kid out of the sun, but first he'd check out the cave.

It was rank. He pulled his tee shirt up over his nose. It didn't help. The tunnel turned, opening into a large chamber. From what he could see, it was trashed. He figured the smell must be coming from a puddle of oily stuff over by a bookcase. He moved the beam around the perimeter of the chamber hoping there was something worth salvaging. His search stopped when the light fell on Sean's body.

"Well I'll be," he said walking up to the boy. "It seems like I'm not the only one done some killing today." This was great. He would drag the other kid up here and then go back to town and say he found them. He'd be a hero by nightfall and those Garcias would pay for it. "Perfect," he said out loud, but a smaller voice inside him warned,

What if someone saw you leave with the kid?

The voice was right. He could say he dropped him off somewhere if the kid just disappeared, but if he knew where he ended up it would be too suspicious. He looked back at the oily stuff that was stinking up the air and had another plan. "No body, no crime." He ran back down to the clearing and snatched up Mark's body. It seemed lighter this time. He brought the corpse into the cave and dropped it near its friend, then he went back down for the bike.

Puncturing the bike's gas tank with his hunting knife, he let a slow stream trickle on the ground as he drove it over to where the bodies were. The cave was deep enough. He suspected, no one would ever hear the explosion or see the flames. He took off his tee shirt and threw it on top of the bike, then went outside and lit the stream of gasoline. He jumped down from the rocky area that concealed the cave and ducked, covering his head as he heard the muffled sound of the explosion. He couldn't tell if flames had come out of the mouth of the cave, but he didn't care. No one was going to find a scorched rock, not with how well that opening was hidden. *Except for the blood.* He went to each rock that had been marked with the drying trail of blood and ground dirt on it so no one would see it. When he got back to the clearing, he checked for the kid's blood. None had spilled on the ground. He was free and clear. Unfortunately, he thought, so were the Garcias.

39

There were a few customers at the photo shop when Sharon, Martha and Anthony arrived. They sat in the Jeep and waited until the shop was empty before then went inside.

"That looks like the last of them," Sharon told Martha and Anthony. "Let's go in before anyone else shows up." Martha was out the door and halfway to the shop before Sharon opened her door.

"She's pretty tense," Anthony said, as if he needed to explain his sister's behavior.

"We all are, I guess," Sharon said turning to the boy. He looked a little anxious himself. Was he afraid of his sister, or for her? Sharon couldn't tell. Martha had found her defensive wall, she had tuned out everything that didn't take her on a direct route to her goal. Anthony was still trying to figure things out. They would be better off following Martha's lead, Sharon decided. Martha had a survivalist mentality now – fear nothing and escape at all cost. It might just be the only thing that would get them across the border.

Sharon and Anthony walked into the empty shop. Martha was standing at the counter. A short thin woman, her straight brown hair pulled back in a pony tail, stepped out from a back room. "Can I help you?" she asked.

"I'm Sharon Clark. We were sent here…"

"This way," the woman said as she turned back toward the door she had come through. Sharon, then Anthony, then Martha followed.

They were led to a room on the east side of the shop. "Wait here," the woman said as she stepped out of the room.

"Just a minute," Sharon said reaching into her bag and pulling out the envelope the woman at the mall had given her. "Can you develop this while we wait?" She retrieved the disk of photos and handed it to the woman.

The woman took the disk, nodded her head and closed the door.

The room was small with a three-sided blank screen. The back of the screen was against a wall, while the two sides angled out. There was enough room for three possibly four people to sit within it. Sharon had seen this type of projection screen before, it allowed the photographer to set up a motion scene that would make the person or persons being photographed look like they were immersed in the setting. The finished product had a more natural look than the standard single backdrop. A large black box was at the other end of the room as well as four light blue plastic chairs. They each took a seat and waited.

Fifteen minutes later, the door opened and a heavy set, balding man, in black pants, black leather belt, and black tee shirt, stepped into the room. He introduced himself as Mel Troullin.

"Mr. Troullin…" Sharon started.

"I know why you're here. If you would just sit quietly while I get ready," he said, cutting her off, as he opened a closet door and pulled out a cart with a camera identical to the ones used at the Identification Processing Center.

"Sit," he told Martha.

"Wait," Sharon said, digging into her bag. "The face recognition program will identify them."

"There's nothing I…"

"I have something." She pulled two unused headbands from her bag and placed it on Martha's head, angled forward. "It's supposed to disrupt the image coordinates."

Mel Troullin shrugged and moved back to his camera. Martha touched the headband and pushed it into place. Sharon checked to make sure its angle was correct, then stepped back.

It took just a moment to snap Martha's picture then he motioned for her to get up and for Anthony to take her place.

As Sharon placed the other headband on Anthony, she looked at the stone face of the photographer. He might be her only communication link in case… *In case you don't make it.* "Mr. Troullin," Sharon said a little more forcefully. "I have a recording of Barbara Sanders' last visit with her husband that I would like to be distributed."

"You do?" Martha asked.

"I can't help you," Troullin responded as he took Anthony's photo. He rolled the cart back into the closet and walked over to the door.

"Well, what about Stan…"

Mel Troullin left the room without letting her finish. He closed the door, resolutely. He would be no help.

Damn him. She'd have to go back to the nursery after she got the kids on the road. Stan would help her. He was Barbara's friend. He'd want to know. Sharon leaned back in the plastic chair. She expected Martha to question her about the recording, but the girl didn't. She was quiet and withdrawn. Anthony, however, was another story. He couldn't sit still. He asked twenty questions about the headband that Sharon couldn't answer while exhaustively examining it. When that bored him, he checked out the photographer's equipment, his hands nervously twitching above buttons and levers. Sharon had to tell him to sit down three times.

It had been over an hour since they had stepped into the small room. Sharon was getting antsy. She couldn't get comfortable. She'd sit then she'd get up and walk around for a minute, then sit again. What was taking so long? She felt like Mel Troullin was purposefully putting her off, pushing her, but why?

"Stay here," she told Martha and Anthony, as she got up and opened the door.

The woman who had greeted them when they first arrived stepped in front of her.

"What are you doing?" the woman snapped. "Get back in there."

"How much longer?" Sharon asked.

"Soon," the woman said and closed the door.

It was another twenty minutes before the door opened again.

Mel Troullin handed each of the kids their IDs. "We deposited a hundred dollars in each of your accounts. It's the best we could do," he said.

Sharon took Anthony's ID from him and examined it. It looked too new, too perfect.

"We need to get you kids new clothes before you leave," Sharon said. "You can't cross the border in the same clothes you're wearing in these pictures. I should have thought of that."

"Don't worry about it," Troullin said. "They won't even notice. All they care about is if it passes through the reader. We've never had a bad one yet."

"Thanks," Martha said as she put the ID in her purse.

"Yeah, thanks," Sharon said holding out her hand to shake

Troullin's.

He looked at her, but did not reach out for her hand. "May I see you alone?" he asked as he turned and opened the door.

Sharon told Martha and Anthony to wait for her then followed the man to a room that held a large white machine. Printed photos were spitting out of it, mechanically being packaged in small booklets. Stan Deitrich was standing behind it going through a set of prints.

"Where'd you get those photos?" Stan asked. Sharon's first impression of relief in seeing him, dissipated quickly. His tone was too authoritative, too demanding.

Sharon walked over to him and pulled some of the pictures from his hand. A young girl was suspended in mid-air. Hoses and wires were hooked up to her naked body. Her stomach had a slight swell. Metal braces hanging from the ceiling had replaced her arms and legs. Scars distorted her face and bald head, but not beyond recognition. Sharon's stomach lurched. She ran to a small sink at the end of the room and vomited.

She stood, her hands on either side of the sink, waiting for another rush of whatever was left in her stomach. It didn't come. She turned on the faucet, splashed water on her face, and rinsed her mouth out. "Oh my God," she said remembering the body in the picture. Stan walked over to her and handed her a towel. Her hands were shaking. She wiped her face and turned around.

"I take it you know who the woman is?" Stan asked.

Sharon remembered the crooked smile of the girl she thought could be her younger sister, the girl in the picture she had shown the inmates at Arpaio. "Bethany Collins. A woman who works at Arpaio Women's Penitentiary gave them to me this morning."

"What's their significance?' Stan asked.

Sharon looked over at the tanned man with his long ponytail. She could tell he was upset. That was good, wasn't it? If the pictures moved him, maybe he would be willing to try and rescue her. "It's the girl's second pregnancy," she said. "The woman told me she had tried to escape and that her baby died. This is a new pregnancy, one they initiated. Evidently, there's some kind of breeding program going on in there."

The two men exchanged glances. "Do you have any other proof?"

Sharon nodded her head. She pulled from her bag the copy of Madison Courtney's pregnancy test and the orders for her genetic blood work. "I met this woman when I toured the prison. She told me she wasn't pregnant, that she had been set up. The woman who works there told me they had ordered genetic testing, and if it came back clean, they were going to send her to a new facility they were building."

Again, the men looked over at one another. She had brought them pay dirt. She could see it in their faces. There was something else too, something she couldn't quite put her finger on, but it screamed caution.

"I'm afraid I need to ask you to give these to me," Stan said.

Sharon looked at each man. She had been prepared to give them copies, to ask for their help in disseminating the material on the disk, but she did not intend to hand them over to anyone. Derek had warned her not to trust anyone, and it was about time she heeded those warnings. She had promised the woman at the mall she would wait another week before making the pictures public. Once she relinquished custody of them, she'd have no say in what happened with the information or when it was released.

She took the papers back from Stan. "I made a promise. After my article comes out, I'd be happy to send you a copy of everything I have. But until then," she said, picking up the pictures of Bethany and putting them in her bag without taking another look at them. "I'm afraid I can't afford to trust them with anyone."

"I see," Stan said. "Well what about the recording you mentioned to my associate here?"

The recording was something different. Barbara made it for her, and Barbara had believed in what Stan and his photographer friend were doing. "Barbara would probably have wanted you to hear this," she said as she took the recorder out of her bag, put it on the small counter, and pushed the play button. She watched the two men as they listened to the conversation between Sanders and his wife. Stan Dietrich's eyes glazed over as the recording neared its end. The photographer turned away.

"She always hated him," Stan said reaching over, pushing the stop button on the recorder.

"She was a brave woman," Sharon said looking down at her feet.

"And that's why you can't publish any of this. We're not ready for it to break. We have many things in place. Twenty years of building. But it's still going to be at least two more years before we can act. If your story breaks, some heads will roll, but only on an individual basis. That's not what we want. We want to show how high the corruption goes. We want to topple the government, not just change it."

Even though Barbara had used the word revolution, Sharon hadn't seen her as a militant. The network Barbara had built seemed more like a well-funded underground movement aimed at stirring up the masses, not conquering them. Sharon didn't buy into the need for toppling the government, her story, her idea was to alert the voters to what was happening and let democracy fix it. Revolution wasn't something she felt compelled to support. Anyway, right at the moment she was more concerned with individuals than the masses.

"What about Madison Courtney? What about Bethany Collins? The only way to save them is by proving what's going on."

"We understand your concern," Stan said. "But you have to realize there are always those lives that must be sacrificed when you're fighting a war."

"Your war, not mine. Not Madison's or Bethany's either," Sharon said louder than she meant to. She was getting mad. She calmed her voice. "I'm going to do what I need to do to save *them*. I'm going to make Sanders and Listner pay for what they've done, and I'm going to expose the breeding factories that are supplying children to the wealthy. And if you don't like it, well then that's just too bad." Sharon grabbed back the recorder. She didn't know if these men were as bad as Sanders and Listner, but they were still about politics and power. She wanted nothing to do with them.

She pushed her way past the men and called for Martha and Anthony. She needed to get out, to get away from the smell of chemicals, and to scream. Someone out there had to care. Someone had to be willing to help her. She thought of Paul, and wondered. He loved Madison, once. Would he be willing to stop being a cop for one day to save her from Bethany Collins' fate?

Sharon felt sick again while picking up the rental car. Anthony asked her what had happened at the photo shop, but she ignored him. She made Martha follow her in the Jeep to a Circle K a few blocks away from the airport. She gave her directions to the Sentinel along with Derek's phone number and made Martha promise to get in touch with him and to let him help them. Sharon still worried about the kids' ability to make it across the border, but had no other choice than to let fate take its course. She had done the best she could for them and now it was time to let them go. She gave each of them a quick hug and sent them on their way.

She stopped by a health clinic and had a second pregnancy test taken then returned to the Basha's to reinstate the satellite tracking. She stared at the results of the pregnancy test while she sat on her bed back at the hotel. The white piece of paper had the word *positive* written next to the pregnant check box. Thomas would want to know. He had the right to know, but she didn't have the energy to tell him. She understood completely what the results meant. She would be held captive by the state whose leaders she planned on destroying. She wouldn't risk the baby's future or her freedom by trying to escape. She would stay and make the best of it, but she wouldn't be stopped from rescuing Madison and Bethany.

She pulled the pictures of Bethany and Madison's test results out her bag along with the recorder. She played the disk while studying what happened to the woman who had become such an important part of her life. She thought about what Paul had said. He was right. She was a novice reporter working for a second rate paper. She had botched most of the assignment and knew it had been sheer luck that she was able to accumulate what lay on the bed in front of her. She no longer thought of Pulitzers or her career. She remembered Phoebe Washington's advice to play by the rules if she wanted to stay out of jail. It was advice she would take, but underneath her smile and sub-servient appearance, she was pretty sure, she would break most of them.

A knock on her door startled her. She looked at her watch. Ten-thirty. It was Paul. She gathered her material, turned off the recorder and packed everything back into the safety of her bag.

40

Martha slowed the car when she saw the lights of the border checkpoint. They had practiced their new names during the three-hour drive. She was Lupe Rodriqez and he was her sister Rachel. Anthony had tried various high-pitched voices that he thought would be a part of his disguise. Martha thought they sounded more frightening than anything else, but she guardedly laughed with him. She didn't have the heart to tell him that his voice was high enough, and he had nothing to worry about. Instead of allowing him to fake a voice that someone might be suspicious of, she told him to let her do all the talking.

They hadn't talked about the present or the past as they drove. All conversation was surface – the type of cars that passed, the scenery, and the music that played on the radio. Martha could tell Anthony was pensive. He had suffered the most while they had been wards of the state, and she knew he was terrified of being caught and being sent back. She, on the other hand, had become lulled by the drive. It gave her time to calm down, to put everything into perspective. She couldn't help thinking of Robert and Mrs. Sanders. Though she had only known them for a few days, they had touched her life like very few other people had, especially Robert. They were dead now, and so was some boy whose name she didn't even know. Dead at her hand.

Martha fought the tears back. She wouldn't let Anthony see her cry. She had to be their strength, she could show no weakness, have no weakness. Robert and Mrs. Sanders had willfully disobeyed Mr. Sanders; and if what Sharon's recorder suggested was true, they had suffered the penalty of treason. It was a valid death during a time of war. She would not mourn them.

The boy was different. She had lied to Sharon when she had told her she had put the boy's killing behind her. She knew it was something that would follow her the rest of her life. She mentally prepared herself to relive the chase in the cave and the blow that ended it every night in her dreams. She also acknowledged how it had changed her.

She was no longer afraid. She had the strength to handle whatever met them at the border, but she would take Sharon's advice and stay calm. There could be no more uncontrolled rages. She had to think before reacting. Only then, would she be in control of the power she believed she had finally attained.

There were very few cars on the road as she pulled up to the guard gate. A long metal, red-stripped pole blocked her from driving through.

"Good evening ladies," a guard said as he walked over to the car and stooped down to look in the window. "And where are you headed this evening."

"To my uncle's in Los Angeles," Martha said looking up at him and smiling. He was rather nice looking she thought. His hair was sandy brown and combed back like Elvis'. He had dimples on either side of his cheeks and bright white teeth. He was older than her, but still he seemed less intimidating than she had anticipated. She would get by him.

"May I see your IDs?" he asked. Anthony handed Martha his and she pulled hers from the purse Sharon had bought her. "I'll just be a minute," he said taking the IDs then stepping into a booth a few feet away. He opened a sliding window and poked his head out. "How long do you plan on being gone?"

"Two weeks," Martha said as she watched him pass her ID through the reader and then type something onto the screen. He hit a button on his keyboard, removed her ID and inserted Anthony's. It took him only a few minutes longer. He came out from the booth with a hand held scanner. Sharon had warned her about this. They were checking for pregnancy, that second life form. It was nothing to worry about. She told Anthony to get out of the car and to meet him on the other side. The guard walked up to her, and pressed the scanner against her abdomen. He held it there for a few seconds. It beeped and a green light went on.

"One down, one to go," he said still smiling.

He walked over to Anthony and positioned the scanner. The seconds beat away like months. Anthony looked at her, his eyes wide with doubt. She shook her head, just a fraction, to tell him to stay still. The scanner beeped, and the green light came on. Martha let out the breath she had been holding.

"Almost done," the guard said stepping back into the booth. Neither Martha nor Anthony moved. This was it. They were almost there.

Martha was about to tell Anthony to get back in the car, when his eyes went wide. "Look," he said. Martha turned. The guard's monitor was flashing. ADDITIONAL VERIFICATION NEEDED – TAKE FINGERPRINTS. The guard saw them looking, held up his finger and mouthed the words, "It will just be another minute." He picked up the phone, not taking his gaze off them.

Anthony grabbed Martha's arm. "Run," he said.

There was no time to think. She followed his lead and holding hands they ran for the Southern California border.

The guard jumped out of the booth, tripping over its small step. "Stop," he screamed. He righted himself, reached back into the booth and hit a large red button.

They were half way across the bridge. Horns blared behind them, but they kept running. Two guards from the California check point on the other side of the bridge stepped out of their booths and ran towards them. Spotlights lit up the road. Anthony started to drag behind. Martha pulled on his arm. "Run faster," she screamed. She could hear the thunder of shoes running behind her.

"Stop or I'll shoot," someone screamed. An engine started. It was only a few more feet. The two California guards had stopped at a yellow strip that marked Southern California's border.

"Hurry," one of them yelled. "He's right behind you."

"Run faster," Martha screamed as she yanked on Anthony's arm. They were almost there. The guards had stretched out their arms as if to grab them and pull them into safety.

A shot rang out. Then another. Anthony flew ahead of Martha then fell to the pavement. Martha tripped then fell on top of him.

"She's been hit," a California guard screamed.

"Get her over here," the other guard yelled.

Martha looked down at Anthony. Blood was pooling on the road. She turned to look behind them. A police car, sirens on, lights flashing was heading for them. The guard that had been so congenial had almost caught up to them. His gun was now aimed at her.

It was no time to be rational, no time to check Anthony's wounds. Martha grabbed Anthony under the shoulders and started to drag him the rest of the way.

"Drop her," the panting guard screamed.

Martha yanked backwards. Two arms grabbed her and pulled her across the yellow line. Two other arms grabbed Anthony by the hips and pulled his feet across the state line. Not so much as a shoelace was left in Arizona.

The Arizona guard, his feet firmly on his side of the line, pointed the gun at Martha's face. "Step this way, Ma'am," he said.

"Stay where you are," the other California guard said, aiming a gun at his Arizona counterpart. "They're in SoCal now buddy."

Martha turned away from the stand off and lowered Anthony down to the ground. Blood covered his clothes. His wig was half way off his head, his eyes closed. He made no sound, no movement. She lay her head on his chest and listened. She couldn't hear his heart.

"No," she screamed as she pulled her brother into her arms.

One of the California guards grabbed her by the shoulders and tried to pull her away from Anthony.

"We'll get an ambulance," the guard said.

It was too late. An ambulance couldn't help. They had taken everything. First their mother, then their freedom, now his life. She would kill them all, make them pay. Slowly she put her brother down on the pavement and stepped away from the guard. She looked at the Arizona guard with the Elvis hairdo. His gun had been lowered. The Arizona state patrol car had pulled up beside him, and three other officers had appeared. They were yelling, hands pointed at Martha then at Anthony.

A scream deep and vile crept its way from the bottom of Martha's soul. Martha grabbed the guard's gun, aimed at her enemy and squeezed the trigger.

The guard whose gun she stole, tackled her from behind and her shot went wild. She was thrown to the ground, the gun wrestled out of her hand, and still she screamed. Her face scraped against the tar, her arm twisted backwards. She heard the snap of bone somewhere off in the distance, before she felt the pain.

The guard let go of her. She turned her head towards her brother's body. A bone protruded from a bleeding gash in her arm, but she didn't see or feel it. She let the arm drag behind her as she pulled herself over to Anthony and lay her head on his bloodied chest.

A hand, smaller than a man's, reached up and touched her face. "We made it sis, we're free."

41

Sharon told Paul the results of her second pregnancy test and that she had decided not to try and fight the state laws. He seemed pleased, and though he kissed her, it was a short friendly one. He told her he'd give her time to decide about their relationship and work things out with the baby's father.

"But," he said. "I'd like to keep seeing you."

Sharon looked at him and smiled. She didn't know how she felt about him. She didn't know how she felt about Thomas, but she liked having Paul with her. It was going to be a long pregnancy if she had to face it alone. Thomas wouldn't leave his job to be with her, would he? No, well maybe, for the child. No. His job was too important. He'd want her to do it on her own.

"I'd like to stay friends too," Sharon said.

They ended up on the bed, fully clothed, with pillows propped under them. Sharon had her head on Paul's shoulder and was contemplating what she was going to do with all the information she had gathered. She would have Derek send someone to Arizona to get her headbands and watch, but she wasn't sure she wanted to hand over the pictures of Bethany or the recording of Barbara's death. What *can* I do with them? She looked over at Paul. He was staring at the blank TV screen. He had connections, but she wasn't sure she really trusted him. He was, after all, a cop.

She looked at the TV screen. If Martha and Anthony had been caught, or if the boy Martha killed had been found, it would make the eleven o'clock news. She decided she didn't want to know. She felt safe for the first time all day, plus she didn't think she could hide her reaction to bad news. She'd wait and read tomorrow's paper.

Paul shifted in the bed, sitting up straighter. She snuggled into his armpit and put her arm around his waist. "You know," he said. "You never did tell me why you went to see Barbara Sanders."

Sharon shrugged her shoulders, but didn't look up at him. She didn't want him to see her face while she altered the truth. "Like I told Grant. I'm a reporter. She was shot and I wanted to know why."

Paul's hand touched the top of her head and he began stroking her hair. "So what did she say?"

"Not much. She was pretty sedated."

"You were in there an awfully long time for her to have said nothing."

Sharon sat up. "Why are you so interested?" she asked.

Paul studied her face for a moment. She didn't like the scrutiny and looked away.

"Look," he said, "just because we don't broadcast everything that happens doesn't mean we don't want to find out the truth. You're the only one who got a chance to talk to her before she died. Sanders wouldn't let us in. If you know anything, you've got to tell us."

Sharon sat back on the bed. *Damn, why don't you trust him? He and Grant could blow this whole thing wide open.* Unless of course, she reminded herself, they were part of it. "There's nothing to tell," she said then got up and went to the bathroom. Paul followed her to the door. She closed it before he could step in.

She didn't want to talk about it. Not right now. The security she felt a few minutes earlier was gone. Something had wrenched itself in her stomach and was turning. Not the nausea she experienced so many times in the past few days, but the sick feeling of anxiety that she got when she thought someone was following her down a darkened street. She turned on the faucet and let the water run for a few seconds.

"Sharon, don't you want her killer found?"

Found and hanged. But would Paul be the one to do it? "I thought they already knew who did it. Some employee of hers and a runaway."

"I don't think you believe that," Paul said through the door. "You know something. I can tell. Either you tell me and let me handle it, or Grant's going to subpoena every picture, note and recording." Paul's voice trailed off on the word *recording*, it was drawn out and extended. There was a hint of question in the way he said it.

Sharon pulled the door open.

"Of course," he said from across the room. He grabbed her bag and dumped it on the bed.

Sharon ran to where he was and tried to stop him, but he pushed her away. The recorder was one of the first things to fall out and he snatched it. Sharon tried to get it out of his hand, but he held it high above her head and pushed the play button.

Barbara and Nathan Sanders' voices began their final conversation. Paul lowered his arm and sat down in the chair beside the bed. There was nothing she could do now, but let him listen. If he was involved in it, she would know soon enough. She put herself between him and the items that had fallen from her bag and started to pick them up. She wouldn't let him get anything else until she was positive she could trust him.

When she finished, she put her bag back beside the bed where it had been, not wanting him to think she had anything else to hide then sat down and watched his face. He was shocked by what he was hearing, she was sure of that, but couldn't tell if it was because of what Sanders was saying or that she had recorded it.

The disk finished and he turned it off.

"How'd you get this?" he asked.

She'd tell him the truth, she decided. She avoided his eyes by looking across the room. He was studying her again, she could feel it.

"I hid the recorder under her bed. When Sanders came in, she turned it on and got every word before he killed her."

Paul didn't say anything for a minute or two. He tapped the edge of the recorder with his fingers, then turned it on and listened again. When it had finished, he took the disk out and put it in his shirt pocket. "Did you make copies of this?" he asked.

Sharon shook her head.

"Look at me," he said. His voice was that of a trained interrogator. Sharon looked over at him. "Tell me the truth. Did you make copies of this?"

She matched his voice with her own. "I told you, no."

"Has anyone else heard this?"

"No. I was waiting until I could get it back to Southern California."

Paul stood up. Grabbed his jacket and headed for the door. "You should have told me about this."

Sharon got up and ran to the door, blocking his way. "What are you going to do with it?"

Paul moved her aside. "Make sure it gets into the right hands. I want you to stay here until you hear from me, and I don't want you telling anyone about this."

Sharon nodded her head and let him leave. She waited at the door until she heard the elevator doors close. She grabbed her bag and ran out of the room. The elevator was already on the first floor. She headed for the stairs and ran down them. She'd see where he took her disk and then decide if she'd tell him more.

Sharon stayed back, letting Paul take turns before making them herself. His car was easy to follow. It was an older model and had separate taillights. He didn't head for the Sheriff's station. Instead he went over the Buttes and headed for North Scottsdale. He turned up a road off Camelback and headed up a small road marked PRIVATE. Sharon waited until she was sure he couldn't see her then drove up the private road to the entrance of an estate named *Camelback Sands*. She didn't know whose home it was, but that horrible sinking feeling in her stomach came back. This wasn't good. She backed her Jeep down the private road and up into another private street. She turned her lights off and waited. If Paul was double crossing her, she'd do the same to him.

42

Norma stood on the roof patio staring out at the lights of the city and the night sky. She was given the day off. They all were. "A time to mourn and pray," Mr. Sanders had told them. She finished her prayers hours ago, but wasn't able to stop mourning. She hadn't loved Mrs. Sanders, not the way she did Mr. Sanders, but she did have feelings for her, deep feelings. The thought that she was never going to come home was too hard to accept and impossible to sleep through.

Her tears and sobs had dried up hours ago, and now she sought the night air for answers. She didn't like Martha, hadn't trusted her from the beginning, but she didn't think she was a threat to the family. If she did, she would have killed her herself. The Sanders were her parents, the ones whose life affected hers, not the whore who gave birth to her and ran off. She wanted to know what had happened and why. She wasn't satisfied with the sketchy answers Mr. Sanders had offered.

The sound of an approaching car interrupted her contemplation of what events must have unfolded to take away the woman she secretly considered her mother. She looked down over the stucco railing to see who would be inconsiderate enough to disturb them at such an hour. The automatic lights came on in the driveway and she saw Paul Matthews' car. She was about to turn and run downstairs to let him in when she saw Mr. Sanders step out from the shadows.

"So what's the emergency?" Mr. Sanders ask as he reached out and shook the detective's hand.

Detective Matthews reached into his shirt pocket and pulled something out. Norma couldn't make it out in the glare from the lights. "Wait till you hear this."

Mr. Sanders invited him inside and the two of them disappeared beyond Norma's view. She thought about going down and greeting him herself. She had always like Detective Matthews. She liked the way he flirted with her and always made her feel special. She had day dreamed about him many times, wondering what it would feel like to have him on top of her, shooting into her his tensions and frustrations with the world. She wouldn't mind being his sin eater, she thought, then blushed at the immorality that had tempted her. She would be sure to say an extra prayer tonight asking God to punish her for such an impure thought. Something she had done many times.

She decided she should return to her room where she could focus on the death of her mistress. As she turned, a second set of lights caught her eye. They were beyond the turn, stopped at the base of the driveway. She ran over to the telescope Mrs. Sanders had bought for the house their first Christmas there and aimed it at the lights. She took a second to focus, then caught the outline of a Jeep. She couldn't be sure, but it looked like the same Jeep she had seen when she followed Robert and Mrs. Sanders into the park the other day. The day she had taken pictures of every stop her lover's wife had made. The day she saw the shaved headed men attack Martha.

The Jeep backed up. Norma followed it for as far as she could, but it soon disappeared between rows of trees, cacti, and homes. She saw the lights go out, and knew the Jeep was hiding, waiting, but for what? Norma decided Mr. Sanders would want to know and hurried downstairs.

She headed right for Mr. Sander's study – he would take the detective there. It was where he conduced all business. She hesitated at the door for a moment, as she had been taught, waiting for the voices behind it to lull so she wouldn't appear intrusive. As she waited, she heard a woman's voice coming from behind the door. It was a voice she knew, a voice she had heard all of her life. It was Mrs. Sanders. She was about to open the door, burst in unannounced, and throw herself in the woman's arms when the words she was hearing started to take form. She remembered Detective Matthews telling Mr. Sanders he had something he needed to listen to. It was a recording. She leaned in closer so she could hear better. Hoping it would answer some of her questions.

"So you did try to have me killed," Mrs. Sanders' voice accused.

"I do whatever I need to do to keep the Lord's word," Norma's lover responded.

Norma turned around, her back to the door. It couldn't be. He wouldn't have arranged for it. No. Martha had done it. Mr. Sanders said so. Norma tried to calm herself. He was a good man, a man of God. He would never have tried to kill his wife. She didn't want to hear anymore, but couldn't pull herself away. She put her ear back to the door and listened.

Mr. Sanders' voice went on to describe how he felt, that he was in the business of saving babies and that he did it to earn money to continue God's work. Mrs. Sanders asked if that money was to kill wives and chauffeurs. He didn't deny it. Instead he called it an "unforeseen expense."

"You have tons of money Nathan," Mrs. Sanders continued. "You sell those babies because you enjoy owning people and having people be owned. Look at the pleasure you get from mounting your own little concubine. What do you think Norma will do when she finds out the truth, that you bought and paid for her? That in your mind she's no more than a whore slave. Do you think she'll..."

Norma pulled away from the door backing up to the opposite wall. She didn't want to hear any more. It couldn't be true. She was born here. Her mother abandoned her. They had taken her in out of love and kindness. She wasn't a whore. She wasn't a slave. She was their daughter, his lover. She slid down the wall and sat on the floor. Muffled voices drifted from under the door. She remembered the first time he had called for her, she was twelve. It was right after her first menses. He told her she was his gift from God, his outlet. That God gave them permission to be together in a way that was private and loving. He taught her what God wanted her to do to him to help release the oppressions Satan put on him every day and how to anticipate his needs. He told her she was a holy vessel, and had the power to absorb all his sins and earthly temptations.

But it was a lie. He bought her. She had not been a gift from God. She felt great shame and repulsion. Her whole life had been a fabrication he designed to trick her into his bed. She thought for a moment of what she would do, what she could do. Then she knew, she would leave. It was against the law to enslave people. She was over eighteen. He couldn't stop her.

She moved back to the door. She wanted to hear the rest. The more she knew, the safer she believed she would be. "How did she get that?" Mr. Sanders ask.

She listened to Detective Matthews explain how someone named

Sharon had hidden it under Mrs. Sanders bed and that Mrs. Sanders herself had turned it on. She had tricked him into giving her recorded proof that he, Nathan Sanders, had been her murderer.

"Does anyone else know?" Mr. Sanders ask.

"I don't think so," Detective Matthews said. "She doesn't trust too many people."

"Good. I want you to get rid of her. I don't care how you do it, but do it quick. We don't know what other information Barbara gave her."

Norma didn't want to hear anymore. She ran to her room, packed her street clothes and grabbed her ID. She had a few thousand dollars in her account, but knew it would barely get her passage to a free state. She took a piece of paper from her desk and wrote a note. *I heard the whole recording, and your plans for Sharon. Put fifty thousand dollars in my account. Do not try to find me. Do not put a lock on my account. If you do I will tell the police everything I heard.*

She put the note on her pillow, then went out the back way, avoiding the sensors that set off the automatic lights, and headed down the hill. She found the Jeep quickly. The woman inside seemed surprised to see someone and turned on the headlights. Norma walked over to the driver's side of the vehicle and rapped on the window. "Is your name Sharon?" she asked.

The woman rolled down the window. "Do I know you?"

"I work for the Sanders. Paul Matthews is going to kill you."

43

Sharon wasn't shocked to hear that the man who wanted to be her lover was now a threatening assassin. Somewhere deep down, she had always known meeting Paul was no accident. Neither were the boys who had attacked them at the park. She and Barbara had been set up all along. Just like Madison Courtney. Was it Madison's rejection that had turned Paul, or was it earlier? Had Madison just been another assignment? She had probably seen through his charade. That was why she had dumped him, and possibly the reason she had been stopped at the border. There had been so much deceit, so many lies, and now there were too many questions. Sharon thought of the young woman busy getting airplane tickets out of Arizona, and realized she had suffered the greatest deceptions.

When the girl first approached the car, Sharon had been scared. She thought she was caught and expected Paul and whomever he was meeting to show up next. She almost bolted, but the girl's face was too distraught, too pale, to be part of anything but what she claimed. When she said her name was Norma and that she had listened to the recording between the Sanders, Sharon knew, that finally, she found someone she could trust.

Norma wanted to know more, and Sharon told her. She explained how Barbara knew about her husband's black market baby business, and then she made excuses for the dead woman, quickly explaining why Barbara Sanders had never stepped in to help Norma. Sharon gave Norma Derek's name and number and told her to contact him when she found someplace to hide. Now it was Sharon's turn to find a way out. She couldn't fly and she couldn't drive across the border. She had only one resource left.

The airport had the usual bustle of passengers trying to get on the red eyes and save money. There was a row of empty phones near the terminal where she left Norma. She pulled the slip of paper with the phone number Barbara had given her at the park then used the untraceable phone card to call.

After the tenth ring someone finally answered the phone. It was a man's voice, husky from sleep and irritated at having been wakened. "You better have a damn good reason for calling this late," the man said.

It was no time for stories. She had to get out tonight. Sharon told him who she was, that she was calling on a secured line, that Barbara Sanders had given her his number, that she was pregnant, and that because of incriminating evidence she had against Nathan Sanders and Senator Listner she had solid proof that one of the detectives from the Maricopa Sheriff's department was going to try and kill her. "I have to get out of the state tonight," Sharon told him.

The man agreed to help her. Barbara had obviously told him all about Sharon and though he hadn't planned on making the run for another week or so, he'd get her across the border, somehow. He wanted her to leave her car in the airport parking garage. "I've been very careful. I have a device that alters my face for the monitors, and have set my GPS tracking position back at my hotel. If I leave the Jeep, they'll connect me to Norma.

"Did you park it?" the man asked.

"Fuck."

"Well, the minute you pay the parking ticket they'll find you. Better to leave it there and have it sit. By the time they find it, both of you will be long gone."

Sharon had made another mistake. She should have just dropped Norma off and found a phone somewhere else, but she wanted to see the girl safely on the plane. Not that she thought she could really protect her against Nathan Sanders, but she believed there was safety in numbers. *No use worrying about it now*, she told herself as she realized the airport was probably the best place to leave the Jeep. Paul had no reason to suspect she had followed him. Even if they knew Norma had flown out, they wouldn't think to look for the Jeep at the airport. Sharon agreed leaving the Jeep in the parking garage was the wisest thing to do. The man barely acknowledged her acquiesces. It seemed to Sharon she had never been given a choice. It was apparent that the moment she made the call, she placed everything in his hands.

He wanted to pick her up in the next half hour. Sharon still needed to get her tote case and see Norma off. She asked for an hour. He gave her forty-five minutes.

Sharon described her appearance and that of her bag and tote case so he could identify her and told him she'd be waiting at the drop off area outside the terminal. He told her to look for a green Ford truck and hung up.

Norma was standing a few feet away anxiously fondling her ticket when Sharon turned around. "Take this," Sharon said pushing the phone card Barbara had given her into Norma's hand. "When you get where you're going, call my boss. He'll help you get a new ID."

"What for?" Norma asked. "I'm going to be getting fifty thousand dollars. If they transfer the money, a new ID wouldn't do any good."

Sharon grabbed Norma by the hand and dragged her into a nearby restroom. She checked to make sure all the stalls were empty before talking. "Norma, you've got to realize by now that Nathan Sanders is a very powerful man. If he finds out you're gone before morning he could have someone waiting for you at the airport. Forget about blackmailing him. I've got enough evidence against him to send him away for life. But even from jail he'll be a formidable adversary. You'll never be safe unless you hide."

Norma shrugged her shoulders. "Where would I hide? I don't know anyone beside the Sanders. I need a place to stay, a job. Without money, I might as well have stayed at the house."

"Don't be ridiculous," Sharon said, then told her what she knew about the revolutionary group Barbara had headed. She gave her Stan Dietrich's name and told her the name of his nursery. "Call him," she told the girl. "Join up with them. They'll help you."

"I don't want to join anything. All I want is my freedom."

"But what about the others?" Sharon asked her. "You weren't the only baby sold into slavery. Don't you want to fight against the people who did this to you?"

"I know who did this to me," Norma said. The venom in her voice striking out in small bullets of spit.

"Use that anger," Sharon said. "Do something with your life. Even if you get the money, how long do you think it will last? A year at the most. Are you willing to risk your life for one year's worth of expense money? Don't be stupid. Call Deitrich and have him help you."

Norma turned away from Sharon. The lights danced off her long black hair. "I'll think about it," she said and walked out of the bathroom.

Sharon tried to follow her, but the girl walked fast. Eventually Sharon gave up chasing her and went to her Jeep to get her tote case.

It was another fifteen minutes before the truck arrived. The man, young, for his deep voice, with acne scars and a twitching left eye, rolled down the passenger side window in his truck and ordered Sharon to get in. He said his name was Jim, and he was going to take Sharon to a safe house. "We'll wait there," he said, "until everything can be arranged. It could take a couple of hours."

After a few minutes of silence, Sharon asked how much the run would cost and how they wanted her to pay them. "Normally," Jim said, "we have clients buy items and donate them to charities we set up throughout the state, but we won't be able to do that with you. Your account's probably already been flagged for any and all purchases. We'll come up with something though, don't worry."

There were no lights on in the house. They entered a two-car garage and waited to get out of the car until the garage door was completely closed. Jim led Sharon through a door into a laundry room and then out into a small kitchen. He made coffee for them then showed Sharon to the living room. There were no pictures on the walls, no knickknacks. The only furniture was a coffee table, a brown tweed couch and an old wooden rocking chair. "Have a seat," Jim told her pointing to the sofa. Sharon sat down.

Jim took his coffee and went back to the kitchen. He sat down at the table, pulled a paperback book from his back pocket and started to read. Every now and then he'd look up at Sharon. Satisfied she was still there, he would go back to his book. Sharon didn't know what to do with herself, nor did she know what would happen next. She was about to lie down on the couch and try to sleep when she heard the mechanical whine of the garage door opening.

Jim motioned for Sharon to stay seated and walked into the laundry room. A car door opened then closed. There were muffled voices, no doubt discussing her fate, then the door opened and Stan Deitrich walked in.

Sharon grabbed her tote case close to her and stood up.

"Well, Miss Clark. Seems you're finally in a position to bargain," Stan said as he walked into the living room.

"It's too late," Sharon told him. "I lost the tape. Paul Matthews of the Maricopa Sheriffs Department stole it from me this evening and brought it to Nathan Sanders."

Stan sat down next to her on the couch. He took her arm in his hand and turned it over. Slowly, he unbuckled her watch. "I seriously doubt you'd let that disk go without making a back up." Jim brought a small black plastic box over to where they sat and handed it to Stan. He turned the watch over, popped out its recording cell and placed it in the box. He pushed a small button on its side and once again Barbara and Nathan Sanders' discussion was heard.

"How'd you know about the watch?" she asked.

"Who do you think got them for you? Derek Robinson? Sorry, he's not that well connected. We supplied them, and to be honest, we never planned on letting you take them out of the state."

Sharon hugged her tote case tighter.

Stan reached for the case, but Sharon held on to it. She knew he would eventually get it, but somehow the little resistance she gave made her feel better. Jim stepped over and they pried the case from her hands.

"What else do you have for us?" Stan asked emptying the case on the floor. He didn't bother with the jewelry or her makeup. He picked up each of the headbands, film cartridges, and recording disks and handed them to Jim. He pointed to the extra recording cells that fit her watch. Jim stooped down and collected them. Stan picked up Sharon's bag and dumped it in a second spot on the floor. He took the pictures of Bethany Collins and Madison's test results.

"There are two headbands missing?" He looked up at Sharon. "Where are they?"

There was no reason to lie. "I sent them with the kids to SoCal."

"Anything on them."

She wanted to lie, to make him think he wasn't getting everything, but as she opened her mouth, she closed it and shook her head. "They were blank."

"Good. You did a better job than we expected," he said standing up and pulling a set of keys from his pocket. He threw the keys to her. "Now it's time for you to make a decision. I'm willing to give you the keys to the truck I brought with me tonight and show you a route out of the state. In exchange you have to agree to say nothing when you get back. You can still write your article against the harsh treatment women at Arpaio are experiencing, but you have to promise that you won't print a word about breeding facilities, Nathan Sanders, or Senator Listner."

"Or what?" Sharon said.

"Or else we drop you off back at your hotel and you take your chances with Detective Matthews."

Sharon looked down at the keys in her hand. She had the baby to think of, Thomas. If she stayed in Arizona, Paul was certain to find her. Without Stan's help she had no way of hiding. Her account would be useless. She had to leave. Everything she fought for was gone. Without solid proof, anything she printed wouldn't be taken seriously. Any effort she made to help Madison would be futile. Stan Deitrich had won.

"I know it may not seem like much now, but I want you to know, Barbara would have wanted it this way. She hoped your article would keep Southern California free and that the upcoming election would prevent any ratification of the constitution, but she wouldn't have wanted you to endanger all she had worked for. Trust me," Stan said reaching over and pulling the headband off Sharon's head. "We can do a lot more with what you were able to accumulate than you could."

"But not for a few years, right? Not in time to save Madison Courtney."

"I'm sorry," Stan said holding out his hand. "Do you mind? I'd like to have the necklace back too."

Sharon reached behind her neck and unfastened the chain. "Actually, this recording," he said tapping the small black box, "was more than we ever hoped for. As well as the pictures of Bethany Collins and your friend's pregnancy test. When we take down Listner and Sanders they're going to fall hard."

"Then why not do it now?"

"The country's not ready. We have to wait until it's at a boil, then strike. There are so many things that still need to be put in place. I hope that when you get home you rethink what we're doing and join us. You'd make a great ally."

Sharon thought of the words she had spoken to Norma before leaving her at the airport. She knew that even once she was in Southern California she wouldn't really be safe from Sanders wrath. It would be easy for Paul to find her no matter where she was. Going underground might be the only hope she had for securing the safety of her child.

"We'll see," she said.

"Good enough." Stan pulled a map from his back pocket. Sharon followed him over to the kitchen table. He laid the paper down and pointed to the route she needed to take.

"This one's empty," Jim said handing Stan a headband.

"Good." He handed it to Sharon. "Wear it until you're out of the state. There are monitors on some of the roads you'll need to travel, it doesn't matter how dark the inside of the vehicle is, the details they capture will nail you in seconds."

Sharon took the headband. Stan focused his attention back to the map.

"Normally we have time to set up better arrangements. This time, I'm afraid we're going to send you on your own. Look here," he said pointing to a section of the Colorado River. "Years ago, before your state had desalinization plants, aqua ducts were used to transfer water from the river to California. We've made some modifications to this one right here," he said pointing to an X marked on the map. Once you're inside, all you have to do is follow it. You'll come out on California soil. There are helicopters that survey the river at random intervals, looking for anyone trying to cross the border illegally. You'll be on foot by the time you reach that area, so always know where your next cover will be before taking off across open desert."

Stan turned the map over to show her a more detailed section of the trail she needed to take to reach the aqua duct. It seemed long. She never liked hiking, nor was she very good at hide and seek. She didn't feel good about the plan, but knew it was all she had. She'd do it, and wait to complain once she landed on safe ground.

"Stash the truck here," Stan said pointing to another mark on the map. "And be careful. The truck's stolen and the plates have been changed. If you get stopped for any reason, the trip's over." Sharon told him she'd be careful, folded up the map and put it in her back pocket.

"Wait until morning before starting the hike," Jim told her as he walked her back to the garage. "If everything goes right and there's no sign of your having been caught, I'll meet you on the other side."

Sharon thanked him, then headed for the truck. She felt naked without her watch and necklace, without her story, but she could feel the warmth in her belly and knew that she wasn't making the journey alone. What she couldn't do for Madison or Bethany, she'd do for her child. And then, when she got home, she'd join Stan's revolution and work with them to ensure her child was given all the freedom and liberty she had sung about at baseball games with her granddad so many years ago

44

It had been a long tiring drive. The truck was uncomfortable, its shocks gone. The freeway had been bearable, but now that she was on back roads, Sharon was being jostled around. Her head and neck ached, and she had to pee. There hadn't been any homes or buildings along the road for quite a while, no street lights, no Circle K's. She was alone in the dark – it was safe.

She pulled over to the side of the road and got out of the truck. It was a moonless night. Anything lurking in the desert brush could be watching her, ready to pounce and she wouldn't have a clue – not until it was on her, tearing at her flesh. A coyote howled somewhere close by. She jumped. Her heart pounded as she strained to see into the night, searching for glowing eyes, a moving bush, but there was nothing. No evidence of being stalked. She listened harder. Tiny footfalls moved in the brush to her right, too small for a vicious dog. Her bladder was about to explode, it was either pee in the truck or brave the pavement. She ran to the center of the headlight's beam. If something was going to get her, it would have to strike through the light. What would it care? She was no safer, and she knew it, but it was a semblance of security, and right now she'd take what she could get. She pulled down her pants and peed.

Nothing came at her, no foot, no barred teeth. The desert made her uneasy. Thankfully, sunrise was only an hour or two away. She put back on her pants, and climbed back into the truck, giving herself a few minutes to let her nerves calm.

She checked her map, then started the truck. The gas gauge was only slightly above E, but she thought she was close enough to the spot where she was supposed to leave the truck to make it. The truck crept along the lonely road, her eyes scanned the sides, the marker had to be here, somewhere. If she missed it, she would run out of gas.

Three miles from where she stopped, she saw the small sign indicating the access road that would lead her into the desert. The road was bumpy and narrow, but clear. She made better time than she expected and arrived at the wash where she had been told to leave the truck. The sky was beginning to lighten with the start of the new day. She was very tired. Every muscle ached from the jostling she took at the truck's expense, and fear. Not so much from what lay ahead of her, but what might be behind her. It wasn't coyote's or snakes she was afraid of, it was the law. If they found her, there would be no escape. Nathan Sanders would see to that.

Sleep was a dangerous luxury, so instead she went through the daypack Stan provided. There were three bottles of water, a packed lunch with two sandwiches, a thermos of coffee and two flashlights. It wasn't much to show for her trip. She had left everything else at the safe house. The jewelry was payment for the truck, her story for her freedom. Had she made the right choice? She rubbed her stomach. There was a baby inside, a baby whose life would make up for all of this. It wasn't as if she had turned her back on Barbara, Madison, and Bethany without a good enough cause. She couldn't jeopardize her child's life for theirs. Besides Barbara was already dead, Bethany might as well be. Madison was the only real consideration. And though Sharon knew she would harbor guilt for having left Madison behind, she could rationalize the exchange. One life for another. Madison's for her child's. It could be justified. Even Madison would have agreed.

She took out one of the sandwiches, poured herself a cup of coffee, and ate breakfast. Thomas was probably still safe in their bed, sleeping, oblivious to his child and to the danger that surrounded it. Sharon rubbed her belly again. "He's going to be surprised when he finds out about you," she said then looked out at the night thinking about the man whose strength she wished was with her. "I should have told him," she said out loud. She rubbed her belly again. "Your daddy would have rescued us."

Sharon looked out the back window. It was too late to turn back, but not too late to change. She knew now she had been wrong about Thomas. Her instinctive distrust towards people had not served her well when it came to Paul Matthews. If she had been wrong about him, then she most certainly had been wrong about Thomas. He loved her, and job or no job, he would have been there. If only she had seen it before. She'd remedy that when she got home, she decided. It was time to tell Thomas about the rape, about Paul, the baby, and her fears of not being worthy of his love. "You're nothing but white trash, what would a man like Thomas want with you," her mother's voice echoed in her head.

"Shut up," she told the nagging image, and in that instant made a life long decision. Mother would never get near her child, she and Thomas would move, somewhere free, somewhere so far away their child would never feel the abuse and distrust her mother had instilled in her. She would be a great mother, and Thomas... She cried when she thought of him, what she had put him through? His love was real, and now for the first time since Granddad died, she realized so was hers. She did love him, and when she got home, she'd make sure he knew it.

The desert began to emerge from the night. Jagged rocks marked the trail that would lead her home. It seemed uninviting, dangerous. Stan had said the trail was easy to follow. Sharon didn't believe him, but forward was the only direction she considered.

"This is it," she said to no one as she repacked the day bag, got out of the truck, and walked into the desert. "We're coming home, Thomas," she said looking to the West.

At first the trail *was* easy. She blocked out the rustling noises she heard, not wanting to think about the thousands of rattlesnakes that would soon be coming out to sun themselves.

A dead cow lay a few hundred feet from the trail. Sharon stopped. Buzzards had descended upon the carcass and were feasting. She tried not to look, but couldn't stop herself. The scavenger's long baldheads dug deep into the cow's body and drew out long red tendrils. The cow's back end was ripped off, its stomach burst. It must have wandered away from the rest of its herd and been brought down by a pack of coyotes. She looked all around. Where were they now?

"Don't go getting paranoid," she told herself. "They're obviously sated."

She continued along the trail for what seemed liked a day's worth of hiking, though she knew by the rising sun it was still only mid-morning. She stopped at the top of a small hill, rested, and checked her map. She should be coming up to another wash soon. From there, she would ascend her final hill. After that, she would be in view of the border patrol's helicopter.

It was starting to get hot. She drank another cup of coffee and then some water before continuing. The walk had left her mind numb. She could think of only one thing, crossing the river, getting home, and seeing Thomas.

She crested the final hill. Remembering Stan's warning, she lay down on the ground and peered over it. She smelled the river before she saw it. The deep musty odor of wet dirt alive with worms and decaying vegetation wafted through the slight breeze. There it was, she could see it, a bluish green line flanked by trees. The sound of its rushing waters sang to her of freedom. She looked across its shore and longed for the land beyond. Home was only a river crossing away, but there would be no wadding across this river. This was the most dangerous leg of her trip. What did people say? Most accidents occur a quarter of mile from home. Well, she wouldn't be a statistic, not today. She would take every precaution and get her baby and herself back to Thomas. The hell with Arizona, the hell with everyone else. Today only three people mattered, two more than had ever mattered before.

The map was in her daypack, she pulled it out and lay it on the ground in front of her. The aqua duct was still at least a mile away. The trail would bring her closer to the river, only a few yards from its embankment, then veer northeast. She listened carefully for the swishing sound of helicopter blades, but heard nothing. It would be safe for a while. The first cover she would head for was a mound of sand covered with low prickly bushes.

"Here goes."

She stood up and ran down the hill toward the mound. By the time she reached it, she was panting. It was hot, the sun had come out in full force, and the trees seemed to move in the heat's haze. She felt light headed, spent. When she got home she'd join one of those aerobic classes for pregnant women, but right now she had to get back her strength. The river was a few hundred feet out of her way, but she couldn't resist the temptation to put her feet in the water and to rest for a few minutes in the shade along its shore. She listened again for any signs of a helicopter. There were none – she was safe. She'd just put her feet in. A few seconds, no more, just enough to revitalize her tired soul. What harm could it do? She pulled herself up from behind the hill and ran.

Halfway there, and still no helicopter. "Almost there," she panted, then, as if pierced by a needle, pain shot through the spot on her neck where she had bruised herself when she fell at the hospital. She placed her hand over the source of pain as she ran. It was hot. A loud ringing noise bombarded her eardrums. Her hands shot to cover her ears, but they didn't help. The pain intensified.

Sharon screamed and fell to the ground. As the pain rose from her neck to her head she felt as though someone had anchored her head in a vise and was slowly tightening it. She cradled her head in her arms, rocked on the desert soil and cried. Somewhere in her brain, something popped and the world disappeared.

45

She awoke in darkness. The air was cold. Whatever was beneath her was soft. Her head still hurt, but it was nothing more than an ordinary headache. She tried to adjust her eyes to the darkness. Her hand moved and hit what felt like steel. She slowly pulled herself up into a sitting position. It was a cot. She remembered some of what happened – the running towards the river, the throbbing in her neck, the pain. She must have fainted again. Someone, hopefully Stan or Jim, found her lying in the desert and brought her to safety. But which side of the river was she on?

She swung her legs over the edge of the bed. Her bare feet felt cold concrete. Her eyes adjusted to the dark. There was a hint of light coming from somewhere in front of her. She forced herself off the cot and stumbled toward the light. She had only taken a few steps when she was able to distinguish the outline of bars.

"No," she screamed running to them and grabbing two between her hands. "No," she cried again, pushing her face between them, trying to see the light. An unseen woman's voice yelled for her to shut up. "No," she said more softly as she crumbled to the floor and leaned against the prison's wall.

Hours went by before any lights were turned on and Sharon could see her surroundings. Her cell held a single bed, steel toilet and a small sink. She was in a hot pink dress, *bubble gum parade*, no shoes or stockings anywhere in the room. Under the dress she had on an oversized pair of cotton briefs and no bra.

It had taken her a while to come to terms with what had happened. At first, she thought Stan had set her up, but then she remembered how the pain started. She touched her neck where the throbbing first appeared. It was swollen and tender. She hadn't hit her head on Barbara's bed rails. They implanted something in her neck. Whatever it was, exploded as she neared the river. She should have known better than to think she would ever escape.

A guard brought her breakfast, sliding it through a small opening in the bars of her cell. It was green mush that she thought was some kind of egg, meat and bread mixture. The sight of it made her sick and she threw up in the sink. When she was done, she pulled away and looked up at the blank wall. *This can't be happening. This can't be my life.* Two sets of heavy footsteps made their way down the cellblock. She wiped her mouth with the back of her hand and ran to the bars.

"Please," she said as the guards approached. "There's been a mistake."

"Only mistake made," one of the guards said as he stopped in front of her cell, "was you trying to kill your baby."

"What? No, you're wrong. You don't understand." She loved her baby and planned to keep it. But that wouldn't matter, would it. She knew how the system worked.

"Step back," the guard ordered as he slid a key card through a slot on the outside of the cell's door.

The other guard stepped forward into the cell. He was holding two sets of chains and shackles. "Arms over your head," he ordered.

Sharon did as she was told. He wrapped a chain around her waist then handcuffing her to it. Shackles were placed around her ankles, separated by a foot of chain. "After you," he said pushing her towards the door.

Sharon walked towards a large steel door at the end of the block. Only four of the other cells held prisoners, all women. One looked pregnant. Another was curled up in a ball on her cot. A small woman in a similar, yet tighter dress gave her a frail smile as she passed. The fourth looked like she could eat her mother for dinner and laugh as she spit out the bones. None of them said anything as Sharon was led out of the cellblock and through the door.

She was taken to a small room with a metal table and two chairs in it. The guard shoved her into a chair that was bolted to the floor. He hooked both sides of her chain belt to steel loops welded to the chair and left the room.

"I told you to stay at the hotel," Paul Matthews said as he walked into the room. Sharon wasn't surprised to see him. He was just another piece of the horrors she knew were waiting for her. Paul moved to the opposite side of the table and sat down. "Now look at the mess you've gotten yourself into."

"Well at least you can't kill me in here," she said with a slight smile.

"Kill you? Why would I do that? I had hoped to marry you."

"Nathan Sanders. I know you gave him my disk?"

"Oh that," Paul smiled. He didn't seem the least bit vindictive or remorseful. "I should have known you would follow me. Someday you've got to learn to trust people."

"Like you?"

"Like me. I would have protected you, but I'm afraid it's too late for that," Paul said standing up. "Your trial's in an hour. They have you on attempted abortion, grand felony theft, falsification of your personal ID, and aiding and abetting murder suspects. The DA's going for life without parole."

"Life," Sharon said choking on the word. "What about my baby?"

"State property."

"Fuck them," she screamed at him, trying to stand. The chains pulled her back down and she hit the metal chair hard. It hurt, but not as much as losing her child. She bent her head over the table and banged it against the metal. Paul walked over to her and grabbed her head after the third hit.

He looked at the guard, then back down at Sharon. In almost a whisper, he said, "I might be able to help you."

Sharon let him lift her head so she could see him. Tears were streaming from her face. Paul pushed away her hair and wiped her face with his hand. "How?" she asked.

"They don't care about you. You're nothing to them. They want the traders who helped you. I could work a deal."

"A deal?"

"Look," he said touching the tender spot on her neck. "You may have figured out by now that you had a transmitter implanted in your neck. It's the newest technology. There are tracers set up all along Arizona's border now, so when anyone with an implant comes within two hundred feet of the border, a beacon goes off and a drug is released into the system that knocks the runner out.

"You were their test bunny. They were sure you'd try and get out of the state, so they decided to use you to see how proficient the system is. Now that they know that it works, within a month doctors

will be implanting these things in all pregnant women. So don't you
see? Next time your friends try and take someone across the border,
they're going to get them. So why not turn them in now, and save you
and your baby?"

Sharon thought about what he said. If it were true, Stan and Jim
would be caught soon enough. Except Stan and Jim didn't make the
runs. They had other people to do that. And if those other people
were anything like Barbara, they'd gladly go to prison to protect the
others.

"Think about the baby," Paul said after a moment's silence.

Sharon looked up into the face that had almost seduced her. She
was thinking about the baby, but not just her own.

"I don't know anything," she finally said.

Paul pounded his fist against the table. "Damn you. Don' t you
know what I'm trying to do for you here?"

Sharon took a deep breath. "I know exactly what you're trying to
do, and what Sanders and Listner are trying to do. You don't care about
me, Paul. You'd probably kill me the minute I was released anyway. All
you care about is power and money." Sharon curled her bottom lip
down and shook her head. "I hope you all rot in hell."

Paul grabbed her face in his hand. "You know that baby of yours?"
His face grew red, a vein was popping on his forehead. "Well your
boyfriend showed up last night. He's going to petition the court for
custody. But it will never be granted."

His fingers dug into her cheeks. She wasn't going to let him intim-
idate her. She looked straight ahead and made no comment about
Thomas' arrival.

"You should have told me he was black."

"Would it have mattered?"

Paul let go of her and stood up straight. "Not to me," he said. "But
I can't say the same for Doctor Listner over at the penitentiary. She
doesn't look too favorably on multiethnic conceptions. Something
about them being unsuitable for adoptions. I think she refers to them
as unholy miscreations."

"That's her problem," Sharon said.

"No, it's your problem. Don't you see? If you don't give up the
traders, you'll be forfeiting both your lives. Why be a martyr?"

*There are always those lives that must be sacrificed when you're fighting a
war.*

"Because it's the right thing to do?" Sharon whispered back, tears
falling down her face.

"Maybe so." Paul walked over to the door and opened it. "I don't think I've heard of one mulatto pregnancy making it through term over there. You think about that. If you change your mind about the traders, you have the guard call me. And do it soon. The minute you walk into that court room, all deals are off."

The door slammed shut. She bent her head back down on the table and cried. There was nothing she could do. If she gave up the revolutionists to save herself and her baby, how many more lives would be destroyed? She remembered the quotation Nathan Sanders had told Barbara about not caring what his opponents thought, that once they had the children they could mold them into anything they wanted. He was right. The children were the key, she wouldn't help them stop the revolutionaries. She couldn't. Her child would survive, it had to. That's where the difference would be made. Stan Deitrich and his friends would prevent what happened to Norma and Martha, from happening to her child, and if not, then at least to any grandchild. Her own life was inconsequential, her fate already decided. She would make no deals.

She put her hands on her abdomen and tried to feel the life within. "Forgive me," she whispered."

Thomas paced the court's lobby waiting for his turn to approach the judge. The lawyer he had retained the minute he found out Sharon had been arrested didn't seem too confident in his ability to get Sharon released. She had been appointed a public defender and the judge had refused to change her council.

The prosecution had shown them videotapes of Sharon back at her hotel room. Everything was there in vivid color, her meeting with Reverend Samuels, her intimacy with a Maricopa County detective, and her attempt at hiding one of her IDs. Surveillance was everywhere, how had she been so naïve?

Seeing her with the detective hurt, but nothing had happened. It wasn't enough to make him stop loving her, or their baby. He understood Sharon, he knew her past and understood her resistance to commitment. The detective had been nothing more than a diversion, Thomas was sure of it. He knew Sharon better than she knew herself, and if he believed anything about who she was, it was that she loved him.

He would do everything he could to save her.

"Mr. Jackson."

Thomas turned around to face his attorney, Ralph Oswald. The man was in his mid-forties, dressed in a gray linen suit, his wavy hair combed back with a slight curl. "I'm sorry. There's no hope for your girlfriend. They have too much on her. The best I can offer is to try and get you custody of the child, and to do that I'll be risking contempt charges by interrupting the proceedings. They refused to give me another hearing date for the baby. Custody is awarded when the mother is sentenced. I'm sorry."

Thomas' knees buckled and he backed up to a wooden bench and sat down. He put his hands over his face and silently cried. Living without Sharon would be impossible. "What type of sentence will she get?"

"Long," Oswald said. "You're best to forget her and decide if you want the child or not."

"Of course I want the child," Thomas said sharply.

"I'll see what I can do," Oswald said then turned to walk into the courtroom.

Thomas stood up. "I'll go with you."

Oswald turned around and put his hand on Thomas' shoulder. "No," he said. "It's best if you wait out here."

"But..."

"Trust me." Oswald smiled then turned and walked into the courtroom.

Thomas sat back down and waited, wondering if hiring Oswald had been a mistake.

"Miss Clark, how do you plead?" the judge, a middle aged balding man in black judicial robes, asked.

Richard Bristol, Sharon's appointed lawyer, had spent only five minutes with her before they were escorted to the courtroom. He was a small man with beady eyes and well-positioned black hair. His blue suit was crisp, his speech impeccable, and though he knew no more about her case or who she was than a complete stranger, he stood, ready to defend her.

"Guilty, your honor."

"What?" Sharon stood up. She had told him what had happened. She had told him the truth. She had never agreed to plea guilty. "Your honor..." Sharon started to step out from behind the table. A bailiff walked over, placed his hands on her shoulders and forced her back down in her seat.

"Mr. Bristol, control your client," the judge ordered.

Bristol leaned over. "I have ten other cases this morning. There's no chance of us winning this one. We're better off admitting guilt. It usually brings a lower sentence."

"No," Sharon stated. "I want a different…"

"Your honor, may I approach the bench," someone said from behind them.

Sharon turned. A man in his mid-thirties, dressed in a light gray double-breasted suit stepped into the aisle.

"Who are you?" the judge asked.

"Ralph Oswald. I represent the father, a Mr. Thomas Jackson. As you know, in Southern California it is legal for unmarried partners to engage in intercourse. Mr. Jackson was above the law when he impregnated the defendant, but was very unaware of the conception. It turns out Ms. Clark willfully withheld knowledge of her pregnancy while she carried on with a new love interest here in Arizona."

"We know all this Mr. Oswald. Get to the point."

"The point is your honor, that my client, Mr. Jackson, wants custody of the child after its birth. He had no prior knowledge of Miss Clarks' attempt to flee the state and to jeopardize the child's life. On the contrary, if he had known about the pregnancy, he would have not only advised her to stay here, he would have paid all the necessary expenses for her to do so."

"And where is the father now?" the judge asked.

"He's waiting outside. But I see no reason for him…"

"Escort Mr. Jackson in please," the judge ordered.

The doors to the courtroom opened. Sharon waited. He had come. Even if he believed everything they had told him, he had come for the child. Only one life would be stolen.

Thomas walked in. He was more handsome, stronger, than she remembered, yet he looked haggard as if he hadn't slept in days. A hush fell over the courtroom.

"Is this the father?" the judge asked, looking at Thomas, then over at Sharon.

"Yes, your honor," Oswald answered.

The judge looked at Sharon. "Miss Clark."

"Yes?"

"Is this the father of your child?"

Sharon looked at Thomas. Their eyes met, and she smiled. His eyes filled with tears as he mouthed the words, "I love you."

"Miss Clark?"

Sharon's lawyer tugged on her arm. "Face forward," he whispered. "The judge is addressing you."

Sharon turned and faced the judge. "Yes sir. It's his child."

The judge shook his head. "Petition denied."

"What?" Sharon screamed.

Thomas pushed past his lawyer. "Your honor."

A bailiff ran up to Thomas and grabbed him by the arm.

"Thomas," Sharon cried.

"Miss Clark," the judge yelled over the high-pitched voices that filled the room.

"I'll get you both out, I promise." Thomas yelled as two bailiffs grabbed him.

"Thomas," Sharon cried out. Thomas pulled free from the bailiffs and turned towards her. "I love you. I've always loved you."

"I know," he said, then the bailiffs grabbed his arms again and dragged him from the courtroom.

"Miss Clark," the judge demanded as he pounded his gavel.

The doors slammed shut. With tears running down her face she turned back to her persecutor. It had been enough that Thomas had come. He hadn't questioned her, he hadn't condemned her, he had stood by her, loving her. Mother was wrong, mother would always be wrong. Love was the most important thing, and finally, for the first time since Granddad died, Sharon felt it. This judge, the state, the Moralists could never take this one moment from her. For the first time in her life, she felt complete.

The judge stood and pointed his gavel at her. The redness in his face made her take a step back. Her lawyer caught her arm.

"You have no defense," the judge hissed through clenched teeth. "You have made a mockery of my court. Whether or not you intended to terminate your pregnancy, you were caught with a counterfeit ID, stole a truck, aided in the escape of two suspected murders by renting them a vehicle, and attempted to illegally exit the state of Arizona. I hereby sentence you to life imprisonment, with no opportunity of parole for twenty-five years.

Sharon fell back in her seat, shaking her head, praying that some day Stan Dietrich would avenge her life, avenge all of their lives. She was to be the individual sacrifice, the one that didn't matter, for in the end, what was one life, one woman, when it came down to it. She had been a fool, now she would be a martyr.

"Stand, Miss Clark," the judge Ordered.

Bristol pulled Sharon to her feet.

"You are to be remanded to the Arpaio Women's Penitentiary until the birth of the child, who will then become a ward of the state. Within one month of the birth, you will be sterilized, and all rights to motherhood, stripped from you. Court adjourned."

The sharp bang of the gavel ended the proceedings and all chances of freedom. Listner, Sanders, and Matthews had won. She was to be the prisoner of a state ruled by a God with no name. As she was led from the courtroom she consoled herself in the fact that her child had a father who would fight to free it from the clutches of the self-chosen people.

46

The processing at the penitentiary went quickly. Sharon was escorted to a private cell and given food. Other than the guard who brought it, no one came to see her on the first day.

The next morning the woman she had met at the mall came into her room with a tray of empty tubes and a long syringe. Her nametag read, Ruth Johnson, Head Nurse. Sharon couldn't see any camera equipment in the small room, but didn't want to take any chances. She was careful not to exchange even the slightest glance with the woman. She looked away as the tourniquet was wrapped around her arm and the nurse searched for a vein. The needle shook as it sought its mark. Sharon wanted to tell the woman not to worry, that she would never tell on her, but decided it would be best if she didn't acknowledge her.

The nurse took five vials of blood then withdrew the needle. As she wiped the puncture wound with alcohol she leaned over near Sharon's ear. "I'm sorry," she said, so low Sharon wasn't positive she really heard it, then Ruth Johnson, Head Nurse, took a syringe full of yellow liquid and shot it into Sharon's arm.

"What's that for?" Sharon asked.

"Just an inoculate," Ruth said, then walked away.

Sharon didn't ask what the blood tests were for, she already knew – genetic testing. Listner had commented on her Aryan genes. Now he owned them. There was no need to fear the prison. It wasn't where she would stay. She would be going with Madison Courtney. "A new facility," Ruth had said at the mall. A new breeding facility.

Sharon laughed to herself as she lay back down on her cot. "My life as a breeder," she said out loud. "One hell of a memoir." It wasn't really funny, and she knew it, but she couldn't stop herself from laughing. She was about to become what she feared most and there was nothing she could do to prevent it. She had made her choice, and they were about to make theirs. All she could hope for was a genetic defect, but unless her mother's alcoholism was discernible in DNA, she was shit out of luck and she knew it.

No one else came in her room throughout the day. Food was slipped through a slot in the floor. It was much better than what she received in the courthouse jail. There was a large helping of vegetables, two pieces of skinned chicken breast, and a large glass of milk. She ate everything – there was no reason to starve.

Her uterus cramped. She placed her hand over where she thought the baby might be and gently rubbed. "Be still," she warned. "Your daddy's coming for you."

The cramps grew worse, and she saw an image of Ruth Johnson's sorrowful face as she shot the yellow fluid into Sharon's arms. "No," she screamed. "Not the baby." Tears fell as she remembered Paul's warning, *I don't think I've heard of one mulatto pregnancy making it through term over there.* "I'm sorry," she whispered to her baby as she curled up in response to the cramps and turned to face the wall.

She could feel the warmth of a second life spill from her. She reached her hand under the maternity dress she wore and felt for fluid. When she pulled her hand out, it was covered in blood.

The door to her cell opened. "Something wrong?" a guard asked.

Sharon didn't answer; she kept her face to the wall and held up her bloody hand.

"Someone get the doc," the voice yelled in a tone that didn't seem either surprised or sympathetic.

The blood continued, but she didn't move, she didn't try to stop it. It was all that was left of her child. She hoped that her life would be drawn with it. An arm grabbed her shoulder and she was rolled over. A woman in her sixties, heavily wrinkled, pursed mouth, and thinning gray hair stood above her. "She's lost it," she said in a deep raspy voice. "Get her cleaned up and moved into the basement.

Hands grabbed her from either side. Her dress was pulled off, her panties thrown in a bloody pile on the floor. Two women washed her while a third stood guard. She didn't help them, she didn't move an arm, or spread her legs without them doing it for her. A haze settled on her mind. She knew she wasn't dead, but she knew too, she was no longer alive.

They wrapped her in a hooded blanket that covered her face and wheeled her into a different building. The wheel chair they cuffed her to was put on a small lift and she was sent to a lower level. Ruth met her at the bottom and moved her down a hall to a small examining room. There was a metal chair with stirrups in its center. Sharon knew the drill and as she was moved over to it, she let her legs be spread and strapped down. Her wrists were strapped as well. An aide walked in and pulled a vacuum hose, similar to the one Simon had at his beauty shop, from a cabinet across the room. Sharon felt the hosing as it entered her and looked away. She couldn't feel the suction as it cleaned out her uterus and readied it for state use.

Her body tensed as the hose was withdrawn. It was over. Her child was gone. She didn't want them to know the anguish she felt or give them the satisfaction of knowing they had destroyed her, so she fought to hold back all emotion, but couldn't. One loud sob escaped. It was short and singular. Her chest heaved and cried for further release, but she fought it.

Ruth handed the vacuum hose to the aide and pointed to a cabinet. "Get rid of it," she said. "Then tell the doctor I think she'll be ready to travel tomorrow."

"Do you want me to send in a guard?" the aide asked as he unscrewed the glass jar that had caught the remnants of the lining that was meant to nourish her child.

"No, she's pretty out of it. I'll be okay. I'll finish up here while you're gone. When you get back we'll move her into her room."

The aide did as he was told and Sharon and Ruth were left alone. "You didn't tell me you were pregnant," the nurse whispered to her.

Sharon shook her head slowly. "I didn't know."

"What happened to the pictures?"

The pictures? *She just killed my child and she's worried about her own skin.* "Don't worry," Sharon told her. "People have them, but they aren't going to do anything with them for a while." Sharon looked into the woman's face. "Madison's screwed. Me too, right?"

Ruth nodded her head. "As of today, you're officially dead. Madison's records show she died two days ago."

"Did she?"

"No. She's in a room down the hall. When they heard they were getting you, they rescheduled her departure date. You'll both be shipped to the new facility tomorrow."

Sharon relaxed back in the chair. Cool air ran up inside her legs. She could feel the numbness of her empty womb and wondered how many times it could produce life before her body would give out. "What about Bethany?" she asked.

"They decided not to take her yet. She's on life support. They're afraid if they try and move her, the baby will be harmed. Since they have you, they decided not to take the risk."

"It's not her baby, it's theirs."

Ruth looked away.

Sharon touched the hem of the nurse's sleeve. "You have to get us...

The aide had returned. He was staring at them through a small window in the door.

47

Ruth Johnson sat in the doctor's office outside the maternity ward listening to the cries of the two babies recently born. She would need to sign their release forms in the morning so they could be taken by the state adoption agency. In another smaller room, a soundproof room, a newborn, secretly created, waited to be picked up by Mr. Logan.

Ruth remembered the conversation she had overheard the day before. The doctor must have been asked by some unknown caller about the risks of having two women die from miscarriages so close to one another. She had responded curtly that coincidences happen. They would claim it was the will of God and they had done their best, then she slammed the phone down and ordered Ruth to ready a new room in the basement. She did as she had been ordered, not knowing its occupant would be Sharon Clark until she entered the cell to give Sharon the abortifacient and to take blood samples.

She had been afraid then. Afraid Sharon would recognize her and scream out. But Sharon had kept her mouth shut, and from what Ruth could tell, always would. There were only two more days before she left for vacation and escaped the insanity of what they wanted her to do. She had no plans of assisting Doctor Listner when they transferred to the *breeding factory*, as Ruth had become to think of it. She would go to a free state and start all over.

She sat back and thought about the past ten years she had been the head nurse at the penitentiary. She couldn't remember how many babies she had aborted, or how many women she had impregnated with someone else's embryos.

White babies were in great demand, the doctor assured her when she first questioned what they were doing. It didn't matter whose body fed them. It was all about genetics and profit. Some minority children were allowed to be born to their natural mothers, but each year it was fewer and fewer. The decision to create the breeding facility and to stop the multi-birth program on prison grounds came from the top. Former inmates were asking questions and starting to publicly speak about their confusion and fears. The factory would house women that were given life sentences, or deemed a threat to society. Both Madison and Sharon filled those requirements. The Collins girl had reacted poorly to the implants, but they had learned a great deal from her. Sharon and Madison would be fitted with joints that would not be rejected by the body. If they survived more than one birth, the program would expand. Dr. Listner hopped for twenty-five sales this first year of full production, and dreamed of hundreds each year after. It was too profitable for them to turn their backs on, the doctor had told her. To profitable, and too easy. The state would never question the high death rate of inmates, nor would they publish it. The state didn't seem to question much of anything.

Ruth had become conditioned to the drug induced breeding that they had been doing. No one was hurt and the profits aided the war against the immoral, but this new facility was different. What they planned to do to these women for convenience sake was as far from godly as she could imagine. "A more quiet, cleaner, environment to produce healthy children," Dr. Listner had told her. Ruth wasn't buying it, and would have no part of it. She would not assist in amputating healthy women's limbs and muting them.

Sharon had asked for her help, but Ruth didn't believe she was strong enough to save her. Doctor Listner took her in when she was young and put her through nursing school. She had always been the perfect prodigy. She did what she was told when she was told to do it. It was only now, now that she couldn't accept the inhumanity they expected of her, that she rebelled.

It took a lot of courage to sneak a camera in and take pictures of Bethany, an inner voice reminded her. *And even more to meet with Sharon.* "I don't have any left," she responded out loud. *You're wrong,* the inner voice replied, and she knew it was right. There was a part of her that couldn't stay seated. A part that required she try.

48

Sharon lay on her cot in the room where she was being stored. She had run out of tears hours ago and held little hope of being rescued. She didn't believe Ruth Johnson was going to help her. The woman was more afraid than she was, and there was no one powerful enough who cared to intervene. She took some comfort in knowing that whatever was going to happen, Madison would be with her. She didn't wish her fate on anyone, but somehow, knowing she wasn't alone, made it easier to accept.

The lock on her door clicked open. Involuntarily she jumped, then sat straight up. Ruth Johnson stepped through it with a silver tray holding a scalpel, pair of tweezers, alcohol swabs, and two small plastic bottles. "More tests?" Sharon asked.

The nurse moved quickly. She sat down on the cot, putting the tray on the bed between herself and Sharon. "Look. I think I know how to get you out. We have to move fast, but first I need to remove your implant."

Sharon put her hand on the woman's arm. If she was getting out, she wasn't going alone. "Madison too." She demanded.

The nurse pulled free of Sharon's grip. "Madison too," she said pushing Sharon's head to the side, exposing her neck. She made a small incision above the spot where the transmitter was, and started probing the wound for it. Sharon winced at the pain, but kept from saying anything.

"Got it," the nurse said, placing a wet cotton swab over the incision and dropping something into one of the bottles she had brought with her. "Stay here while I get Madison."

Sharon held the cotton to her neck and watched the nurse leave. She didn't believe Ruth would be able to pull the escape off. But, she'd rather be killed trying than live the life they had planned for her. There were no bags to pack, no personal items to collect. She had nothing to do but wait.

Minutes passed like hours. Sharon got up and walked to her door. She tried to open it, to find out what was taking so long, but it was locked. Frustrated at not knowing what was going on, she began pacing the small cell. Finally, she heard the click of the lock and Ruth opened the door. Madison was standing behind her in a hot pink maternity dress. She didn't say anything when she saw Sharon, nor did she act surprised.

"Okay," Ruth said. "I have my truck pulled into the docking bay. I told them I was moving supplies for the doctor. You can hide in some big boxes I took out of storage. They never check my equipment. Without the implants, they won't know you've left the compound until someone goes to check on you in the morning. By then we'll be in Navajo country. I think we can hide out there until we find a way to get out of the state undetected."

Sharon was impressed with the nurse's plan. It could work, if luck, fate, God, destiny, or whatever it was that played with her life, would allow it. Yet, deep in her gut she knew she would never escape. She knew her future. It had nothing to do with freedom. *But, I'm still going to try.* "I can get us new IDs," she said playing along with the fantasy.

"I have connections, too" Madison said. "You get us out of here, and we can do the rest."

The nurse nodded her head. "Okay. We need to be real quiet. There's an aide in the nursery. We'll have to pass right by him."

Sharon was ready to go when she remembered one of the reasons she had come to the prison the first time. Bethany Collins. She couldn't leave without seeing her. "Wait a minute. What about Bethany?"

"What about her?" Ruth asked. "We can't do anything for her."

"I can," Sharon said. "Which room is she in?"

"Over there." Ruth pointed at a door at the end of the hall. "Forget it. We don't have time."

Sharon ran down to the door. Madison and the nurse followed. "Open it," she told the nurse. Madison agreed. Ruth looked at both of them, then passed her key card through the lock.

Sharon looked at the disfigured sleeping face, hanging from metal poles. The room stank of infection. The sockets where Bethany's arms once were raw and wet. "

"Oh my god," Madison turned away and sank to the floor.

"That's is what they plan for us, isn't it?" Madison asked.

"I'm sorry," Ruth said.

Sharon stared at the young face, the face a father loved and the state owned. She purposely avoided the bulging abdomen and the life it held, a life Bethany had not initiated.

"Hurry up," Madison said from the hall.

Sharon leaned over and kissed Bethany's forehead. "Bethany," she whispered. "Your father loves you. He's sorry he wasn't able to save you, but wants you to find peace now," she said, then removed the IV tube attached to Bethany's arm and unplugged the respirator. The monitor attached to her chest began to buzz.

Ruth reached over and unplugged it, then grabbed Sharon's arm. "We have to go."

Sharon wanted to stay, to make sure Bethany was free, but it was too risky. She followed the two dark haired women down the hall and up the stairs. Ruth went ahead to see if an aide was in the nursery. She nodded to them that there was, then motioned for them to wait for her signal.

Ruth disappeared through the door. "Look here? This baby's jaundiced. Put it under the UV lamp for ten minutes."

"She looks fine to me," the aide said.

"Well she doesn't look fine to me. Now, do as I say."

"Yes, Ma'am."

Ruth reappeared, waved them on, then went back into the nursery. Sharon went first, then Madison. They stopped when they reached the exit and looked back at the nursery.

"I'm leaving now," Ruth called. "Watch that baby carefully."

"I will," the boy called back.

Ruth came out of the room and met them at the end of the hall. She held her finger to her mouth, and slowly opened the door. "Okay," she whispered then fell in behind them as Madison and Sharon stepped into another long hall "This way." They followed Ruth through two long corridors lined with empty examining rooms and offices. Ruth stopped in front of a metal door, fumbled with a key ring, and unlocked it.

"I parked the truck in here. No one will see us," Ruth said as she pushed opened the door. The three women entered a large darkened storage facility with a docking bay and headed toward the silhouette of a pick up truck. A light snapped on.

"Going somewhere?" a deep raspy voice asked.

Ruth jumped back. Sharon almost laughed. Doctor Listner stood beside the garage door. A guard, his gun drawn, was next to her.

"How'd you know?" Ruth stammered.

Dr. Listner and the guard walked over to where they stood. "I didn't," Listner said shaking her head. "I was suspicious though. You changed after that one was bought in." She pointed at Madison. "And then you were seen talking to the Clark woman. I've been monitoring your coming and goings Ruth. I was called when you returned here tonight. What were you thinking?"

"It's wrong," Ruth said.

"It's not our place to decide what's right and wrong."

"Oh really," Madison said taking a step forward. The guard matched her step, the barrel of his gun within an inch of her chest. "What do you think the world would say when they find out what you're doing?"

Listner smiled. "They would be appalled. But then we never expected them to understand, or know. That's why I'm afraid you girls are going to return to your cells and first thing in the morning be shipped out to start your work for the Lord. And you Ruth, I'm sorry to say, will be going with them."

"I'll die first," Sharon said.

"I doubt that." Listner nodded toward the guard.

He reached his arm up to Madison's shoulder. Her knee came up and at the same instant she grabbed his wrist and twisted. The gun fell to the floor.

Sharon dove for it. Her knees struck the tiling hard as her hand reached for the gun. She could feel Listner above her and knew the doctor was about to pounce. Her body tightened in anticipation of the assault. But none came. Instead there was a loud thud to her left. Sharon rolled toward it. Listner lay beside her, blood freely flowing from a large crack on the top of her skull. Ruth stood above them, a large metal cylinder raised over her head. Before Sharon could cry out for her to stop, the cylinder came down hard on Listner's head. There was a loud crack, then splatter, as Dr. Listner's head broke open spilling blood, bones, and brains onto Sharon's pink maternity dress.

"Sharon," a hushed voice called as if from some far away place. "Sharon."

Slowly, Sharon sat up, and turned towards whoever was calling her. Madison had the guard on his knees, his right arm pulled tight behind his back. That was something she could grasp, could deal with. She stood up and walked over to the guard. The gun felt foreign in her hand, its handle cold and hard, but still as if it were a natural position, her finger found the trigger. She walked over to the guard. With her hand a lot steadier than she felt it should be, she placed the tip of the barrel against his temple. Tears welled in his eyes, his mouth opened and closed, like a fish gasping in air.

"You're going to do exactly what we tell you. Isn't that right?"

He nodded his head.

"Good." Sharon handed Madison the gun then turned to face what Ruth had done.

Ruth was sitting next to what was left of the doctor's head, pulling bloodied chips from the woman's gray hair. "I'm sorry," she mumbled over and over again.

"Ruth," Sharon said quietly. "Ruth we need to go. What can we do with the guard?"

Ruth didn't look up at her.

The guard cried out. Sharon swung around. He was laying on the floor, his arms stretched out in front of him. Madison stood next to him, holding the barrel of the gun. "What should I do with this?"

Sharon shook her head and looked down at the guard. He was still breathing.

"We'll have to take him with us. Drop him off in the desert somewhere so he won't find help until morning," Madison said as she laid the gun on the top of some boxes. "I hit him hard enough. He won't wake up before we clear the compound.

Sharon nodded. It was a plan at least. All they needed to do was get Ruth cleaned up and stable enough to pass the guard at the gate. Madison walked over to where the doctor lay and offered her hand to Ruth. "We have to go know," she said. Ruth looked up at her.

"I couldn't let her do it."

"I know," Madison said. "Come on, you need to wash up. Sharon and I will move the guard into the truck.

Ruth nodded and stood then slowly walked backed toward the entrance to the hall.

Sharon and Madison carried the guard over to the back of Ruth's truck. It was an old truck with a large bed. There were seven large boxes in the back. One held long metal braces, another plastic hosing. Two contained Fetal Heart Monitors and another was filled with metal canisters simply marked as a high protein food source.

"For us?" Madison asked.

Sharon didn't answer. She didn't want to acknowledge where they had been headed. That would be saved for later, once they were safe. She shrugged her shoulders and opened another box. It was empty.

"Let's put him in here."

The guard was heavier than he looked and it took them a few tries to get him in the bed of the truck. "He'll be sore when he wakes up," Madison said.

Sharon looked back where Dr. Listner lay. "He should be grateful." She stared at the blood surrounding the doctor's head. She waited for nausea, disgust, anything to force her to turn away, but it didn't come. "Are we just going to leave her there?"

"We don't have time to clean it all up. Hiding the body wouldn't do much for us."

"I guess not." Sharon turned and looked up at Madison. "There's no going back now, is there?"

Madison pulled the hosing out of its box and threw it on the floor next to the truck. "I don't know. Ruth said we've been declared dead. To legally come after us, they'd have to admit they lied. That would expose a cover up. Or so I'd hope."

"Our resurfacing would do the same thing. They'd have nothing to lose."

"Probably not," Madison said as she stepped into one of the empty boxes.

Ruth walked over to them slowly. "Get in the boxes," she ordered.

Madison and Sharon exchanged a quick glance, then Madison crouched down in her box. Sharon folded over the flaps of its top and stepped into the box that had held the hosing. Ruth pulled herself into the bed of the truck and walked over to Sharon. "Get down," she said. Her face was pale, and heavily lined. Her voice seemed harsher, almost raspy. Sharon knelt in the box, using her hands to keep her steady. She lowered her head thinking about the death of Listner, when it dawned on her. "Wait," she said holding up her hand. She stood up. "What if she left word not to let you leave the prison?"

Ruth pushed down on Sharon's shoulder. "It's a chance we'll have to take."

Sharon looked into the nurse's eyes, they were glazed but steady. Her grip was tight. If there had been no order to retain her, Ruth would get them through. She was beyond fear.

Light diminished quickly as the flaps of the box folded over. The bed rocked as Ruth jumped out. Madison's box or maybe the guard's jammed against Sharon's, but didn't topple it. Sharon tried to resituate herself as the engine of the truck turned over. It was going to be a very uncomfortable ride. The hum of the garage door opening, then the forward momentum of the truck offered some sense of safety, but not enough.

The truck pulled to a stop. Sharon held her breath and prayed to anyone that would listen that the guard would remain silent as well.

"Miss Johnson," a voice said to her right. "Dr. Listner was looking for you."

"She found me." Ruth's voice seemed lighter. "I was watching after a sick baby. She took over and sent me home. I have to deliver these boxes to another facility in the morning."

"Very well," the guard said, his voice trailing off as if he were walking away. There was another hum and the clanking of the gate unlocking.

"Oh," Ruth called out. "I forgot. Dr. Listner said no one is to bother her. She's planning on sleeping in a chair in the nursery."

"I'll pass the word."

The truck pulled forward. Sharon let her breath out, and thought she heard Madison do the same.

There were no sirens, no bells, just the constant crunching of gravel beneath the tires. Then there was calm. They had hit pavement. Sharon lowered herself in the box, the muscles in her body relaxed. "We made it," she thought she heard Madison say over the noise of the truck.

Tears ran down Sharon's cheeks, the bitter salt finding its way to the corners of her mouth. She rubbed the area on her stomach where she had once thought her baby to be. "Forgive me," she whispered into the stale air.

Her legs and arms were numb, her back ached. They had been driving for what seemed like hours before the truck veered off onto another gravel road. Sharon waited a while until she felt sure they were a safe enough distance from the road. She pushed open the flaps of her box and stood up. Madison had already opened her box, but was still crouched down inside it. She opened the box that held the guard and checked on him. He was still out cold.

"How hard did you hit him?"

Madison stood and peered into the guard's box. "Pretty hard. He's still breathing isn't he?"

Sharon reached over and placed her hand on his chest, it was moving. "Yeah," she said then turned her attention to the desert. It was dark, and she couldn't see far beyond the truck's headlights, but she could feel its danger, not from the animals or the cactus, or the killing heat, it was from what surrounded it, those who controlled it.

They drove behind a small hill splattered with cactus and stopped. Ruth didn't turn around, or get out of the truck. Madison was the first to jump down.

"We'll leave him here. Ruth, do you have any water?"

The door of the truck opened and Ruth dropped a plastic milk container out of the door. Sharon jumped down from the truck and walked over to pick up the water. She looked up at Ruth as she did. The woman's face was blank, the knuckles of her hands white. She was staring forward. The top of her blouse was wet and stained with eye makeup.

"She took me in when my mother died. Raised me like I was hers. I killed her."

"She was about to do worse to you," Sharon said without feeling any sympathy or remorse for the dead doctor.

Ruth nodded her head. "Still…"

"Sharon, grab the bottom of the box. He'll be safer if we leave him in it," Madison called to her.

Sharon reached up and put her hand on Ruth's arm. "If you hadn't done it, the three of us would be worse off than dead. Ruth, you did what you had to."

"I know," Ruth said, "but…"

Sharon turned away. She didn't want to hear how Ruth had loved the woman, how Ruth had aborted babies deemed lacking, inseminated women without their consent, or helped in creating the living corpse of Bethany Collins all because she loved a monster. It wasn't a good enough excuse, and although Sharon was grateful for what Ruth had done, she could not accept her grief or offer solace.

"We'll put these other boxes around him, so no critters will find him." Madison pushed the box forward. Sharon grabbed its edge to keep it from falling. Madison jumped down and together they moved the box to a clearing to the side of the road. They brought the other six boxes and placed them up against the guard's. When they returned to the truck, Ruth was gone. The keys swayed in the ignition.

"Ruth," Madison called.

Sharon looked around, but there was no sign of the nurse. A gunshot filled the night air, and they ran toward it. Ruth lay against a cholla tree, its spines tearing her dead flesh. The guard's gun had fallen by her feet, her dark hair covered her tear stained face.

Sharon turned and walked away. "Madison, are you coming," she called.

Madison ran up beside her. "We can't just leave her."

"Yes we can," Sharon said. "It's what she wanted."

Madison drove. They were headed for the Superstitions. There was a working underground there that would help them leave the state.

Once home Sharon vowed, she wouldn't sit silent waiting for the likes of Stan Dietrich and his stagnant revolutionaries to act. She wouldn't hide behind false pretences like Barbara Sanders had either. She would strike out and expose Senator Listner, Nathan Sanders and all the others who manipulated, controlled and destroyed the lives of everyone under the guise of their man made God.

49

Martha Garcia sat in her cell waiting for the guards. Her extradition hearing was in two hours. Arizona had demanded she be sent back to stand trial for the murders of Barbara Sanders and Robert Hernandez.

The locked door to her row opened. The hard clanking of metal made her jump. She stood up on shaky legs, determined not to let anyone see her fear. A guard appeared before her cell and the door slid open.

"Garcia, follow me," he said. There were no hand cuffs, no leg irons. A second guard fell in behind them.

She was escorted down a flight of stairs to a small window with a clerk behind it.

"Sign here," the clerk said pushing out a package of new clothing. Martha took the packet and signed the form.

"You can change in there," the clerk said pointing to a door behind them. The guard that had led her down the hall opened the door.

"What's going on?" she asked in a slight whisper.

"You're being released. All charges have been dropped."

"What?"

"Get dressed. Your lawyer's waiting."

Martha dressed as quickly as she could with only one good arm. The shirt was sleeveless and the splint fit through it. She stopped for a minute and took a breath to absorb what was going on. She was being set free, free in a free state. If they had dropped charges against her, they would have to do the same for Anthony. She was more nervous now than she was when she thought she'd have to stand trial in Arizona.

As promised, her lawyer was waiting for her in a car outside the prison gate. Another man sat in the back seat.

"I'm Derek Robinson, Sharon Clark's boss."

Martha thought she remembered the name, then she did. He was the man she was supposed to contact once she reached California. "Did Sharon make it out okay?"

Derek shook his head. "She was arrested trying to get across the border. At first they told us she was dead. Then three days later it was retracted. According to the Arizona press, she had conspired with a nurse at the prison to forge her and another woman's death certificates, and then the three of them murdered the prison's doctor and a guard. Supposedly she and this other woman, a Madison Courtney, then killed the nurse."

"What?" Martha leaned forward. "How? I don't…"

"They said she was pregnant. I'm sorry Martha, but Sharon's in deep trouble. Her face has been splashed across every newspaper in the country. It worked out for you though." Derek offered a half smile. "The Arizona authorities have decided to put Barbara Sander's death on Sharon instead of you and your brother. Seems she was the last to see Barbara before she died. They claim she suffocated her."

"That's not what happened. Sharon…"

Derek held up his hand. "It doesn't matter Martha. I know the truth, there's nothing we can do about it. Sharon's on her own. They found her boyfriend bludgeoned to death in a hotel room in Arizona. They're pinning that one on her too."

Martha turned away and looked out the window of the car. Sharon hadn't done any of it, but escape, she was sure of it. "Is there anyone else she'd go to?"

"Me, maybe, but SoCal police are working with Arizona on this one. My house is under surveillance, my phones tapped. I'm grateful actually."

Martha turned and stared at him hard, her upper lip curled. "You're afraid of Sharon."

"Hell no. I'm afraid of Listner. The doctor was his sister." He turned away this time and in a shallower voice said, "I don't want to end up like Thomas."

Martha relaxed a little, he was right to fear them. "How's Anthony?"

Derek's voice lightened and he looked back over at her with a smile. "Recovering. You can go see him tomorrow. I've made room for both of you at my house. I promised Sharon I'd look out for you."

"Thanks," she said then turned back toward the window. The remainder of the ride to Derek's house was taken in silence.

A room had been made for her. It was small, but homey. She wouldn't be staying long. As soon as Anthony was better, she'd make sure he could stay with Derek, then she'd take off on her own. Sharon was out there somewhere, hiding and probably afraid. She would find her. And when she did, it would be her turn to be the hero, her turn to stand up to the bastards.

Martha pulled off her shoes and threw herself down on the soft bed. It was the first comfort she had experienced in years. She lay there for a few minutes embracing the protection of her new room, of her new life. Unbidden, scenes from her last week in Arizona played in her mind: Finding Andrew near death; discovering his mutilation; killing the boy in the cave; the small body of her brother jerking forward then falling when they shot him. The vision that came back to her most often was her own action when thinking Andrew dead. The gun in her hand, the surety that she could pull the trigger and kill the bastard coming at her. She threw the pillow on the floor and lowered herself to it.

Comfort was not something she could afford. Not something she would allow until Sharon was safe. She raised her arms as far as the splint would allow and clasped her hands. With her broken arm's index fingers pointing towards the ceiling, she pulled an imaginary trigger and smiled. There was one comfort, one pleasing thought. With a slight whisper, her mouth lingering on each syllable, she embraced her new mantra. "Revenge."